The PHANTOM DETECTIVE COMPANION

The PHANTOM DETECTIVE COMPANION

BY

TOM JOHNSON

WITH

EDMOND GOOD
EVERETT HIBBARD
MATT MORING
WILL MURRAY
LIN STREETER
CHARLES S. STRONG
AL TONIK
HAROLD WARD

BOSTON

ALTUS PRESS

2009

© 2009 Altus Press

———————————————

Printed in the United States of America

First Edition—2009

Visit AltusPress.com for more books like this.

———————————————

EDITED AND DESIGNED BY
Matthew Moring

ABOUT THE COVER
This cover was reworked from Murder of the Clergyman's Mistress
by Anthony Abbot (Popular Library #286).

THANKS TO
*Bruce Brenner, The Grand Comic-Book Database, Art Hackathorn, Ed Hulse,
Jack Irwin, Tom Johnson, Chuck Juzek, George Martin, Will Murray, Rick
Ollerman, Andrew Pepoy, James Reasoner, Bob Sampson, Kurt Shoemacker,
Bill Thom, Al Tonik, Mark Trost, Virgil Utter, the Estate of Harold Ward &
The Who's Who of American Comic Books.*

TABLE OF
CONTENTS

All chapters by Tom Johnson unless otherwise noted.

Here They Are!

THE
THRILLING
GROUP
of magazines
for every taste and
for every member of
the family—

FEATURING
the best novels and
stories being
written today
by America's most
popular authors—

ASK FOR THEM
at your newsstand—
low in price,
high in quality!

You can't go wrong
when you read

The Thrilling Magazines
EACH ONE THE BEST OF ITS KIND!

CHAPTER I

THE ORIGINAL
MASKED MARVEL

IN EARLY 1932, D.L. Champion, writing as G. Wayman Jones, wrote a series of nine short stories for *Thrilling Detective* about a young, rich-man-about-town who turned to bullet justice when his father was murdered by a group of hooded master crooks known as the Murder Club; men who controlled the crime and politics in Newkirk City.

The nine stories began in the February 1932 issue, and ran in monthly installments until the October 1932 issue; the story titles were "Alias Mr. Death," "The Affair at City Hall," "Midnight Marauders," "Dead Man's Drop," "The Long Arm of Vengeance," "Death's Race," "Mr. Death, Gangster," "A Rendezvous with Death," and "Death vs. Death." The short stories were all published in hardback at the close of 1932, as *Alias Mr. Death*. At the end of the story, Mr. Death was supposedly killed in a plane fight with the leader of the band of crooks. However, in 1939 Mr. Death was brought back to the pages of *Thrilling Detective* in the April and May issues, in stories titled "Death Takes the Wheel" and "Decks of Death," respectively. Readers were told that Mr. Death had survived the plane crash by parachuting out over a river mist that hid his escape from the eyes of the police.

Mr. Death was actually a rich playboy named Jimmy Gilmore, and he fought the criminals in disguise and, later, while wearing a frightening hood. Joining him in the stories were his fiancée, Sally Fortune, and his father's oldest and dearest friend, Mr. Clyde Bates. The stories concerned the retribution he inflicted against the nine members of the Murder Club, one member per story, until he fought and killed the leader in a dogfight high above the city of Newkirk.

Mr. Death was nicknamed the Phantom Killer.

Leo Margulies, head editor of the Thrilling Group of Standard Magazines was looking for a hero to run in competition with *The Shadow* over at Street & Smith. The character of The Shadow was selling out at the newsstands, and Standard wanted in on the action. They needed a pulp hero. With a few changes in the Mr. Death stories, Leo Margulies and D.L. Champion worked out the Phantom Detective, changing Jimmy Gilmore's name to Richard Curtis Van Loan, his girl friend's name from Sally Fortune to Muriel Havens, and his father's oldest and dearest friend from Clyde Bates to Frank Havens. The basic plot would remain the same: after the death of his parents, and the end of World War I, young Van Loan, super athlete, with incredible intelligence and a restless soul, with more money than he could possibly spend in ten life-times, was searching for meaning to his life.

At the encouragement of his father's oldest and closest friend, Frank Havens, the young Van Loan had been asked to investigate a crime that was giving the police trouble in solving, as well as giving Havens' newspaper, the *Clarion,* a scoop on the other papers. Frank Havens was starting a campaign to clean up crime in New York City, and needed someone to help him. A few days later a mysterious man had walked into the police station with the crook in tow. The crime had been solved. The police were grateful, and the newspapers nicknamed the mysterious manhunter the Phantom Detective! Jimmy Gilmore's Mr. Death had become Richard Curtis Van Loan, the Phantom Detective.

The Phantom would fight crime for twenty years, and solve 170 cases. The Shadow and Doc Savage would have more cases in their careers, but they wouldn't last twenty years. The Phantom Detective was the longest running of any of the pulp heroes. However, the series was also the most uneven.

The series can be split into two periods; the first ten years, February 1933 to December 1942 (covering 114 stories), and the second ten-year period, from January 1943 to the Summer 1953 (with 56 stories). The first ten years were the most chaotic. D.L. Champion was responsible for the first three years, 1933 through 1935, although his stories would be broken up by individual stories from Anatole France Feldman, Norman A. Daniels, and George A. McDonald. One other, the September 1933 story, "Cities for Ransom," was by neither of the named authors. The strong aviation theme in this story, and Standard's new pulp series appearing at the same time, *The Lone Eagle,* leads me to believe the new writer for the new pulp series was given a test by letting him write a *Phantom Detective* story to see if he could handle his own novel-length series. If this is actually the case, then the September 1933 *Phantom* author is possibly the same author who started *The Lone Eagle*—was that F. E. Reichnitzer? Interesting.

Anatole France Feldman was a good friend of D.L. Champion's and probably helped Champion write some of the 1933 to 1935 stories. Both George McDonald and Norman Daniels were probably brought into the series by Leo Margulies.

The year of 1936 was the first big shake up for *The Phantom Detective.* One reason was undoubtedly the results of a mysterious individual named Marcus Goldsmith, a rich backer of the *Phantom Detective* series who purportedly supplied financial aid for the series to keep it going regardless of sales. In fact, Goldsmith actually paid many of the authors himself. He thought of himself as Frank Havens, the backer of the Phantom, and he accepted or rejected the stories that were brought to him. He would send out a call to the writers when he wanted some changes in their stories. When the writers received such a summons, there was probably a red signal light of warning flashing through their minds.

In 1936, D.L. Champion and Anatole France Feldman were replaced, though it's possible Champion—or perhaps both—did some writing for Leo Margulies afterwards. Norman Daniels had at least one story rejected in 1935, and several in 1936 were heavily edited. George McDonald appears

Richard Curtis Van Loan/The Phantom

to be the only one to pass muster during this period, and he did write some excellent stories.

Some of the changes that took place were lasting ones. Steve Huston, a young reporter on Frank Havens' *Clarion* became a regular player in the stories, the red signal light atop the *Clarion* Building that flashed a signal when the Phantom was needed also became a regular feature. Steve Huston was actually the culmination of the previous three years of a search looking for a sidekick for the Phantom. Several individuals had been tried, including a character named Jerry Lannigan that was brought in for several stories. But the character of Steve Huston stuck.

The two top *Phantom Detective* stories appeared in 1936: "Dealers in Death" (July 1936), and "Death Rides the Blizzard" (November 1936).

Unfortunately, 1937 to 1942 was the most unsettling period. During these years, everyone in the pulp field wrote a *Phantom Detective* story. Or so the story goes. Actually, the story probably isn't far off. However, we'll probably never know who all wrote *Phantoms* in this period, but there were many.

The years of 1937 & 1938 were mediocre years for *The Phantom Detective*. Many of the stories during this period are mere carbon copies of each other. By the end of 1938 there is another shake up of some kind; a Dan Fowler story is re-written into a *Phantom Detective*, another story is started by one author and finished by another. Why, we don't know, but it's possible the author passed away before finishing the story. He had written a previous story; this was the November 1938 story, "Death Glow." And a few other stories sneak in without meeting previous novel guidelines. Something had happened.

A super crook makes two appearances in 1939, plus 1939 sees the introduction of yet another addition to the main characters. He is Chip Dorlan, who the Phantom meets in San Francisco. This character would survive for a number of years, then mysteriously disappear during the war years, and be brought back in for a while afterwards, his absence explained by military service.

The years of 1940, 1941 and 1942 are a hodge-podge of stories. Again, the authorship is questionable on many of these. They were just more of the same from previous years. A total period of six years, 1937 to 1942, with mostly mediocre stories by anyone who could write, were turning in *Phantom Detective* stories. Some were okay. Indeed, some were outstanding. But there weren't many of them.

The second ten-year period is different. Finally, the series takes shape. Some outstanding writers turn in some outstanding stories, and the Phantom becomes more three-dimensional, with substance. Fewer authors are involved, and the stories follow more to pattern. The characters can be expected to act the same way story after story. Discounting, of course, hair color, eye color, and that sort of thing. I don't think any of the authors could remember what color Muriel's hair was, or the Phantom's eyes, including Norman Daniels who kept file cards on all the characters he was writing. The Phantom's eyes were blue or gray, or dark; and Muriel went from being a brunette in one novel, to a blonde in the next novel.

But all this could be overlooked. What mattered were the stories, and the stories were good during the second half of the series. With the January 1943 story, I believe that Charles Greenberg comes back, alternating with C.S. Montayne and Norman Daniels until Stewart Sterling is brought in at the end to bring sexual content into the stories. Though these last few stories were good, the sexual content is a little distracting. And by this point, I would guess that Marcus Goldsmith had either passed away, or was no longer interested in the direction the stories were going.

I'm sure that Stewart Sterling wrote stories prior to 1943, but it would be difficult to pick them out. However, the stories now are easy to identify. Though Charles Greenberg appears to write in the same formula, and his new stories revisit some old plots, he is a much better writer now. Montayne goes a step more by copying plot devices by both Greenberg and Daniels. Montayne did have some originality with his stories, though. He just borrowed from past novels.

Regardless, what we got were three great authors—Greenberg, Daniels, and Montayne—writing solid, interesting, and action-packed adventures. Even the Sterling stories are good, discounting the sexual content. And I should add at this point that the new editor, supposedly a woman, wanted sex added to the stories, and Sterling merely complied.

Actually, there is only one story during this period that is somewhat questionable. I'm not sure who the author is for the Summer 1949 story, "Murder Set to Music"; it's anyone's guess. Although this author uses some of C. S.

Montayne's plot devices, the writing does not appear to be that of Montayne.

Besides the two 1936 novels I've already picked as being the best in the series, I don't want to leave the impression they were the only ones. Norman Daniels wrote many exciting stories, and two of his most outstanding novels were undoubtedly "The Circus Murders" (March 1936) and "The Doomed Millions" (Spring 1952). Greenberg's "Stones of Satan" (March 1943), and Montayne's "The Chinese Puzzle" (January 1947). D.L. Champion's "Thirteen Cards of Death" (August 1933), and Anatole France Feldman's "The Sinister Hand of Satan" (October 1933), are all good picks.

The two stories featuring Clifford Boniface, "Murder at the World's Fair" (June 1939) and "The Forty Thieves" (July 1939), plus a previous story, "Cavalcade of Death" (August 1937), were all excellent. As was "The Sampan Murders" (September 1939), by Laurence Donovan, in which Chip Dorlan was introduced.

If I picked one stinker from the series, it would be an easy choice to make. True, there were a number of stories published that shouldn't have been. But the worst of them all had to be "Murder Calls the Phantom" (March 1941), by Ralph Oppenheim. That one takes top honors.

With the story of C.S. Montayne literally falling dead over his typewriter while typing "The Black Ball of Death," I thought I'd ask Norman Daniels about the story, and following is Norman's interesting letter in response to my letter, dated July 21st, 1993:

> About this writer Montayne. I know almost nothing about him. Nor do I have any idea of how many *Phantoms* he wrote or when he wrote them. Remember, this was about fifty years ago and my memory of this occurrence is not perfect.
>
> However, I recall that Leo Margulies gave me these pages of uncompleted *Phantom* and asked me to finish it. I agreed and I studied the pages he had written—a first draft—and I do recall one interesting thing. I was also supplied with his version of a synopsis. It was an almost unreadable scrawl on the inside of a folding match container. I recall also that he died suddenly, falling over his typewriter. At any rate, I heard that he was a reliable, talented writer and Leo thought very highly of him. I accepted no payment for my part in the production of this story. I'm sorry I can't help you more.
>
> But I can supply you with some interesting background which nobody seems to have knowledge of. The main reason behind this Phantom was an elderly and very rich man named Marcus Goldsmith. He was financially involved with the series. Perhaps the entire organization, for all I know. He was certainly odd, and not very well-liked at the office.
>
> I found him to be a fine gentleman even though he read every *Phantom* and was picky and rather unversed in writing fiction. He had a habit of making a writer do over a certain amount of pages, always in the middle of the book. They were unnecessary rewrites, but he insisted. So I would write in some foolish midsection of the novel and have the correct sequence ready. When he spotted the none-to-good sequence and called for a rewrite, all I had to

do was insert the pages which I had extracted and which were the real part of the book.

I found Marcus Goldsmith to be a gentleman in every respect and I liked him. He used to have me come to his apartment on West 72nd Street. We plotted some *Phantoms* there. He thought of himself as Frank Havens, the Phantom's backer and he loved living this part. He maintained an elaborate apartment and he usually insisted on giving me a cigar. Since he hadn't smoked in about twenty years, the cigar would have exploded if I'd lit them. But mysterious as he was, he was respected in the office.

As proof of this, I sometimes asked for an advance. He always agreed and always handed ma a bit of paper torn from anything on his desk. On it he had written "Give Norman three hundred." It drove the girl who wrote the checks mad. It highly annoyed Ned Pines also, but they did as he demanded.

The scenario that Norman mentions in his letter probably went on for years. And Mr. Goldsmith's secretary that he alludes to in his letter reminds me of the later stories in particular, those by Greenberg and Montayne. These authors must have found the secretary quite annoying and gave Frank Havens a similar type secretary, often named Miss Marsh. She often met the Phantom at the front desk and refused to admit him. I could not help but connect this fictional secretary, Miss Marsh, to Mr. Goldsmith's secretary, and her being annoyed at signing checks over to the authors. I would guess that this had been the case with Greenberg and Montayne, as well as with most other writers who lived in the New York City area. My guess is that Goldsmith had died by the time Stewart Sterling took over, as I doubt that he would have approved of these later stories. As it is, with the last published novel, "Murder's Agent" (Summer 1953), Frank Havens is not in the story, and we are told that he now has no active involvement with the Phantom's cases, and now Richard Curtis Van Loan was the Phantom's backer.

CHAPTER II

THE MAIN
CHARACTERS

A S WITH ALL continuing series, there were certain main characters
introduced to flesh out the stories. *The Phantom Detective* was no exception. Most characters in the Standard line of pulps were really interchangeable
from one series to another; so Frank Havens, Van Loan, Muriel Havens, and
Steve Huston could suddenly become F.B.I. Director Hoover, Dan Fowler,
Sally Vane, and Larry Kendal (from *G-Men*) with ease. In fact, the spot drawings were often switched from one series to the other, so Muriel Havens picture was used for that of Sally Vane, and vice versa.

Of curious note, when Jerry Siegel and Joe Shuster fleshed out the characters in Superman, they knowingly or unknowingly borrowed the characters from *The Phantom Detective:* Perry White of the *Daily Planet* was Frank
Havens of the *Daily Clarion;* Lois Lane was Muriel Havens; Jimmy Olsen
was Steve Huston; and Superman/Clark Kent was the Phantom Detective/
Van Loan.

There was also a rumor of a movie serial being planned for the Phantom
Detective, but one never appeared. However, on another curious note, Republic's 1947 *The Black Widow* strangely has some similarities. A newspaper, the
Daily Clarion was investigating spider-poison killings. They called in Steve
Colt to unravel the murders. Assisting the detective was one of their reporters,
a young girl named Joyce. When I watched this 13-chapter serial, I was immediately reminded of the Phantom Detective. Unfortunately, Steve Colt does
not wear a domino mask.

With the series running for twenty years, a number of characters popped
up for a few issues, then disappeared again as mysteriously as they had appeared. However, the main characters were present, off and on, for most of the
long run.

RICHARD CURTIS VAN LOAN: A dilettante, clubman-about-town,
and one of the wealthiest young men in a city of wealth, finished his swim and
reached for the chromium guard rail at the end of the green-tiled pool in the
gymnasium of the ultra-exclusive Patroons Club.

Climbing out, with the water dripping from his magnificently proportioned body, which was an ideal example of physical perfection, he reached for his terry-cloth robe. Pushing his feet into cork clogs then, Van, as he was affectionately known to his host of *Social Register* friends, hurried off to the locker room to dress for his dinner appointment.

Van was well-known wherever he went, throughout the length and breadth of the land, as well as on his numerous trips to foreign climes, as one of the most eligible bachelors in the city of his birth, and

The Phantom

smiled at indulgently for what was believed to be his disinterest in anything except amusing himself. Therefore those who had never had an opportunity of seeing him in a swimming pool like that he had just left would have been surprised at that superb physical condition of his.

Not an ounce of superfluous weight was carried over the expanse of his six feet of coordinated brawn. Muscles flowed and rippled as he toweled himself briskly in the dressing room.

Frank Havens, thinking back, could never forget that evening, for it marked the birth of one of the most dramatic personalities alive today.

Van had come to him for advice, since Havens had been his father's best friend. In an almost desperate manner, Van had admitted to Havens that his life had neither meaning nor direction. The great fortune he had inherited upon his father's death precluded the necessity of earning a living. He had been bored with the inane society playboy life he had been leading. He had wanted to do something. But what? What could he do that took brains and courage, and was exciting?

Havens had been stumped. Then his eyes had fallen on a headline in a newspaper on his desk. A vicious killer, who had already claimed four victims, had still been thumbing his nose at the police. An entire section of the city had been in terror, and all efforts of the police to catch the clever fiend had been fruitless.

Purely as an experiment, without putting much faith in it, Havens had pointed at the headline and suggested that Van try his hand at catching the murderer. The result of that suggestion had made dramatic history!

Van had succeeded where the entire Police Department had failed. Twenty-four hours after Havens had pointed to the headline, a man had entered Police Headquarters, dragging by the scruff of the neck a snarling specimen of vicious humanity. The killer!

There were many versions of the beginning for the Phantom. In the early years, the emphasis had been on the period following World War I. Van Loan had flown missions in war-torn Europe during the great war, and upon return to civilian life, had found that the war had created something in him that could not be satisfied in civilian life. He needed danger, action, a reason to exist. In the later novels, the war had been forgotten and never mentioned in recounting his beginnings.

Van lived in an apartment on Park Avenue. At times, depending on the author, the building was owned by Van Loan, or he merely rented the apartment, but paid a large fee for the penthouse apartment, and a secret elevator to the street side entrance, that was only used by him as he came and went about his business of being the World's Greatest Sleuth.

These quarters he maintained were in a cloud-bumping apartment at the very apex of the building on aristocratic Park Avenue. In a way it was a rather curious set-up. To reach his high suite, Van had a private elevator, a private entrance—something no other tenant boasted. For these privileges he paid well. There was a reason for them, but that reason was a closely guarded secret. A velvet-quiet elevator rushed him skyward. Fireproof doors opened and in little more than a round of seconds Van was in his room.

Twilight gathered, laying a paint brush dipped in purple over furnishings and decorations so charming they might have come out of a colored page from one of the better magazines devoted to interior decoration. Around him, in artistic groupings were things he had collected with discernment and exquisite taste. Pictures, objects d'art, mallow furniture. All blended into a perfect mélange.

Below the windows, and the jut of a red flagged terrace, set with awning and shrubbery, the city streets lay far below. Their sounds were faint, murmuring echoes. Here, quiet and tranquility prevailed.

Van, who lived alone and liked it, noted the time as he switched on lights in parchment-shaded lamps. He dropped the copies of the *Clarion* on the pumpkin-brown top of an ancient tavern table, lighted a cigarette, and made himself comfortable in one of the upholstered chairs.

Van snapped on the lights in his exquisitely furnished rooms. Each piece had been selected personally, each was a treasure. Tonight, though, he hardly noticed the glimmer of old glass, the crackled surfaces of his paintings, the glow of tapestries and rugs as he went on through the living room to his Empire bedroom. As he closed the door behind him a change came over him. It was almost as if he had thrown off a mask of blasé indolence and become another man. As a matter of fact, in his changing attitude, he did assume another character.

This other self came more fully into being a few minutes later—after the touch of a hidden button slid back a cleverly constructed, movable wall panel. Behind the panel was revealed an inner room, small and windowless, that was a combined workshop, laboratory, arsenal and dressing room.

Many suits of clothes hung in a long line in the wardrobe. A triple-mirrored dressing table was in the foreground, the same sort of table usually found in theater dressing rooms, complete with make-up and like materials in great variety. In addition chemicals in jars and all the paraphernalia of a scientific research laboratory in miniature made an orderly clutter on all sides of the room, which was made light as day by indirect lighting.

As the Phantom, Van carried three items on his person at all times; one was the world famous badge, known by police departments all over the world. This badge was set on a platinum shield, with diamonds, emeralds and rubies shaped like a domino mask. The other two items were a domino mask and a make-up kit, all hidden in secret pockets that were immune to searches by anyone. The badge he showed off at least once in every story as it became necessary to identify himself to the police. In the early novels, he often put on the domino mask when he wanted to hide the Van Loan identity from the police or someone else. In the later novels, he seldom, if ever, wore the mask. However, the make-up kit usually came in handy at least once during each novel; again, in the early novels, the Phantom changed disguise every other page. But in the later novels, maybe once or twice was sufficient.

The Phantom maintained three super-charged black automobiles in a garage near his Park Avenue penthouse. The owner of the garage was a man named Rogers, who thought that he was some kind of government agent, always in disguise. He knew the identification signal of tugging the lobe of his left ear (a signal the Phantom used to identify himself to everyone who was familiar with his work).

In appearance the car was deceptive. It was an expensive car, true, but there was more to it than that. Under its rakish hood was one of the finest and most powerful motors built. The body was constructed of bulletproof steel and in the rear were gadgets Van had designed for the Phantom's use—a folding makeup table built into the back of the front seat, a compartment for guns, and a space for two or three suits of clothing and other necessities. All of his cars were similarly equipped.

In the early novels, we never knew what type of gun the Phantom would carry. Depending on the author, some times he carried a .45 automatic, or a .38. Later the problem with what caliber gun (or guns at times, when he wore double shoulder holsters) he carries was somewhat taken care of by the including of a gun cabinet in his hidden room. His other accessories were his master-key, a clever contrivance invented by a Viennese locksmith, capable of manipulation so that it could turn the lock behind any keyhole into which it was inserted; his pocket flashlight, wallet with money and his gun.

He selected this last item from a well-stocked arsenal where lethal weapons, loaded, oiled and ready for use, were racked according to size and shape. He had only to slide back a panel in one of the cabinets and there they were, in a neat array. Guns small enough to decorate a woman's purse, large enough to bring down a mountain lion. Guns of all manufacture, all calibers, all handiwork. He merely selected one for the current case. After all, the Phantom was a master with any caliber, big or small.

In the early novels, the Phantom changed disguise every few pages. He could do this in the dark of an alley as easily as if he were sitting before his triple-mirrored desk. He went to great pains to alter his features, and assume the character of anyone he had seen and heard only once: few people were as expert in altering their features as the Phantom. He lived the roles he took, and depended greatly on skillful acting in putting over each identity he created. False whiskers, heavy appliances and cumbersome artificialities were not for him.

Deftly he applied a cream to his face. Instantly it became shades darker. Shadow pencils changed both the color and shape of his eyebrows. Highlights made his cheekbones seem more prominent and his face thinner. An expertly contrived denture gave his lower lip a slight bulge and his chin appear slightly retreating. A dye, which could be quickly removed, made his hair as black as night.

That was all the Phantom needed, and an utter stranger had been created out of those tubes, bottles and jars. The keenest eyes could have detected no trace of a disguise.

The Phantom did maintain several stock disguises, which he applied to certain aliases he used. In the early days he created the alias of Lester Cornwell, actually used first by Norman Daniels in 1934, but used by the other authors at the time. Very likely this was a decision at the editorial level. This alias did not last long, though.

In 1936, again whether by author, editor or rewrite person, the alias of Gunner McGlone was instituted, and again, it didn't last too long. Actually, the alias was only "mentioned" in reference to previous cases at first. However, in the novel, "Cavalcade of Death" (August 1937), the Phantom actually used the disguise. Unfortunately, it was seldom used, though, and soon forgotten entirely. Although in a later story, the alias was even mixed up by changing the alias from Gunner McGlone to Gunner Malone. This alias had a strong resemblance to *The Spider's* Blinky McQuade, and would have worked nicely as an alter ego for the Phantom.

In the later novels, the authors decided upon an alias first used in a Charles Greenberg story, that of a "Mr. Gray," a name the Phantom used when he made contact with Frank Havens, Steve Huston, Chip Dorlan, Inspector Gregg or someone over the phone that he wanted to know he was the Phantom.

Undoubtedly, the longest running alter ego was that of Doctor Paul Bendix, an older gentleman scientist who maintained a warehouse in the Bronx, near the Westchester boundary. This alias was created as part of the changes from the 1936 period, and was maintained throughout most of the series after that, although the character was seldom seen, except in the vicinity of the warehouse.

Van was off to the Bronx laboratory that he had rented and outfitted in the guise of gray-bearded, stoop-shouldered Doctor Paul Bendix. Only Frank Havens knew that the owl-like Bendix and the Phantom were one and the same.

The Bendix role played a major part in the Phantom's varied cases. Many times the disguise of the bearded ancient helped Van penetrate deeper into baffling mysteries and follow through to smashing, brilliant solutions of bewildering crimes.

It was in the Bronx building which housed Doctor Bendix's laboratory that Van kept many bulky reference books and huge files for which he could not have found room in his Park Avenue penthouse. In these files were the complete life stories of every man of note in the country, as well as clippings on everything that had happened to which he might have occasion to refer.

In the small building that stood alone, close to the Westchester line, Van looked around his private laboratory. It was as he had left it. A little more dust, perhaps, a few more empty nuts on the hearth of the big fireplace, dropped by busy squirrels from the woods nearby.

Early in his career the Phantom had realized the necessity of having a headquarters remote from the throbbing heart of the city and had arranged for this place. Here he could work without interruption, in secret. At his disposal were the most modern scientific instruments available. Ray machines, microscopes, and a completely stocked chemical lab for his research work. Arsenal and wardrobe, photographic dark room and filing cabinets containing every scrap of information necessary to him in his war against crime.

Although the badge of the Phantom was mentioned from the very beginning of the series, another object connected to the Phantom of equal popularity was that of the red signal light atop the *Clarion* Building that called the famous crime fighter to another case, novel after novel. This was another of those long-running gimmicks we saw created in 1936, such as in the story from July, "Dealers in Death." The signal light would either be used or mentioned over the coming years, and would last until the last few years of the series.

In the early novels, there was a hodgepodge of gimmicks used in contacting the Phantom in an emergency, from the use of two-way radios, commercial radio broadcasts, traffic lights all over the city being turned on to the red signal to attract his attention. But it was the light atop the *Clarion* Building that eventually worked and became a clarion call for the Phantom.

A couple of curious notes about the famous badge: in an early story, one by D.L. Champion, the Phantom lost the badge for a while, and a man he was with had been wounded and was dying. In order for the Phantom to escape and bring the crooks to justice, this man grabs the badge from the Phantom and leaps to his death from an airplane. When his dead, disfigured body is found, with the famous badge, the crooks believe it is the Phantom Detective. In a later story, "The Grim Shadow of Hate" (June 1941), the Phantom and a group of victims are locked in a basement shelter, cemented and steel-lined, while a fire burns that will kill them all. The Phantom uses his badge to make an atomic bomb by melting it down with certain other chemicals, and blowing a hole in one of the walls to allow them to escape.

FRANK HAVENS: Dignified and handsome, though past middle age, Frank Havens pulled his chair up to the table. Gray-haired and stocky, Havens was the personification of a prosperous business tycoon. For years the *Clarion,* as well as the string of other papers he owned from coast-to-coast, had been a dynamic factor in a campaign against crime.

Frank Havens

Time and again the unceasing crusade of Havens and his editors had done much to expose criminals who otherwise might have escaped the penalties for their wrongdoing. On their activities the *Clarion* had trained a clear, white light, exposing their intrigues and sinister plotting—and was continuing to do so.

Not the least of the success of Havens' unending warfare, however—the greatest element, he would declare himself—was due to the efforts of a character known as the Phantom Detective. This scientific, brilliant and mysterious crime detective, called in by the newspaper owner when police methods were unsuccessful, had crowned the *Clarion's* battles with crime with the glittering laurels of triumph.

Frank Havens was mentioned from the very beginning, and was actually the longest running main character within the series, besides the Phantom, of course. However, he was not always present in the stories. Sometimes he was merely mentioned in passing, or talked with the Phantom over the telephone. At other times, he would not be brought into the story until the very last minute as the Phantom brought the case to a close. Then Frank Havens, the police, and all others involved would appear as if by magic.

From the very beginning we were told that Frank Havens was responsible for creating the Phantom Detective, and that Havens himself sponsored his cases. Usually, an old friend of Havens' would call upon the publisher requesting that he call in the Phantom to solve some terrible trouble that was plaguing him and his friends. From murder to espionage. It was always big crime and super crooks that the police could not handle.

At the very end of the series, with "Murder's Agent," Frank Havens has been set aside. His involvement with the Phantom was to be no more. He was a fascinating character, nevertheless. He had been the perfect model for other pulp father-figures, as well as the movie chapter plays. The pulps and the cliffhangers were very similarly plotted. And Frank Havens was undoubtedly a model for many of them.

> In Frank Havens' lofty office in the *Clarion* Building, the publisher's secretary spoke to her employer over the inter-office communication system.
>
> "Mr. Van Loan to see you, Mr. Havens."
>
> Back came the robust, familiar voice of Van's old friend. "Send him right in, Miss Sawyer. I'll see him immediately."
>
> Van opened a door on the left side of the anteroom and crossed the threshold. The publisher's office was more like a study or library in a private home than a place of business where the intricacies of newspaper publishing were conducted. The draperies at the windows, the plain taupe rug underfoot and the dull-rubbed furniture were set off by the pickled pine bookcases, the wood-burning fireplace with its polished andirons, the framed sporting prints on the walls.

Of course, the office changed considerably over the years, as did the name of the secretary. Some times the secretary was a male, later a female; many names were given to them, until Miss Marsh became something of a regular. At one time there was a secret door in the office that allowed the Phantom to enter from the street straight up to the office without going through the secretary. At one time there was a hidden room in Havens' office, where he could hide people for the Phantom; this room had all the comforts of home.

MURIEL HAVENS: The only child of Frank Havens, Muriel had been mentioned from the very beginning of the series, and it was always known that she was the love interest of the Phantom/Van Loan. However, she was seldom seen in the stories. There were only a couple of appearances during the first ten years, and when she did appear, she often had blonde hair, blue eyes, or dark hair, dark eyes.

Her main status in the beginning was to sit with Van Loan when he visited her father on occasion. In 1936 there was a period when she almost took an active part in the stories, especially in "Sign of the Scar" (September), in which she was returning from a long stay in Europe. Crooks kidnapped her and tied her in a remote-controlled car filled with dynamite and sent it towards a bridge that the crooks were planning on blowing up. This was straight out of the *Operator #5* stories, in which that hero was always rescuing Diane Elliot from horses or cars laden with explosives.

Still, it wasn't until Ralph Oppenheim's story, "Murder Calls the Phantom" (March 1941), that she really sees active duty with the Phantom Detective, and for a period from 1941 through 1942, she was often with the Phantom,

Steve Huston and Chip Dorlan assisting with the investigations.

From 1943 to the end of the series, she was in quite a few of the stories, and quite active. But during the Stewart Sterling period, she was even more available to the Phantom than was normal, as Sterling gave the readers a strong sexual content, and Muriel is no longer the virtuous young girl of the early years.

In "The Silent Killer" (Winter 1952), Muriel discovers the Phantom's true identity, although she had suspected it for

Muriel Havens

years. Towards the end of the story, after the Phantom rescued Muriel from a drug dealer, we read this exchange between the Phantom and Muriel:

> She looked up at him questioning, "You told 'em that Joey Harris couldn't have killed Bob Warren. Have you forgotten that I was present when the murder was committed? Or not too far away. It certainly looked as if Joey was guilty and yet you are so sure he wasn't."
>
> "I know," the Phantom said. "But I saw more than you did that night. I saw the drug peddler, the real murderer, going over the alley fence."
>
> "I see. But you didn't tell the police when they got there did you, Van?"
>
> He was looking out the front window and from where he sat, he could see Inspector Gregg's car pulling up.
>
> "At the time I wanted to work on it myself. I—" He looked at Muriel with a startled expression on his face. "What did you call me just a second ago?"
>
> "I said that you didn't tell the police you saw that man going over the fence. Did you, Van?"
>
> "So you know," the Phantom said quietly.
>
> "I've suspected for a long time, Van. Oh, I admit you fooled 'em wonderfully for years. Richard Curtis Van Loan, sportsman, society man, polo player with scads of money and no ambition. There certainly wasn't any resemblance between him and the Phantom. Perhaps Van Loan was the last person I'd ever have associated with the Phantom Detective. Up until a few months ago."
>
> "Look here, Muriel," he said. "I'm glad the masquerade is over. But I would

like to know how I betrayed myself."

"In a way you'll probably never understand, Van."

"But I'll try, Muriel."

She smiled happily. "You see, I knew Richard Curtis Van Loan well. I knew the Phantom equally well. But how could a girl fall in love with two men at the same time and have no doubts at all but that she really loved both of them? You had to be one person. I could sense it."

So the cat was out of the bag. Norman Daniels is the author who wrote this story, but my guess is that the decision for him to disclose the Phantom's identity to Muriel came from the editorial office. The secret identity had been protected for almost twenty years, with only Frank Havens knowing the secret. This is another reason I believe that Marcus Goldsmith was probably dead by now. I don't think he would have allowed the secret to be let out.

STEVE HUS-TON: Steve was introduced in the novel, "Dealers in Death" (July 1936). In this story, Steve is described thusly: a keen-faced youngster with dark hair and eyes that were very alert. He was a legman for the *Clarion;* a hell-for-leather newshound who used to boast that he was "Hard-Boiled" Huston.

Steve is elevated to crime reporter when the *Clarion's* crime expert, Ace Duveen, was murdered. From then on he

Steve Huston

would be a main player in many of the novels to come. Although he would not always be around, he was usually mentioned. At times, the Phantom would call Steve on the phone and ask that he run down information on certain individuals connected to the case. At other times, he was trouble-deep in the cases and loved it. Always wanting to assist the Phantom in all of his cases, he accepted danger over the mundane job of sitting behind a desk and typewriter.

In the later novels, Steve would become a small, redheaded and wiry ace crime reporter, and the protégé of Frank Havens. In the novel, "Homicide Town" (Fall 1950), a novel reading like Charles Greenberg tells us that Steve's home town was Wainboro, New York. In this story, Steve returns to his hometown for a vacation, only to find corruption and crime running rampant in the city of his birth.

In "Doomed Millions" (Spring 1952), author Norman Daniels lets Steve learn the true identity of the Phantom. In a spy novel, Steve had been captured and was being held as a possible bargaining tool for a master Russian spy. He was rescued in the darkness late at night by the Phantom. But when they come into the light, it is the face of Richard Curtis Van Loan that Steve sees. The Phantom tells Steve openly that he is Van Loan, thus revealing the secret again.

In the following novel, also by Norman Daniels, Steve is still aware of the secret identity of the Phantom. But in the Stewart Sterling novels, he does not know the secret once again. And these were to be Steve's last involvements in the Phantom's cases. He was not even mentioned in the last story, "Murder's Agent" (Summer 1953).

Overall, Steve was a welcome character in the series. For years the editors had searched for a sidekick for the Phantom, trying many men in the role, but it was Frank Havens' ace crime reporter that they eventually settled for.

CHIP DORLAN: A young rebel from the streets of San Francisco, Chip tried to shoot the Phantom, thinking he was a crooked judge that had sentenced his big brother to die on a framed-up charge. Bugs Dorlan had actually been framed by the mob, and the judge was expected to convict Bugs for the crime.

The face of the gunman was as scrawny and pinched as his hand. It was also as dirty. Black eyes that looked too big for the pinched features showed in the shaded light.

The starved, gaunt young body, the thinly

Chip Dorlan

drawn white lips, and the tousle of black hair made it difficult to fix the small gunman's age. The Phantom judged him to be somewhere in his early twenties.

Chip did not remain "gaunt" for long. The Phantom had him sent to New York where Chip became the protégé of the Phantom and worked with him on many cases.

After Laurence Donovan, the author to introduce Chip in "The Sampan Murders" (September 1939), dropped out of the series in the early 40s, so did Chip Dorlan. While Donovan was not the only author to use Chip, the character was almost like he belonged to him, and when the author left the series, Chip was not used long after. In the late 40s, C.S. Montayne brought him back, supposedly after Chip had served in the war as an intelligence officer, where he gained maturity and experience. Unfortunately, Montayne appeared to not like the character of Dorlan, and you could feel it in his writing. It was as if Chip Dorlan had been forced on the author. Actually, Montayne had introduced a character named "Skip" Nolan into his *Phantom* stories, and this could have been the reason that Chip was brought back in. Possibly, the editors had told him to drop Nolan, and use Chip Dorlan instead. Whatever, this Nolan character disappears, and back comes Chip Dorlan—for a little while. His last appearance was in the Fall 1949 story, "The Black Ball of Death," and he was mentioned in the Summer 1950 story, "The Deadly Diamonds," and after that, Chip Dorlan was no more. Chip lives in a Forty-third Street boarding house.

INSPECTOR THOMAS GREGG: The Inspector was a grizzled, middle-aged man with a ruddy complexion and a perennially worried look. His first appearance was in July 1937, "The Beast King Murders," and then appeared off and on until the end of the series. However, Gregg would be replaced off and on with names like Iverness, Inverness, Farrugut, and numerous other inspectors. But, by 1943 Inspector Gregg would be established until the end of the series, and it's his character that is the best known of the police officials to have helped the Phantom in his many cases.

JERRY LANNIGAN: This character was brought into the series in 1936 as a possible choice for a sidekick to the Phantom Detective. He was introduced in "The Sign of the Scar" (September 1936).

The Phantom's shifting eyes centered calculatingly upon a human figure swinging, gorilla-like, along the criss-crossed girders. "Who's that up there?" he demanded.

"A fellow from the engineering department who volunteered to keep checking those girders until the last minute. I've looked up the lad's records myself. He's okay. He was an army mechanic before he went to work for the city ten years ago. I had him stripped and searched before we let him go up there," the inspector said.

The red-haired girder tester had come to the surface and was swimming near Van Loan and the Phantom got a second good look at him. The man's beefy face was bronzed and leathery, and enormous freckles showed beneath his tan. He was staring about with bright, narrowed blue eyes, but there was a big grin on his face.

The man had been chief mechanic in Van Loan's air squadron during the war. He had a penchant for telling tall tales, mostly true, but somewhat exaggerated.

He had been in New York since the war, and knew Van Loan also lived there but had not been able to contact him. He did not know the Phantom's identity, but called the Phantom, "Skipper," and Van Loan called him, "Champ."

He only made three appearances: "The Sign of the Scar," "Empire of Terror" (October 1936), and "The Torch of Doom" (February 1937). It's possible that the author was Emile C. Tepperman. Sgt. MacTavish, from Tepperman's Purple Invasion within the *Operator #5* series, was very similar to Jerry Lannigan.

"SKIP" NOLAN: Created by C.S. Montayne, the character was introduced in the second half of the series. Skip Nolan was an ex-boxer; he began as a minor character, but later became a helper of the Phantom and Steve Huston. His job was to hide away some crook—keep him on ice for as long as the Phantom needed him hidden. There was little to Skip Nolan, but he did appear in four stories, "Murder of a Marionette" (December 1944), "Death to a Diplomat" (October 1945), "The Case of the Poison Formula" (December 1945), and "Death Rides the Winner" (August 1946).

ANDY: Keeping in company with the other authors, Stewart Sterling also brought in a character for his stories. Andy worked on Van Loan's yacht, as its captain, and really performed about the same duties as Skip Nolan. However, he was only in one story, "The Staring Killer" (Winter 1953).

One other item should be mentioned, and that is a place called Longacre Square, in New York City. Apparently, there were many clubs and eating establishments in this area, as the Phantom was often entering the area to meet with one of his contacts, Steve Huston, Chip Dorlan, or Frank Havens. I'm not sure just what all was located in the area. The author, C.S. Montayne usually mentioned "near Longacre Square." This eventually became Times Square, of course.

Some of the clubs mentioned in the later novels were: Toni's, the Pilgrims Club, the Green Spot, Patroons Club, and the Publishers Club. There were many others.

1933
1934
1935
1936
1937
1938
1939
1940
1941
1942
1943
1944
1945
1946
1947
1948
1949
1950
1951
1952
1953

CHAPTER III, SECTION A

THE G. WAYMAN JONES PERIOD: 1933-1934

WITH ALL THE research done on the great hero pulp series from Street & Smith, as well as Popular Publications, and the *Secret Agent "X"* novels, the main characters which are left are from the Standard Magazine group, in particular, are the *Phantom Detective* stories and the early Dan Fowler novels. With no records bring available for us to research, we are left with purely our ability to pick out and identify certain penmanship of certain authors as probable writers of the stories in question. Many times we fail, which is not surprising as a number of authors wrote alike or even copied the writing styles of others—not to mention the possibility of editors and rewrite personnel having their own input to the finished story. So our personal research is often full of flaws. However, we do what we can while the information is available for us to research. What we put down on paper today can be studied tomorrow and, hopefully, more facts added.

The character of the Phantom Detective debuted with the February 1933 issue featuring the story "The Emperor of Death" by G. Wayman Jones. The magazine was copyright THE PHANTOM DETECTIVE, Inc., 570 Seventh Avenue, New York. It was published by Ned Pines, and the editorial director was Leo Margulies. The character of the Phantom Detective was conceived at least as early as 1932. In fact, there was a previous novel published late in 1932 under the G. Wayman Jones name, titled *Alias Mr. Death,* that reads a lot like the future *Phantom* novels.

This hardback edition was published by The Fiction League, and listed previous stories by the same author as *The Phantom Stalks, The Doomed Island,* and *Hell's Mansion.* Though G. Wayman Jones was a house name, it is still very possible that the four stories were by the same author, as we will see in the review of the 1933 *Phantom Detective* stories. There is little question of who wrote *Alias Mr. Death.* In his obituary in the *New York Times,* March 23, 1988, D.L. Champion was credited for writing *The Phantom Detective, Alias Mr. Death* and "Run the Wild River."

Fortunately for researchers, D.L. Champion's early writing style is quite unique and easily identified. His usage of the written word is quite colorful: The scenes become "pregnant with excitement, pregnant with rage, or there is

20

a pregnant silence." Or these:

> ...the legato roar of a machine-gun... Van's own pistol roared obligato... mounted on its diurnal journey through heaven... a silent footstep evanesced into the darkness... the ado of the minute... a machine-gun rattled its ominous threnody... the epitome of all the evil in the world, the apogee of all the hate... tense febrile excitement... shrieks of pain sounded obbligato above the confusion... the scooting cavalcade of cars eschewed the suburban section... a savage obligate to the legato of the engine... the perfidious secretary fell backwards... a smashing right to the jaw ere the other could recover... a banshee wail of bullets... fleet as a dear... deep in the odoriferous filth...

Where most writers of pulp fiction used common words, Champion looked for the less common, words that would send you seeking a dictionary; the action doesn't become feverish, but Champion gives us "febrile" excitement. And how many authors used the word "evanesced?" Not many I bet! Here are some more: apoplectic, exigent, genuflect, expostulated, inured, avidity, ignoble, inured, indubitably, perspicuity, perspicacity, ubiquitous, and perturbation. And there are others. With this information in mind, we can assemble the following list of novels with the possible author(s):

1. THE EMPEROR OF DEATH

VI #1—February 1933
Written by D.L. Champion

Place: New York City; Baltimore, MD; Edgetown

Main characters: The Mad Red, Alexis Hesterterg, Kennel, "Cokey" Day, Sligo, Isaac Block, Silas Bursage, Carl Wooley, Peter Schyville, Clairborne, Mearson, Judge Pinelli, Lewis Bond, Arthur Remis, Naylor, Carson, Ruby, Conners, Manning, Inspector Demaree, Inspector Armitage, Det.-Sgt. O'Neal, Richard Curtis Van Loan/the Phantom, Frank Havens, Muriel Havens

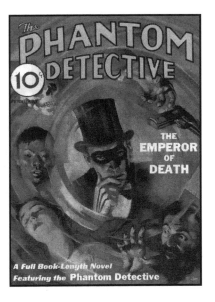

Through Frank Havens, the Phantom is called into the presence of the President of the United States; it appears that a mad scheme is afoot, one that will put world power into the hands of one man—one man known as The Mad Red, a Russian. This mastermind is seeking millions for Russia, plus there are some important documents that he must have in order to blackmail the heads of other nations. The President turns over to the Phantom all the known information about this mad scheme.

From his very first move, it appears that gangdom knows his every turn, and

1934
1935
1936
1937
1938
1939
1940
1941
1942
1943
1944
1945
1946
1947
1948
1949
1950
1951
1952
1953

1933

1934

1935

1936

1937

1938

1939

1940

1941

1942

1943

1944

1945

1946

1947

1948

1949

1950

1951

1952

1953

he is stopped on every maneuver. But through a small criminal dive, the Phantom uncovers the Mad Red's hideout, where are found the drug addicts and small time hoods which are at his disposal. But the game is world conquest, and all of gangdom is at the bidding of this evil genius of crime.

The adventure comes to a climax in Edgetown, where the Mad Red and his criminal army of gangsters have captured the town's inhabitants; they are being held under guard in the local church. The Phantom calls out the National Guard to surround the town and a fierce battle takes place between the combatants.

Notes: Frank Havens is a tall, gray-haired man of about 42. The Phantom wears a Masonic ring. When the Phantom becomes excited, his pulse kicked out a steady hundred and thirty (this would be used often by Champion and others). The Phantom gives some kind of a hand signal to identify himself, but the signal is not described. He has black snapping eyes, and is a skilled hypnotist. Muriel is captured but rescued. Van Loan smokes Egyptian cigarettes, but this is the only time that brand is mentioned. And Muriel has blonde hair.

Availability: *Pulp Classics* #20 (published by Robert Weinberg, 1979), *Thrilling Novels* #16 (published by Fun Stuff Imaginations, 1996), *Wildside Pulp Classics: Phantom Detective* #1 (published by Wildside Press, 2005), *Phantom Detective* #1 (published by Girasol Collectibles, 2007).

2. THE CRIME OF FU KEE WONG

V1 #2—April 1933
Written by D.L. Champion

Place: New York City/Pleansantville

Main characters: Fu Kee Wong, George Rawson, Lee, Hip Lee, Charlie Eadie, Ah Sing (or Ah Chin), Hung Yat Low, Lee Chang, Sen Fong, Hung Mee, Lin Poo, Low Yuen, Soy Foo, Ruth Eadie, Inspector Simmons, Inspector Armitage, Smythe (Haven's butler), Richard Curtis Van Loan/the Phantom, Frank Havens, Muriel Havens

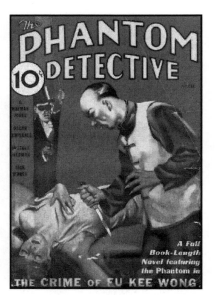

Prophecy spoke of a coming world leader of Chinese ancestry who was destined to rule the world. The Phantom is called into the case by a seating of world ambassadors who have requested his aid in stopping the bloodshed that was soon to erupt if the prophecy came to pass. A while later, a private citizen also requests the Phantom as he has received a threat from the mysterious Fu Kee Wong—a threat of death!

The Phantom locates one of the headquarters of the evil genius and penetrates the hideout several times. He is in disguise as Yat Sen, a Chinese tong man, but is soon captured and put in a cell. Next to his cell, however, is a young girl (Ruth Eadie) who is also a captive. Fu Kee Wong comes seeking the girl for his pleasures but she refuses his advances. The Phantom tells the girl that on the next visit from Fu Kee Wong she is to accept her fate, though when Fu Kee Wong brings her past his cell, she is to push him towards the Phantom. She does, and the Phantom is able to escape and take the girl with him.

Fu Kee Wong is later identified as a white man.

Notes: Muriel is slim and blonde, her mouth a crimson arch. The ring is still present, but now it's the Phantom's identifying symbol. The mastermind rigs up electrical wires to electrocute people on a train while his minions rob it of a load of gold (he also needs the funds to finance his fight for world conquest). This scene strangely enough will be used again in a later story, plus the Spider will also combat a criminal who uses this trick in one of his adventures ("The Corpse Cargo," July 1934).

Availability: *Action Adventure Stories* #79 (published by Fading Shadows, Inc., 2000), *High Adventure* #79 (published by Adventure House, 2004).

3. THE SCARLET MENACE

V1 #3—May 1933
Written by D.L. Champion

Place: Zenia City

Main characters: Mayor Robert Kenwall, Joe Corrigan, Andy, Perkins, Hicks, Jenkins, Hastings, George L. Richards, Ardmore, Simmons, George L. Mawson, Tombs, Naylor, John Lawton, Rogers, Tomers, Hoche, Lombardi, Grey, May, Lacey, Holmes, Leech, Maynard, Richard Curtis Van Loan/the Phantom; Frank Havens is only mentioned

This is a re-wroking of the novel, *Alias Mr. Death*. The town of Zenia City is being ruled by a murderous group known as the Scarlet Menace (it was known as The Murder Club in *Alias Mr. Death*). The mayor went to New York on a secret mission—that of contacting Frank Havens and requesting the help of the Phantom Detective. He has done this without the knowledge of the Scarlet Menace, and suddenly the Phantom is in their midst and causing trouble. They round up every stranger in Zenia City and take them to a theater where they tell the Phantom Detective to step forward or they will kill everyone in the theater (about two hundred people).

Before Van Loan can step forward, though, another man claims to be the Phantom. Before the gangsters can shoot him however, the Phantom saves the

1933
1934
1935
1936
1937
1938
1939
1940
1941
1942
1943
1944
1945
1946
1947
1948
1949
1950
1951
1952
1953

1934

1935

1936

1937

1938

1939

1940

1941

1942

1943

1944

1945

1946

1947

1948

1949

1950

1951

1952

1953

day—along with those two hundred people. The gang has been checkmated, and they still don't know who the Phantom is.

During a bank robbery, the Phantom uses a gas gun to capture one of the crooks and save the booty for a short time. This is the only time a gas gun is used in these early novels.

Notes: The Phantom uses the aid of a man named Rogers, who had the courage to step forward when the gang was looking for the Phantom in that theater. The Phantom has mocking eyes, like chips of crystal. There is a scene where "his heart stood still."

Availability: *The Scarlet Menace* (published by Jim Hanos, 1986).

4. THE ISLAND OF DEATH

V2 #1—June 1933
Written by D.L. Champion

Place: San Francisco; the Philipines; the Island of Death

Main characters: Matsiami, George Rath, Messman, Sen, Yamo, Rawlins, Ricci, Stern, Penwall, Roberts, Wells, Ito, Yigo, Bomers, Ralph, Marie Desplains, Manners, Ruffing, Astsi, Inspector Reeves, Richard Curtis Van Loan/the Phantom; Havens is only mentioned

The Phantom is requested by Washington to assist in their investigation of Matsiami who plans a plot to control the entire Pacific rim—he plans on seizing the Philippines and all military bases in the Pacific. The Phantom has a rendezvous with a Secret Service agent in San Francisco, captures important documents from the enemy and turns them over to the agent. But just as quick, the agent is killed and the papers are stolen.

Five scientists are kidnapped, each an expert in some field of warfare. The Phantom is captured by Matsiami and left on a ship that is to be sunk in the Pacific, while Matsiami and his minions escape by an airship. However, before the ship explodes and sinks, a sailor rescues the Phantom and the two hide aboard the airship. They are taken to the Island of Death but are recaptured. As they steal an airplane and escape from the island, the sailor is fatally wounded. He grabs the Phantom's badge and jumps to his death from the airplane. His body is later found and identified as the Phantom.

Notes: This was one of the better 1933 *Phantom* stories. It involves the second type of theme that Champion was using in these early *Phantom* stories—that of high adventure, as will as mystery. This was also the first appearance of the badge.

Availability: *Action Adventure Stories* #119 (published by Fading Shadows, Inc., 2002), *The Phantom Detective V2N1—Pulp Facsimile* (published by Adventure House, 2009).

1934

1935

1936

1937

1938

1939

1940

1941

1942

1943

1944

1945

1946

1947

1948

1949

1950

1951

1952

1953

5. THE JEWELS OF DOOM

V2 #2—July 1933
Written by D.L. Champion &
Anatole France Feldman

Place: New York City; India

Main characters: The Rajah, Charters, Winton, Louie Senton, Conners, Hari Sigh, George R. Champion, Rossi, Knowles, Iraq, Putra, Akbar, Major Hammersly, Inspector Ralph, Richard Curtis Van Loan/the Phantom, Frank Havens

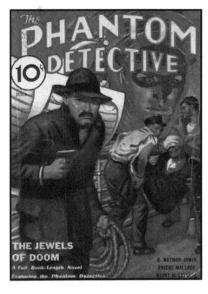

This is a fine novel, although it appears that Champion may have only written the first few, and last few chapters of the story. Feldman may have written the middle chapters of the adventure. It involves, at first, the robbery of a Rajah's fortune in jewels. The Phantom foils the robbery by placing fake jewels in the safe instead of the real jewels. But just as quickly, the real Rajah and the real jewels are stolen before the Phantom can turn around. And just as quickly it appears that a new author is at the helm.

The adventure takes on a deeper meaning than just the theft of jewels. Now it appears that a syndicate is about to lose its control over the trade dealings between America and India. One of the syndicate leaders plans to dispose of the current Rajah, replacing him with a man he can control. New York gangsters are used in the beginning and are taken to India as the adventure switches to that locale. The jewels now mean the success of the overthrow of the current Rajah.

The Phantom is captured in New York City as he boards a submarine belonging to the enemy. He is held captive until the sub approaches India. At this point the Phantom escapes his cell and escapes through a torpedo tube in the sub, floating to the surface in an air-bubble, then swimming to shore. But once on land he enters the presence of the evil mastermind and is dropped through a trap door and falls into a basement of horror—in which a prehistoric giant spider has his den. The Phantom fights his way from this trap, after killing the spider with an improvised club, then trails the criminals through the jungle to a mansion owned by the current Rajah. Here a weird religious ceremony is performed in which a dead Rajah (dead thousands of years) is to rise again and place his crown (jewels) on the new leader of India. But the Phantom arrives in time to save the old Rajah and unmask the syndicate boss who has

1933

1934

1935

1936

1937

1938

1939

1940

1941

1942

1943

1944

1945

1946

1947

1948

1949

1950

1951

1952

1953

masterminded the plot.

Notes: This was an exciting adventure, even with the science fiction elements. There were a number of plot devices that appeared in the story that makes me think Feldman had a hand in this. First is the scene in a morgue. Second is the room of horror—in this case the giant spider in its den. The idea of the Phantom being shot through a torpedo tube, then floating to the surface within an air bubble was a little far-fetched—but then, so was the giant spider! Just how much of the story was actually written by D.L. Champion, there's little telling. Again, his writing style is present for the first couple of chapters, then it appears again toward the end chapters. But the middle section does not conform to his writing style. The Phantom has wavy brown hair. There is new a secret closet entrance/exit to Haven's newspaper offices that the Phantom can use undetected by the office personnel. A similar morgue scene is used in the upcoming novels, "The Sinister Hand of Satan" (October 1933) and "The Tick-Tack-Toe Murders" (March 1934).

Availability: *The Jewels of Doom* (published by Jim Hanos, 1986).

6. THIRTEEN CARDS OF DEATH

V2 #3—August 1933
Written by D.L. Champion

Place: New York City; Hollywood, California

Main characters: Richard Summers, Trent Wells, Norwell Rains, Martin, George Winters, Mango, Foo Chang, Carson L. Downes, Ward Rochamber, Ruthie, Maynard, Inspector Harlow, Inspector Finley, Richard Curtis Van Loan/the Phantom, Frank Havens, Muriel Havens

Again, the *Alias Mr. Death* plot; this time there are thirteen members of a group who use a deck of cards as their identities. They each wear a hooded suit with a symbol of a playing-card heart—the ace of hearts, King of hearts, queen of hearts, etc. They each draw a name from a hat (each name is that of a millionaire) and the name that each has drawn belongs to that individual. A threat of death is sent to that person, and he is told that he will die if he doesn't turn over a hundred thousand dollars at a certain time. They figure that ten out of thirteen will capitulate, so the group will receive one million dollars with each drawing from the hat. The group immediately frames the Phantom as one of the killers. The police quickly arrest Frank Havens, while they start a manhunt for the Phantom Detective.

Notes: The story ends in something of a battle on an island get-away the group maintains, similar to the story of "The Emperor of Death" (February 1933). Typical of Champion's stories, this small group has big plans. Plus they launch an attack on the police headquarters—and get away with it! During these early novels, Frank Havens' part is actually quite ridiculous. He is a man of importance, yet he is arrested without thought, and not allowed bail, for no apparent reason—except that the Phantom is suspected of a crime. Remember, Havens is a millionaire himself, and the owner of a chain of national newspapers. Maynard is listed as Haven's butler—Champion has forgotten he named him Smythe previously. Muriel is now a brunette. Champion did not remember what color her hair was from one novel to the next. Also, Muriel seldom has any speaking parts to the action. In "The Crime of Fu Kee Wong" (April 1933) she did have a conversation with Van Loan. She had gotten on the young man for not visiting with her for such a long time. Van had replied that he had been very busy, to which Muriel replied, "Busy at what, clipping coupons?"

Availability: *The Phantom Detective V2N3—Pulp Facsimile* (published by Adventure House, 2008).

7. CITIES FOR RANSOM

V3 #1—September 1933
Written by Arthur J. Burks

Place: San Francisco; Haiti; Metropole City (this is either New York or near Miami, FL)

Main characters: The Black Admiral, Leslie Nadal, Timothy Malarskey, J. P. Lowman, Natalie, Brandon, Harry Klein, Al Graham, George Billingsley, Fannard Bogart, Simon Legarto, Jad Leontes, Pierre Tombe, Petit Goave, Laos, Anses-a-Pitre, Tumiseau, Plaisance, Asa Mordant, Richard Curtis Van Loan/the Phantom, Frank Havens; Muriel Havens is only mentioned

Metropole City is under siege by a mysterious person known as the Black Admiral. He is blackmailing the city for millions of dollars—pay or face mass destruction. The world isn't safe as long as this dastardly devil is allowed to run loose. The Phantom is quickly called—the mayor of that city calls Frank Havens in his office in San Francisco and requests that he contact the Phantom Detective. The Phantom is with Frank at the time, and says that he will fly immediately to Metropole City. No sooner does he leave in Van Loan's personal airplane, but an enemy aircraft is sighted heading for San Francisco—loaded with bombs. The Black Admiral has already figured that the Phantom will be called in and sends an airplane to wreak havoc on San Francisco. Van Loan has a short battle

1934
1935
1936
1937
1938
1939
1940
1941
1942
1943
1944
1945
1946
1947
1948
1949
1950
1951
1952
1953

1933
1934
1935
1936
1937
1938
1939
1940
1941
1942
1943
1944
1945
1946
1947
1948
1949
1950
1951
1952
1953

with this enemy aircraft, crashing it before reaching the city proper. Shortly he lands in Metropole City where everybody knows Richard Curtis Van Loan by sight. Then he appears in the mayor's office as the Phantom. He finds that the city is in dire need of a leader and quickly assumes that position.

He quickly triangulates a radio massage that appears to be coming from Haiti. With little ado, he jumps back in Van Loan's airplane and heads for Haiti. Somewhere he has obtained certain lights that are wrapped around his airplane that when turned on resemble a giant snake. This frightens the local natives into thinking that the snake has attacked the flying bird and is bringing it down to earth. It also keeps them away while the Phantom tracks into the jungle where he suspects the enemy is headquartered. There is a battle and he is captured by the Black Admiral's men. The Phantom escapes right after his enemy departs in a plane. So it's back into the air and a swift flight back to Metropole City.

The Phantom learns that an old prophecy had foretold the arrival of a white-faced black man who would rule the world—or some such nonsense. Anyway, the Black Admiral believed that he was this prophesied person. Fortunately, the Phantom makes quick work of him. The Black Admiral sets a blast that destroys his skyscraper in Metropole City, but he is in it when it explodes, and we never learn his identity—nor do we really want to.

Notes: It's easily understood that whoever this present author is, it isn't D. L. Champion. It can also be assumed that he probably read the novel "Island of Death" (June 1933) to get a feel of the series before writing the story, as that was the story in which the Phantom starts the case while in San Francisco. So our present author probably believes that this is the location of Havens' offices and the home of the Phantom. Local criminals in Metropole City give their support to the city officials in combating the evil Black Admiral, plus the black community also wants him caught, as they want nothing to do with this crazed black man. Such sentences appear as "I wear no man's collar... I've made my bed... look for me when you see me coming... in all the Bulls of Bashen." When he is captured he does not hide his identity as that of the Phantom. No sooner is he captured than he says, "I am the Phantom!" The Black Admiral says things like "...babes in the woods to handle masters of men." Police are called "coppers." Machine-guns are called "tommies." Guns are "gats."

8. THE SINISTER HAND OF SATAN
V3 #2—October 1933
Written by Anatole France Feldman

Place: New York City

Main characters: D-R-X, Leslie Stephens, Dr. Charles Frazer, Norman Striker, Doctor Weintraub, Jukes, Maida, Capt. Meehan, Sgt. Norbeck, Dr. Hale is the Medical Examiner, Armitage is the D.A., old Bolton works the night shift at the morgue, Richard Curtis Van Loan/the Phantom, Frank Havens; Muriel is only mentioned

From the X gland comes a chemical that rejuvenates body cells, making old men young again—for a short time, then another X gland is required! And the

X gland comes from... the human brain!

A famous doctor is found in his laboratory—dead. His brain is exposed and there appears to have been an operation performed on the brain. Almost immediately other people are found throughout the city dead with similar operations performed on their brains. There appears to be no connection between them, as they come from varied lifestyles, from the poor to the rich, from the ranks of the homeless, to men of importance. The police are baffled and call in the Phantom.

Notes: D.L. Champion does not appear to be connected to this story in any way. Someone in the story asks the Phantom, "Who—what are you—man—devil—or—?" To which Van Loan replies, "Neither, I'm just... the Phantom!" This new author says things like "murder has been done—foul murder." Newspapers don't just run headlines, they run "ebon" headlines. Frank Havens is now thirty years older than Van Loan. In the beginning Frank Havens was given the age of 42, which, if he is now thirty years older than Van Loan, would have made Van Loan 12 years old. Anyway, Frank Havens is more realistically around 55 to 60. Havens' newspaper, the *Clarion*, is now called the *Daily Clarion*. The character of Armitage, once an inspector in the police department, is now the D.A. The morgue is at City Hospital, and will play an important role in upcoming stories, as a plot device of this current author. The Phantom has broad shoulders, the lithe sinewy build of the professional athlete. Beneath a slouch hat, set at a jaunty angle, are piercing black eyes. Old Bolton was the night attendant at City Morgue. The Phantom wears two automatics on his hips. Sentences become a little more colorful now: "...he turned a livid purple... red fires of rage... ballets sang a dirge of death... spider's web of steel." There is more melodrama in this story than any of Champion's. You might recall the fight scene in "The Jewels of Doom" (June 1933) between the Phantom and the giant spider. A death-defying fight takes place on the wing of a plane in this current novel. The Phantom swims out to a plane at rest on the water, a plane under the control of the mastermind, being piloted by one of his minions. As the Phantom reaches out and grabs hold with one hand, the plane takes to the air. Van Loan holds on with one hand as the plane quickly rises to three, then five thousand feet in the air. But with one hand he holds on until the pilot starts doing stunts in an attempt to throw him from the wing. In one

1933
1934
1935
1936
1937
1938
1939
1940
1941
1942
1943
1944
1945
1946
1947
1948
1949
1950
1951
1952
1953

maneuver the pilot makes a mistake and Van Loan is able to grasp the wing with both hands. Now he crawls along the wing, as the plane attempts loops and other maneuvers, until the Phantom reaches the cockpit and pulls the pilot from the plane, throwing him to his death five thousand feat below! Van Loan then takes the controls and lands the plane safely.

There is a clue of a broken hypodermic needle. This clue would surface in a number of other Phantom stories as well as the Dan Fowler novels, and it is probably the same author in most cases. Van Loan's fingers drummed a silent tattoo. He uses gunpowder—from spare bullets—to blow his cell door open. The girl, Maida, is the daughter of Armitage, the D.A. The scene in the morgue is quite dramatic, too: Van Loan is examining a dead body when a supposed corpse comes up from a nearby slab and tries to stick a knife into him. This is one of the mastermind's individual minions from his army of corpses; men who had lived after their X glands had been removed. There is also a scene in a room of horror where this mastermind had performed earlier operations on poor dead souls in the past. Also, in the laboratory of the first victim, there are cages of giant rodents, from some secret experiments being performed. A lot of material from this story would work its way into future novels as well, so this current author is giving shape to the character at last. Actually, I think this novel helped give some kind of steady continuation to the series, where it was becoming stagnated with Champion's entries alone. This is probably the same author that contributed to "The Jewels of Doom."

9. GAMBLERS IN DEATH

V3 #3—November 1933
Written by Anatole France Feldman

Place: New York; New Jersey

Main characters: The Big Shot, Lucky Paul Clayborne, Kid Carey, Johnny Hopper, Steve Yates, Harry Fagin, Skyhigh Billings, Roy Gates, Ponzi Revelle, "Red" Stephen McLarnin, Allan Forbes, Monty Forsythe, Mrs. Greehan, Doyle, Grogan, King Terry, Simmons, Capt. Valentine, Fradzen, Turrner, Marty Farrell, Morton, Lefty Martin, Lou Goldstein, Fink, Frick, Nelson, Wilson Marden, Jerry Fagin (probably the same character as Harry Fagin, the author just forgot the first name), Curtis Parker, Gil Porter, Sgt. Flynn, Smythe, Flanagan, Croyden (now the D.A.), Martin Christie (Phantom alias), Richard Curtis Van Loan/the Phantom, Frank Havens, Muriel Havens, Police Commissioner Farrar

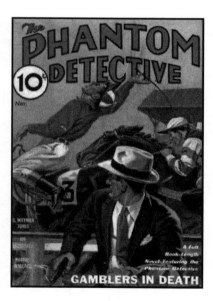

The story is pretty good, but remains a minor entry. The case involves murder and big crime around the sporting arenas—horse racing, boxing and oth-

1934

1935

1936

1937

1938

1939

1940

1941

1942

1943

1944

1945

1946

1947

1948

1949

1950

1951

1952

1953

ers. The Phantom must find out who is controlling and fixing events in the racing and boxing arenas, and doing all the killing to reach his own ends. The police should have been able to handle this one.

Notes: This is the first use of the plot device of gathering all of the suspects into one room. Another plot device is that of an important meeting taking place—with the Phantom in attendance—when a messenger arrives bringing death—poison in the letter, or some such. An attempt at murder, or a murder accomplished. Again, there is a clue of a broken hypodermic needle, which goes back to the last issue. Crooks say "jeez." And the Phantom burst out with "gosh." Van Loan is also dropped through another trap door, which will become a common occurrence in the series. The Phantom has a habit of blowing kisses (sarcastically) at the crooks. Police are "coppers." There are colorful sentences; a mottled purple, red rage, etc. And Van Loan winks at himself and others. Van Loan and Muriel go to the theater, but there is no recorded conversation between them, nor is she described in any way. The Phantom uses the disguise of Martin Christie. Again, the question, "Are you man—devil—or—?" And again, Van Loan replies, "Neither, I'm just... the Phantom!" I'm not positive that this is the same author as last issue, but many of the same clues are in both stories, which leads me to conclude that both stories are by the same author. I can't discount a rewrite person adding these clues that I'm finding. The character of Grogan is that of a gorilla-type individual, which will also be used again. And Smythe is back as Havens' butler.

10. THE YELLOW MURDERS

V4 #1—December 1933
Written by D.L. Champion &
Anatole France Feldmen

Place: New York

Main characters: Ching Po, Morton Clay, Judson Snell, Mark Heiner, Jed Martin, Jake Lingle, Cronin, Wong Lee, "Turk" Sam Yassiff, Fu Yat Len, Toy Soo, Hip Sing, Ming Soy, Clayton Burwell (Phantom alias), Lui Hun, Sing Wu, Wah Poo, Wo Li, Singapore Sal (first of the femme fatales), Ah Ling, Soo Ching, Ling Yum, Jasper Ayehorn (Phantom alias), Lu Potaru, Yuen, Sgt. Michael Xavier Quinlin, Nevers, Becker, Norman, Capt. Svenson, Ruby DeViere, Richard Curtis Van Loan/the Phantom, Frank Havens

This novel involves murder and big crime around the liquor and dope racket. Sam Yassiff, the "Turk," runs illegal liquor for a living. He has a paramour named Ruby DeViere in the beginning. But we learn that five years ago he had gotten into the drug trade, and a

1933
1934
1935
1936
1937
1938
1939
1940
1941
1942
1943
1944
1945
1946
1947
1948
1949
1950
1951
1952
1953

big gang war between Yassiff and a Chinese gentleman named Ching Po broke out which resulted in many deaths, and the disappearance of the Chinese leader, Ching Po. However, it appears that Ching Po is back now, and with him is Singapore Sal, a half-caste beauty who was once Yassiff's paramour until he kicked her out. Ching Po and Singapore Sal have teamed up together to take back the drug trade—and to kill the Turk at the same time.

Notes: The novel starts out in typical Champion style, with all the clues present—for the first chapters, then there appears to have been another author take over the story. It begins like previous Champion stories about the Chinese, Japanese and Indians, but then the story takes a critical turn. Champion's writing style is in full steam but after only a couple of chapters the writing switches drastically away from the known Champion style. Ruby DeViere is quickly forgotten by the new author and he brings in his own woman character, femme fatale Singapore Sal. Nor does the writing style of Champion return. If Champion wrote more than the first few chapters, then I would guess that Feldman threw out the later chapters in order to work his own story to a satisfactory conclusion. The Phantom's badge is back. The *Clarion* is the *Daily Clarion*. There are colorful sentences again: His face turned green. A purple cicatrix. Phantom uses the disguise of Clayton Burwell. He winks. Another disguise he uses is that of Jasper Ayeborn. Though Feldman did a fairly nice job on the story, compared to Champion's previous entries of "The Emperor of Death" (February 1933), "The Crime of Fu Kee Wong" (April 1933) and "The Island of Death" (June 1933), I can't help but feel that if he had completed "The Yellow Murders," we'd have a better story than this little entry. Again, just how much of this story was by D.L. Champion and how much belonged to Feldman, I don't know. But from the writing style, I would say that Champion only wrote the first few chapters. A minor clue of an apartment numbered 3-D appears in the story; I've seen mention of an apartment 3-D in previous stories—whether by Champion or Feldman.

Availability: *The Phantom Detective V4N1—Pulp Facsimile* (published by Adventure House, 2007).

11. THE SIGN OF DEATH

V4 #2—January 1934
Written by D.L. Champion

Place: New York; New Jersey; No Man's Plain, KY

Main characters: The Titan, Charles Raymond, George Burtis, Tactin, John Cleary, Charles Cleary, Harry Roberts, Bill, Joe, Maynard, Malloy, Harding, Slade, Genners, Ricci, Loring Hellman,

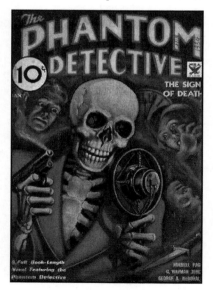

Samuel Karns, Ronald Crane, Stern, Chalmers, Andrews, Rawlins, Regina Crane, Richard Curtis Van Loan/the Phantom, Frank Havens

This is a similar story to *Alias Mr. Death*, "The Emperor of Death" (February 1933) and "The Scarlet Menace" (May 1933). Again, a secret group, ruled over by a mastermind, has big plans of controlling the worldwide trade of liquor. He has a printing press to make counterfeit liquor stamps, and a radio network to broadcast to his minions all over the United States. As in "The Emperor of Death," there is a big finale at the mastermind's hideout in an area of Kentucky known as No Man's Plain. The police and militia surround the area while the Phantom works from the inside.

Notes: The badge is present. The girl, Regina, performs a similar rescue of the Phantom as did Ruth Eadie in "The Crime of Fu Kee Wong" (April 1933). Also, the girl hums "The Prisoner's Song." This was similarly done in a previous novel, probably "The Crime of Fu Kee Wong."

12. DEATH'S DIARY

V4 #3—February 1934
Written by D.L. Champion

Place: Chicago, IL; New York City

Main characters: Larry Shane, Caswell, Charlie "Cutting" Short, Robert Glebe, Professor Burgmeister, Richard Curtis Van Loan/the Phantom, Yegg Drummond (Phantom alias), Segnor Perrini, Capt. Scooner, Slicker Thomas, Inspector Kelly, Kondo, Stewart Allmon, Valerie West, Harlow (Phantom alias), Welsh, Charter, Naiada, Cummings, Frank Havens, Muriel Havens

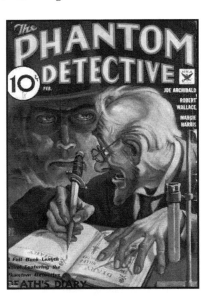

In a novel with some similarities to "Thirteen Cards of Death" (August 1933), a man disguised as the Phantom murders another man in front of witnesses, and with the Phantom framed for the murder, the police immediately start after Frank Havens, demanding that he reveal the Phantom's identity.

Actually, the story begins at a fair in Chicago, as an important businessman leaps to his death from a carnival ride high in the sky. Van Loan is visiting the fair and witnesses the death. He immediately recognizes it as a murder and starts his investigation. However, just as quickly, and with no fanfare, the action switches to New York City—where the Phantom gets framed for the murder.

Notes: As with "Thirteen Cards of Death," Frank Havens is hounded by the police to turn the Phantom over to them. The Phantom uses the aliases of Yegg Drummond and Harlow, plus disguises himself as a black man. Van

1933
1934
1935
1936
1937
1938
1939
1940
1941
1942
1943
1944
1945
1946
1947
1948
1949
1950
1951
1952
1953

1933

1934

1935

1936

1937

1938

1939

1940

1941

1942

1943

1944

1945

1946

1947

1948

1949

1950

1951

1952

1953

Loan speaks with Muriel Havens over the telephone, plus she makes an appearance during the novel, stepping out of an elevator as a crook rushes by her. At one point, when it was necessary for the Phantom to climb a tall building, he attaches rubber suction cups to his shoes, which allow him to climb the granite wall like a human fly. The "Diary" of which this story is all about, appears to contain only blank pages; however, the Phantom discovers that with special glasses he can read invisible printing on the pages. (Champion uses a lot of secret writing, and gimmicks that are needed to read it.) One of the crooks, Kondo, has no ears. On the local radio, there is a program that is known as *The Frank Havens Hour,* sponsored by Havens and features orchestral music. During this hour, if the Phantom is needed, a certain signal is flashed and the Phantom will call on Havens immediately. The Phantom, on a Coast Guard boat, chases the villain across the water to a place called the Isle of White Orchids, where the typical Champion ending takes place. Of interest is a young man named Chalmers, who aided the Phantom in the story; at the end they bargain to be life-long friends, and the Phantom promises to call on him when he is needed. This incident not only recalls similar characters from previous stories, but is a prediction of the future. In later stories, especially in 1936, the editors were looking for a companion for the Phantom. So numerous men were introduced into the stories, but none would be accepted until 1936, when the kid reporter Steve Huston makes his appearance and becomes the Phantom's right-hand man. D.L. Champion introduced a lot of women named Ruth, Ruby, Regina, or others with an "R." Why he did this, I have no idea, but it could be important.

Availability: *The Phantom Detective V4N3—Pulp Facsimile* (published by Adventure House, 2007).

The early stories of the Phantom, at least these by Champion, did not allow the Phantom to grow in characterization. There was little change during the first year. But when the new author started writing the series—or at least filling in for Champion—we find the first real changes. Changes that would shape the series in coming years. With the exception of "Cities for Ransom" (September 1933), thankfully. By the end of 1933, with new author(s), the Phantom is starting to take shape and becomes more three-dimensional. In 1934, the Phantom would be worked out to how the character would flesh out in the years ahead. The 1933 novels, except for their uniqueness, can be overlooked as great Phantom novels. They weren't. The real Phantom took shape in 1934. But 1933 was a unique year, and a lot of fun. D.L. Champion was an interesting writer, regardless of his faults, and he did create the series. Unfortunately, he did not have the imagination to build upon the character—this would be done by others. One other small clue I did notice in Champion's novels—he used a lot of Second National Banks in his stories instead of First Nationals and other titles.

1933

1934

1935

1936

1937

1938

1939

1940

1941

1942

1943

1944

1945

1946

1947

1948

1949

1950

1951

1952

1953

CHAPTER III, SECTION B

THE ROBERT WALLACE YEARS: 1934-1935

WITHOUT WARNING, THE G. Wayman Jones name is suddenly dropped from the series, and Robert Wallace will become the house name used for the remainder of the long run. There is no explanation; G. Wayman Jones will be used on other series in the future, as well as individual stories, so it wasn't abandoned completely. Just dropped from *The Phantom Detective*. If I were to hazard a guess, I would propose that the mysterious Marcus Goldsmith might have had something to do with the change in author names. It's very likely that Mr. Goldsmith did not like the Jones moniker, and ordered the switch in names. But who can say?

13. THE TICK-TACK-TOE MURDERS

V5 #1—March 1934

Written by Anatole France Feldman

Place: New York City

Main characters: The Ghoul, Judge Victor Pastor, Jon Piazza, Dan Parkis, Paul Silver, Jenkins, Mark Farrington, Flash Raleigh, Raymond Turner, Grimes, George Coombs, Robert Patrick, Joe Martin, Arthur Carrin, Will Buckley, Tobias Grime, Featherstone, Det.-Sgt. Rafferty, Inspector Walsh, Brady, Petrucci, Ryan, Norris is the medical examiner, Smythe is back as Havens' butler, Richard Curtis Van Loan/the Phantom, Frank Havens

This story is very similar to "The Sinister Hand of Satan" (October 1933). Men are found murdered throughout the city, some poor, some rich, some important, others not. The murders seem random. The mastermind immediately sets a trap for the

Phantom, captures him, brings him to his hideout and challenges him to a game of death, then has him released.

Notes: Again, we have a story full of melodrama. The sentences are more colorful—people have purple faces, the scarlet red of blood, green shades; a lurid flash of heliotrope exploded; he fought against the black abyss; brain is consumed by liquid fire; incipient pains swept over him; evil, malevolent eyes; stroked his Mephistophelian chin with prehensile fingers; fires of hell raged in his eyes. The Phantom thinks of himself as the Hand of Judgment, Righter of Wrongs, Flaming Sword of Retribution. The mastermind and his henchmen are ghouls. There is another horror room, and the now-familiar scene in the morgue. Similar to "The Sinister Hand of Satan," one of the Ghoul's minions is caught and takes a poison capsule to commit suicide before he can be questioned. The *Clarion* is the *Daily Clarion*. His fingers drum an impatient tattoo. The inspector pulled at the lobe of his left ear (the first time for this practice); the Phantom pulled meditatively at an ear. Another clue (which has happened before, but not recorded by me) is the Phantom giving bills of sizable denomination to cab drivers. Again, the clue of a broken hypodermic needle. There is a character that is described as a gorilla-type (similar to Grogan in a previous novel). Flash Raleigh is a notorious gambler. Again, we have an apartment numbered 3-D. Plenty of melodrama. Certainly the same author as "The Sinister Hand of Satan," plus there are clues that tie it in with "Gamblers in Death" (November 1933), possible connections to "The Jewels of Doom" (July 1933) and "The Yellow Murders" (December 1933), which had been started by Champion but finished by someone else.

Availability: *The Phantom Detective V5N1—Pulp Facsimile* (published by Adventure House, 2009).

14. MURDER CITY

V5 #2—April 1934
Written by D.L. Champion

Place: Covington; New York City

Main characters: JAF, Ralph Summers, Police Chief Harner, Doctor Jammers, Joe Rivers, Evelyn Reid (Drake), Mayor Greyson, Frank Havens, Richard Curtis Van Loan/the Phantom, Sloane, David Drake, Latson, Luigi, Gotha, Eben Jasper, Herbert, John Albert Finley, Doctor Richards, Robert Simpson, Kigos, Lucas

Yet another story patterned after *Alias Mr. Death* and "The Scarlet Menace" (May 1933). The mayor of Covington contacts Frank Havens in New York City, requesting help from the Phan-

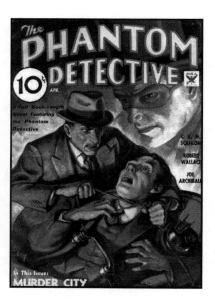

1934

1935

1936

1937

1938

1939

1940

1941

1942

1943

1944

1945

1946

1947

1948

1949

1950

1951

1952

1953

tom: a wave of mysterious murders have occurred in his town, while other important citizens appear to have lost their minds. The only clues are a mysterious bearded man with hypnotic powers, and a woman wearing a thick veil.

The Phantom heads for Covington. Along the route he picks up a remote-controlled automobile with a figure sitting at the wheel meant to represent himself. This car is ambushed as they near town, but the Phantom, operating the remote control from his car in the rear, shoots it out with the ambusher. From there on the Phantom is involved in a mad, violent rush to solve the case before others are killed or driven insane.

At the bottom of the mystery is millions in inheritance, impersonation, and sudden death.

Notes: Sloane, the city editor at the *Clarion*, is killed in the *Clarion* building; this is a plot device that will happen over and over again.

Availability: *High Adventure* #52 (published by Adventure House, 2000), *The Phantom Detective V5N2—Pulp Facsimile* (published by Adventure House, 2009).

15. THE CRIMSON KILLER

V5 #3—May 1934
Written by D.L. Champion

Place: New York City

Main characters: Frank Havens, Police Commissioner James Hapwood, Inspector Hulfweig, Richard Curtis Van Loan/the Phantom, Red Monk, Dudge, Ralph Norwood, Tom Nolar, Harris, Dave Walsh (Phantom alias), Craig, Mr. Ventrusco (D.A.), Smiling Sam, Arthur Mullens, Police Chief Mallow

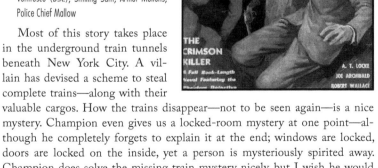

Most of this story takes place in the underground train tunnels beneath New York City. A villain has devised a scheme to steal complete trains—along with their valuable cargos. How the trains disappear—not to be seen again—is a nice mystery. Champion even gives us a locked-room mystery at one point—although he completely forgets to explain it at the end; windows are locked, doors are locked on the inside, yet a person is mysteriously spirited away. Champion does solve the missing train mystery nicely, but I wish he would have also let us know how the man disappeared from that room!

The story actually has similarities to several of Champion's 1933 stories. Very little new material. In most of Champion's stories, the Phantom will be captured and taken to a criminal hideout near a large river or other body of

1933
1934
1935
1936
1937
1938
1939
1940
1941
1942
1943
1944
1945
1946
1947
1948
1949
1950
1951
1952
1953

1933

1934

1935

1936

1937

1938

1939

1940

1941

1942

1943

1944

1945

1946

1947

1948

1949

1950

1951

1952

1953

water. When he escapes, he is swept away so fast he has no idea where the hideout had been. In this present story, he is captured while underground and is spirited away to some underground chamber. When he escapes, he climbs to the top of a speeding train that is flashing by. Once on top of the train he passes out, and is swept away from the area, so he will have no idea where it was he had been held captive. A neat switch from the water escape theme.

Notes: Ralph Norwood is Frank Havens' nephew. Every so often Champion drops the use of the word "febrile," and uses feverish instead. A possible sign of the future, as I'm not so sure the editor liked for him to use those fifty-cent words that he was so proud of. Still, he does continue to get in an occasional febrile and evanesced, as well as a few others. Van Loan removed the powder from his bullets and made an explosive charge. There are some plot devices from "The Emperor of Death" (February 1933) and others. For instance, the villain from "Emperor" was the Mad Red while in this current story he is called the Red Monk. The character of Craig is similar to Bomers, a character from "The Island of Death" (June 1933), and is killed early in this story. There is a scene in the story where hungry hounds are chained in a tunnel passageway to guard the entrance to the hideout. The chains are inserted through a small hole in the wall of the cavern, and can be pulled inward—forcing the hounds against the walls, allowing crooks to pass when they enter or leave the hideout. The Phantom uses the alias of Mr. Walsh. The badge of the Phantom is present in all of these 1934 stories.

Availability: *The Crimson Killer* (published by Jim Hanos, 1985).

16. DIAMONDS OF DEATH

V6 #1—June 1934

Written by D.L. Champion

Place: New York City

Main characters: King of Diamonds, Waldo Reiner, Frank Havens, Deputy Police Inspector Graves, Richard Curtis Van Loan/the Phantom, Colton, Lawrence Rivers, Alvin Mathews, Federal D.A. Hallway, Josiah Glebe, Richard Stanton, Ralph Naylor

Again, Champion relies on old plots. This current story has similarities to "Thirteen Cards of Death" (August 1933), "Death's Diary" (February 1934), and others. A criminal known as the King of Diamonds has sent out notes of doom to certain men of wealth. The notes request a certain sum of money to be paid or they will die.

Aiding the mastermind is a group of African warriors who kill with spears. These men appear completely devoted to the King of Diamonds, and willingly die for him.

Notes: Havens broadcasts a call for the Phantom on the police radio band. This phrase is new: "...invisible Damoclean thread...." The Fourth National Bank (Champion either disliked using First National, or the editorial staff did not want First Nationals used. Makes me wonder if possibly Mr. Goldsmith had something to do with it?). The girl involved in the case is never identified or named. The interior artist is not named, but his work will appear from now on. Will Gilbert was the interior artist in all previous issues. The use of Africans is in keeping with Champion's previous novels that featured Chinese, Japanese, Indians, and Russians. Perhaps to give the stories an international touch. In this case, the Africans ware actually handled fairly well. Except for the tired old cliché of the black slave who is completely devoted to his white master, Champion gives them a heritage of proud warrior blood. When the Phantom and a giant African entered into combat, it was man against man. The Phantom was not "superior" because he was white.

Availability: *The Phantom Detective V5N1—Pulp Facsimile* (published by Adventure House, 2008).

17. THE TALKING DEAD

V6 #2—July 1934
Written by D.L. Champion

Place: Hollywood, CA

Main characters: Assistant D.A. Trivers, Mysto, Richard Curtis Van Loan/the Phantom, Gernsback, Harley, Joe, Greyson, Police Chief Foster, Paul Powers, Doctor Strathers, Madame Kalin, Frank Havens (mentioned only), Clayton Harris, Richard Burr, Henry Harper, Stephen Crier, Elmer Barnes, John Hastings (Phantom alias), Jenkins, Blanche Powers, Jeff Webster, Henry Rauerback

Van Loan is again on vacation, this time in Hollywood, California, when he sees a dead man in the window of a store. The man is not who he is supposed to be. The man was supposed to be Mysto, a human corpse who uses drugs to go into a cataleptic state. The real Mysto escapes when the police are called. Upon investigation more dead bodies are found in the area.

The case appears to involve the mastermind in a plot to hold certain men of wealth in a state of near-death to obtain profit from their next of kin.

The Phantom is captured and taken to the crooks' hideout, where he quick-

1933

1934

1935

1936

1937

1938

1939

1940

1941

1942

1943

1944

1945

1946

1947

1948

1949

1950

1951

1952

1953

1933

1934

1935

1936

1937

1938

1939

1940

1941

1942

1943

1944

1945

1946

1947

1948

1949

1950

1951

1952

1953

ly escapes—again, near a body of water similar to those rivers found in New York City. The Phantom is found shortly after his escape by a man named Harley (one of the crooks). The two fight, but the crook falls into the rapids where he would have died if Van Loan had not jumped in and saved him. The crook gets the upper hand again, but lets the Phantom go for saving his life. But later in the story, they again face each other, and this time the confrontation ends in a shooting. It is the Phantom who is the victor. This scene was straight out of the novel, *Alias Mr. Death*.

At first, the story appeared to be a non-Champion entry, but his fingerprints quickly become evident. This is the second case in which Van is on vacation outside of New York City, and becomes involved in a case on his own, and not from a request from Havens or the police. And though there were the similar water escapes, and other Champion touches, it does appear that he is trying some new plots in the series, or there is, indeed, a ghost writer involved.

Notes: Criminals force an ambulance off the road and steal two bodies before they are taken to the morgue. The Phantom uses the alias of John Hastings. Phantom's weight is first given as 170 pounds, but later in the novel it is given as 180 pounds. (This was a continuous problem within the series, keeping the Phantom's weight, height, and other vitals the same from one story to the next.) At one point in the story, the author mentions the Golden Gate (Bridge?) in a scene. Did Champion place the Golden Gate Bridge in Los Angeles, or was this some other Golden Gate? The next day I did flip through the story looking for this passage again. At the first of Chapter 7, we have this: "Dawn streaked the eastern sky over the Golden Gate."

18. THE SILENT MENACE

V6 #3—August 1934
Written by D.L. Champion

Place: New York City; Rockville, NJ

Main characters: Five of Clubs, Frank Havens, Richard Curtis Van Loan/the Phantom, Harry Chalmers, Inspector Rolph, Ronald Rolland, Hammersly, Sgt. Horton, McKay, M. L. Monson, Somers (Phantom alias), George Prentiss, Williams, Hennessy, Lane

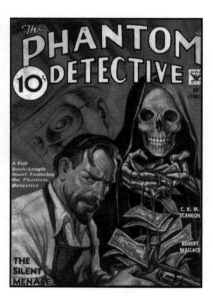

Another very typical Champion story, similar to "Thirteen Cards of Death" (August 1933), "Diamonds of Death" (June 1934), and others. Killers wearing hoods with the design of the Five of Clubs are murdering men who appear to be members of their own gang. The Phantom finds a giant counterfeit scheme in the works. From New

York City the case moves to Rockville, New Jersey, where the story comes to a typical Champion ending. Little new in this story.

Notes: Minions of the mastermind go by numbers, which is similar to many previous stories. The Third Federal Bank. The Phantom uses the alias of a man named Somers. As in "Death's Diary" (February 1934), hidden writing in coded messages must be figured out by using some gimmick—in this case, holes cut in a five of clubs playing card.

19. SPAWN OF DEATH

V7 #1—September 1934
Written by unknown; possibly Edwin V. Burkholder or D.L. Champion

Place: New York City

Main characters: The Black One (sometimes called The Silent One), Garros Rex, The Fer-de-Lance Gang, Evelyn Jardine, Hawks, Franklin C. Pace, John Hutton, Jose, Pedro, Police Commissioner Henry, Professor Atwell, Raynor, George R. Tate, Juan, Raymonde, Mameloi Perine, Tallent, Papa Nebo, Dion Valero, Detective Sergeant Malone, Richard Curtis Van Loan/the Phantom, Frank Havens (mentioned only)

This one had me going. First, it has all the fingerprints of a Champion story. His writing shows throughout. But the plot is certainly different, and at times I could swear someone else is writing the story.

Two men of evil, one with aspirations of becoming a king, the other after riches. A Cuban revolution has that nation in turmoil, while in the United States a renegade Cuban has tied up with an American, both after their own gains. The Cuban leads a group of followers known as the Fer-de-Lance gang, and they use this deadly snake to do their killing. Once bitten, the victim will fall dead immediately.

Notes: The Phantom disguises himself as a Cuban bandleader and directs the orchestra. He is a competent musician. The City Central Bank. The Phantom carries a hidden hypodermic needle in the lining of his coat, plus another one in a cavity of the sole of his shoe. Though la savate is not named, it is said that the Phantom uses the French fighting technique used by the French Apaches. This, of course, is la savate. Appears to be a new plot, though it again uses a group of foreign agents, this time Cubans. Typical Champion at times, not typical Champion at other times. Very possibly a ghost writer. The use of venomous snakes and spiders will be a recurring plot device from now on.

Availability: *Action Adventure Stories* #90 (published by Fading Shadows, Inc., 2001), *The Phantom Detective V7N1—Pulp Facsimile* (published by Ad-

1933
1934
1935
1936
1937
1938
1939
1940
1941
1942
1943
1944
1945
1946
1947
1948
1949
1950
1951
1952
1953

venture House, 2009).

20. MERCHANT OF MURDER

V7 #2—October 1934
Written by Norman A. Daniels

Place: New York City

Main characters: The villain is called many things: the Voice, the Menace, the Murder Merchant, the Merchant of Murder; Russell Monson, Commissioner Fowler, Richard Curtis Van Loan/the Phantom, Frank Havens, Ernest Potter, Dr. McLarney, Jepson, George Knapp, Joseph Jewell, Carl Phelps, Windy, Dr. Richard Kleiner (Phantom alias), Arnold Baldwin, Grayson, Capt. Brady, Austin (Phantom alias), Roger Robertson, Jimmy Patton, Lester Cornwell (Phantom alias)

Certain men of wealth are kidnapped and given a poison, then released. Now they must pay a certain amount in order to receive the antidote. The police broadcast a call for the Phantom on their radio band. Meanwhile, Frank Havens' best friend has been kidnapped and held on the threat of death if Havens calls in the Phantom, so Van Loan must keep a low profile while investigating the case. The Merchant not only poisons his victims, but poisons his minions as well. They are given the antidote after each successful mission. If they don't get the antidote, they die.

While disguised as Dr. Richard Kleiner, the Phantom is captured and given the poison. The mastermind tells him that his antidote has been mailed to a location in California, and he has just enough time to catch a plane and reach California for this antidote. If he remains in New York City he will die.

Notes: Daniels uses the Second National Bank. The Phantom uses the alias of Dr. Richard Kleiner, Austin, and Lester Cornwell (the Cornwell alias will be used quite often). Van Loan had studied chemistry in college and was exceptionally proficient in toxicology. Van Loan has private servants in his home, but they only perform their duties in the morning, and then leave. He also maintains a second residence on Twenty-third Street, near the river; this second residence was a workshop, but within was a hidden room containing medical lab equipment, among other items. Jimmy Patton is Havens' private pilot. Crooks say, "Lift your dogs," when telling the Phantom to climb steps. The Phantom changes disguise every few pages in the story.

Availability: *Action Adventure Stories* #144 (published by Fading Shadows, Inc., 2004).

21. THE TOMB OF DEATH

V7 #3—November 1934
Written by George A. McDonald

Place: New York City; Chinatown

Main characters: Li-Hung, Luther Lane, Richard Curtis Van Loan/the Phantom, Eric Lane, Tom Wong, Inspector Crowley, Frank Havens, Randolph Fowler, Eddie Higgins, Roy Manson, John Twanbly, Charles Young, Wilson, Sing Lee, Finney, Kennedy, Lawton Marsh, Dugan, Empress Quon Shang (long dead, only mentioned)

1933

1934

1935

1936

1937

1938

1939

1940

1941

1942

1943

1944

1945

1946

1947

1948

1949

1950

1951

1952

1953

This story is modeled after that of "The Crime of Fu Kee Wong" (April 1933), though much better written, and has greatly improved plotting. Again, it appears that a Chinese mastermind is at the bottom of the crimes, until he is unmasked at the end and turns out to be...

The case appears to center around the death of a young pilot flying across China when his plane crashes. His father believes it was murder and that a white man is behind it. He asks for help from the Phantom. Since Van Loan had been a friend of the dead pilot, he takes the case. He is captured several times by the Chinese tong in Chinatown. It appears is that Li-Hung, the Tong leader, is working for a white man, but when the case comes to an end, the Phantom is not surprised at the true identity of the real leader.

Notes: The "Fu Kee Wong" plot is when a white man takes on the guise of a Chinaman, looking for some great wealth or world leadership. Li-Hung fits this description. In the December 1933 story, "The Yellow Murders," Ching Po did not fit this description. Li-Hung does. Killings by the Phantom become a little more graphic: he shoots one man through the neck, another between the eyes. Phantom wears a pair of shoes which have been invented by Houdini that help in escapes. There is a "queer coterie" of people. In one scene the Phantom walks the streets wearing his mask, dines at a restaurant while wearing his mask. Everyone knows he is the Phantom. The Five Finger Tong. The police wagon is called the *Black Maria*. His thought was one of savage fury. The presentiment of danger had not been generated by nerves. Police are called the white ghosts. The knockout blow Van "parked on his chin." Again, the second hideaway on West Twenty-third Street. The Sun Tsay Tong. The Phantom is called "the Black Ghost." His belt contains a kit of many items to enable him to escape from traps. The Rocky Cave Cemetery. A lot of new ideas, which certainly sound like a new author, while Champion's fingerprints are still all over the story. The plot and many scenes are those of Champion's, but the writing appears to be that of McDonald. When I first read the story I noticed the similarity to other Champion stories, especially "The Crime of Fu Kee Wong,"

1933

1934

1935

1936

1937

1938

1939

1940

1941

1942

1943

1944

1945

1946

1947

1948

1949

1950

1951

1952

1953

and would have given this novel to him completely, even with the many new ideas and the strange writing style that was emerging, except for Will Murray giving me the clue to McDonald. After researching his style, I had to agree with Will that the new author involved was probably McDonald. The traces of Champion could merely be that McDonald read a previous Phantom of his.

Availability: *The Phantom Detective V7N3—Pulp Facsimile* (published by Adventure House, 2008).

22. THE CRIME CASTLE

V8 #1—December 1934
Written by George A. McDonald

Place: New York City

Main characters: The Crime King/Big Shot, J. Perry Montague, Peggy Manning, Inspector Crowley, Ted Welden, Tommy Dagmar, Orrin Wilkerson, Lester Cornwell, Phil Scarponi, Richard Curtis Van Loan/the Phantom, Frank Havens, Artie Dubuis, Frankie Gillis, Joel Stratta, Blind Pete (Phantom alias), Capt. Tim O'Mara, Carl Krug (The Fixer), Dave Dominick, Joe Wailer, Joe Dominick, Tony Marinito, Ike

An important New York banker requests the aid of the Phantom—something to do with a rash of deaths—supposedly suicides—in and around New York City. Police are baffled. The Phantom arrives to speak with the banker, but that gentleman is immediately killed. However, before his death he mentions the name of a young artist he was thinking of helping financially but had some doubts. The Phantom follows the lead to the Village where he encounters a number of suspects, including an ex-counterfeiter.

The case involves a giant scheme of counterfeit bonds. Young artists are hired to work on the bonds, while other young people are initiated into the group by a promise of lots of money. Their job is to push the counterfeit bills. Some have refused after being told of the criminal activities, and they are the supposed suicides that surround the mystery.

A number of new ideas, some old ideas, and a very strange novel in that this new author is like a chameleon in that he adopts ideas from previous novels, while at the same time bringing new ideas of his own to the story.

Notes: Inspector Crowley makes his second appearance. His first was in the previous novel, "The Tomb of Death" (November 1934). The Phantom uses the alias of Lester Cornwell, first used in Norman Daniels' story, "Merchant of Murder" (October 1934). The many suicides around town appear to have little or no connection with each other. They are people of varied walks of life (similar to those Anatole France Feldman stories). Someone yells, "Johosophet—it's the Phantom!" A club in the Village is called the Hi-de-Ho Club. A security agency is used by a rich man to guard his home, called the Homes Service Patrol. Van's spine tingled. A detective is a shamus. The Phantom has a hideout on West Eighth Street. A deep "V" showed between his brows. Someone yells, "Great Gods!" The car slowed to the curb. Inspector Crowley tells the Phantom that a crook had taken a poison capsule after being captured (again, the connection to Feldman). The Phantom uses a new identity, that of a character known in the underworld as Blind Pete. This was a character that Van Loan had established in the underworld very similar to Blinky McQuade from *The Spider*. Blind Pete was known in most of the dives as a pleasant-mannered, harmless old fraud that had a penchant for going off on alcoholic jaunts whenever his begging brought him enough for a spree. It was in this way that his numerous disappearances were accounted for. He wore a grimy, threadbare suit, a dingy black hat over his tousled mop of greying hair. He wore the dark glasses associated with the blind. This alias, and that of Cornwell, are both compromised in the story. Plus, when Blind Pete gets into a brawl in one of the dives, the crooks know immediately that he is other than he appears. Van can read lips. Cold chills run up and down his spine. "Ga-ga." With his West Eighth Street address compromised, the Phantom moves his hideout to Carmine Street. Van Loan assumes the identity of Dave Dominick, the brother of murdered Joe Dominick. The first mention of the French fighting technique of la savate, originally hinted at in the previous novel, is now labled. "Will-o'-the-wisp." Everyone calls each other "feller." Apartment 1D. He tugged at his lower lip. Has a razor-line strip of steel in the cuff of his coat. The young girl is found murdered. His belt contains the make-up kit. As one crook is dying, the Phantom asks him a question, to which the gangster tells him to "go to hell," as the Phantom had been responsible for the capture—or death—of one of his pals. A nice fight scene takes place in one of the dives while the Phantom is disguised as Blind Pete.

Availability: *Action Adventure Stories* #113 (published by Fading Shadows, Inc., 2002), *The Phantom Detective V8N1—Pulp Facsimile* (published by Adventure House, 2009).

23. DEATH ON SWIFT WINGS

V8 #3—January 1935
Written by Norman A. Daniels

Place: New York City

Main characters: The Gargoyle, Richard Curtis Van Loan/the Phantom, Magda Defoe, Frank Havens, Dr. Antonio Andres, Gibbs, Police Commissioner (not named), Ted Collins, Bert Warren, Blackie Burns, Jessup, Chick, Lester Cornwell (Phantom alias), Pedro DeMaiz, Lefty, New Jersey State Policeman Prescott

A super criminal plans to steal a death ray and offer it to the highest bidder, regardless of which country makes the highest offer. A scientist and his assistant are both killed and the machine is in the hands of the spy ring. The

1933
1934
1935
1936
1937
1938
1939
1940
1941
1942
1943
1944
1945
1946
1947
1948
1949
1950
1951
1952
1953

Phantom must run down the mastermind and either get back the death ray or destroy it.

The case comes to an end on a mountain top in New Jersey, as the Phantom and State Police assault the house of the mastermind; this was very typical of many of the Champion endings, but the story is totally that of Daniels—Champion had nothing to do with it.

Notes: The White Death, a death-ray machine; a crook that Van impersonates has a missing finger, which gives the Phantom's disguise away; a man, disguised as an old hag, guards the entrance to an old house that is being used as a hideout by the gangsters; Phantom weighs 170 pounds; a rattlesnake den is used as a trap to kill the Phantom. Lester Cornwell alias is used by the Phantom.

Availability: *The Phantom Detective V8N3—Pulp Facsimile* (published by Adventure House, 2007).

24. THE HOUSE OF MURDERS

V9 #1—February 1935
Written by D.L. Champion

Place: New York City

Main characters: James Thorpe, Harker, Colonel John Laval, Murray Thorpe, Richard Curtis Van Loan/the Phantom, Frank Havens, Amos Thorpe, Doris Thorpe, Ricci, Slade, Simon Wayman, Francis Thorpe, Florence Thorpe, Charles Thorpe, Dr. Graham Hamilton, Ralph Thorpe, Inspector Crowley, Garner, Rolph, Drone, Prudence, Muriel Havens (mentioned only)

This story has similarities to "Spawn of Death" (September 1934), in that people are being murdered by the bite of black widow spiders. The case centers around the Thorpe family mansion. Clues surface about an old family hatred, but the Phantom believes the murders may have something to do with the future, not the past.

As with the bite of the fer-de-lance snakes in "Spawn of Death," once a victim has been bitten by a black widow, they immediately drop dead. Actually, the black widow does not kill that quickly—if it kills at all. The author also says that the spider only comes from the Montana and Idaho regions, but I would imagine he could have found plenty of the spiders in dear old New York at the time.

Notes: As with "Spawn of Death," this could have been one of Champion's ghost writers, but his fingerprints are all over the story. A similar scene from "The Crimson Killer" (May 1934) shows up where hungry hounds are chained in an entry way to a house (part time they are chained outside, too), with small openings in the walls where the chains can he pulled through to allow people to pass through the area way. There is a "queer coterie" of people (this was used in "The Tomb of Death" (November 1934), so could either be a Championism or a McDonaldism. If it belongs to McDonald, then he may be the ghost for this story, too.

If Champion isn't involved in the writing, I may be reading clues from an editor or rewrite person.

Availability: *High Adventure* #68 (published by Adventure House, 2003).

25. THE HOLLYWOOD MURDERS

V9 #2—March 1935
Written by D.L. Champion

Place: Hollywood, CA

Main characters: The Ghoul, Larry Phail, June Markham, Von Arnheim, Graig, Armstrong, Marilyn Hall, Inspector Wolf, Somers, Frank Havens (mentioned only), Ruth Rambo, Richard Curtis Van Loan/the Phantom, Downing, Marjorie Hart, Ralph Nearing, Higgins, Dorothy Madsen, Drago, Sgt. Burman, Arthur Arkwright, Hammond, Jimmy Kelly, Armond Kator, Arthur Rich, Sam Foster, Ray Estor, George Kudos, Lester Trent, Dexter Scow, Dick Quelles, Jordan, Noble Johns, Jenkins, O'Brian, Ike

After "The Talking Dead," I would have been surprised if a similar plotted story had not appeared. Well, this is it. Big men in the making of Hollywood movies are being blackmailed into paying large sums of money, or their actors will be killed. After a few murders the local police send a message to Frank Havens in New York City, requesting the help of the Phantom: he flies immediately to Hollywood to take on the investigation.

1933

1934

1935

1936

1937

1938

1939

1940

1941

1942

1943

1944

1945

1946

1947

1948

1949

1950

1951

1952

1953

It is very similar to the novel, "The Talking Dead" (July 1934), so Champion (with or without a ghost writer) continues to use old plots over and over. But it's a good story, nevertheless. The Phantom is captured and escapes the normal amount of times, and we get a behind-the-scenes look at the making of movies, however fictional it is.

Notes: He uttered four words—"My God—he's dead!" Champion does this a lot, quite really. I just forget to mention it in previous notes. Sometimes it's "he uttered two words," or "he uttered three words," etc. Champion was sneaky with cussing too. Some curious ways in which he handled things like that would be like this: one of the crooks would be surprised by the Phantom and they'd start saying something like, "You son of a...." At which the Phantom would finish for them: "Son of Satan? You're right!" In other cases, Champion would say that the Phantom uttered three words to the gangster that would make a real man want to fight. I'll leave these words to your own imagination as to what they might have been. The Phantom stabs a gangster through the heart with a knife in the story. Another phrase was, "roaring of a Bashan bull." The villain remained hidden when he spoke to the Phantom and others, and actually speaks from a hidden room through the use of a speaking system that is used in the movie business.

1933

1934

1935

1936

1937

1938

1939

1940

1941

1942

1943

1944

1945

1946

1947

1948

1949

1950

1951

1952

1953

CHAPTER III, SECTION C

THE NORMAN DANIELS PERIOD: 1935-1936

D ARKNESS WAS DESCENDING. Shadows began to fill the small room as the skylight above his head darkened with the approach of night. The pulp author sitting behind the desk slipped another sheet of paper into his typewriter as he turned on the small lamp to illuminate his work area.

For on the desk, and around the room, were piled stacks of pulp magazines that he was writing for: *The Phantom Detective, Black Book Detective, Ten Story Detective*, and many others. Titles long forgotten. Pen names he favored. House names that hid him behind many masks and identities. Series characters, formula fiction, blood and guts avengers who fought crime, solved mysteries. After all, he was a pulp fictioneer.

"Chapter 1," he typed; and immediately below that, "Blood from the Mummy." Then his hands began to flash across the keys as the story began to unfold.

"In broad daylight the Egyptian Room of the Central Museum was a grim, silent place where visitors walked lightly lest they disturb the long dead. The wrinkled, blue-black faces of mummies, encased in glass, looked out upon the world with ageless remoteness."

So simple a beginning, yet before the story comes to an end, the Phantom Detective would put his life on the line for all humanity. He would be captured, escape, shot, fight, and finally, in the end, unmask this latest terror that stalked the innocent people of New York City. The story is "The Pharaoh's Mark," and the author is Norman A. Daniels.

Pick up any pulp magazine and chances are you will see the name of Norman Daniels on the cover. One of the most prolific pulp writers who ever came out of the pulp magazine era, Daniels wrote for most—if not all—the pulp houses of the day. Some magazine issues had two or more of his stories inside, under different names of course. The April 1943 *Detective Novels* for instance, had "The Man From Ludak" by Daniels, and "The Dangerous Gamble" by Frank Johnson (also Daniels, writing under a house name). The latter story featuring the very popular character of the Crimson Mask. In the June 1941 issue of *Detective Novels* there was "The Crimson Mask and the Vanishing

Men" by Frank Johnson (featuring the Crimson Mask), and "Fur-Wrapped Murder" by John L. Benton (featuring the very popular Candid Camera Kid). Both novels were written by Norman Daniels! And these two series characters were the hottest properties appearing in *Detective Novels* at the time.

To mention pulp magazines without speaking of Daniels is quite difficult. He wrote all genres, including science fiction and aviation. And when you bring up the heroes—Doc Savage, The Shadow, and their kin, well, Daniels fits right in there. There was the Black Bat from 1939 to 1953, which Daniels wrote almost exclusively. And then there was *The Phantom Detective*, 1933 to 1953 (of which, he wrote at least 36 of the stories). The already mentioned characters of the Crimson Mask and the Candid Camera Kid. The Masked Detective. Don Winslow of the Navy. And Dan Fowler, ace of the g-men in *G-Men Detective*. And most of the Captain Danger, soldier of fortune novels in *Air War*.

Though Daniels' records only show 36 *Phantom Detective* novels, there could certainly have been more. The fact is Daniels was being groomed to take over the *Phantom Detective* series in 1934. All clues point in that direction. D. L. Champion had been responsible for *The Phantom Detective* from the very beginning. Champion was possibly bringing in ghost-writers, and might have been collaborating with Anatole France Feldman. In truth, I highly suspect that Standard Magazines brought in McDonald. But whatever the case, Daniels was brought into the series in early 1934, with his first story being published in the October 1934 issue. By 1935, he was writing the series—with some fill-in novels by D.L. Champion. The status looked simple: D.L. Champion was on the way out, and Mr. Daniels was on his way in. It was the normal evolution for the *Phantom Detective* series.

Neither Champion nor Feldman were doing bang up jobs on the stories. Evidently, there might have been problems with McDonald also. Champion's novel, *Alias Mr. Death*, that gave birth to the *Phantom Detective* series, was in reality a series of nine short novelettes. It's very possible that Anatole France Feldman appears to have missed a deadline in early 1934 and been removed from the series. Just a suspicion. So, if the series was to survive, I'm sure the editors at Standard decided to bring someone else into the series, with eventual plans to replace D.L. Champion as the main author. Norman Daniels was the perfect choice! Unfortunately, he wouldn't last long, either.

If I were to be asked to describe Norman Daniels in one word, that word would be "professional." Daniels approached his writing career with that word as the basis in everything he wrote. The novel lengths were no problem for him. He made it look easy. The stories didn't ramble, or roam in confusing directions. His stories moved smoothly, with rational sequences of action, and ended in a tight solution to the case. He included the appropriate number of captures and escapes required by editorial dictates. The villains brought chills to your spine. The Phantom becomes a master of disguise, a ruthless fighter against the evils of the crime-infested scumland. As Richard Curtis Van Loan, he was the top-hatted, young, rich, man-about-town, gay (this meant fun-lov-

1933 1934 **1935** 1936 1937 1938 1939 1940 1941 1942 1943 1944 1945 1946 1947 1948 1949 1950 1951 1952 1953

ing back then) socialite playboy of the New York set. As the Phantom, he was
fearless, strong in body and spirit, moral in all that he did and thought—but
he could fight fire with fire when dealing with the killers of gangland. This was
Norman Daniel's Phantom Detective.

Though I only have Anatole France Feldman listed on a few of the stories,
it is quite likely that he was involved in many of the 1933 and 1934 stories
with D.L. Champion. In fact, many of these stories read like a collaboration
between Champion and someone else—and that someone else is very likely
Feldman. From what I have been told, the two men were good friends and
worked together in some way. As I mentioned earlier, it is quite possible that
Anatole France Feldman helped Champion lengthen the *Phantom* stories. But,
regardless, where I have listed Champion, he had something to do with the
story. His fingerprints are all over the stories.

26. MASTER OF THE DAMNED

V9 #3—April 1935
Written by Norman A. Daniels

Place: New York City

Main characters: The Master/the League of
the Damned, Lewis Rister, Capt. Burke, Limpy
McCue, Sock Malone, Squirmy, The Weasel,
Richard Curtis Van Loan/the Phantom, Ronald
Trueman, Jack Curtin (Phantom alias), Frank
Havens, Leon Talbot, Commissioner of Police
Crowley, Dick Pritchard, Lester Cornwell (Phantom
alias), Dr. McGreer, David Burnham, Lyman Cady,
Horton, Benjamin Dewell, Madame Blanchard

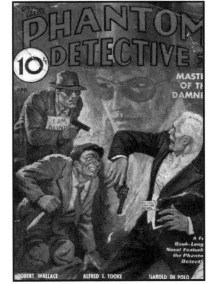

Wealthy men are ordered to
pay $100,000 a day to a private
sanitarium, and will face death on
the day they cannot pay. Aiding
the Master are local gunmen, plus
a number of cripples (the cripples are promised that their disabilities will be
cured if they follow orders).

There were two motives behind the case; one was the re-opening of a rich
mercury mine, and second, revenge from years past.

Notes: The Master supposedly cures the cripple, makes the blind see, the
lame walk; Phantom uses the aliases of Jack Curtin and Lester Cornwell; the
dresser in his apartment has a secret compartment containing all of his make-
up material; Inspector Crowley is now the Police Commissioner; the McGreer
Sanitarium for Cripples; he called a number that "is very familiar to New
Yorkers"—Spring 3100 (probably similar to our current 911 system).

1933

1934

1935

1936

1937

1938

1939

1940

1941

1942

1943

1944

1945

1946

1947

1948

1949

1950

1951

1952

1953

1933

1934

1935

1936

1937

1938

1939

1940

1941

1942

1943

1944

1945

1946

1947

1948

1949

1950

1951

1952

1953

27. WRITTEN IN BLOOD

V10 #1—May 1935
Written by D.L. Champion

Place: New York City

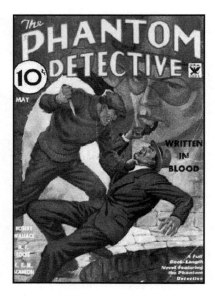

Main characters: The Avenger, Elias Crowther, Martens, George Renault, Frank Havens, Richard Curtis Van Loan/the Phantom, Inspector Wolfe, Brightson, Paul, Harlow, Albert Tanner, Loft, Herbert Waite, Wellington, Blackwell, Gene Rawson, Charles Ballston, Surliss, Isabelle Rawson, Crimmins, Le Grande, Police Commissioner Crowley

This story probably originally had "The Crimson Scar Murders" as its title, as that is what the murders are called. Nothing new in this story, either. Very similar to several previous adventures; previous plot devices are an escape through a sewer system below a hotel, a trick of placing a note inside his food in hopes that whoever finds the note will take it to Frank Havens for a reward. Very similar to "The Sign of Death" (January 1934), and others.

Notes: People are hard-faced and feral-eyed; cicatrix; strange deaths—a man drowns in a flop house where there was no water, another starves to death while locked in a storage room containing food and drink; there is "an unseen Damaclean threat"; the scene was pregnant with fear; he issued a laconic two-word statement: "He's dead"; a Bashan voice; the mastermind uses a gimmick when placed on a telephone, which allows his voice to be transmitted like a loud speaker system; Crimmins is Havens' butler; the Longman's Hotel, at 119th Street; a crimson scar appears on the victims.

Availability: *Action Adventure Stories* #70 (published by Fading Shadows, Inc., 2000).

28. NOTES OF DOOM

V10 #2—June 1935
Written by Norman A. Daniels

Place: New York City

Main characters: The Faceless One, Victor Carmody, Capt. Blane, Police Commissioner Crowley, Boston Lefty, Richard Curtis Van Loan/the Phantom, Biff, Whitey, Gerati, Jams Buckley, Uncle Charlie, David Lockwood, Arthur Carlton, Frank Dygert, Charlie Prout, Claude Sinters, Ben Armitage, Lt. Decker, Thomas Joray, Frank Havens

During World War I, an assignment was given an army officer to penetrate the enemy lines: the officer was selected by lot, "I.O.U.s of Death," and it seems that one man had rigged the drawing to insure that one particular man would be selected. That man was supposedly killed during the mission (date of November 16, 1917). Now it appears that the supposed dead man was back, and killing the other men who had been in the lot.

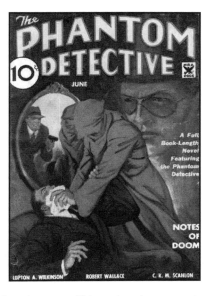

1933

1934

1935

1936

1937

1938

1939

1940

1941

Notes: This was one of the best *Phantom* stories to date, and future *Phantom* writers would rely on this plot device in their own stories. This was also very similar to the *Secret Agent "X"* story, "Plague of the Golden Death" (December 1937), written by Wayne Rogers. In fact, a future *Phantom* writer would write two such *Phantoms* with similar stories (these stories will be covered in the next segment); one of the first uses of the name "Carmody" that Daniels would use in many of his stories; the army unit was the Two Hundred and Twentieth Regiment.

Availability: *Wildside Pulp Classics: Phantom Detective #28* (Wildside Press, 2008), *The Phantom Detective V10N2—Pulp Facsimile* (published by Adventure House, 2008).

29. THE PRINCE OF MURDER

V10 #3—July 1935
Written by Norman A. Daniels

Place: Washington D.C.; New York City

Main characters: The Black Prince, Ivan Kossov, Miss Sullivan, Lester Cornwell (Phantom alias), Frank Havens, Richard Curtis Van Loan/ the Phantom, Moriarty, Edward Vogel (Phantom alias), Barney Temkin, Louis Haber, Chris Clague, Nikolaus Radoch, Julian Dmitrich, Natasha, Senator Edward Owen, Peter Brundage, Howard Clarke, Hollister, Janatis, Nina Jarvis, Perry Reisfield, Lt. Wilson, Capt. Dunham

International intrigue as a foreign spy hopes to throw America into a war with an unnamed country. In the end the Phantom, using the voice of Senator Owen, gives a speech over the radio to calm fears by

1945

1946

1947

1948

1949

1950

1951

1952

1953

| 1933 |
| 1934 |
| **1935** |
| 1936 |
| 1937 |
| 1938 |
| 1939 |
| 1940 |
| 1941 |
| 1942 |
| 1943 |
| 1944 |
| 1945 |
| 1946 |
| 1947 |
| 1948 |
| 1949 |
| 1950 |
| 1951 |
| 1952 |
| 1953 |

talking of peace, not war, and tension is smoothed between the peoples of both America and the unnamed country.

Notes: A Russian diplomat is killed in the outer office of the Secretary of State; the Secret Service chief enlists the aid of the Phantom; the alias of Lester Cornwell is used, as is Edward Vogel; Senator Edward Owen becomes Senator William Owen by the end of the story.

Availability: *The Prince of Murder* (published by Jim Hanos, 1985).

30. THE PHARAOH'S MARK

V11 #1—August 1935
Written by Norman A. Daniels

Place: New York City

Main characters: Richard Curtis Van Loan/ the Phantom, Jack Arnold, Dr. Arthur Temple, Flanagan, Frank Havens, Philip Mayne (Phantom alias), Rocks Alden, Chanda Rhi, Peter Conway, Colonel Lourtier, Raoul, Pierre, Lester Cornwell (Phantom alias), Franz, Commissioner of Police (not named), Scheff, Jacques

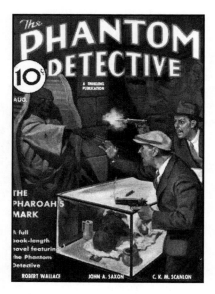

A Pharoah's mummy has been brought to the New York City Central City Museum. It had recently been discovered in Egypt. But even before it arrives at the museum, strange deaths occur. It appears that one gang of French Apaches are after a hidden secret that may be worth millions, but they—and others—are being killed by what appears to be the mummy's curse—golden arrows are shot into their necks by a strange creature wearing the robes of an Egyptian king.

Notes: Aliases of Lester Cornwell and Philip Mayne are used by the Phantom; a curse of the mummy—the imprint of a scarab on the head of the victims; a Pharaoh, dead thousands of years, appears to be mysteriously killing men with bronze arrows, while another gang of ruthless French Apaches are also involved for unknown purposes.

Availability: *The Phantom Detective V11N1—Pulp Facsimile* (published by Adventure House, 2008).

31. MASTER OF THE WORLD

V11 #2—September 1935
Written by Norman A. Daniels

Place: New York City

Main characters: Le Diable Boiteuz—the Lame Devil, Walter Hanna, Frank Havens, Richard Curtis Van Loan/the Phantom, Billy Hill, Gibbs, Colonel Thorne, Shifty, Ape, Mike Copra, Sidney Lucas, Fred Arnold, Calvin Tuthill, John Allyn, Heinrich Krause, Lester Witham, Con Courtney, Herbert Budd, Grover Fellows, Police Commissioner (not named), Tom Water (this character's name suddenly changes to Tom Matera with no warning)

An international spy is killing inventors and stealing their inventions—super war weapons—to sell to the highest bidder, regardless of what country they represent. Very similar to "Death on Swift Wings" (January 1935).

Notes: Billy Hill, a test pilot, was a personal friend of Van Loan's—they had flown together in the war-torn skies of France; call comes over the police band radio for the Phantom; hell-for-leather.

Availability: *The Phantom Detective V11N2—Pulp Facsimile* (published by Adventure House, 2007).

32. THE ISLAND OF SUDDEN DEATH

V11 #3—October 1935
Written by Norman A. Daniels

Place: Washington D.C.; New York City

Main characters: The Black Gang, Robert Allen, Slasher, Matthew Cramer, Richard Curtis Van Loan/the Phantom, Roswell Crane (Phantom alias), Brady, "Ape" Norton, Goss, Snate, Johnson, Palache, Steve Hennessy, Frank Havens, Grant Page, Harry Brooks, Fleming Lambert, Chester Ives, Thomas Manning, Police Commissioner (not named), Rogers, Blackmore, Bradley

The Phantom is requested by the Secret Service in Washington D.C., and upon arrival, he is immediately captured by the Black Gang, but just as quickly, he escapes. And no sooner has he arrived in Washington, than the scene switches back to New York City for the remainder of the story.

1933
1934
1935
1936
1937
1938
1939
1940
1941
1942
1943
1944
1945
1946
1947
1948
1949
1950
1951
1952
1953

1933

1934

1935

1936

1937

1938

1939

1940

1941

1942

1943

1944

1945

1946

1947

1948

1949

1950

1951

1952

1953

The Secret Service had wanted the Phantom's aid in tracking down the notorious Black Gang who has been robbing armories of weapons and explosives.

Notes: The story felt all wrong. For one thing, released at the same time as this story was the first Dan Fowler (*G-Men*) adventure, "Snatch," in which was introduced the government feds battling the notorious Grey Gang. It is very possible that Daniels had been asked to write an early Dan Fowler story with this plot, only to have the George Fielding Eliot story used, and Daniels turned his story into a *Phantom*. No proof of this, but it's very suspicious to have two similar stories appear at the same time—one a *Phantom* and the other a Dan Fowler. It's also interesting to note that the first Lynn Vickers story, "The Red Raiders" (*Public Enemy*, December 1935), was released only two months later, in which Vickers fought the Red Gang! The Lynn Vickers stories were written by George McDonald, who had been writing the *Phantom Detective* stories off and on. This is one of the first appearances of a crook named Snate (this was the crook's name who was responsible for blinding D.A. Tony Quinn—the Black Bat!); the Phantom uses the alias of Roswell Crane; shoe-laces are actually stiff wire covered with silk, which the Phantom uses to unlock doors; Phantom physically breaks a thug's neck; the "island" as mentioned in the title does not appear until Chapter X—Pirate Island, located off the Georgia coast; Phantom weighs 160 pounds—probably a typo by the editors.

33. MURDER CRACKS DOWN

V12 #1—November 1935
Written by George A. McDonald

Place: New York City; Charleston, SC

Main characters: Public Enemy Number X, Andrew Quincy, Hubert Ainsley, Mrs. Sweetland, Ole Jorgensen, Leon Rinaldo, Horace Manton, Grace DeHand, Frank Havens, Richard Curtis Van Loan/the Phantom, Ed Borden, Bill Flynn (Phantom alias), Dot Gwyn, Capt. Nielson (sea captain), Scar Lipp, J. Franklin Draper, Olsen, Lewis Fink, Capt. Brower (sea captain), Grew, Capt. O'Brien (sea captain), Chief of Police Harkness (Charleston)

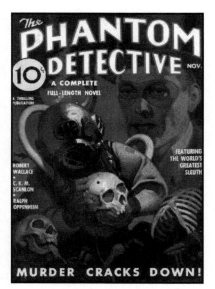

The case involves a sunken ship, supposedly loaded with millions in gold, and the crew of a salvage ship planning on retrieving the gold. There are two gangs at work: one a powerful syndicate, the other is quite mysterious, but may be a pirate crew running guns to South America in exchange for illegal whiskey and rum.

Notes: There are a lot of similarities with this one and McDonald's "The Crime Castle" (December 1934); an accident that happened to an individual years before is a plot device used quite often by this author—during the accident there appears to be a change in the victim's personality, either someone else has taken his place, or the accident has caused him to undergo a change in his own personality (from good to evil); throughout the story, the Phantom is thought to be a g-man, no one is aware that the Phantom is at work on the case; "feller"; the Village again; a powerful syndicate; Grace DeHand is a reporter with the *Clarion;* pile-driver blows; Apartment 3D; the Phantom has a secret hideout on West 8th Street; bullets are angry hornets; "Skipper"; once, twice, three times; Havens publishes the *Charleston Star* in Charleston, SC; Van touches his chin with thumb and forefinger in secret signal to Frank; the use of the apartment 3D is a strange throwback to those 1933 novels, especially "Gamblers in Death" (November) and "The Yellow Murders" (December), so my guess is that maybe the author read those back issues, or an editor or rewrite person is to blame. The Phantom uses the alias of Bill Flynn.

Availability: *Action Adventure Stories* #127 (published by Fading Shadows, Inc., 2003), *The Phantom Detective V12N1—Pulp Facsimile* (published by Adventure House, 2008).

34. THE MURDER EMPIRE

V12 #2—December 1935
Written by Norman A. Daniels

Place: San Diego & San Francisco, CA; Tia Juana, Mexico

Main characters: Richard Curtis Van Loan/ the Phantom, Jim Woodson, William Maitland (Phantom alias), Frank Havens (on the telephone), "Slick" Mitchell, Lt. Pelman, Leslie Banks, Philips, Gramercy, Police Commissioner Trent (CA), Ah Yuen, Kwan Kim, Colonel Thorne, Chau Wing, Manuel Corroba, Dill Moxon, Kohl, Guy Lawson, Bock Wan (Phantom alias), Pedro Sanches (Phantom alias), Kalligan, Kane, Chun Moy, Martin Gillian, Blane, Wah Yuan

Van Loan is vacationing in California with a Secret Service agent. While they are on a fishing trip, Agent Woodson is killed, and the Phantom discloses his identity to the dying agent, and promises to avenge his death.

It appears that opium and Chinese are being smuggled over the border through Mexico and then into California, where most of the aliens end up in San Francisco's Chinatown district. From there they disappear into the Chinese community.

Also causing a problem in the Chinese community is a reputed ruler of old

1933

1934

1935

1936

1937

1938

1939

1940

1941

1942

1943

1944

1945

1946

1947

1948

1949

1950

1951

1952

1953

China, who would be—if still alive—over 130 years old! Chun Moy claims to be Kwan Kim (the long-dead ruler), and promises the people a new China. But he must have much white man gold and silver. A gang of American mobsters lead the illegal Chinese in robberies of train shipments carrying government gold and silver.

The gangs use a radio ray gun that can stop engines of airplanes, automobiles and trains.

Again, this would-be Chinese god turns out to be a white man in disguise. His aims were not for a new China, but rather riches for his own pockets.

Notes: The Phantom uses the alias of William Maitland; Havens owns a ranch near San Diego; a gun is a roscoe; also uses aliases of Pedro Sanchez and Bock Wan; Phantom travels to Tia Juana as a Chinaman, then lets the system smuggle him into San Francisco.

Availability: *The Phantom Detective V12N2—Pulp Facsimile* (published by Adventure House, 2007).

35. THE DIAMOND MURDERS

V12 #3—January 1936
Written by Norman A. Daniels

Place: New York City

Main characters: Clayton Crowder, Richard Curtis Van Loan/the Phantom, Sgt. Hawley, O'Brian, Johnson, Dutch, Mervin Day, Frank Havens, Samuel Lee, Dr. Zaharov, Sebastian, Kieffer, Foster Bancroft, William Miner, Bernard King, Roy Stoddard, Lt. Boswig, Police Commissioner Ellis, Minch (Phantom alias), Keller

THE DIAMOND MURDERS

Diamonds are flooding the market, causing great concern among a diamond syndicate; four of the syndicate leaders are murdered in a mysterious way—apparently shot with a silenced gun, but no bullets are found, and the medical examiner states that the wounds appear more like knife wounds than bullet wounds—it turns out that the mastermind is using diamond bullets!

Notes: Havens is captured by the gang; Phantom carries a police badge that had been given to him by the Police Commissioner; Phantom uses the alias of Minch; he saves Sgt. Hawley's life—and the sergeant reminds me of Captain McGrath from the Black Bat (that would appear later); people reply "laconically"; right there and then—this is a phrase also used by Charles Greenberg (in later novels), and I was curious that Daniels also used it (but again, it could have been an editor or rewrite person); when someone makes a mistake, they are called "boners."

Availability: *The Diamond Murders* (published by Jim Hanos, 1986).

36. THE CHATEAU OF CRIME

V14 #1—February 1936
Written by Norman A. Daniels

Place: New York City

Main characters: Duke Snate, Whitey Munger, Dawson, Gregory, Mellata, Monk, Dopey, Leroux, Frederick Frink, Bob Richards, Clark Griffing, Sanders, Gus Hyatt (Phantom alias), Edward Wheeler, Theodore Zorg, Singe, Tully, Richard Curtis Van Loan/the Phantom, McGonnell, John Chater, Foster (T-Man), Gates (T-Man), Frank Havens

Begins with a similar scene from Daniels' later Dan Fowler stories, in which a gunman runs up the steps of a government building and is shot down by gangsters before he can pass on his information. This is a plot device often used by Daniels.

A printing expert, hired by the government, is being held by gangsters and forced to make counterfeit bills. But he is able to get a message out on one of the bills, giving the address where his wife and children are being held captive.

Notes: One gangster is a machine-gunner, with a pet Tommy gun, which would also be a plot device for Daniels' later novels; a bank examiner switches counterfeit money for real money; the Phantom goes through the novel disguised as Gus Hyatt, a counterfeiter who recently died in prison—they had faked a prison escape in order for the Phantom to assume his identity; the mastermind wears a red hood to conceal his identity; again, a crook named Snate appears—this one dies with the Phantom's bullet between his eyes; a room is rigged up like a checkerboard floor, with some squares being electrically charged, while others are safe—in order to escape, the Phantom must know which squares he can touch!

This year was, perhaps, the most solid year of novels. Daniels had brought sanity, along with professionalism to the series finally. Why the coming changes I cannot imagine. But the next segment will cover 14 stories, those that take us through the fiftieth issue. This will be the upheaval period. The period of violent change. Both D.L. Champion and Norman Daniels will be dropped. New authors brought in, and new characters introduced. Some of the changes are welcome, but others are not. I feel that Standard's choice in dropping Dan-

1933
1934
1935
1936
1937
1938
1939
1940
1941
1942
1943
1944
1945
1946
1947
1948
1949
1950
1951
1952
1953

1933

1934

1935

1936

1937

1938

1939

1940

1941

1942

1943

1944

1945

1946

1947

1948

1949

1950

1951

1952

1953

iels was a great mistake. The series should have been his.

As we return to that small room, with the desk, the stacks of pulps, the dim-lighted lamp, Daniels closes out "The Pharaoh's Mark" with this final scene:

> Havens noticed his weariness. He took Van by the arm and led him up the steps through the museum that was now rid of its murder menace.
>
> "You saved my life, Van," he said earnestly. "It isn't the first time, either. I'm grateful."
>
> "And you," Van smiled, "gave me life when you helped me create the Phantom."
>
> "May he live and fight crime forever." Havens' voice was almost a prayer.
>
> Both men were silent, heedless of the radio cars that were screaming their way through the early dawn toward the museum of death.

Daniels sighs, removes the last sheet of paper from the typewriter, sets the manuscript on the edge of the table in a neat stack. He smiles as he thinks of his lovely wife, Dorothy, who, tomorrow will go over his latest manuscript, make corrections and changes, cleaning it up before mailing it to the editorial department at Standard Magazine. Another *Phantom Detective* story has been written. As he reaches for the light switch on the lamp to turn it off, for a second he imagines that he caught a glimpse of a bat in the room—a bat that strangely resembles a man. He pauses for just a moment, then shakes his head in the negative. "No," he says. "Just my imagination."

Well, after all, it is only 1935.

1933

1934

1935

1936

1937

1938

1939

1940

1941

1942

1943

1944

1945

1946

1947

1948

1949

1950

1951

1952

1953

CHAPTER III, SECTION D

THE UPHEAVAL PERIOD: 1936-1937

U PHEAVAL. CHANGE—VIOLENT CHANGE! The editors want more for the series. All of a sudden new characters are added— brought in by editorial demands. Someone, an editor likely, does heavy editing to the stories. Norman Daniels doesn't sound like Norman Daniels. Whoever did the editing—it may have been Charles Greenberg—did a disservice to the author. But be that as it may, after a while Daniels leaves the series, along with D.L. Champion and Anatole France Feldman, and a new author comes into the series. And Charles Greenberg—who was doing some editing for Leo Margulies at the time—decided he could write the stories better and so he turned out some of his own *Phantom* novels. Some of these changes are okay, others are not. But changes are here, nevertheless.

Once again, I want to caution the readers not to take my findings as gospel. The authors I've listed are who I believe them to be. For instance, when I first read "The Death-Skull Murders" (May 1936) and "The Golden Killer" (April 1937), I thought they were possibly written by Wayne Rogers as they corresponded strongly with the *Secret Agent "X"* story that Rogers wrote, "The Plague of the Golden Death" (December 1937). I might add that I read many of these Phantom stories during this period out of order, so my notes were a jumble of information. After borrowing several of the stories from Bob Sampson, I was terribly confused about Wayne Rogers' involvement. I decided to take a break and set the *Phantoms* aside while I did other research. With the *Phantom* authors on hold, I re-read that *Secret Agent "X"* story by Rogers and found no similarities to his writing and any of the *Phantoms* up to this time. So Wayne Rogers was out.

"Cities for Ransom" (September 1933) should really be easy to identify. With the aviation theme so strong in the story, it is very likely the author was one of the early authors for the *Lone Eagle* series. The key clues to the author (see the first segment of this article series) should be easily picked up by searching the authors found in the early issues of *Thrilling Detective* if not through *The Lone Eagle*. I think this author will be identified before long. As for the author of "The Criminal Caesar" (April 1936), there are fingerprints of D.L. Champion, although agent August Lenniger claims this story was

1933

1934

1935

1936

1937

1938

1939

1940

1941

1942

1943

1944

1945

1946

1947

1948

1949

1950

1951

1952

1953

written by one of his clients. Will Murray advised me that among Lennigers' clients were Norman Daniels, G.T. Fleming-Roberts, and E. Hoffmann Price. There is no proof that any of these authors wrote the story, though they could have. I am uncomfortable with the story because of Champion's fingerprints, though. If a new author submitted this story through his agent, and it needed to be re-written for some unknown reason, why would the editors have sent it to Champion for re-write—unless, of course, D.L. Champion was working as an editor during this period. But I'm not comfortable with that explanation, either. D.L. Champion was leaving the *Phantom* series at this time. Though he would possibly write more *Phantoms* throughout the coming years, as well as Dan Fowler stories, I'm not sure that Leo would have employed him as a re-write editor for the Phantom series. Who knows.

There are also some problems with the Norman Daniels stories during this period. "The Circus Murders" (March 1936) gave me trouble identifying it as Daniels', even though it is on his list as belonging to him. Actually, it more resembled a story more like those of Anatole France Feldman. But, again, an easy explanation could be that Champion—and Feldman—may have had something to do with re-writes during this period. Daniels' "Six Prints of Murder" (March 1936), and "Specter of Death" (August 1936) may also have had some heavy editing. But now Daniels drops out of the *Phantom* series until at least 1939. He may have contributed to the Dan Fowler series during this period.

It was during this period that two new characters were brought into the series. First was Steve Huston, introduced in "Dealers in Death" (July 1936), and Jerry Lannigan, introduced in "The Sign of the Scar" (September 1936). Another character—really, an alias—was suggested by the editors (probably Leo Margulies), and that is Dr. Paul Bendix, sometimes called a professor, who has a laboratory where the Phantom often performs experiments. The character is often mentioned, though in reality, seldom seen. This would be an alias that would last throughout most of the remaining series. Steve Huston would also become a main character until the end of the series, though he is not always present. Jerry Lannigan only lasted for three issues, but the character is a strong typical Emile C. Tepperman creation.

One last change during this period is a long-lasting one. It is the beacon light atop the *Clarion* Building that would call the Phantom to action in many—though not all—of the adventures from now on. The authors had a field day with the beacon light, putting the Phantom in all kinds of situations (usually with some beautiful girl) when he suddenly notices the light calling him to action. Through some excuse, he would bid his farewells to the party he is with and contact Frank Havens for his latest adventure. These episodes were quite comical at times, and were repeated often. The author just re-wrote the scene from a previous story he had written. This beacon was created in "Dealers in Death," written by a new author, but possibly suggested by Leo Margulies. Who knows?

37. THE CIRCUS MURDERS

V14 #2—March 1936
Written by Norman A. Daniels

Place: New York City; Philadelphia, PA

Main characters: The Crimson Clown, Det. Sgt. McCarthy, Det. Lambert, Albert King, Richard Curtis Van Loan/the Phantom, Frank Havens, Charles Wagner, Paul Dransfield, Inspector Iverness, Ansielmo, Major Barnard, Tom Higgins, Luke Towers, Novey, Curtis Connington, Knuckles Martin, Gus Gillon, Cliff Grendon, Jarvis, Mueller, Ben Harlan, Zandow, Deputy Police Commissioner Martin

1933

1934

1935

1936

1937

1938

1939

1940

1941

1942

1943

1944

1945

1946

1947

1948

1949

1950

1951

1952

1953

Story actually begins at a circus Big Top in Philadelphia, as a man is mysteriously killed inside a lion's cage—by the lion, of course. The scene swiftly switches to New York City, where the Phantom is called to battle this new outbreak of mysterious murders.

Known as the Circus Murders, the Crimson Clown is killing off old circus partners of his from an earlier period in time: one man dies as an elephant steps on him, another from the mauling of a lion, and yet another falls from a high trapeze.

A lot of melodrama once again, and at one point the Phantom must fight the Crimson Clown while the two swing on a trapeze high above the crowds of spectators.

Notes: Carnival of death; unholy aura; Mmm; a bullet "sang like an angry wasp"; right here and now; with the name of the Crimson Clown as the villain, it would be very easy to assign this one to Johnston McCulley, who had a character named the Crimson Clown. But this one reminds me too much of many of those early 1933-1934 stories by Champion and Feldman. Though there is not a scene within a morgue, there is a similar type scene featuring wax dummies—and a corpse—that could have been right out of one of Feldman's novels. And the Phantom's fight with the Crimson Clown on the trapeze is another strong Anatole France Feldman fingerprint. And there are fingerprints belonging to Champion. Nothing about the story reminded me of Norman Daniels, even though this one's in his records (and it must be his), I am also certain that someone touched it up. Very strange.

Availability: *Thrilling Novels* #25 (published by Fun Stuff Imaginations, 1996), *The Phantom Detective V14N2—Pulp Facsimile* (published by Adventure House, 2007).

1933

1934

1935

1936

1937

1938

1939

1940

1941

1942

1943

1944

1945

1946

1947

1948

1949

1950

1951

1952

1953

38. THE CRIMINAL CAESAR

V14 #3—April 1936
Written by unknown; possibly Anatole
France Feldman or Charles S. Strong

Place: New York City

Main characters: Ron Bennett, Richard Curtis
Van Loan/the Phantom, Happy Hilliard, Donald
Carter, Jasper Stevens, David Grimm, Wayne
Gaynor, Tom Water, Inspector Wolfe, Sellers, Larry
Horton, Lenny Harris, Marshall Breamer, Raynor,
Frank Havens, Kaiser, Waxman, Herman, Allen,
Miller, Elva Stuart, Benny Matters, Harry Lane,
Wallie Ware, Calkins, Burke, Conklin, Willis

THE
CRIMINAL
CAESAR

The Criminal Caesar is head
of eight men of crime, each man
an expert in some field: a chemist,
an attorney, an engineer, an inven-
tive genius, and others. They are demanding money from radio actors or they
would be killed. Frank Havens and Van Loan are on vacation in Maine, fishing and relaxing from a long work period, when they receive a request for the
Phantom over their radio. They immediately set out for New York, but a plane
appears in the sky and bombs the road in front of their car—the criminal mastermind had intercepted a telephone call from Havens, and knew that he and
the Phantom would be traveling by a certain route.

Notes: A very strange novel. Actually, it reads like a similar plot to a later Dan Fowler story, "Station D.E.A.T.H." (December 1938), plus the plot
would be used again with a *Phantom Detective* novel, "The Radio Murders"
(April 1939). Agent August Lenniger credits this story as by one of his clients,
although there appears to be some touches of both Anatole Feldman and D.L.
Champion's fingerprints toward the latter half of the novel. The Phantom is a
tall, well-built man; radio station WAAZ; the motor roared diminuendo; cold
fingers of fear touched his heart; "a reign of terror brooded over the..."; a sopo-
rific effect; an expectant silence, pregnant with some menacing significance;
muffed the job; the "double-noose" torture device; the Phantom goes on the
air in place of a nationally famous comedian; Wallie Ware is the gossip columnist for the *Clarion;* there is a visit to the morgue, which strikes as Feldman's
involvement; morgue attendant is named Charlie; the Phantom runs in long
galloping strides; phlegmatic attitude; telephone number AU-98906; Intersection of Lamar & Jackson Avenue; the *Evening Star,* another New York City
newspaper; he hummed, "Just Before the Battle, Mother"; a lot of Champion,
some Feldman, and there has to be someone else, too. Looking at this story
again, I see touches of Jack Byrne, so my guess is the editor is making changes
to this novel and causing all my confusion. The beginning starts out like one

of Byrne's later Blue Ghost novels (see page 198). Wallie Ware is another clue. Byrne chose a lot of first and last names with the same initials—W. W., etc. But if he only made changes, who was the actual author?

39. THE DEATH-SKULL MURDERS

V15 #1—May 1936

Written by unknown; possibly Edwin V. Burkholder, George Fielding Eliot or George A. McDonald

Place: Long Island & New York City

Main characters: Frank Havens, Richard Curtis Van Loan/the Phantom, Steffan Barret, Clyde Cummings, Thomas Stark, H.H. Taber, Adam Keesler, Raymond Wilkins, Gregory Cummings, Senator Steele, Parker, George Chester, K. K. Oaks, Mr. Spaulding, Police Commissioner Crowley, Clawson, Frederick Klemper, Hobson, Pete, Hawker, Mike

On May 7, 1918, five men escaped from No-Man's Land in France, leaving a sixth man—their buddy—lying in a foxhole, supposedly dying from wounds he had received in combat. Now the other five men are being killed off, these many years later, and it appears that the sixth member of their squad has survived and is now taking his vengeance on those five who had left him behind during the war.

Notes: This novel is almost a complete steal from Norman Daniels' entry, "Notes of Doom" (June 1935). Even the appearance of Police Commissioner Crowley is a throwback to that novel, as that was the last appearance of this police commissioner. And this story, combined with the fiftieth *Phantom* novel, "The Golden Killer" (April 1937), had me almost convinced that the two stories were by Wayne Rogers, as the two stories combined read a lot like that *Secret Agent "X"* adventure Rogers wrote in December 1937, "Plague of the Golden Death." The Five Days Club; a bullet is "a messenger of death"; within an ace of; the Phantom, while searching through a desk, finds "a couple of well-thumbed detective magazines"; weasel eyes; action moves at a tremendously fast pace, with the Phantom taking many unnecessary chances in his fight—which was a strong give-away to Tepperman's action scenes; people explain, "by jove!"; eyes become saucers; here and there and everywhere; just calls Frank "Havens"; people speak in grunts more in this novel—"What?" he grunted; lips came together in a thin line; hell-for-leather; gun barked three, four times. Again, there is evidence of Jack Byrne's hand in the story, but who the actual author is, I'm not sure.

Availability: *Action Adventure Stories* #62 (published by Fading Shadows,

1933
1934
1935
1936
1937
1938
1939
1940
1941
1942
1943
1944
1945
1946
1947
1948
1949
1950
1951
1952
1953

Inc., 1999).

40. SIX PRINTS OF MURDER

V15 #2—June 1936
Written by Norman A. Daniels

Place: New York City

Main characters: Edwin Philips, Cantwell, Inspector Callahan, Richard Curtis Van Loan/the Phantom, Capt. Brady, Meade, Johnson, Paul Lambert, Capt. Scrutton (sea captain), Woodly Young, Marshall Newton, Police Commissioner (not named), Rose, Earle Jackson, Frank Havens, Manuel Cruz, William Cresbon, Herman Dimmock, Don Alvarez, Jose Zarilla, Lawrence Carter, Harry Bruges, Bob Robinson, Alex Rudman, Allen Falk

In a story very similar to "Murder Empire" (December 1935), a criminal mastermind identifies himself as a man long dead, and the story appears to involve a planned revolution in the Philippines, where it is thought this leader is planning on taking control of the country. To his henchmen, it is believed the leader wants the white man's gold and money to finance the buying of many weapons for the revolution. Instead, this supposedly long-dead leader plans on destroying his henchmen and keeping the riches for himself!

Notes: Darts are shot through blow pipes; the morgue wagon is stopped along the highway and a dead body is removed and spirited away; Earle Jackson grave at the Tranquility Cemetary; Philipinos use a gas gun; Don Alvarez was a man long dead, and his name is now being used by the mastermind to further his quest for greed; the Phantom and Captain Brady work together on the case, as if they were supposed to be a team—probably yet another attempt by the editors to give the Phantom a side-kick (or another Dan Fowler/Larry Kendal *G-Man* story); pygmy headhunters, aborigines of the Philippine jungles are used by the mastermind to do his killings.

41. DEALERS IN DEATH

V15 #3—July 1936
Written by Jack Byrne & Norman A. Daniels

Place: Brandford, CT; New York City; Palm City, FL; the Everglades, FL

Main characters: The Big Guy, Elliott Taber, Moira Taber, Major Geoffrey Talcott, Genevieve Linke, Gregory King, Helen Taber, Inspector Iverness, Det. Sgt. Hawley, Steve Huston, Ace Duveen, Frank Havens, Feeney, Nita Wayne, Richard Curtis Van Loan/the Phantom, Dr. Paul Bendix (Phantom alias), Gunner McGlone (alias

1933

1934

1935

1936

1937

1938

1939

1940

1941

1942

1943

1944

1945

1946

1947

1948

1949

1950

1951

1952

1953

is mentioned), Mr. Austin (Phantom alias), O'Conner, Griffith, Dario Paiz, Ellstrom, Katherine Wilde, Rosloff, George Helwig, Rocco Spoldi, Wallace Stevenson, Osgood Vance, Joel Nickolas, Flanagan, Ackermann, Benny, Dr. Vallejos (mentioned), Dutch, Ellis Carbon, Roscoe Foley, Duster, Archambault, Walter Stevenson, Francis X. Muldowney, J. Jarvis Petrie, Miles Bambrick, Davey Alkoff, Colonel Worthing, Inspector Brixton (C. I. D.), Dave Mornier

At first this appears to be a simple murder/robbery mystery, as crooks hold up a party in a rich residence. The Tears of the Virgin, a valuable necklace, is stolen from the hostess, and then she is killed as she goes to her husband when he is hit over the head by the crooks.

It appears that a giant jewel theft ring is in operation, as well as a mysterious organization known as Crime Consolidated, with the jewel gang offering their organization to the organized crime bosses—for a price.

But there is a much deeper mystery to this than first meets the eye. The Phantom is hard pressed to follow the crime spree, as he goes from New York City, to Connecticut, and then to Florida and into the Everglades, where he finally unravels the mystery during a meeting of the jewel gang and Crime Consolidated.

Notes: This is one of four top-notch novels during 1936. The other novels being "The Sign of the Scar" (September 1936), "Empire of Terror" (October 1936), and "Death Rides the Blizzard" (November 1936). However, in both "Death Rides the Blizzard" and this current story, there are clues pointing to Jack Byrne, who was probably working as rewrite editor at the time. But I am just as positive that many of these new ideas now surfacing have been created by him. The Dr. Bendix alias is used for the fist time, the red light atop the *Clarion* is used for the first time to call the Phantom to action, and the reporter, Steve Huston is introduced in this story and would become a mainstay in the series until the end. Jerry Lannigan, introduced in "The Sign of the Scar" was probably a suggestion by the editors, as they were looking for a side-kick for the Phantom.

Though the two stories are by different authors, the best I can figure it, both of the characters are the culmination of the search for a side-kick for the Phantom. Nita Wayne will also appear off and on from now on. And Dr. Paul Bendix appears for the first time, along with the mention of the Gunner McGlone alias; Five silent men; like ghosts out of nowhere; spine cold as ice; "Ummm"; hell-for-leather; Crack, crack, crack; snake-quick; breathed

1933

1934

1935

1936

1937

1938

1939

1940

1941

1942

1943

1944

1945

1946

1947

1948

1949

1950

1951

1952

1953

flame; the *Clarion* call for the first time; Mr. Austin is used as an alias, while the Gunner McGlone alias is only mentioned as being one the Phantom had used in a previous case—this would be mentioned often during this one period, as the Phantom contemplates his past adventures—this one in particular involved a Dr. Vallejos; Van is with a girl named Nita Wayne—he would be with her often in future stories; fingers tapping against his knee; Havens' secretary, Griffith, is murdered outside of the publisher's office; a presentiment of failure; Apartment 3E; femme fatale has sea-green eyes; "we're going by-by"; gangsterdom; a feeling in my bones; Joel Nickolas is a shady detective—he collects rewards on returned stolen jewelry (very similar to a previous McDonald character); Nameless as the night wind—elusive as a shadow; "In your hat, brother."; "Not me. I don't fall for stuff."; Greenwich Village (also an area used in the previous McDonald story); his belly ate the bullets; cabbie says, "Keep feeding me these an' I'd trail the devil to hell for yah!"; a blind man in a house used as a "gun drop" has a cat named Blackie as a companion; very melodramatic fight scene between the Phantom and the blind man in a dark cellar was somewhat reminiscent of Phantom's fight with the giant spider in "Jewels of Doom" (July 1933); a small-time gangster is effeminate; police wagon is a Black Maria (also used in previous McDonald story); pince-nez; Van calls Havens, "Mr. Havens"; story focuses on criminals as well as Phantom—this is the first time in the series that the Phantom is not always at the main scene of action in the story; the Phantom had been responsible for sending gangster's pal to the hot seat; Camp Flamingo; straight-as-a-die; held in a plaster cast; swart detective; a watery grave escape is very similar to plots used in many G.T. Fleming-Roberts stories—this particular escape was within the swamp of the Everglades, as the crooks toss him overboard to a watery grave with the gators.

This was definitely a well-plotted and well-written story. One of the best to date. I was often reminded of the stories by Fleming-Roberts as I read it, and others by the same author; the green-eyed vamp that was such a trade-mark for Fleming-Roberts' *Secret Agent "X"* stories, the escape trick the Phantom used was also quite typical of many of those used by Fleming-Roberts' heroes. And "Death Rides the Blizzard" will again have many of the Fleming-Roberts tie-ins. Unfortunately, there is no proof that Fleming-Roberts wrote any *Phantom Detective* stories, and we do have several similarities to previous McDonald stories, so they may be his, though a lot of the changes were done by Jack Byrne.

42. SPECTER OF DEATH

V16 #1—August 1936
Written by Jack Byrne & Norman A. Daniels

Place: New York City; New Jersey

Main characters: The Chameleon, Colonel Marrs, Lefty the Sneaker, Clark Darnleigh II, Tommy Alord, Frank Havens, Richard Curtis Van Loan/the Phantom, Polly Darnleigh, Edward Page, Logan, Brophy, Fred Ryerson, Louis Malone, Limpy Shea, Police Commissioner Wade, Major Exter, Henry Chapman, Paul Radcliffe, Peter Mantoza,

Charles Seddon, Anderson, V. Santos, Roderigue Ramir, Rex Derek, J. Mayer, Franz Leibert

Robberies of armories are taking place around America. It appears that a South American revolution is about to happen and many weapons are needed. Actually, the guns are being swapped to South American revolutionists for exchange of illegal drugs.

Notes: The red signal light atop the *Clarion* calls the Phantom to action; a man has a bovine face; snap along; feller; Phantom uses a gas gun; icy eyes; slat-eyed; the Black Claw Bar; "Remember me in hell!"; killer gives his victims a red poppy when he kills them; this novel is listed in Daniels' records, and his writing is evident at times. However, someone—probably an editor—re-wrote a lot of the story. You can almost see where Norman Daniels' writing leaves off and another writer's begins. Again, this recalls "The Circus Murders" (March 1936) and "The Criminal Caesar" (April 1936), in which there seems to have been heavy editing. Maybe too much editing!

Availability: *Specter of Death* (published by Jim Hanos, 1985).

1933
1934
1935
1936
1937
1938
1939
1940
1941
1942
1943
1944
1945
1946
1947
1948
1949
1950
1951
1952
1953

43. THE SIGN OF THE SCAR

V16 #2—September 1936
Written by unknown; possibly George A. McDonald or Emile C. Tepperman

Place: New York City

Main characters: The Scar, Debrette, Richard Curtis Van Loan/the Phantom, Frank Havens, Vernon, Lester Cornwell (Phantom alias), Police Commissioner Otto Miller, Fenworth, Carlton Porter, Capt. Gray, Emanuel Vince, Gleason, Samuel Haxton, James J. Hardigan, Jerry Lannigan, Watson, Knuckle Hogan (Lannigan alias), John Twembly, Dexter Daly, Muriel Havens

The Scar demands five million dollars from the city of New York, or he will wreck destruction in critical areas. It appears that a real-estate coup may also be planned by the mastermind.

Muriel, returning from a long stay in Europe, is kidnapped by minions of the Scar, then is placed in a remote-controlled automobile loaded with explosives. The Phantom and Jerry Lannigan rescue her and stop the explosives from destroying a bridge. This is right out of Tepperman's *Operator #5* adventures as Diane Elliot or Nan Christopher is tied to a horse, car, or other vehicle, with explosives. It is then left up to Operator #5 to rescue the girl.

1933

1934

1935

1936

1937

1938

1939

1940

1941

1942

1943

1944

1945

1946

1947

1948

1949

1950

1951

1952

1953

Notes: With the exception of a morgue scene, there is no evidence of this story being a ghost of Champion, so Standard might have brought Tepperman into the series, if this is he; the police put shadows on all of the suspects at the Phantom's urging; Jerry Lannigan calls the Phantom, "Skipper," and the Phantom calls him, "Champ"; snaked out his own rod; Jerry Lannigan uses alias of Knuckle Hogan—he is also very typical of Sgt. MacTavish from the Purple Invasion stories from Tepperman's *Operator #5* series; the Phantom is called by the red light atop the *Clarion;* Havens is a small, nervously aggressive man of fifty; the Phantom uses alias of Lester Cornwell again; slewed around; One Sutton Place; carte blanche; Police Commissioner Miller is murdered and is replaced by James J. Hardigan; a cop is a dick; Van's right fist flashed upward with the kick of a pile-driver; "You've heard of the Phantom," he snapped. "You're looking at him!"; men of the Scar are Eurasians—East Indians, with their tongues cut out; "nerts to him"; Jerry Lannigan had been Van Loan's chief mechanic in his air squadron during the war; though Lannigan wasn't a bad character, I think the final decision to use Steve Huston instead of Lannigan was the better choice. Also, the Phantom uses a strand of hair as evidence—and appears to be an angrier Phantom than before.

Availability: *The Sign of the Scar* (published by Jim Hanos, 1985), *High Adventure* #91 (published by Adventure House, 2006).

44. EMPIRE OF TERROR

V16 #3—October 1936

Written by unknown; possibly George A. McDonald or Emile C. Tepperman

Place: Rock Canyon Dam, AZ; New York City; Washington, D.C.; Mountain View, PA

Main Characters: The Imperator, Lt. Howard, Mort Lewis, Frank Havens, Muriel Havens, Richard Curtis Van Loan/the Phantom, Lundbalm, Jim Doran (Phantom alias), Toby, Jack Bluebold (warden), Judkins, Dr. Maurice Jessup, Congressman Harry Arnold, Lester Gimble, Dr. Waldo (often switched to Dr. Hugo) Jones, Rotz, Simmons, Capt. Walters, Jackson, Dr. Paul Bendix, Snakey Willow, Jerry Lannigan, Gunner McGlone (mentioned), Jud Marks, Lucky Luke Lamar, Maxie Herman (mentioned), Trigger Dwyer (mentioned), Professor Kag (Gulliver Vonderkag), Flannigan, Jimmy Lance, Rowan, Killer Kline, Sam Robbins, Joe Sholz, Governor Young, Muldoon, O'Hara, Colonel Leusik, Dr. Harold Armster

A dam explosion, a prison reform, and a scientist who is experimenting on

a new metal alloy: these are problems facing the Phantom as he
investigates the mysterious group
calling themselves the Invisible
Empire. The leader of this invisible
empire calls himself the Imperator,
and he holds his minions in the
mine tunnels beneath a state pen.
He hopes to obtain world leadership through terrorism, and his
army of criminals obey his every
command. He has promised his
men that if they are killed, their
family members will be taken care
of for seven generations by his
world authority when he comes
into power.

Notes: Straight out of *Operator #5*, of course; the emblem of
the invisible empire is a small gray seal cut in the shape of an hour glass—
these emblems are pasted on the foreheads of their victims; the Invisible Empire calls itself the Two Americas; the *Clarion* signal light is used to call the
Phantom to action; there are two Tobys—one operates the private elevator
to Havens' top floor office in the *Clarion* Building, and the other is an assistant radio engineer—typical of Tepperman, too many names, far too many
people; Judkins is Havens' private secretary; cyclonic confusion; icy voice; "I'll
see you in hell!"; a pencil is used as a gas gun; guns are roscoes; the Phantom
contemplates the memory of the case involving Dyer; again, the nicknames
of Skipper and Champ between the Phantom and Lannigan; the Phantom
takes the place of Killer Kline, a notorious killer about to be put to death in
the state pen; people have green eyes; there's a hunchback; a babble of voices;
the Phantom uses alias of Jim Doran; this is another good story, with some
similarities to McDonald, but a lot of clues point to Tepperman, and they read
like *Operator #5;* again, a more angry Phantom than usual—he snaps at people,
including Frank Havens.

Availability: *Action Adventure Stories* #8 (published by Fading Shadows, Inc.,
1997), *High Adventure* #57 (published by Adventure House, 2001).

45. DEATH RIDES THE BLIZZARD

V17 #1—November 1936
Written by unknown; possibly Jack Byrne & Ray Cummings

Place: New York City; Quebec, Canada; Isle of Orleans, Canada

Main characters: Pierre Georges, William Cane, Wilfrid LeMieux, Wessel, Richard Curtis Van Loan/the Phantom,
Steve Huston, Frank Havens, John Claridge, James Blaine Vandergrift, Jenkins, Roy Dalbert, Nita (Wayne?), Dr.

1933

1934

1935

1936

1937

1938

1939

1940

1941

1942

1943

1944

1945

1946

1947

1948

1949

1950

1951

1952

1953

Paul Bendix, Inspector Iverness, Gunner McGlone (mentioned), Robert Worthington, Murphy, Jeane Hamel, Sgt. Ainsley, Tim, Red, Beaufort, James (John?) Rance, Mr. Allen, Mac, Francis Porquet

Frank Havens and two other newspaper owners are kidnapped. A French Canadian outlaw is suspected. The Phantom believes the case is heading towards Canada, plus a mysterious young girl appears to be heading in that direction, as well. The Phantom, with Steve Huston, follow on a train, but she escapes from them at a sudden stop en route. The Phantom has a fight with three of the outlaws under the train, and though he wins through, the train starts up and he is forced to ride underneath the boxcars in freezing, bone-chilling.

In Quebec, the Phantom and Steve make contact with the girl again, and eventually the action leads them to a small island where the newspaper owners are being held, and the story comes to a great climax as the Phantom races to the rescue riding a dog sled over the frozen snow and ice!

This is the best *Phantom* story to date, and possibly the best in the entire series. Again, I was reminded of G.T. Fleming-Roberts as I read the story; green-eyed people, the villain has three identities, and the final scene was so reminiscent of the later *Secret Agent "X"* stories (in particular, the August 1937 *"X"* story, "Satan's Syndicate"):

"Wait!" Jane Lenox put a detaining hand on "X's" arm. "You... you're going?"

He nodded. "I must. There's more ahead—more adventures, more criminals."

"Can't I..." She dropped her eyes and whispered... "Would you take me with you? I mean, perhaps I could help..."

"X" took both her hands in his. "No," he said gently. "You've done more than your share already. I have my duties—you have yours. Some day, perhaps, our paths may cross again. Until that time..."

"Satan's Syndicate" (August 1937)

And then he found Jeanne standing before him. "So you—you're really the Phantom?"

"Yes, that's what they call me."

She clung to his hand. "But won't I ever see you again?"

He hesitated, then he smiled gently. "If you're ever in New York, you tell Mr. Havens. He generally knows where to find me."

"Death Rides the Blizzard" (November 1936)

Notes: The newspapers involved are the French Canadian *Le Matin*, the *Clarion* and the *New York Star;* a hunchback is involved; again, Van Loan is with a girl named Nita when the story begins; the *Clarion* call; 125th Street and Lennox Ave. (the girl in the *"X"* story was named Jane Lenox, another strange coincidence); a silly-ass Englishman; "allez au diable"—"go to hell" or "go to the devil," freely translated; will-o'-the-wisp; feller; a babble of voices; polyglot babble; the Phantom uses smoke signals to send a dot and dash message to Steve; the Phantom drives a dog-sled to reach the crooks' hideout; one problem that the author had was placing the mastermind in three different places at the same time. Still, this one is my favorite *Phantom* stories. It will take a good story to beat this one.

Availability: *Action Adventure Stories* #25 (published by Fading Shadows, Inc., 1998).

46. THE SILENT DEATH
V17 #2—December 1936
Written by Ryerson Johnson

Place: New York City

Main characters: Silent Death, J. Dewey Rennsylier, Jertz, Hannihan, Richard Curtis Van Loan/the Phantom, Steve Huston, Tompson, Joey Fioretti, Ace Duveen (mentioned), "Pockets" O'Doud, Inspector Werners, Frank Havens, Sgt. Nelson, Morris Friedlander, John Rhodes Hill, Eric Garth, Rene Du Bois, Santiago de Ceva, Dr. Paul Bendix, G. Fillmore Clayton, Okada, "Specks" Haffrey, Flag Miller, Gunner McGlone (mentioned), Snag Gerlash, Crespe, "Angel" Lunt, Louie Alterie, Goldie, Mr. Harker, Frankie, Shoemaker Max

What is the bulletless death? Certain men of wealth are suddenly killed, with a small hole appearing in their foreheads. But no sound is heard, and no bullet is found in the wound.

Millions in gold have been hoarded by several men. Now someone wants it—and they are killing for it. At the bottom of the case is another revolution in South America, with the villain planning to take control of the unnamed country and keep all the gold.

Notes: a gun is a gat; people are sooty-eyed; a "Lawyer's Lulu"; a hop-hound out of hell; palooka; "aah-ghgh-gh"; Van does a tap dance routine to entertain

1933
1934
1935
1936
1937
1938
1939
1940
1941
1942
1943
1944
1945
1946
1947
1948
1949
1950
1951
1952
1953

1933

1934

1935

1936

1937

1938

1939

1940

1941

1942

1943

1944

1945

1946

1947

1948

1949

1950

1951

1952

1953

his friends at a party; the *Clarion* call; the Phantom is a lone wolf, avenging phantom; saffron flame; the *Wraith* is Van Loan's personal fast speedboat; mobsters are gun-uglies; there are some similarities to "Spawn of Death" (September 1934), though Ryerson did not write that one—however, it is evident that "Spawn of Death" is the novel he read prior to writing his *Phantom* story; the villain is called the Silent One, or the Black One; also, a revolution is taking place in Cuba; even the fer-de-lance snake is mentioned in the story—that snake had a big part in "Spawn of Death."

Availability: *The Phantom Detective V17N2—Pulp Facsimile* (published by Adventure House, 2008).

47. THE MURDER CARAVAN

V17 #3—January 1937
Written by Charles Greenberg

Place: New York City

Main characters: Ralph Bankhead, Madeleine Bankhead, Steve Huston, Richard Curtis Van Loan/the Phantom, Mac, Mike, Lehman, Jackson, Arnold Berber, Tommy Berber, Clyde Parrish, Frank Havens, Jeffery Clark, Emil Stephano, Jamison, Hugh Keller, Gary, Stanley Peterson, Martha Parrish, Inspector Farragut, Frank Capardy, Hugo, George H. Clifford, Henry Husing, Kohler (mentioned), Tom Fenton, Baron, Slasher, Mary Hastings, Chris Muller, Otto

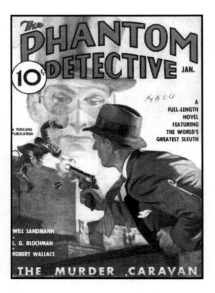

The families of rich, powerful men in the drug business are being kidnapped. The kidnappers are demanding large quantities of illegal drugs (which these men control in their companies), cocaine and opium, in return for their loved ones.

Notes: The crook allows a prisoner to escape in order for that person to "see" the supposed mastermind unmasked, but the man they see is actually a dupe they've set up to make the prisoners believe that who they saw was the actual mastermind; the mastermind is said to resemble a giant bat; right there and then; author calls him "the Phantom Detective" instead of merely "the Phantom" in connection to the hero; Jamison is Havens' secretary; his left hand tugged at the lobe of his ear (this has been used before, but it's possible that Charles Greenberg created the idea); a bullet is a flesh-seeking missile; "Revelry in Hell" is the title of a poem the mastermind wrote; the killer's eyes closed, opened, closed again; a lost soul in torment; within an ace of...; "Hell's bells!"; Steve says, "Rich man, poor man, beggar man, thief—he comes and he goes, and who he is nobody knows," when the Phantom enters the scene—this was cute, but it didn't catch on, thankfully; palooka; whistles "Annie Laurie";

torture device is called the Devil's Bathtub; slap, slap, slap; house of cards; since Charles Greenberg was also an editor for the *Phantom,* many of these same clues possibly pop up in stories by other authors, as he could've easily stuck his own favorite quips into a sentence.

48. THE TORCH OF DOOM

V18 #1—February 1937
Written by unknown; possibly George A. McDonald or Emile C. Tepperman

Place: Indianapolis, IN; New York City

Main characters: The Torch, Al Harran, Nick Gold, Big Tim Tangway, Paul Gleason, "Hi-card" Guffy, Naomi Carloff, Felix Goerner, Capt. Wander, Richard Curtis Van Loan/the Phantom, Joe Riley, Frank Havens, Blockman, Jacks, Lyman Sack, Rip Sosne, Bill Buckley, Jerry Lannigan, Packy Miles, Pedro Lorenzo, Gregg Fowbin, Phillip Norton, Dopey, Beefer, Police Commissioner (not named), Jerry Lang (Lannigan alias), Bert Standish

A twisting and fast-paced story involving the Indianapolis 500, a super car, and a new fuel invented to give higher performance to an automobile, as well as more miles to a gallon. Agents from Europe are searching for the inventor—who has mysteriously disappeared—while New York gangsters are running a stolen car and illegal gas and oil racket. A second gang appears to be trying to muscle into the operation.

At the head of the crime spree is a masked killer called the Torch, who is kidnapping important people in the race industry, holding them for millions of dollars in ransom—he needs the money to buy into the big corporation which controls the new fuel.

Notes: Crime-deep; the *Clarion* call for the Phantom; Havens calls Van, "Dick," instead of the more commonly used "Van"; Havens makes a clicking sound with his tongue; the Phantom wears a skin belt next to his waist that contains several zippered pockets that hold his many gadgets; fella; hells bells; the Phantom sometimes calls Havens "Chief"; Phantom carries a Colt; the Phantom says, "Ripley or not"—meaning "believe it or not"; Hiyah; muffed it; "Gosh," the Phantom said; a more angry Phantom than usual, but at times I questioned this one as being by Tepperman; Jerry Lannigan uses alias of Jerry Lang; Skipper and Champ nicknames are used; Phantom sometimes snaps at people, including Frank Havens.

Availability: *Action Adventure Stories* #1 (published by Fading Shadows, Inc., 1997).

1933
1934
1935
1936
1937
1938
1939
1940
1941
1942
1943
1944
1945
1946
1947
1948
1949
1950
1951
1952
1953

49. THE HENCHMEN OF DEATH

V18 #2—March 1937
Written by Charles Greenberg

Place: New York City

Main characters: Chris (later changed to Tony) Moreno, Straus, Dutch Gorman, Kellerman, Red Munson, Honeyboy Clinton, Butcher Malloy, Warden Thomas, Father Ryan, Richard Curtis Van Loan/the Phantom, Frank Havens, Joshua Hendricks, Judson, Eddie Marlow, Henry C. Richman, Roger Blaine, Wilbur Kennedy, John Stuart, Nina La Mar, Hugh Weber, Ruth Hollis, Gregory Hollis, Hugo, London, Nancy Marlow, Brandt, Harmond, George Hargreaves, Allhoff, Wesley, Brandford, Ivans, Clark, Foreman, Johnson, Foley

A dozen killers on death row are rescued from prison. The Phantom is called to the home of an important banker a few days later, where he finds one of the escaped killers present; there is a raid on the house by the other killers, and the banker is killed.

A clue leads the Phantom to a masquerade ball, where again the escaped convicts are on hand to kidnap an important man and his daughter. A mysterious woman promises the Phantom a solution to the mystery, but she is killed before she can reveal everything.

A giant counterfeit scheme is at the bottom of the mystery. One of the killers rescued from the death house was a master engraver. Inside men in the banking system were supposed to pass the counterfeit money, while the real money was to be spirited away.

Notes: One man is effeminate; an ex-dancer in the story had been financed by a rich man who was in love with her; people have green eyes; an underground cavern—similar to an incident from "The Criminal Caesar" (April 1936)—that could have been a plot device by Greenberg; at one point the crooks plan on electrocuting the Phantom; a message is left on a Dictaphone, similar to a previous Greenberg entry; straight as a die; bullets are angry hornets.

Availability: *Action Adventure Stories* #32 (published by Fading Shadows, Inc., 1998).

50. THE GOLDEN KILLER

V18 #3—April 1937
Written by unknown; possibly Paul Chadwick or George A. McDonald

Place: New York City

Main characters: Golden Killer/Golden Death, Francis B. Corbin, Richard Curtis Van Loan/the Phantom,

George Travers, Duke, Joe, Paul Corbin, Frank Havens, Gregory Prescott, Police Commissioner Crowley, Mary Corbin Wright, Harold Corbin, William Corbin, Monk, Charles Dwyer, Dr. Carver, Miss Jackson, Bradberry, Jane Brown, Dip, Mulligan, "Bullet" Baker, John Brown, Jake, Ike

In 1895 a bold robbery of a shipment of gold took place. One of the outlaws, "Bullet" Baker, was eventually captured and sent to prison. He kept his secret of where the gold was hidden until his death while in prison, at which time he sent a map detailing the secret location to one of his heirs (which one received this map, the mastermind does not know).

The mastermind had been a partner of Bullet Baker at one time, and wanted the gold that had been hidden away for all these years, and was willing to kill for it.

Notes: Again, this novel had a number of similarities to the *Secret Agent "X"* novel, "Plague of the Golden Death" (December 1937), as well as a Dan Fowler story, "Golden Harvest" (July 1939), but the story has strong clues to McDonald, not Paul Chadwick; a date, October 4, 1895, is stenciled in gold across the victims' backs; interpolated; between the devil and the deep blue sea; hidden button in his car, when pushed will cause police license plates to appear; there was no *Clarion* call in this one; the Phantom uses a trick sleeve gun; barked his shin; bullets are wasps and hornets; supposedly a previous story had involved the Bradberry case; one suspect has green eyes; helter-skelter; split hairs; birthstone in Phantom's ring is a tear-gas powder; he has fittings for both a wrist and ankle gun; the mastermind uses a blow pipe to shoot poison darts; National City Bank.

Availability: *The Phantom Detective V18N3—Pulp Facsimile* (published by Adventure House, 2008).

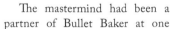

1933

1934

1935

1936

1937

1938

1939

1940

1941

1942

1943

1944

1945

1946

1947

1948

1949

1950

1951

1952

1953

1933

1934

1935

1936

1937

1938

1939

1940

1941

1942

1943

1944

1945

1946

1947

1948

1949

1950

1951

1952

1953

CHAPTER III, SECTION E

AUTHORSHIP BECOMES MORE COMPLICATED: 1937-1939

FROM NOW ON the authorship is going to be more difficult to identify. Although I think I am fairly certain on most identities of the authors involved, a lot of editorial involvement, new ideas entering the series, and some of the changes could either be from new writers, using styles from previous writers, or the same writers adding editorial changes and new ideas, making their stories harder to identify. Whatever the case, the Phantom does enter into a new period.

After such outstanding stories as "Dealers in Death" (July 1936) and "Death Rides the Blizzard" (November 1936), many of these 1937 and 1938 stories fail to make the same grade. In fact, many of these, such as "The Beast King Murders" (March 1937), "The Corpse Parade" (December 1937) and "Fangs of Murder" (January 1938) and others, are almost carbon copies of each other. The crooks' dialogue is the same from one story to another; though the author has devised new plots, with new scenes, we can still see the same things happening. For instance, in one story, the action may be taking place in an underground tunnel, while in another story it is taking place on the skeletal frame of a tall building. Different areas, but the setting, dialogue and action is the same in both cases. One explanation for this could be the fact that the author was churning these Phantom stories out like an assembly line. In fact, some of the Lynn Vickers titles sound a little like the Phantom stories: If this author is McDonald, it could be the result of his work elsewhere. For instance, "Fangs of the Cobra" over in *Federal Agent* (January 1937), sounds a lot like "Fangs of Murder."

Several new authors become involved at this point, too. The June 1937 story, "The Dancing Doll Murders," involves the mastermind sending little "dancing" dolls to his victims. Will Murray told me that he believes this to be the same author who wrote the Jim Anthony novel, "The Horrible Marionettes" in *Super Detective* (June 1941). In the *Phantom* story, "The Phantom's Gamble With Death" (February 1940), the mastermind sends his victims miniature coffins. Some authors may only be one-shot *Phantom* scribes. Laurence Donovan becomes a big factor very quickly. There are a number of entries that have touches of *Doc Savage;* Laurence Donovan's for sure, and possibly some others.

It is also at this point that something must have happened at the *Phantom Detective* section of Standard. With the October 1938 story, "Graduates of Murder," we have a re-written Dan Fowler story. Too many clues jump at the reader; a character named Daniels, a woman detective (Sally Vane, of course), and the Phantom uses too many F.B.I. techniques to be our "Famous Detective." Then comes the November 1938 story, "Death Glow," which has some Champion clues. Did the editors suddenly find they were without *Phantom* manuscripts for some reason, thus had to change a Dan Fowler story into a *Phantom Detective* while Champion completed the manuscript for "Death Glow"? Another clue that an author may have died during this period.

"The Murder Syndicate" (December 1938) was a treat, but I cannot imagine who the author could be here, either. The story was odd in that the Phantom is never captured throughout the story, something that the editors demanded! How this author got away with this, I'll never know, except that and again, this story follows "Graduates of Murder" and "Death Glow," when something was happening at Standard. Again, they must have needed a story very badly, or they never would have let this slip by them. But it was a good story!

Suddenly Charles Greenberg is back with several stories, plus possibly Tepperman, and other repeat authors, so Standard seems to have bounced back from a sudden slump. "The Radio Murders" (April 1939) is our last mystery during this period. But it is a strange mystery. First, the story appears to be a re-written "The Criminal Caesar" (April 1936), as it has the same format and plot. There is a single incident of D.L. Champion's fingerprints showing up, but it is almost overlooked, so I doubt that he had much (if anything) to do with the story. Second, the story relies heavily on incidents from the earlier "Death Glow" plot. But this is not our mystery author, nor is it totally a Champion story. But I can't help but feel that whoever this new author is, he was provided with a copy of "Death Glow" and possibly even "The Criminal Caesar," to read before he turned in "The Radio Murders." Something I might add, I've heard that Champion became a better writer after leaving the Phantom series for a few years, so if he has returned, I may not be recognizing his style at this point.

Just to touch a bit on "Murder at the World's Fair" (June 1939) and "The Forty Thieves" (July 1939): in these two novels we are introduced to Clifford Boniface, the only character who fought against the Phantom twice—and Boniface is merely a remake of another character that was used in "Cavalcade of Death" (August 1937) named Dike Patton. Curiously enough, "The Forty Thieves" is basically the same story as "Cavalcade of Death." Another curiosity regarding these two stories is that Boniface is introduced in "Murder at the World's Fair," and, as can be assumed, the World's Fair is involved. However, in our next segment, we'll cover a story titled "The Sampan Murders" (September 1939) that takes place at another World's Fair, this one in San Francisco, and in which the lad Chip Dorlan is introduced. I might add that "The Sampan Murders" is by Laurence Donovan. Again, I will make an unconfirmed conclusion that the character of Chip Dorlan—and the setting at World's Fairs—were

1933
1934
1935
1936
1937
1938
1939
1940
1941
1942
1943
1944
1945
1946
1947
1948
1949
1950
1951
1952
1953

1933

1934

1935

1936

1937

1938

1939

1940

1941

1942

1943

1944

1945

1946

1947

1948

1949

1950

1951

1952

1953

probably suggested by editorial staff, and not the author. And this goes back to such events that happened in 1936, such as Steve Huston coming into the series, and the introduction of the signal light atop the *Clarion* Building that would call the Phantom to action in story after story. The character of Gunner McGlone was probably a suggestion from the editorial staff, too. Originally, the alias of Gunner McGlone was merely a name the authors were to refer back to, although the Phantom does use the disguise in one story, "Cavalcade of Death." Some other examples are some of the other aliases used at odd times, like Lester Cornwell that was used many times by all authors involved. Another problem was with the Police Commissioner and Chief Inspector; different authors were using different character names. Eventually, Inspector Thomas Gregg would become a regular in the series, and was probably suggested by the editors. This had to be done. More and more authors were coming into the series now, so the editors had to have some kind of continuity to the stories.

51. HARVEST OF DEATH

V19 #1—May 1937
Written by unknown;
possibly Ray Cummings

Place: New York City

Main characters: Francis Green, Gloria Green, Jim Crawford, George Carrington, Señor Alcatraz, Frank Havens, James Grant, George Montague, John Wylie, Capt. Franklin, Guttierrez, Richard Curtis Van Loan/the Phantom, Luis Angelo Palegrino, John Torrence, Robinson, Ramon, Winton Rand, Jones, Peter Blair, Dr. Paul Bendix, John Philip Worthington, Winnie Wayne, Tolly Marks, Inspector Iverness, MacDougall, Jake Wayne

Men connected with a South American country, Aldara, and an engraving company, are being murdered. It appears that a giant scheme is being worked out to counterfeit the new money that is being printed in America for their government. Millions of dollars in Aldaran currency is at stake, and not only is there a mastermind involved in the scheme, but it also appears that there is a rival gang after the foreign currency.

Notes: The Phantom moved like same jungle cat; a bullet sang a whining whizz of death; the scene is electric with excitement, anticipation; leprous in the fog; audible; time becomes crowded seconds; pseudo-breathing; the Black Cat Restaurant; again, there is no *Clarion* call for the Phantom; this actually reads like an earlier *Phantom* entry, possibly written prior to the *Clarion* signal light being written into the stories, but it could be simply that it wasn't used.

Availability: *Action Adventure Stories* #16 (published by Fading Shadows, Inc., 1997), *Wildside Pulp Classics: Phantom Detective* #51 (published by Wildside Press, 2008).

52. THE DANCING DOLL MURDERS

V19 #2—June 1937
Written by Paul Chadwick

Place: New York City

Main characters: Esmond Caulder, Don Winstead, Eben Gray, Reggie Winstead, Orville Tyler, Jason Squires, Inspector Farragut, Steve Huston, Det. Sgt. Nelson, Frank Havens, Richard Curtis Van Loan/the Phantom, Wally, Dr. Paul Bendix, Alex Barry, Mike Keogh, Judd Moxley, Simon Blackwell, Sarah, Blackie Guido, Bowers, Dopey O'Banion, Joe Vanzanni, Warburton, Dolly DeLong, Hog-Face, Rodney Post, Marie, Fanny Green, Svendal, Symie, Sheehan

Family members receive miniature mechanical dancing dolls just prior to their murder. It appears that someone is after the inheritance. The mastermind had stolen these dolls previously, and was responsible for sending them to the intended victims. However, at one point a crook leaves one of them for the Phantom without the mastermind's knowledge.

Notes: The mastermind appears from below water in a mansion swimming pool to give instructions to his minions. He wears a diving suit for this purpose, and has a secret entrance into the mansion and pool; get gay about death; a swift parabola; ultra-smart; people say, "Great God!"; spavined; a ghost from hell; presentiment of doom; Van Loan sings to the music of an orchestra on board a yacht with his friends; elusive as a shadow, as hard to hold as the night wind; Wally is a young friend of Van Loan's group; pulled the lobe of his ear; mist, blue-lidded, sinful eyes; lynx-eyed; machine-gun yammered; within an ace of; Washburn 7-9292; a missing finger gives the Phantom's disguise away; carnival of murder; rocked on his heels; billet-doux; "Great Scott!"; *Clarion* signal light is used to call the Phantom.

Availability: *Phantom Detective* #2 (published by Corinth Regency, 1965), *Wildside Pulp Classics: Phantom Detective* #52 (published by Wildside Press, 2008), *The Phantom Detective V19N2—Pulp Facsimile* (published by Adventure House, 2008).

1933

1934

1935

1936

1937

1938

1939

1940

1941

1942

1943

1944

1945

1946

1947

1948

1949

1950

1951

1952

1953

1933

1934

1935

1937

1938

1939

1940

1941

1942

1943

1944

1945

1946

1947

1948

1949

1950

1951

1952

1953

53. THE BEAST KING MURDERS

V19 #3—July 1937
Written by George A. McDonald

Place: New York City

Main characters: Jason B. Lammond, Duke, Marty Short, Red, Deputy Chief-Inspector Thomas Gregg, Ralph Mortimer, Richard Curtis Van Loan/the Phantom, Morrisy, Larry Wells, Mrs. de Ruyster, Frank Havens, Adams, Kirk H. Cunningham, H. H. Struthers, Thomas Rathbone, Peter Loring, Mark Bannister, Melvin Thorpe, Henry Crawford, Wayne, Max, George Hamilton, Lou, Jeff Horgan, Roderick Fenton, John Ryle, H. C. Smith

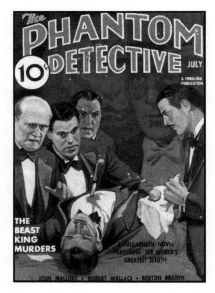

Men are being killed, apparently mauled by lions. The Phantom learns that ten men had been on a safari in Africa when they happened upon a native chief who was hoarding a cache of diamonds. They plan on murdering the chief—well, maybe it wasn't murder, after all he was nothing more than a savage—or so these ten men had told themselves.

They did steal the diamonds, but one of the men had been killed, supposedly mauled by a lion, while another had been beheaded by the tribe for the murder of their chief and the theft of the diamonds. Now, the remaining eight men have hidden their stolen jewels in a vault, each man holding a key that will open the vault, but it takes all eight keys to open it, and give access to the jewels.

Notes: Atavistic savagery; swart faced; abattoir; pulls at the lobe of his left ear; Adams is the city editor of the *Clarion;* feller; symbol of a globe—the Adventurers' Club that the men belong to; Larry Wells is the *Clarion* crime reporter; pug-ugly face; Phantom is tossed from a window ten stories above the street, but uses window awnings to slow his fall and crash through a window on a lower floor—very similar to previous escapes; cops are "dicks"; Havens owns the Kimberly Star, a very large and expensive diamond; some similarities to G.T. Fleming-Roberts again: signal light atop the *Clarion* calls the Phantom to action; date of September 4th, 1920 (?) is used.

Availability: *Phantom Detective* #3 (published by Corinth Regency, 1965), *The Phantom Detective V19N3—Pulp Facsimile* (published by Adventure House, 2009).

54. CAVALCADE OF DEATH

V20 #1—August 1937

Written by Paul Chadwick

Place: New York City

Main characters: The Voice, the Bent Car Mob, Ben Moore, Swain, Frank Havens, Richard Curtis Van Loan/the Phantom, Anne Calvert, Mrs. Carson, Arnold Calvert, Lance Beadle, Saki, Huntress, Inspector Farragut, Basil Jarvis, J. Wesley Troop, Edward Garvey, Big Al Diamond, Gunner McGlone (Phantom alias), Rose LaFlamme, Albert Diamaonni, Dike Patton, Dr. Paul Bendix, Jones, Symes, Farlin

Automobiles are being stolen and torn down, changing them enough in appearance to re-sell here and abroad. With the wanton killing that the Bent Car Mob is doing in their raids and automobile hijacking, the Phantom becomes interested in the case. But it is after Havens' chauffer is murdered in the theft of Havens' car, that Frank Havens decides to call in the Phantom.

Notes: This is a story that would be re-written later, as "The Forty Thieves" (July 1939), in which Clifford Boniface is involved. In fact, Dike Patton is the forerunner of that character. Debouched; cacophony of screams; as elusive as a shadow, as hard to follow as a zephyr; Van Loan drives a Duesenberg; the "merry-go-round" torture; Van Loan is with Anne Calvert at the beginning of the story; the *Clarion* signal light calls the Phantom to action; tugged at the lobe of his ear; people clip, guns bark; Phantom actually uses the alias of Gunner McGlone in an active part; feller; "in your hat"; Jeez; heel of shoe contains steel blade; bullet is a messenger of death; miasma; the Village; gimlet-eyed; Hell's bells; "Karist!"; one of the henchmen is a hunchback. Author uses "febrile," but this could've been the editor.

Availability: *Action Adventure Stories* #108 (published by Fading Shadows, Inc., 2001).

55. HAMMERS OF DOOM

V20 #2—September 1937
Written by George A. McDonald

Place: New York City; Hopeton, PA

Main characters: The Grey Hood/Big Shot, Lefty, Slug, Joey, Pedro, Carl, John T. Russell, Chief Inspector Gregg, Paul Kennedy, Steve Huston, Frank Havens, Richard Curtis Van Loan/the Phantom, Dr. Norton, Jackson, Robert Matthews, Adams, Miss Reid, Tony, Peterson, Dr. Paul Bendix, Harvey Pierce, Joseph Wyatt, George Cameron, T. H. Taggert, Max Atchison, Benjamin Rowe, Manuel, Wilder, Capt. Thomas Radlow (sea captain), Juan de Hernandez, Lollita, Brown, Bert, Pete, General Uriburu

1933

1934

1935

1936

1937

1938

1939

1940

1941

1942

1943

1944

1945

1946

1947

1948

1949

1950

1951

1952

1953

AUTHORSHIP BECOMES MORE COMPLICATED: 1937-1939 83

In a story with similarities to "The Golden Killer," South American gold is being hoarded by eight men, while another man wants it—wants it all! The gold had been hidden in a mine owned by another—yet only the eight men had maps to the hidden treasure.

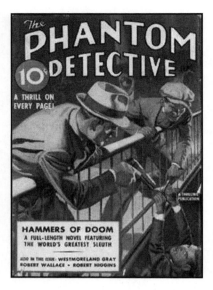

Men are murdered with their hands riveted together, each at a location connected to their own businesses. This horrible torture was supposed to throw suspicion towards one man, but the scheme backfired, and while the Phantom closes in on the criminal he switches suspicion to yet another.

Notes: This story had a lot of similarities with "The Sign of the Scar" (September 1936) and "The Torch of Doom" (February 1937). People are swart-faced; pug-faced; crack, crack, crack; *Clarion* light flashes heliographic message telling the Phantom to go somewhere in particular, where a murder had taken place; Adams is the city editor; Miss Reid is a woman secretary to Havens; Phantom carries a Colt .45; a dye in a scarf points to an area in Argentina—plus, a perfume points to South America; there is a recording disc; rat-ta-tat-tat; "What devil—" someone says. "I," said Van grimly, "am the Phantom." Very similar to some early 1933 stories; the South Americans use bolas; a fight on the docks is similar to a scene from an earlier story, and the rescue by a police boat is also the same; a native uses curare poison to kill himself; helter-skelter.

56. DOUBLE-STAMPED DOOM

V20 #3—October 1937
Written by unknown; possibly Robert Sydney Bowen

Place: London; Paris; New York City

Main characters: Big Boss, Pierre Caballe, Inspector Hardy (Scotland Yard), George Walters, Tapling, Lapham, Ed Duncan, Armitage, Stephen Le Roy, Kernan, Barker, Harrison, Frank Havens, Richard Curtis Van Loan/the Phantom, Inspector Farragut, Olsen, Steve Huston, Joe Burns, Sheriff Hogan, Eric Martin, Courtney Burke, Nada Le Roy, Arthur Hind, Henry Quarl, Pete Grogan, Gus Lody, Pete, Hank, Ronald Starbuck, B. K. Miller, Roger Closs, Colonel Green, Hawker, Jackson, Henderson (Bronxville Police Chief), Frederick von Elm, Fritz

A fairly nice entry, with the mystery involving the theft of rare and valuable postage stamps from collections around the world. Some of the stamps are then counterfeited and sold to rich customers who collect stamps, even if they are stolen, never suspecting that they are being duped.

The mastermind kills with a type of gas gun that shoots a stream of liquid oxygen that freezes the heart muscles and brings instant death. The Phantom works from a clue of the victim's watches being 15 minutes slow—the freezing effect of the liquid oxygen slows its inner workings.

Notes: The Johnson Hospital; "Huh, huh?"; oke—this spelling of okay was used by one of the Dan Fowler authors; the Phantom crosses an open space by hand-walking along electric lines from one point to another; eyes became saucers; similar to Charles Greenberg, characters repeat when talking, "that's right, that's right"; people talk in a lot of grunts; the nth degree; geez; the dragon of crime and death that preys on honest men and women. The Phantom is blunt with Frank Havens, which is not normal—"Goodbye, Frank," and Havens will immediately leave as though he has been dismissed. Robert Sydney Bowen had several plots very similar to this, and I'm pretty sure this one is his.

Availability: *Action Adventure Stories* #48 (published by Fading Shadows, Inc., 1999).

57. MINIONS OF MURDER

V21 #1—November 1937
Written by George A. McDonald

Place: New York City

Main characters: Inspector Gregg, O'Toole, Ryan, Steve Huston, George Banning, Frank Havens, Brady, Mrs. Reusaler, Richard Curtis Van Loan/the Phantom, James Kendricks, W. B. Harrison, Samuel Quayne, Sprayer, Miss Davis, John Harkness, Philip Worthing, Floyd Benson, Nick, Kenneth Raymond, "Horseface," Charlie, Neal, Miss Evans, Dr. Bendix, Curly, Lucius B. Peters, Jim Allen, Hal, Mrs. Pears, Henry Baker, Emil Baker, Paul Baker, Walter Baker, Ralph, David, Eli, Dr. Hugo, Frenchy, Amelia Baker

Years previously, a well-to-do

1933

1934

1935

1936

1937

1938

1939

1940

1941

1942

1943

1944

1945

1946

1947

1948

1949

1950

1951

1952

1953

family secretly assumed new identities and businesses, while they kept up munitions work for America and foreign countries. When their real family business began sinking, they threw everything into their secret identities and supposedly killed off all the family members in a fake accident. Now it appears that one family member wants everything and is really killing off the whole family!

Notes: The signal light atop the *Clarion* calls the Phantom to action; fog horn from a ship also calls the Phantom; people speak crisply, or in clips; beetle-browed eyes; okay; geeze; Star Warehouse; pince-nez; Van Loan is personal friend to heads of the war department, also able to fax material over the phone to them from Dr. Bendix's warehouse laboratory; the Phantom has a dead gangster secretly removed by the police—a plot device by this author; a gun battle in a cemetery, which is another plot device I've encountered before; too many similarities to "The Golden Killer" (April 1937), for it not to be the same author.

Availability: *Thrilling Novels* #35 (published by Fun Stuff Imaginations, 1996).

58. THE CORPSE PARADE

V21 #2—December 1937

Written by unknown; possibly Robert Sydney Bowen or George A. McDonald

Place: New York City

Main characters: Big Shot, Squinty Martin, Beef, Ato, Nat, Thomas J. Reynolds, Capt. Shea, Inspector Gregg, Adams, Miss Wilson, Kenneth Trask, Elliot Brockton, Jackson, Anne Trask, Dr. Bendix, Niles, Hillary Leonard, Willett Bascomb, Ralph Herndon, Charles Foster, David Rutledge, Geoffrey Daniels, Joseph Edmunds, Larry Kanes, Harry, Hearn, Frank Havens, Richard Curtis Van Loan/the Phantom

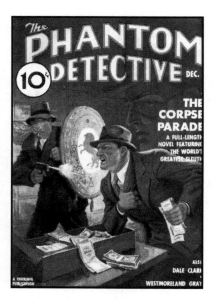

Men are killed in a strange fashion: their right arm is amputated just above the elbow, then their body is chained behind a city truck to be dragged through the streets of New York City. Clues point to a Greek legend, as well as an Ethiopian custom of dealing with thieves.

Several Americans had made a deal with an Ethiopian prince to deliver weapons for a deed to valuable oil lands in Ethiopia. After obtaining the deed, the Americans reneged on delivering the weapons to the prince. It appears now that the prince is killing them for being thieves of his land.

Notes: Baleful eyes; Adams is city editor at the *Clarion;* Miss Wilson is the switchboard operator for the *Clarion;* the *Clarion* light is not working at this time, so Havens has all city traffic lights show red to alert the Phantom that he is needed; the Phantom carries a Colt .45; pince-nez; calls Frank, "Mr. Havens"; oke; presentiment of danger; again, people speak in grunts, or they "crisped out" when they speak. Same plot as previous McDonald entries, but also some similarities to the author of "Double-Stamped Doom" (October 1937). Confusing!

Availability: *Phantom Detective* #22 (published by Corinth Regency, 1966), *The Corpse Parade* (published by Jim Hanos, 1986).

59. FANGS OF MURDER
V21 #3—January 1938
Written by George A. McDonald

Place: New York City

Main characters: The Fang/Big Shot, "Scars" Ricco, Monk Gorman, "Dutch" Kaltz, Flowers Gursh, Big Boy Rinaldi, Gus, Inspector Thomas Gregg, Albert Millett, Carl Fenwick, Clyde Dickson, Bernard J. Andrews, Paul Corbin, John Gifford, Gordon Drake, Kenneth Meade, Bernice, Benjamin Marcy, Lyle Marcy, Capt. Donaldson, Capt. Waltham, Tony, Choppy, Eddie Collins, Pete, Richard Curtis Van Loan/the Phantom, Frank Havens, Lt. Donovan, Queen Stella, Count Karnov, Dr. Bendix, Spike, O'Brien, Estella Millett

Twenty years previously, a group of circus freaks formed a club—the Gargoyle Club. One circus performer was a reputed wild young man with buckteeth who was nicknamed "the Fang." This man was involved in petty crime. He also married the trapeze star, but she died after giving birth to their daughter. The daughter and her father disappeared afterwards. Now some of the showmen are being killed in strange ways, while a sabretooth is left at the scene—denoting "the Fang."

Notes: A torture called the "Ladle"; some similarities to "The Criminal Caesar" (April 1936) as well as some more recent stories. Very probably the same author of "The Corpse Parade" (December 1937), regardless. A man is effeminate; a carnival ride called the "Leap-for-life"; Milady's Salon; Crowley & Buckill circus; bugaboo; hullabaloo; people again grunt when they speak, or they "crisped" out; The Golden Slipper; Eddie Collins works as the *Clarion's* newspaper cartoonist—he's killed at the *Clarion* where Frank and Van Loan see him die; the Gargoyle Club; Palladium Club; gruesome murders—two men are possibly killed by ax blows (though it never reveals how they were killed while surrounded by many people), while another has a crowbar supposedly driven through his head (this was actually an earlier accident which made

1933

1934

1935

1936

1937

1938

1939

1940

1941

1942

1943

1944

1945

1946

1947

1948

1949

1950

1951

1952

1953

1933

1934

1935

1936

1937

1938

1939

1940

1941

1942

1943

1944

1945

1946

1947

1948

1949

1950

1951

1952

1953

him a freak at a circus—how he was really murdered is never explained); left at the scene of the murders are sabreteeth; Phantom carries a Colt .45.

Availability: *Phantom Detective* #12 (published by Corinth Regency, 1966), *Wildside Pulp Classics: Phantom Detective* #59 (published by Wildside Press, 2005).

60. TYCOON OF CRIME

V22 #1—February 1938
Written by George A. McDonald

Place: Kansas; New York City

Main characters: Tycoon of Crime, Slick, Luke, Pat Bentley, Ape, Max Garth, Bill, David Truesdale, Nancy Clay, Inspector Gregg, Vincent Brooks, Leland Sprague, Joseph Ware, Paul Talbert, Donald Vaughan, John Eldridge, James Strickland, Charles Jenson, Andrew Harvey, Richard Curtis Van Loan/the Phantom, Muriel Havens, Frank Havens, Elwood Mason, Winston B. Garrison, Dr. Bendix, Dr. Carl Ferris, Shirley Keenan, "Frenchy" Jacques Barac, Maxie, Kitty

A group of scientists, while making maps for the U.S. government, locate a rich area of pitchblende ore on land owned by a railroad company. The company is going broke and quickly accepts the scientists' offer to buy stocks in the railroad. The scientists, of course, merely want controlling interests through the stocks in order to control the rich deposit of ore. However, it appears that one of them wants it all—and he is willing to kill the others for it!

Notes: Pat Bentley, now an airline pilot, was at one time a reporter for Frank Havens' *Clarion;* ballyhoo; Van made a clucking sound with his tongue; Muriel has dark hair, dark liquid eyes—this story contains a nice description of Muriel; Pat Bentley's dead body is left outside Van's apartment building, and he takes this as a direct challenge; carries a Colt .45; Van had mastered judo from the Japanese champion, Soji Kamura; the Phantom tugs at lobe of his ear to identify himself to Havens; a black ledger—the case book of Richard Curtis Van Loan; sometimes calls Frank, "Mr. Havens"; will-o'-the-wisp; feller; the radio eye-witness report of the crash "of a great air ship" is featured in the story; oke.

Availability: *Phantom Detective* #4 (published by Corinth Regency, 1965), *Wildside Pulp Classics: Phantom Detective* #60 (published by Wildside Press, 2005).

61. THE MASTER OF DEATH

V22 #2—March 1938
Written by Charles Greenberg

Place: Westchester, NY; Water City (NJ?), the World's Playground—might be Atlantic City, NJ

Main characters: The Secret Six, John Travis, Benny the Duchess, Frank Havens, Richard Curtis Van Loan/the Phantom, Joe O'Keefe, Paul Kendall, Jennings, Inspector Friar (Westchester), Gregory, Dr. Barrett, Hugh Gregg, Mike, Robert White, Nick Matteo, Hennessy, Harris (police chief of Water City), O'Brien, Harrington, Walter Claridge, Jeffery Murdock, Henry Arlen, Bentley, O'Hara, "Frenchy" Henri Duval, Sing Woo, McNair, Scotty, Lefty, Nina LaMar, Emil Kruger, Chris Allison, Cappy

A very good story, and something of a take-off on Champion's *Alias Mr. Death* plot. The Secret Six are controlling Water City politics and finances, but now one of the Six may be planning on taking over complete control—and eliminating the other five members.

The newspaper chief on Havens' local newspaper, the *Water City Herald*, travels to Westchester, NY, where Havens has his estate, to confer over some hard editorials the chief wants to run in the paper about the corruption in the city. In the meantime, he has been followed by mobsters from Water City, who gun him down in the presence of Frank Havens and Van Loan. The Phantom accepts the challenge and, assuming a disguise as Mr. Havens' new editor of the *Herald*, arrives in Water City to meet a top-notch, red-headed reporter (merely a replacement for Steve Huston). But the mobsters immediately throw suspicion on the Phantom for a murder, thus the editor disguise is dropped for another almost immediately. With the drop of the disguise, the red-headed reporter is forgotten just as quickly.

The story comes to a nice, though somewhat sudden ending.

Notes: A man is effeminate; Havens is in his fifties again; Water City is probably Atlantic City; the Apollo Cabaret; once, twice, three times; bullets are angry hornets; no *Clarion* call; Jennings is Havens' butler; right there and then; Gregory is Havens' chauffeur; Havens has a Swedish couple who are his cook and housekeeper; the Imperial Hotel, room 1919; Dr. Barrett is Havens' family doctor; Joe O'Keefe is a red-headed reporter on the *Herald;* the Boardwalk is mentioned in Water City; collapsed like a house of cards; overall, this is a nice story, even if there are a lot of inconsistencies. It does have some strong characterization. One of the fascinating aspects did not involve the story itself, but rather the cover by Rudolph Belarsk. The scene depicts a man wearing a

1933

1934

1935

1936

1937

1938

1939

1940

1941

1942

1943

1944

1945

1946

1947

1948

1949

1950

1951

1952

1953

1933

1934

1935

1936

1937

1938

1939

1940

1941

1942

1943

1944

1945

1946

1947

1948

1949

1950

1951

1952

1953

diving suit being shot by gangsters in a passing automobile. The scene does not appear in this current novel. But it does appear in the very next issue, "Milestones of Murder" (April 1938). Evidently, Belarski was given the wrong details to illustrate a scene for "The Master of Death." I wonder how often this happened. The cover for "Milestones of Murder" was not done by Belarski.

62. MILESTONES OF MURDER

V22 #3—April 1938
Written by George A. McDonald

Place: New York City; Passaic, NJ

Main characters: Zarago, Komuri, Nate, Kerry Randolph, Richard Curtis Van Loan/the Phantom, Douglas Winfield, Inspector Gregg, Capt. McGuire, Paul Taber, Robert Balline, Dr. Charles Stanhope, Robert Brown, Jackson, Rischi, John Simon, Nicky, Nicholas Jones, Dr. Bendix, Jerome Kelland, Louis Gordon, Sam, Tompkins, Miquel Larchardo, Joe, Ralph, Pete, Shorty, Jimmy Grant, Marty, Johnson, Vince, Gomez, Frank Havens

Men are found murdered with strange carved knives in their chests. The case appears to involve the silk trade—in particular, the Japanese silk business, and the manufacture of raw silk.

Several men have banded together and are attempting to start producing raw silk with the secret technique used by the Japanese. They try to buy land in Cuba, where they hope to manufacture their Japanese silk. Now, it appears that someone else is killing them off to get the secret that they hold.

Notes: People have baleful eyes; carried a Colt .45; swarthy-faced; pince-nez; people "crisped" or "grunted"; no *Clarion* call for the Phantom; Van takes the role of a dead actor to finish some remaining scenes; the Star Warehouse; Jimmy Grant is a reporter on the *Clarion*, and is also a diver (deep sea diving experience). "Milestones of Murder" has a lot of similarities to the Dan Fowler story in the November 1935 issue of *G-Men Detective*.

Availability: *Milestones of Murder* (published by Jim Hanos, 1985).

63. THE MOVIE LOT MURDERS

V23 #1—May 1938
Written by Charles Greenberg

Place: Hollywood, CA; Nevada desert

Main characters: Emil Kroft, "Apache" Joe, Joe Gorman, Claude Finch, Black Eagle, Christopher Thorpe, Viola Stewart, Paul Drake, Michael Palmer, Running Deer, Frank Haley, Patsy Scott, Keefe, Frank Havens (mentioned), Andrew Becker, Richard Curtis Van Loan/the Phantom, Johnny Patterson, Hugh Gregory (Phantom alias), Red Cloud, O'Malley, Landis, Doc Saunders, Lion Marshall, Stephenson, Crosley, Morton, Josephs, Carlotto, Mendez, Garrison, Roger Scott

Frank Havens and Van Loan are vacationing in Hollywood, when the Phantom is requested by a movie studio to find their kidnapped young star. Though Frank Havens is mentioned, he does not make an appearance. Instead, Van Loan goes with the studio people to a location in the Nevada desert where the young girl has been kidnapped from the set.

Van Loan assumes the identity of Hugh Gregory and accompanies the studio men in a plane. As the airplane lands in the desert, they are attacked by Apache Indians. The action was too fast to follow, and too much was happening for the novel to sound very realistic. Everything seemed to happen within minutes, when days should have passed. Very unreal.

Though the police had been called in, they were not around when they should have been, are suddenly present when it seemed they shouldn't be, and are suddenly gone again. This is a problem with more than one story by Charles Greenberg.

Phantom does not wear his domino mask, and only uses the one disguise throughout the story. He was more like a private detective than the famous Phantom, and I was constantly wondering if maybe this novel had been re-written from something else. The story will be re-written later as "Death in the Desert" (June 1943), and will be a better story—Charles Greenberg very likely wrote the re-written story, too.

Notes: Again, I felt that this was a false *Phantom* story; a man is effeminate; Mammoth Films; once, twice, three times; bullets are angry hornets; dishabille; people often "clipped" when they talked; right there and then; eyes looked balefully; story does not recall the ever-present background information on the Phantom; his jaw muscles stood out in hard little balls.

64. THE FRONT PAGE MURDERS

V23 #2—June 1938

Written by unknown; possibly Paul Chadwick

Place: New York City

Main characters: Grover Lane, Mungo, Heinie Manush, Pie Traynor, Paul Waner, Nicky Yergez, Dan Powers,

Frank Havens, Judge Landis, Lester Carteret, Jack Lowe, Richard Curtis Van Loan/the Phantom, Rush Miller, Terry Stoneham, Horace Stoneham, Clyde Johnson, Abel Curtiz, Fred Lassiter, Ramon Montez, Cecil Smith, Sally Cateret, Herman Swanstrom, Smoke, Ernie, Robert Craig, Jimmie Loomis, Winnie Gunch, Henry Jordan, Keeling. The following are all baseball players in the story: Sam Leslie, Dick Bartell, Mel Ott, Hubbell, Wally Berger, Mickey Cochrane, Walter Brown, Pancho Snyder, Cy Blanton, Brubaker, Vaughn, Lloyd Waner, Young, Suhr, Lieber, Joe Moore, Ed Brandt, Jensen, Leslie

THE FRONT PAGE
MURDERS
A FULL-LENGTH NOVEL FEATURING
THE WORLD'S GREATEST SLEUTH

A very nice entry, but certainly a strange one! The case appears to surround a current pennant race between the Giants and the Pirates, as the players are forced to throw the games. They refuse, and after one is murdered, the Phantom enters the case. The police are not aware of the criminal activity, or at least are never in the investigation, until the very end, when the Phantom calls them in for the final round up.

A good blow-by-blow of the baseball game gives the impression that the author may have been a regular sports-story writer for the sports pulps. Who knows?

Notes: This is the same author who will write the first quarter of the novel, "Death Glow" (November 1938); atavistic horror; the *Clarion* is the *"Morning" Clarion;* carries a Colt .45; a hangout called the Fighting Cock; the Phantom has a "young-old" face, a common description of Secret Agent "X," not of the Phantom until this story; the *Clarion* signal light calls the Phantom; okay; the Phantom takes the place of one of the players on the Giants' team in a game with the Pirates; the Phantom reads a copy of *La Vie Parisienne*, a magazine freely translated to read "Parisian Life"; the Phantom removes a bullet from his own arm and treats the injury himself; the Phantom is six foot two inches tall.

Availability: *Action Adventure Stories* #142 (published by Fading Shadows, Inc., 2004).

65. YELLOW SHADOWS OF DEATH
V23 #3—July 1938
Written by Charles Greenberg

Place: New York City; San Francisco, CA

Main characters: Sin Lui, Jackson, Frank Havens, Harkness, Dr. Sue Yat, Lin Young, Chang Young, Police Commissioner Joe Bayliss (San Francisco), Richard Curtis Van Loan/the Phantom, Paul Craig, Sergoff, Big Bill Donahue, Miss Ryan, Roger White, George Rodney, Lal Kurda, Tony Ricco, Mike Ricco, Walter Kennedy, Stella

Kurda, Red, Judge Jeffery Stewart, Chris Herrick, Bill Parrish, Lefty, Dutch, Jeff, Kelly, Lonnigan, Joseph P. Schmidt, Borelli, Joe, Hugo, Pete, Smitty, Sin Foy, Lambert, Spike Henley

A robbery takes place in San Francisco, by a mob supposedly led by Sin Lui, a Chinese hero known as the Robin Hood of Chinatown. Two leading Chinese merchants in New York request the Phantom in helping them solve the case before America turns against the whole Chinese race.

The Phantom heads for San Francisco, accompanied by Chang Young, a young Chinese youth who has asked to assist in the investigation. But upon arrival in San Francisco, the Phantom finds much more to be involved than a simple robbery. An earlier kidnapping for which someone had received $50,000 in ransom, plus there is an upcoming mayoral race that could be at the bottom of everything.

Notes: Harkness is Havens' secretary; carries a .45; an old Chinese gentleman has a pet cockatoo perched on his shoulder; Sin Lui is thought to be a Robin Hood of Chinatown; the On Leong Tong; people "clipped" when they talked; the Sergoff case took place two years previously, we are told; his jaw muscles stood out in hard little balls; a boat named the *Dolphin*—this boat has appeared in previous stories; escape through a trap door in a furnace, coming out beneath a parked automobile; Hugo is a man who is half giant, half midget—Greenberg uses similar characters in other stories; there is a black panther named Jetan; Greenberg introduces a lot of international intrigue, usually in the form of a beautiful vamp who is stringing along several men at the same time, or is married to one, having an affair with another; no *Clarion* call for the Phantom; no background history on the Phantom; once, twice, three times; characters sometimes repeat themselves—"I get it, I get it."

Availability: *Phantom Detective* #9 (published by Corinth Regency, 1965), *Yellow Shadows of Death* (published by Jim Hanos, 1985), *The Phantom Detective V23N3—Pulp Facsimile* (published by Adventure House, 2009).

66. THE BROADWAY MURDERS

V24 #1—August 1938
Written by Laurence Donovan

Place: New York City

Main characters: Loder, John L. Dolan, Inspector Thomas Gregg, Capt. McGuire, Andrea Hoyt, Richard Curtis

1933
1934
1935
1936
1937
1938
1939
1940
1941
1942
1943
1944
1945
1946
1947
1948
1949
1950
1951
1952
1953

1933

1934

1935

1936

1937

1938

1939

1940

1941

1942

1943

1944

1945

1946

1947

1948

1949

1950

1951

1952

1953

Van Loan/the Phantom, O. T. Young, Ronald, Frank Havens, Seymour Bryan, Lark Grayson, Samuel Hawther, Luke Graves, Amos Hoyt, Brutus Bolo, James Roselyn, Joseph Sterne, Elsie Dolan, Audrey Hoyt, Ralph Stevens, Charles Thornton, Barbara Dolan, Lafe Donner, Steve Huston, Cato, Dr. Bendix, Joe, Cane, Marty, Buck, Chalk

The case stems from the burning and sinking of the *Carrantic*, a cruise ship, at which time a number of people were severely injured, and others killed. Now several of those who were injured—most of who are heads of a big insurance company—are apparently being murdered in a possible revenge plot. However, the Phantom uncovers a big insurance blackmailing plot to be at the bottom of the case.

The story is highly suggestive as being by a *Doc Savage* author, as the Phantom uses many devices similar to Doc's exploding capsules that release a gas, and the Phantom uses nerve centers to render crooks unconscious.

Notes: Piggishly pale eyes; fella; joy-mad; the Sunny Seas Cruise Line; some do grunt when they talk; the call for the Phantom comes from the light atop the *Clarion* Building; the Phantom has quiet eyes; two or more minutes; shoe-button eyes; Van manipulates nerve centers to cause people to sleep or awaken from sleep; elucidating; Junoesque proportions; fish tank in Dr. Bendix's laboratory has a small hidden camera inside to take pictures of anyone entering the building—again, highly suggestive of gimmicks used by Doc Savage; a double-barreled headache; "Great God, Phantom," he ejaculated; carries a .45; Phantom uses gadgets like gas bombs in tiny capsule form; though Steve Huston is assigned to the case by Frank Havens, he is never active in any of the action—merely mentioned, and seen from afar.

Availability: *Phantom Detective* #5 (published by Corinth Regency, 1965), *The Phantom Detective V24N1—Pulp Facsimile* (published by Adventure House, 2009).

67. THE COUNTERFEIT KILLER
V24 #2—September 1938
Written by Paul Chadwick

Place: New York City

Main characters: The Skipper, Grover Dorsey, Pauline Dorsey, Madame Erika Jardin, Ralph Dorsey, Rhea Cabot, Nita (Wayne?), Professor Max Lenbach, Richard Curtis Van Loan/the Phantom, Craig Garner, Frank

Havens, Dr. Bruno Hahn, Dr. Wilfred Burns, Ellis Homer, Inspector Gregg, Blake, Dolly, Alec, Clark Carey, Slade, Thomas Marshall, Hugh Burke, Jay Putnam, Joe Haggen, Conlon, John Simon, Marie, Dr. Paul Bendix, Tony, Joe

At first they appear to be strange, unrelated crimes: a jewel robbery from a well-to-do crowd at a party, the kidnapping of several deaf-mutes from an asylum, and the theft of records from a psychiatrists office—and it appears that there were inside helpers in each case—inside, at the top.

Frank Havens calls in the Phantom when a witness at one of the scenes attempts to bring photographs he had secretly taken of the jewel robbery is shot and killed outside the *Clarion* Building.

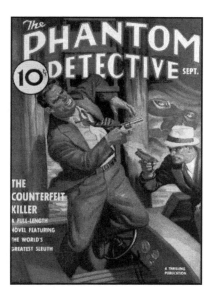

At the bottom of the case are counterfeit cosmetics. The mastermind is blackmailing leading men in the cosmetic industry that have been treated by a psychiatrist, who don't want their medical records known to the public. Wanting to keep their innermost secrets from the media, these men assist the mastermind in obtaining what he wants.

Notes: A man is effeminate; without kith or kin; the *Clarion* call for the Phantom; tugged at the lobe of his ear; he clicked his teeth; okay; fella; hell bent for leather; eyes like polished agates; the truck slewed; sometimes people repeat themselves like in Greenberg's stories, but this has similarities to "Dealers in Death" (July 1936).

Availability: *The Counterfeit Killer* (published by Jim Hanos, 1985).

68. GRADUATES OF MURDER

V24 #3—October 1938
Written by Paul Ernst

Place: New York City; Makon, OH; Dayton, OH

Main characters: "Pop" Terry Brassey, Macey, George Creighton, Mitchell, Mary Haines, Richard Curtis Van Loan/the Phantom, Frank Havens, Amos Overby, Robert Martin, Dr. Bendix, Simon Stigler, "Frenchy" Dubios, Dannie Regan, Harry Seymour, Rake Malone, Bat Luden, Chief of Police Amos Negley (Makon), Blanchard, Ripman, Henry Barber, Bill Rand, Daniel Clarke (F.B.I.), Doris Wellman, Patrick Moller, Adelia Carson, John Claridge, O'Rourke, Jack, Thomas Walthan, Eli Corsener, Leroy Elmo, Ike, Kelly, Pinkie Benz, Grogan, Elias T. Scott, Cap Stryker, Sam Johnson, John Kubin, Bill Bates, John Carter, Emma, Patelli, Theodore Fowne, Dugan, Henry Boyle, Jack Collins, Mimi, Milton

A bank robbery brings the great detective into the case. He arrives in Makon, Ohio and assumes the identity of a local police detective from the department. From then on he acts more like Dan Fowler of the F.B.I., using techniques of the F.B.I., scientifically examining clues, and generally being more of a federal agent than the Phantom Detective.

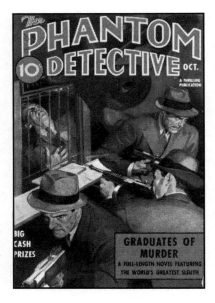

To complicate matters, there is an F.B.I. agent involved at first, named "Daniel" Clarke, who is working with a female private investigator named Adelia Carson (Sally Vane and Dan Fowler, of course). But if this is a re-written Dan Fowler story, the Phantom takes over the roles of both Dan Fowler and Larry Kendal, the two operative from that series. The author has the female investigator sent away, and the F.B.I. agent is murdered, so the author now has the Phantom doing all of their work in the story.

The crooks act like graduates of a school in which crime is taught. All of their actions are coordinated into one unit, with each man knowing his assigned tasks, and all wear the same clothing to make individual identification impossible.

Notes: Darn, but this story had clues to just about everybody! And several clues even pointed towards Norman Daniels, though I don't believe this one is his. For instance, the Phantom makes a point to visit the local gangster boss, which Daniels often did. And another clue that pointed to Daniels was that the crooks used a plan—or blueprints—to set up a mock scene for the gangsters to use in practicing the upcoming crime; this was used in "Blueprints of Crime" (Spring 1950), a Black Bat story Daniels wrote. But there were equally enough clues for any of the main authors already writing the *Phantom*, including McDonald and others. He said lugubriously; what the deuce; insouciance; Webber's Perfect Bread; "Good cripes"; laconically; okay; a queue of people; fella; there was the call from the *Clarion* signal light; Acme Food Company; Best Welt Shoe Factory; a crime school; the Apache Club; that's a darb; factotum; Hiltonia Hotel; loquacious frame of mind; "you're aces"; enough to make a preacher cuss; not worth a finger snap; National Manufacturers' Detective Association; perforce; Second National Bank; dollars to doughnuts—used a lot by the Dan Fowler author(s); Phantom's eyes glinted ice-gray; 190 pounds; variest; fatuously; corner of Miller & Hastings; a hypodermic needle is used; Moloch of crime; the Black Swan; will-o'-the-wisp; unholy din; bullets are angry hornets; people grunt, they crisp when they speak; crook takes a poison pill at end.

This was probably a regular *Phantom* writer—just look at some of the names of the characters, but the story was definitely a Dan Fowler story originally, and only changed to that of the Phantom after it was written. You can almost see where action should have involved Fowler, Kendal and Sally Vane.

69. DEATH GLOW

V25 #1—November 1938
Written by Norvell W. Page

Place: New York City

Main characters: The Blue Light, Roger Arkwright, Baron Nuffield, Det. Sgt. Conners, Ambers, Monash, Locke, Richard Curtis Van Loan/the Phantom, Stryver, Rayner, Alwyn, Ruth Langdon, Needam, Van Sittart, Gattle, Anderson, Frank Havens, Thomas Lightfoot, Inspector Gregg, Harold R. Langdon, Grover Jordan, Robert F. Grandley; Max S. Burman, Richard Winston, Arthur Lane Donovan, L. Hammond Dwight, Patrick McSorley, Ricco, Dr. Bendix, Wolfe, Robert Lord, Agatha Tibbetts, Steve Huston, Wyliss

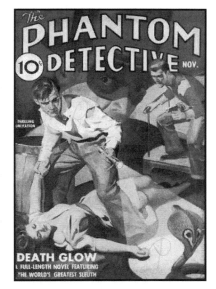

A strange killer who slays with a knife during almost total darkness, with only a dim, blue light visible to his victims.

Eight men belonging to a corporation are slated for death. Is the killer one of these eight men? With each death, half a million dollars from the estate and insurance goes into the company, not to the family or relatives. Meanwhile, the killer, known as the Blue Light, seems to be almost superhuman. Can the Phantom bring him to justice?

Notes: Well, just following a re-written Dan Fowler story turning up as a Phantom story, I was shocked at how much this one resembled a re-written *Secret Agent "X"* story. The early part of this story sounded so much like our Secret Agent "X," I was thrilled thinking that maybe I had found yet another *"X"* adventure that had been turned into a *Phantom*. Then suddenly the Phantom is full blown, and I find heavy traces of editing. I was not discouraged, though. My first thought was that a *Phantom* author may have attempted an *Agent "X"* story, but the manuscript was rejected so he turned it into a *Phantom*. My second thought was that the author had a *Phantom* author re-write the story. However, as already mentioned, I found that both these ideas were likely incorrect.

The beginning of this story starts out with a ghostly atmosphere: Champion liked to start his stories with the character of "Death" looking over the

1933
1934
1935
1936
1937
1938
1939
1940
1941
1942
1943
1944
1945
1946
1947
1948
1949
1950
1951
1952
1953

scene. On the other hand, Paul Chadwick's atmosphere was more that of a ghostly atmosphere, with fog and eerie drama. Still, the novel had other strong similarities to the *Secret Agent "X"* series, even to the name of the mastermind—the Blue Light. In "Kingdom of Blue Corpses" (December 1935), "X" battled the Blue Spark.

The car slewed; nerves are darting quick-silver; the car slued; ghostly atmosphere; limpid eyes; Johnny-on-the-spot; jack-in-the-box; out of the blow's orbit; Consolidated Life Insurance Company; Peru, Indiana; there is no *Clarion* call—the Phantom is suddenly in the story; Van Loan's background changed—no mention of his military service during the war—this was almost an every-issue formula within the Phantom stories; a tryst with death; indigo glow; eerie atmosphere; made war on women; the *Morning Clarion*—this was also used in "The Front Page Murders" (June 1938), normally, it was simply the *Clarion*—in Anatole France Feldman's stories, it was the *Daily Clarion;* beat a thoughtful tattoo; Third National Bank; Phantom has black hair; he sallied forth; the Phantom and Ruth are imprisoned in a cellar with a King Cobra. The snake bites the girl and she dies—the cobra was only one of several that were taken off a ship near where they were held prisoners—these cobras will be in "The Radio Murders" (April 1939), which is coming up; noblesse oblige, one of Champion's favorites; typical Champion ending; a woman who had impersonated Ruth is never named or mentioned again. Could Champion have attempted an "X", but it was rejected, and he turned it into a *Phantom?* Or did one author start the novel, and it was completed by Champion or someone else? This is one strange novel.

Availability: *Phantom Detective* #16 (published by Corinth Regency, 1966).

70. THE MURDER SYNDICATE

V25 #2—December 1938
Written by unknown; possibly
Emile C. Tepperman

Place: New York City

Main characters: The Dollar Man, Chris Ringold, Charley Schiebert, Mike Bittro, Victor Purcell, Fennell, Samuel Slater, Tim Connors, Judge Treadway, Jerome Phillips, Bert Forman, Charles Gale, Frank Havens, Inspector Gregg, Richard Curtis Van Loan/the Phantom, Harry Marn, Linda Treadway, Phil Carter, Miles Corey, Joe, Susan, Praugwittz, Peter H. Antom (Phantom alias), Smokey, Fritz Danton, Wilks, Dr. Bendix, MacNiell, Lloyd Merriwell, Smith

A syndicate controls horse betting, while a mysterious crook

1933 1934 1935 1936 1937 **1938** 1939 1940 1941 1942 1943 1944 1945 1946 1947 1948 1949 1950 1951 1952 1953

known as the Dollar Man has devised a way of fixing each race in order to make millions. Unknown to the large "books" around the country, they still follow his orders, and allow larger bets than usual on the favorite horse to win, knowing that the Dollar Man will make sure that the favorite will not win, but instead it will be a long shot, making the books a fortune. They willingly pay the Dollar Man for his "service."

This new author gives us a strange story: the Phantom is never captured, is never really in danger, although he does have some narrow escapes in action. In truth, the crooks never made a fuss about the Phantom being on the case—if they even knew.

The mastermind hands out discs to his men and the victims. These discs contain a substance that can be exploded by short wave signals, and can kill who he wants when he wants. A nice entry, but strange!

Notes: Off a tangent; Tuckerton Detective Agency; okay; Van carries a .32; owns a Daimler; the Black Swan Inn; his Daimler can be quickly changed into an Issotta-Fraschini; parabola; the Phantom carries a Webley; vermilion; munificence; stereopticon; the Phantom had operated in India, Armenia, Constantinople, Paris, Moscow, Buenos Aires; the Phantom had published books on psychology through Havens' *Clarion* publishing company, as Peter H. Antom; the Phantom is five foot ten inches tall; there was no *Clarion* call.

Again, this is the third strange novel in a row, giving me the impression that something was wrong at Standard during this short period.

Availability: *Action Adventure Stories* #104 (published by Fading Shadows, Inc., 2001).

71. THE YACHT CLUB MURDERS

V25 #3—January 1939
Written by Charles Greenberg

Place: Near Haggensville, NY

Main characters: The Bat, Joe Wessley, Jeff O'Malley, Whitey, Stanley Ross, Walter Kruger, Clyde Emerson, Andrew MacDowell, Robert Finney, Oscar Garvin, Clyde Manning, Chester Grattan, Hugh Ware, George Sheffield, Richard Curtis Van Loan/the Phantom, Frank Havens, Muriel Havens, Dr. Bendix, Claire Grattan, Donald Henley, Benedict, Miss West, Joe Bartlett, Steve, McCarthy, Lopez, Alice Craven MacDowell, Limpy, Deacon, Inspector Trevor (State Police), Bob Henley, Manuel, Mr. Jones, Chris, Ryan, Irene Craven, Mr. Porter

Murder and mystery surrounds

1933
1934
1935
1936
1937
1938
1939
1940
1941
1942
1943
1944
1945
1946
1947
1948
1949
1950
1951
1952
1953

1933

1934

1935

1936

1937

1938

1939

1940

1941

1942

1943

1944

1945

1946

1947

1948

1949

1950

1951

1952

1953

a well-to-do Yacht Club. A group of men, each owning a percentage of the interest in the Club, and all apparently in need of money, have been offered a large sun of money for the land where the club is located. But the majority refuses to sell, regardless of their need for money. Now, they are being murdered. Presumably to eliminate those who will not sell.

The Phantom is attending a party at the Yacht Club with Frank and Muriel Havens when the first murder takes place. He is quickly brought into the case and starts his investigation. However, Muriel Havens is kidnapped by the Bat—the villain wears the costume of a batman; hood and rib-caged cape—to force the Phantom out of the investigation, so he must assume the identity of someone already known within the group in order to continue the investigation.

Notes: One character is a dwarf; a man is effeminate; right there and then; okay; once, twice, three times; people repeat themselves—"all right, all right"; and again, the love triangle between the men and a woman involved in some way; a house of cards; crooks have a hideout underground on the shore, can be entered only at low tide when the water does not cover the entrance—this plot device is used quite often in both the *Phantom* and Dan Fowler stories.

Availability: *Behind the Mask* #3-5 (published by Fading Shadows, Inc., 1990).

72. THE WEB OF MURDER

V26 #1—February 1939
Written by Emile C. Tepperman

Place: New York City

Main characters: Wilson Dennison, George Cheltenham, Lance Vickers, Alexis Konstantin, Cookey, Sackett, Doris Madeleine Dennison, Bunny Driscoll, Blane, Frank Havens, Dudley Yerkes, Richard Curtis Van Loan/the Phantom, Walter Morse, Magda Helmuth, Johnny McGuire, Limpy Teed, Semple, Joe Polittio, Harold Barrat (D.A.), Hiram Bendix, Mr. Bilbo, Inspector Gregg, Andrew Gerard, Vincent Stephenson, Baron von Helmuth, Harvey Stephenson (probably should be Vincent, author just changed his name), John Lewison Ardsmore, Pete Cook, Judge Wilberforce, Fannie Davis, Policeman Burns, Melissa Williams, Det. Slocum, Harry Moon, Dutch Hargan, Maloney

Stockholders in a company own a large piece of land in India, supposedly a rice-producing area. But the stockholders are suddenly involved in murder and are being arrested. An upcoming defense attorney is successfully defending them in court and they are found not guilty—of course, for a large sum of money that the defense will cost them. Unfortunately, the murder victims are also stockholders in the company. The mastermind is killing off some, while breaking the others because they have to sell their stockholdings in order to obtain enough money for the lawyer. From their financial ruin, the mastermind is coming out ahead all around.

Notes: Mills bombs are used—mills bombs were used a lot in *Operator #5's* Purple Invasion; machine-gunner has a pet machine gun he calls "Betsy"; okay; inveigled; the *Daily Clarion*—odd for this to pop up again; Frank calls Van, "Dick"; anathems; Johnny McGuire works in the *Clarion* Building as elevator operator/building detective, though after being brought into the story, he is just as quickly forgotten; the Phantom uses a special camera; hue-and-cry; expostulating; the Phantom gives cab driver a large sum of money; grim-lipped, cold eyed; ratiocination; Dr. Bendix's real first name is "Paul," not "Hiram," but I doubt the author remembered the name, so he picked the wrong one; the actual murder is recorded on film; off on a tangent; eyes rested balefully; people grunt and speak crisply; peroration; a policeman is reading a copy of *College Humor* in one scene; a bitter pill to swallow; staccato, trip-hammer cadence of the tommy gun's deadly refrain; within an ace of; tenterhooks; the Phantom drives a Daimler automobile, though this is not the first time the Phantom was said to have one; there is no *Clarion* call; mastermind is an expert swordsman. At times this appeared to be a new author, but all clues point to Tepperman, and since his last *Phantom* was probably back in 1936, this could account for the strangeness to the story.

73. THE CHAIN OF DEATH

V26 #2—March 1939
Written by Charles Greenberg

Place: Key West and Palm Beach, FL

Main characters: King of the Everglades, Joe Moffat, Lottie LaMar, Duke Henley, Frank Havens, Richard Curtis Van Loan/the Phantom, Steve, McCarthy, Sam Allen (Chief of Police, Palm Beach), Roger Bailey, Jeff Donahue, Clancy, Walter Cameron, Chris Todd, Bill Smiley, Bill Gerard, George Winslow, Clyde Walker, McHugh, Riley, Palmer, Nick Moreno, Governor Dwight, Mayor Justin, Harrigan, Mr. William Grey, Nickie Tulio, Sam Littel, Chris Forman, Boris, Warner, Bill Andrews, Pat Allen, Dolores Costa, Slim, Lin, Barney, Max, Dusty

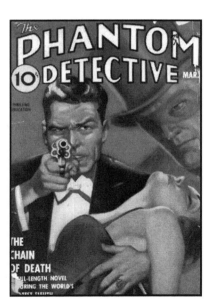

In South Florida a would-be king hopes to take over a multi-million dollar hotel chain, as well as a leading bank in town. Using the Everglades as his hideout for his henchmen, the Phantom must endure gators and water moccasins to battle the criminal un-

1933
1934
1935
1936
1937
1938
1939
1940
1941
1942
1943
1944
1945
1946
1947
1948
1949
1950
1951
1952
1953

derlings, unmasking the mastermind in their final encounter.

Notes: Okay; once, twice, three times; villain keeps a pet water moccasin in his pocket—he calls the snake "Cleo"; a tiny tube shoots a poisoned sewing needle; phonographs are used; he spoke acridly; people repeat—"all right, all right"; a woman is in a love triangle with the mastermind and another.

Availability: *Action Adventure Stories* #100 (published by Fading Shadows, Inc., 2001).

74. THE RADIO MURDERS

V26 #3—April 1939
Written by Emile C. Tepperman

Place: New York City

Main characters: Somers B. Faulkner, John Rand, Homer Blythe, Myron Wilkes, Carson Dexter, Steven Logan, Dr. Hall, Heather Heath, Veda Marsden, Muriel Havens, Harry Marsden, Frank Havens, Jerry Dobbey, Richard Curtis Van Loan/the Phantom, Timothy Perkins, Dr. George Saltus, Inspector Gregg, Max, Louis, Cass Locke, Tim Brody, Tony Risso, Sherman, Lt. Nevins, Jacob Cole, Elizabeth Faulkner, Chet, Walsh, Bat, Dr. Bendix, Sam White, Sheila Baker, Sheldon Chambers, Charles Lothar, Sgt. Black, Lt. Ward, Steve Huston, Jigger, Benito Bruno, Tiger, Race, Codfish, Hicks

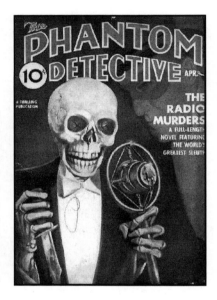

In a novel that seems almost a re-write of "The Criminal Caesar" (April 1936), owners of a radio station are being murdered. They call in the Phantom, naturally. However, it appears that the mystery had actually started about a year earlier (their estimation) when some cobras had been stolen out of crates from a ship's warehouse on the waterfront (remember "Death Glow," November 1938). This story ties in very nicely with the earlier theft of the cobras, although the new author does not refer back to the novel itself.

The Phantom uncovers a double crime: one man appears to have been blackmailing the others, but he is killed by the current mastermind. The Phantom also uncovers a drug ring being operated on a giant scale. Ships bring in drugs, dropping them in the water near the port of the harbor, then a radio announcer will read a coded message over the airways directing the gang where they are to pick up the drugs; strangely enough, a Fleming-Roberts *Secret Agent "X"* story, "Death's Frozen Formula" (February 1937), has a similar plot line in that the drug pushers/addicts have devised a plan to give notice as to where drugs can be picked up each day from coded clues on the newsreels at the local movie theater; if you will recall, agent August Lenniger claimed that "The Criminal Caesar" was one of his writers, and Will Murray says that

Lenniger's main writers at the time were Norman Daniels, E. Hoffmann Price and... G.T. Fleming-Roberts.

The stolen cobras are milked for their venom, and the poison is used to kill the victims in the story.

Notes: I detect clues to D.L. Champion but whether he has anything to do with the story, I just don't know. I do believe we have a new author here; he opened his mouth, shut it again; clucked his tongue; "Great God!"; he spoke crisply; Van calls Muriel "Honey" and "Darling"; Van is with Muriel when he sees the *Clarion* call; baleful eyes; cul-de-sac; okay; he snapped; a ship named the *Eastern Star;* tenterhooks; there is a visit to the morgue, which has throwbacks to Anatole France Feldman; the cobra venom is injected through the use of a blow gun; on a tangent; he barked; rat-tat-tat; wears a ring containing a spring-knife; gewgaws; "heh, heh"; "Holy Smoke"; aces in my book; he grumted; tear gas is contained in his shoe; once, twice, thrice; bullets are missiles of death.

Will Murray ran across information that Don Cameron wrote a *Phantom* in 1939, which could have been "The Radio Murders." But why the similarities to a previous writer?

Availability: *The Radio Murders* (published by Jim Hanos, 1989).

75. MURDER AT THE CIRCUS

V27 #1—May 1939
Written by Charles Greenberg

Place: New York City; Philadelphia, PA; Tulsa, OK

Main characters: Pompii, Leopold, Colonel Flick, George Coleman, Frank Havens, Richard Curtis Van Loan/the Phantom, Nick Farrel, Smith, Manning, Slim Eaton, Barney, Inspector Gregg, Bill, Steve Huston, McCleary, Harry Morton, Shaw, Police Commissioner Johnson (Philadelphia), Matteo, Lola Dare, Beppo Riverdi, James Thorne, Victor Shaw, George Verez, Donato, Todo, Joe, Donahue, Professor Hugh Wessley, Henry Forbes, Weatherby, Irene, Bishop, Kurt Muller, Rodney Stone, Paul Trevis, Howard Lyman, Bill O'Malley, Merrill

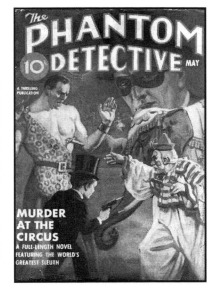

Two circus performers, a midget and a giant, observe someone starting a fire at the Big Top. After they go to investigate, they hear crooks talking about children being killed at the Big Top on the following day. They are able to stop the fire, though the owner now thinks that they started it, and fires them.

They head for New York City and make contact with Frank Havens who

1933
1934
1935
1936
1937
1938
1939
1940
1941
1942
1943
1944
1945
1946
1947
1948
1949
1950
1951
1952
1953

1933
1934
1935
1936
1937
1938
1939
1940
1941
1942
1943
1944
1945
1946
1947
1948
1949
1950
1951
1952
1953

calls in the Phantom. But in his first battle with the crooks, the giant is killed. The midget ties in with Steve Huston and the Phantom to solve the crime.

At the bottom of the mystery is a piece of land in Oklahoma with a rich oil find secretly hidden away.

Notes: Okay; people repeat, "all right, all right"; once, twice, three times; .45 is carried by the Phantom; when police should be around, they aren't—this was a big problem with Greenberg's stories—two men are killed on the circus grounds, everybody comes running, then everything is back to normal as if nothing had happened, no police, not even another mention of the killing; the Beneficial Order of Pinta (the B. O. P.); Havens' newspaper in Philadelphia is the *Star-Herald;* will-o'-the-wisp; no *Clarion* call.

Availability: *Action Adventure Stories* #41 (published by Fading Shadows, Inc., 1999).

76. MURDER AT THE WORLD'S FAIR

V27 #2—June 1939
Written by Whitney Ellsworth

Place: New York City

Main characters: The Unseen, Clifford Boniface, Enrico, Richard Curtis Van Loan/the Phantom, Frank Havens, Dr. Clement Hersch, Professor Arnold Dane, Rodney William, Inspector Thomes Gregg, Horace M. Caldwell, Helen Lee Caldwell, Tony, Mae, Randolph Faversham, Thomas Peyton, Jones, Robert Marlin, Luigi, Francois, Major Frank Tarleton, Reynolds, Barney Stagge, Donaldson, Delmar Overman, Bryant, Miss Brown, Schaeffer, Benny, Cranston, Joe, Red, Snuffy, Mallow

The opening of the New York's World's Fair coincided with a convention of world police heads meeting in recognition of the "World's Most Famous Sleuth," the Phantom Detective! The Phantom has already given his speech—something to do with some detective work in which he was an expert—and had just been replaced on the stage by two scientists. It seems that they had been working on an invisibility machine, and chose this meeting of the world's police heads to demonstrate the invention. But during the demonstration, gunmen suddenly appear and kill one of them and steal the invisibility machine when the lights are knocked out.

It's all sleight of hand, though: there is no invisibility machine. It is all done with illusions and mirrors. And the real scheme is to make the world believe there actually had been such a machine, while the mastermind kills and robs while supposedly... "invisible!" With the stolen money he hopes to take over control of a large company located near the World's Fair.

Unfortunately, there is little to do with the World's Fair. At one point, a crook, disguised as the Phantom, is killed when the other crooks run him into the lance from a statue. This scene is featured on the cover, by the way.

Notes: Very strongly representative of *Doc Savage* stories in which Doc is giving a lecture to visiting scientists, musicians, or other giants of which he is considered greater than them all. Van is Havens' protégé; the Churchill-Dunlap Building; "No-o"; irascible; wattle-necked, bald-headed; beetle-brows; lamps in Van's apartment blink on and off when the Phantom is needed—the *Clarion* signal light is also mentioned; Frank calls Van, "Dick"; hm-m; fists are pile-drivers; paradoxical as it may appear; two-for-a-nickel; Boniface has limpid blue eyes; the Phantom throws gas pellets in his escape; Boniface enters the story around the half-way mark; okay; Boniface uses the alias of W. Cranston; one of the first mentions of the Mafia in the *Phantom* series; laughed in unholy glee; a missing finger gives the Phantom's disguise away.

While a captive of Clifford Boniface, the Phantom asks if he can smoke, and Boniface lets him. The escape comes soon afterwards. This was also used in the next story, too, so Boniface had not learned from the first mistake.

Here we have a good write-up of the Phantom's ideals:

"Every man," he said, "has a price. I'm a wealthy man. Maybe I could meet your price for forgetting all this."

The Phantom kept his eyes on the road. His answer came between clenched teeth.

"I've got a price," he said, "that will make me leave this business forever. It's a high price, though, Faversham. Too high for you to meet."

"Name it," urged Faversham, eagerly.

"My price," said the Phantom, "is an end to all crime! A society free of greed or violence or want. A civilization that would have no more need for a gun or a knife or a policemen's billy than we have for flint and steel or a stone ax. A world in which war would be recognized as the horribly ridiculous thing it is. An era in which hunger and squalor would be remembered only as witch-burning is remembered now. That's my price, Faversham!"

"Oh," sneered the manacled man. "An idealist, eh?"

At the end of the story, Clifford Boniface escapes, but leaves a note for the Phantom:

"Please excuse the abominable writing, but I'm carrying one of your souvenirs in my right hand, and it's a bit difficult writing this note.

"That second shot of yours, incidentally, didn't do much but tear a hole in my perfectly good jacket and rip some flesh from my shoulder. How did you like my death agonies? I should have been an actor, eh?

"Sorry to have to run off like this, but it seems I have made an unholy mess of this job. Oh, well, we all mess up sometime. Maybe the next time, it'll be you.

1933
1934
1935
1936
1937
1938
1939
1940
1941
1942
1943
1944
1945
1946
1947
1948
1949
1950
1951
1952
1953

"And there's going to be a next time, my dear Phantom. Depend on that!"

And Boniface does come back in the next story, thus becoming the only real supercrook to face the Phantom twice. There is a city named Boniface, somewhere on the East Coast. I remember seeing the city—or town—mentioned in an obituary only recently. Unfortunately, I didn't keep the notice, so do not remember the state. But New Jersey does sound right. I wonder if our author could be from near that town? Something else that shouldn't be overlooked is the name "Churchill," which crops up in the story. There is an Edward Churchill writing about this period of time. However, this was a good entry in the series.

Availability: *Action Adventure Stories* #55 (published by Fading Shadows, Inc., 1999).

1939

1940

1941

1942

1943

1944

1945

1946

1947

1948

1949

1950

1951

1952

1953

77. THE FORTY THIEVES

V27 #3—July 1939
Written by Whitney Ellsworth

Place: San Francisco, CA; Newport; Detroit, MI; New York City

Main characters: Clifford Boniface, Alice, Johnson, Poe, Jones, Monk, John Joseph Altridge, Frank Havens, Hendricks, Jay Armington, Jake, Richard Curtis Van Loan/the Phantom, Mr. Dorson, Fred, Riley, Thompson, Bert, Mooney, Harvey Lord, Tom Banks, Roger Dale, T. L. Peavey, Guilermo, Jiminez, Thomas, Capt. William Olney, Tresk, Joe, Gomerra, Will Hysler, Mike, Juan, Gomez, Estelle Hysler, Sgt. Stone, Peter Dale, Jorgesen, Joe Borgonowicz, Carson, Inspector Francis X. Cassidy (Detroit), Inspector Gregg, Capt. Felipe Martinez (sea captain), Jorge

A would-be dictator of South America (somewhere) brings his army of revolutionists to America where, with the help of Clifford Boniface, set up their operations all around America, and call themselves the "Forty Thieves."

At first, jewels are stolen to finance their operation for buying guns and other instruments of war. Then they hijack shipments of new automobiles from Detroit; the Phantom learns that one automobile company has made a deal with the South American country to sell them a large shipment of cheaply made cars at a low price. The stolen automobiles are being torn down to become parts for the building of the cheap cars to fulfill the contract. With rebuilt automobiles, the stolen jewels and the revolutionists are to be smuggled back into the South American country hidden on board a ship.

Notes: This is the second and last appearance of Clifford Boniface; okay;

once, twice, three times; he lipped; yah; ennvi; Van Loan drives a Bugatti; Van Loan runs a red light and is given a traffic ticket in New York City; the *Clarion* signal light calls the Phantom to action; Frank calls Van, "Dick"; a bullet sounded "cor-rang"; slewed to a stop; the crooks' password is "Como Dios a Liberted"; holy smoke; Van and Frank speak Esperanto when conversing over a telephone; a new tangent; "By Harry!"; a man cries at the death of another, also kisses dead man's hand; crooks use radio wavelengths to send messages to the forty thieves around the country; a narrow squeak; "Fah!"; "Huh!"; his badge is known from here to there—you pick the names, Seattle to Tampa, etc.; fairly similar plot to a number of Dan Fowler stories, too. Boniface is effeminate.

Availability: *Phantom Detective* #20 (published by Corinth Regency, 1966), *The Forty Thieves* (published by Jim Hanos, 1985).

78. DEATH UNDER CONTRACT

V28 #1—August 1939
Written by Charles Greenberg

Place: Hollywood, CA

Main characters: Mr. X, Emmet Polling, Godfrey Hodgson, Reardon, Brown, Richard Curtis Van Loan/the Phantom, Red Cardigan, Hugh Gray, Frank Havens (mentioned only), Judge Andrews, Nash, Paddy O'Hara, Police Commissioner Jim Eaton (Hollywood), Christopher Nolan, Robert Quigley, Gail Montrose, Donald Thurber, Jaws Coleman, Dr. Eric Sturm, Ivan Tarloff, Netta Palmer, Richard Lowel, Chester Grange, John Keith, Inspector Hawkins (Hollywood), Clyde Morrison, Forbes, Nicholas Bryan, Pat, Jackson, Emma Newton, Roger Sanders, Capt. Bennett (LAPD), Stanley Long, Claire Hammond, McCrea, Dayton, Mike, Lefty, Peterson, Joe Finch, Murphy, Slim, Marge

The Phantom, arriving in Los Angeles for a meeting with a friend, watches a scene being played out for the benefit of witnesses. But he recognizes a murder plot and, though in L.A. on a scientific study, he decides to investigate. The investigation takes him to Hollywood and the motion picture film industry, with hidden motives behind killings, kidnapping, and the control over actors and studios within the theater crowds.

Patterned a lot after "The Movie Lot Murders" (May 1938), but the action takes place in the city, not the desert.

Notes: No *Clarion* call for the Phantom, of course; Stellar Picture Studio; a woman involved in a love triangle; Superba Productions; he clipped; the filming of "The Dawn Came Late"; a bitter pill to swallow; okay; Audubon Films;

1933
1934
1935
1936
1937
1938
1939
1940
1941
1942
1943
1944
1945
1946
1947
1948
1949
1950
1951
1952
1953

1933

1934

1935

1936

1937

1938

1939

1940

1941

1942

1943

1944

1945

1946

1947

1948

1949

1950

1951

1952

1953

Black Swan Tavern; people repeat themselves, "all right, all right"; made a clucking sound with his tongue; with the snap of his fingers; bally-hoo; come-uppance; the woman vamp has green eyes; situation is pregnant with anticipation; fighting tooth and nail.

Availability: *Phantom Detective* #21 (published by Corinth Regency, 1966).

Okay, this concludes another segment of the *Phantom Detective* series. I have merely dissected the stories to make some kind of sense out of the authorship. Identifying authors is a risky business. With little to work from except the rumor that everyone wrote a *Phantom* novel it is easy to sit back and not bother with trying. I am not totally satisfied with my own research. Though I believe I have separated certain authors for their involvement, I could certainly be wrong in my findings. For instance, the September 1937 story, "Hammers of Doom," could be by McDonald or another author entirely. I will leave it up to future researchers, or, by chance, to records being revealed some time down the road. I listed "Double-Stamped Doom" (October 1937) by Robert Sydney Bowen, along with a couple other questionable entries that could be his or McDonald's. In truth, the authorship is becoming harder with each new issue I research. There are so many possibilities. Standard had a stable of good writers who were churning out stories for Leo Margulies, and Leo could have pulled from any source. The Dan Fowler stories in *G-Man/G-Men Detective* were so closely akin to the *Phantom Detective* stories, that a switch could be accomplished with merely changing the names of their main characters. And rewrite editors were doing some heavy rewrites, causing me to pull out my hair in frustration.

I think that Laurence Donovan comes into the series strong by our next segment, but he could already be present in some of the novels I've gone through. I'm sure that Robert Sydney Bowen is one of the mystery writers, and I'm not ruling out Alan Hathway and William Bogart, for now or in the future. There are some strong *Doc Savage* influences in some of these stories. Jean Francis Webb and Edward Churchill were also suspects.

CHAPTER III, SECTION F

WE PASS THE 100
MARK: 1939-1941

1936

1937

1938

1939

1940

1941

1942

1943

1944

1945

1946

1947

1948

1949

1950

1951

1952

1953

W E'VE COME A long way from our first segment covering the series, and I am still surprised at the thought that we may have identified as many of the authors as we have. I am satisfied that the identities uncovered are fairly accurate. Though some of the authors may still be questionable, I feel that we now have a base on which future research can be established. I look forward to someone else doing a more in-depth study, and hope that I have provided a place for them to start from.

My main problem up to this point is that many of the stories were read out of sequence. Because many of them were not in my collection, I read the ones I had while searching for the missing titles. Thus, I had to refer to my notes when I read the issues that were loaned to me. I think I would have been more accurate if I had been able to read the stories in order. Thankfully, a lot of this will be eliminated in the next half of the series.

Perhaps I should have named this segment the Laurence Donovan period, as this author is very active during our current set of stories. However, we also have some oddities. For one thing, I have some doubts about some of the stories. For instance, the author of "The Phantom's Gamble With Death" (February 1940) has a final scene in the story when the Phantom calmly goes to sleep in a chair while others look on. Then, with "The Phantom and the Crime Legion" (October 1940), that reads so much like the McDonald entries, the Phantom does the exact same thing in the last scene of the story. So we have two stories, that sound like two different authors, but they use the same scene at the end—or at least very similar. Now, again, with "The Trail to Death" (May 1941), that also reads a lot like McDonald, the Phantom politely goes to sleep at the end. Plus, we have another little oddity; this story also is a throwback to "The Dancing Doll Murders" (June 1937) and "The Phantom's Gamble With Death." So is this McDonald, or yet another writer who is imitating McDonald? I don't know. But I did do some research into other authors, and the only one who sounds anything like the author in question is—Robert Sydney Bowen! Could "The Phantom's Gamble With Death," "The Phantom and the Crime Legion," and "The Trail to Death" be his stories? I wish I could say for sure. Unfortunately, there are no records we can check.

1933

1934

1935

1936

1937

1938

1939

1940

1941

1942

1943

1944

1945

1946

1947

1948

1949

1950

1951

1952

1953

Also in my records, I have "Murder Calls the Phantom" (March 1941) identified as by Ralph Oppenheim. In this current research, I read this story for the second time, and felt better about it than I did the first time. The first time I read it, I thought it was awful. Two things I remembered about the story: a big fire that burns a mansion to the ground, and all other action stems from that incident. Second, towards the end of the story, the Phantom enters the home of one of the suspects (the reader is not told which suspect), where the Phantom knocks the person out and goes through his belongings for clues, then leaves. This happens in order for the Phantom to positively identify the master crook before the story comes to an end. Okay, so that gives us a clue that this could be Oppenheim. Now the problem; in the next story, "The Murder Bund" (April 1941), we have a fire that destroys a mansion, which seems to be the center of the story. Then, towards the end of the story, the Phantom goes to the home of one of the suspects, knocks him cold, goes through his belongings and then leaves. Later he has the clues that prove this was the bad guy! Same author? I would say so. But now we run into problems. Both stories read a lot like Donovan, at least the writing does, if not the plot devices. In the second story, guess what the master crook is called? The Murder Prophet. Okay, we knew that this is a favorite of Laurence Donovan! Did Donovan have something to do with both stories? I'm at a loss for an answer. I'll discuss both stories more a little later. Both appear to be by the same author, and both do have touches of Donovan, but the story plot devices appear to be new. My guess is that both are by Oppenheim.

Henry Kuttner writes one of his two Phantom stories during this period. He wrote both "The Sabotage Murders" (July 1941) and "The Medieval Murders" (July 1942).

Laurence Donovan gives us some new plot devices during this period. Actually, several of his entries are so much like *Doc Savage* stories I had to wonder (as I read them) how Doc would have fit in the story. For the Doc Savage fan, give "The Thousand Islands Murders" (August 1941) and "Death Over Puget Sound" (September 1941) a read. In some of his other entries, he brings in characters that leave a lasting impression on the reader; a character in "Race Horses of Death" (October 1941) tosses pennies into the street to make Mexican children run in front of cars to retrieve them; in "The Black Gold Killers" (November 1941), one killer keeps tarantulas and scorpions in his pockets; and in "The Phantom and the Curio Murders" (February 1941), a killer keeps a white mouse in his pocket, while always eating popcorn.

Oh, and with "Murder Calls the Phantom" (March 1941), which is listed by Oppenheim, one crook keeps a large Shepherd dog as a pet, and there is a scene in which the Phantom is on a boat with the crooks and the dog. This recalled a very similar incident in the Black Bat series (if I'm not mistaken), in which a crook kept a large dog, and while on a boat the dog attacked the Black Bat and they both went overboard. Unfortunately, I do not recall the title of that particular Black Bat story, or I would read it again for research. Perhaps someone out there can help?

1933

1934

1935

1936

1937

1938

1939

1940

1941

1942

1943

1944

1945

1946

1947

1948

1949

1950

1951

1952

1953

This series of stories run into two categories; only about half of them take place in large cities, while the other half take place in particular settings—an isolated island in "The Thousand Islands Murders," the wilderness of Washington in "Death Over Puget Sound." Race tracks were the center of two stories: "The Grim Shadow of Hate" (June 1941) and "Race Horses of Death." In "The Grim Shadow of Hate," the Phantom had to destroy his badge by melting it down to form the compounds for an atomic bomb, which he uses to blow out a wall where he and some other captives are being held. (Only in the pulps, right?)

All in all, 1941 was a very interesting year. Hardly any outstanding entries, to be sure. But there was enough entertainment in the stories from this year to possibly bring life back into the *Phantom Detective* series if it was faltering on the newsstands. It is Laurence Donovan who is most visible in 1941, and he was a good writer, even if uneven at times. He brings in Muriel Havens for some action scenes in some stories, then forgets her in several others. Frank Havens does not always appear in the stories, and sometimes only comes in towards the end of the story, as if he has been present during the entire action of the adventure. The Phantom is a physical superman in many of Donovan's stories, with rippling muscles, a master of nerve centers, a genius at the scientific tables, and inventor of many of his own weapons in fighting crime—in short, a masked Doc Savage. He wrote some good stories, and it's no wonder that his Doc Savage stories were considered good. He knew how to turn out entertainment month after month.

79. THE SAMPAN MURDERS

V28 #2—September 1939
Written by Laurence Donovan

Place: San Francisco, CA

Main characters: Luy Wong, Judge H. T. Wandersee, Tony Decano, Lomar Sunderson, Aturis Camaris, Carlos Zandu, Frank Havens, Richard Curtis Van Loan/the Phantom, Mr. Roker, Mr. Kee, "Happy" Beylor, "Scrum" Golan, Ty Hu, Ku Soo, Lora Wandersee, Chee Lo Wang, "Gunner" Charles Lorton, Ching Lung, Inspector Murphy (San Francisco), Dr. Paul Bendix, Chip Dorlan, Bugs Dorlan, Mart Connors, Homer Howard, "Smoker" Hennessy, Luke Carter, Lee Tai

At the San Francisco World's Fair, great treasures are stolen, while men are killed by the mysterious "hole-in-the-eye" death. The Phantom, as Van Loan, and Frank Havens are attending the Fair when the action starts.

At the bottom of the mystery lies the theft of great oriental treasures, along with the blackmail of certain individuals who are trying to hide their past.

Though a minor story in the series, it is important in that a new character is introduced to the series. The Phantom likes what he sees in young Chip Dorlan and would later send him to a military school, where he would study to become the Phantom's protégé. Also in the story is Chip's brother, Bugs Dorlan, who had been arrested and charged with a crime he did not commit.

Notes: For years I thought that this was the same author who created Clifford Boniface. There are several things that seemingly tie those stories together. For instance, "Murder at the World's Fair" (June 1939), which brings Boniface into the series, and this novel, both take place during a "World's Fair." And in this novel, Lomar Sunderson is described as "bony-faced." An unholy smile; Mark Connors works for the *San Francisco Clarion;* a red signal of danger; White men masquerade as Chinese; Great glory; okay; Idol of the Seven Sacred Suns; the Lee Tai Tong; the Phantom immediately identifies himself as the Phantom to people who could be an enemy; the Phantom uses nerve center pressure to subdue people while on the case; he has a jiu-jitsu fight with a Chinese guard—very good fight scene; carnival of blood and murder; a luminous light precedes the hole-in-the-eye murders; Phantom is tortured, but reveals nothing, so the crooks begin to torture a beautiful young girl instead; vibraphone; Phantom stops a gun from firing by putting the fleshy part of his hand between the firing pen and hammer of the gun; Chip Dorlan enters the story during the second half (again, as with the case of Boniface); Phantom tugs lobe of left ear; Frank calls Van "Dick"; hunting falcons are used in the hole-in-the-eye murders; gimlet eyed.

80. THE PHANTOM STRIKES BACK

V28 #3—October 1939
Written by Willis T. Ballard

Place: New Orleans, LA; Fort Knox, KY

Main characters: The Domino, the Mysterious Five, Maurice Perette, Albert Laporte, Gilbert, Martin, Michael, Tom, Arsin LeFete, Steve Huston, Harry, Richard Curtis Van Loan/the Phantom, Frank Havens, Marie Perette, Gaston Charles, Timothy Perkins, Chester Diller, Allan St. John, Boyer Joyce, Raymond Charles, Robert LeBoeuf, Franklin Demoyer, Fred Pettie, Jose Hernandez, Dr. Manuel Hervel, Montague Saunders, Jacques, Dr. Bendix, Muriel (mentioned), Borsten, Hal Franklin, Alger, Pennman, Sgt. Fogarty, Arthur Green, Al, Rico, Olson

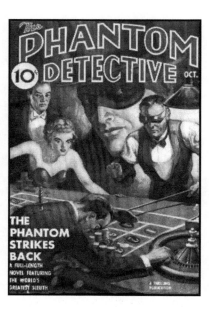

Communication are lost, roads

washed out, bridges gone, all ordinary currents of every day life are paralyzed, helpless, broken down. In a story more suited for an *Operator #5* adventure, it is almost alien to *The Phantom Detective*. The southern central States of America are flooded by heavy rains after dams are dynamited by an unknown group organized by a mastermind.

A hidden mastermind is behind a raid on Fort Knox, where our gold reserves are stored. The Phantom, investigating two murders in New Orleans, comes across the gigantic scheme. However, New Orleans is suddenly cut off from the rest of the country, with telephone lines down, radio communications disrupted, and inter-state transportation at a standstill.

Taking a plane to Fort Knox, the Phantom is forced to crash land in what has become a swamp from all the rains. He soon finds a horse and rides by horseback the rest of the way. Meanwhile, the military assigned to guard the gold have been ordered out to help rescue people from the flooded areas. And before the Phantom can reach Fort Knox, men dressed in strange garb attack the remaining soldiers at the fort. They release a poison gas that penetrates the soldiers' gas masks and kills them. The Phantom arrives while the gang is looting the vaults, and is captured.

While Frank Havens waits for word from the Phantom in his newspaper office in New Orleans, his star reporter, Steve Huston is traveling by riverboat to write a feature for Havens' newspaper on the nationwide flooding. Somewhere during the trip, Steve is knocked out by crooks. He wakes up in his bed in his cabin, though, as if nothing has happened, and rides safely the rest of the way. The Phantom figures that this incident was for the gang to divert the riverboat to an area near Fort Knox where the gold could be loaded on to the boat.

The story comes to a climax during the Mardi Gras parade in New Orleans, as the killer is unmasked.

Notes: His ring contains a spring-knife; one man who is killed by poison also has a knife stuck in his back to confuse the murder; "hold it," he ordered, and the Phantom "holds it"; no *Clarion* call, as Phantom is already in New Orleans; Havens' affiliate newspaper in New Orleans is the *Tribune;* propitious; gesticulating; a bullet is an angry bee; shadow-like; shoe contains tear gas; pig-like eyes; scotch their plans; stentorian voice.

Availability: *Wildside Pulp Classics: Phantom Detective #80* (published by Wildside Press, 2009).

81. MONEY MAD MURDERS

V29 #1—November 1939
Written by Laurence Donovan

Place: Miami, FL

Main characters: The Shark, Marty Thurston, Burke, Sgt. Moran (Miami), Morton T. (Mort) Andras, Connors (F.B.I.), Richard Curtis Van Loan/the Phantom, Jacklin Burton, Lamont Shrove, Hermann Lister, Lola Saunders, Dorr Murtroyd, "Honest" Joe Arden, Arthur Crayton, James Rocklin, Mrs. Colver, Carter, Ramon, Mr. Randall, "Satan"

1933
1934
1935
1936
1937
1938
1939
1940
1941
1942
1943
1944
1945
1946
1947
1948
1949
1950
1951
1952
1953

Crass, John Mogrum, Frank Havens, Jake, Martin, Johnson, Margie, Capt. Mahoney (Miami), Pokpla, Rodum

Frank Havens and Van Loan are vacationing in Miami when a series of murders occur; one at a horse race, and another on a gambling ship off shore. One man, a bank clerk, is given counterfeit money as part of his winnings at the racetrack. He also discovers another oddity during this time that will later result in his own murder.

It appears that two gangs, both in the counterfeiting business, are operating around Miami; one has their printing presses hidden in the Everglades, while the other gang operate their presses on barges that ply the vegetable trade along the shore line. Both operations are nicely hidden.

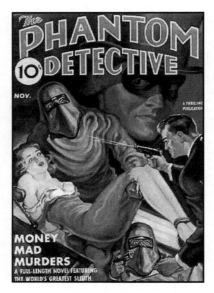

Notes: At times, Phantom has some similarities to Doc Savage; okay; gambling ship, the *Golden Dream;* eyes like gimlets; she trilled; Van has careless brown eyes; Ripley—believe it or not; Chip Dorlan has been placed in a military school—story refers to "The Sampan Murders" (September 1939) in which Chip was introduced; facile fingers; no *Clarion* call; drives a Bugatti—also drove a Bugatti in "The Forty Thieves" (July 1939), a novel with Clifford Boniface; tugged lobe of left ear; he said, laconically; Swamp Angels; the Phantom snorted; Van and Frank use mixed words when talking on the phone; Van toed over; Great glory.

Availability: *Money Mad Murders* (published by Jim Hanos, 1985), *The Phantom Detective V29N1—Pulp Facsimile* (published by Adventure House, 2009).

82. MURDER RIDES THE SKIES

V29 #2—December 1939
Written by Norman A. Daniels

Place: New York City; Blue Mountain, NY

Main characters: The Protector, John Sigrid, Raymond Mogarth, Samuel Parsons, Bill Evans, Brenda James, Tragano, Joe Harper, Renee Mogarth, James Clark, Slim Montague, Huber, Monte Lamer, John Mogarth, Lon Crowler, Chic Sardonia, Artie, Richard Curtis Van Loan/the Phantom, Dr. Bendix, Burney, Frank Havens, Homer James, Henry Horan, Sgt. Braddock, Chip Dorlan, Calloway, Joe, Mocker, Nick Arlo, Monk, Chuck, Homer Maxwell, Clement Darnton, Choker, Tom, Jevins, Burke, Randall, Raber, Randolph Boyle, Charles Montague, Christobal Montague-Anderson, Raslie Clark, "Trig" Young, Ann Meadows, Warden (prison) Jones, Ferguson, Jack, Steve Huston, Samuels, Arthur Thurston

Murder and kidnappings are taking place in an area of ski lodges in the Blue Mountain resorts. Ransom is asked for the return of the kidnap victims, but when they are returned—they are dead! A protection racket is also in the plot—the resorts are told to pay $3,000.00 a season for protection. Also in the offing is the release—soon—of a well-known mobster from prison.

It appears that the mobster had hidden millions in loot somewhere in the mountains before he went to prison, and some of his old pals were merely waiting for his release, to trail him to the hidden millions and take it away from him.

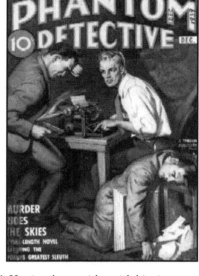

Notes: He slewed; the *Clarion* call; Van ice skates with a girl; his ring contains a blade for cutting rope; in one escape, the Phantom becomes a giant snowball descending a steep mountain that terminated in an area of large rocks—the snowball around his body protected him from injury when he struck the rocks; Chip uses ju-jutsu and knowledge of nerve centers; Great glory!; Phantom carries a .45; Van and Havens speak in unintelligible sentences over the telephone; "it's all right, all right"; toward the end of the story Chip Dorlan returns to New York and Steve Huston comes into the story to replace him.

Availability: *Action Adventure Stories* #129 (published by Fading Shadows, Inc., 2003).

83. THE PHANTOM COMES THROUGH

V29 #3—January 1940
Written by unknown; possibly Robert Sydney Bowen, Don Cameron or William Hopson

Place: New York City; Carboro, NY

Main characters: The Earless Man, Jim Prior, Gloria, Hugh Masterson, Bob Owen, Bertram Kline, Hiram Humboldt, Frank Havens, Baldy Koretz, Richard Curtis Van Loan/the Phantom, Oliver Trask, Joe, Mickey, Tony, Tip Bailey, Paul

1933

1934

1935

1936

1937

1938

1939

1940

1941

1942

1943

1944

1945

1946

1947

1948

1949

1950

1951

1952

1953

Corday, Rusty Graham, Randolph Travers, Steve Charters, William Merrick, Miles Merrick, Chip Dorlan, Fred, Nicky, Blane, Veyden, Mitchell Simons, Sam Foster, Martha Ralston, Kendrick, Alan Foster, Taylor, Remsen

The case appears to stem from an incident twenty years previously, when a posse had caught the wrong man and shot his ears off before the mistake was discovered. Now it appears that this "earless" man is after revenge on those who did this to him.

However, the earless man is only a red herring. Actually, someone is reading wills from lock-boxes in a bank. It appears that when a rich man has a weak son that can be blackmailed, the father is killed and the son is framed for a crime he didn't commit. The crooks then obtain the fortunes through the weak sons of the rich men.

Notes: I've got a strong suspicion that this novel was written by one of the western authors, probably someone we are already very familiar with, say, the Jim Hatfield or Rio Kid stories; people are glinty-eyed; okay; could also be Robert Sydney Bowen—from the name of the character B(ob) Owen; "you're stealing my thunder"; crook tugs at lobe of his ear; peril of the most intense nature; as signal, the Phantom lights a cigarette then tosses the match into the air; the Phantom wears his top hat and tails and mask often in the story; a gun battle takes place in the cemetery; Chip Dorlan is the Phantom's protégé; gangster has a knife in a scabbard behind his neck; cab driver says, "for twenty bucks I'd follow a rocket car to the moon"; no *Clarion* call. Some clues to a previous author, which again brings up Robert Sydney Bowen.

Availability: *Action Adventure Stories* #96 (published by Fading Shadows, Inc., 2001).

84. THE PHANTOM'S GAMBLE WITH DEATH

V30 #1—February 1940
Written by George A. McDonald

Place: New York City

Main characters: The Flame King, Glidden, Coleman Graves, James Cartier, Amos Beardsley, Bernice Walters, John Graves, Frank Havens, Claude Weldon, Bill Bolton, Henry Gear, Bonny Doonan, Dave Williams, Richard Curtis Van Loan/ the Phantom, Kosta, Peter Sardin, Tony Moreno, Roy Rader, Glenda de Ruyster, Adams, Count Elmo de Esteban, Felix Tomlinson, Steve Huston, Miss Walters (a secretary who is mentioned, although there is already a character named Walters in the story), Jules, Laurelton, August Strafer, Lee, Colonel Ritchie (state police), Perez, Richard Beardsley, Russell, Lt. Hotchkiss (state police)

The weapons factories in America appear to be sabotaged by

an unknown agent called the Flame King. He kills his enemies with a blue flame while witnesses are present. The Phantom is called into the case as there may be foreign agents operating in America, but he soon decides that the case may involve money and revenge rather than international intrigue.

Notes: He triggered twice; a gun-slug; "By George!"; victims receive miniature coffins prior to their murder, similar to "The Dancing Doll Murders" (June 1937) case—this could be the same author, plus it also has similarities to "Murder at the World's Fair" (June 1939); a rolly-polly body; quavered; the *Clarion* call, as well as a radio stations broadcast for the Phantom; ennui; Van is with a girl named Glenda de Ruyster when action starts; apoplectic; Phantom carries a .38; Adams is the city editor at the *Clarion;* faces were fish-belly white; a pile-driving punch; Phantom is buried alive in a coffin—Dan Fowler suffered a similar fate in J. F. Webb's "Murder's Hex Sign," *G-Men Detective* (November 1940) in this same year; tugged the lobe of his ear; a yacht, the *Flame Queen;* mouse-colored hair; strangely sounds like a Dan Fowler story at times, and would be more reasonable for an F.B.I. agent to be called in on possible foreign agents sabotaging American factories than a private investigator; a ship, the *Valdemere;* the Hawser Saloon; fella; Russell is the *Clarion's* pilot; "Great Scott!"; villain wants to be called, "His Majesty," and kills with electricity (a blue flame) again, the similarity to the *Secret Agent "X"* story, "Kingdom of Blue Corpses" (December 1935); as chary as himself; he clipped; a tissue of lies; rigmarole; at the end of the story, the Phantom calmly goes to sleep in a comfortable chair in the murder house while others are looking on.

Availability: *The Phantom's Gamble With Death* (published by Jim Hanos, 1985).

85. THE PHANTOM'S MURDER TRAIL

V30 #2—March 1940
Written by Ray Cummings

Place: Isle of Rest, Bermuda; New York City; Garth Cove, CT

Main characters: John Torg, George Prince, Peter Frantz, Uriah Atwater, Parker Hunt, Lee Banning, Alan Edwards, Richard Curtis Van Loan/ the Phantom, Frank Havens, Peter Gilbert, Asher Frost, Robert O. Bainbridge, Dr. Bendix, Jones, Steve, Tom Swanson, "Blackie" Ross, Red, Rollie, Hobart Reed, Inspector Gregg, Jackie Banning, Sgt. Rawley, Spike, Long John Lannigan, Arthur Powers, Ybarra Gutierrez, Sir Edward Dean (Bermuda Police Chief), Ingram, Sgt. Grant, Davis, Anita Gutierrez

Men of wealth are being kid-

THE PHANTOM'S MURDER TRAIL
A FULL-LENGTH NOVEL FEATURING THE WORLD'S GREATEST SLEUTH

1933
1934
1935
1936
1937
1938
1939
1940
1941
1942
1943
1944
1945
1946
1947
1948
1949
1950
1951
1952
1953

1933

1934

1935

1936

1937

1938

1939

1940

1941

1942

1943

1944

1945

1946

1947

1948

1949

1950

1951

1952

1953

napped and held for ransom. Van Loan is with Frank Havens on a private yacht, with three other rich men when they are all captured to he held for ransom. But the Phantom escapes, rescuing Frank and the other three men in time.

But the case has some strange twists. Several of the kidnapped men end up—supposedly—as skeletons. Other clues lead back to the sinking of a ship, the *Lady Helen,* that had been involved in the smuggling of illegal aliens. Now it appears that the people once associated with the smuggling activities are involved in another scheme of kidnapping and the disappearances of others. And there appears to be two different gangs at work, each after the same things.

Notes: The yacht, the *Adair;* Van is Havens' protégé; when crime reared its ugly head—may have been used in the previous story; weasel-faced; "you muffed it"; a Niagara torrent in his head; slewed around; hue and cry; will-o'-the-wisp; crooks' hideout located in underground cave near the shore, and can only be reached at low tide when the water does not cover the entrance—this was used in Charles Greenberg's "The Yacht Club Murders," but this is not by Greenberg; mastermind uses deadly piranha fish to strip the bones clean of flesh—this was used in Fleming-Roberts' "The Case of the Walking Skeleton" *(The Green Ghost Detective,* Spring 1941); an underground cave was also used in J. F. Webb's Dan Fowler story, "Crossroads of Crime" (March 1939); with the girl's father missing, and she is searching for him, it reminded me of the November 1936 *Phantom* story, "Death Rides the Blizzard." And this scene was very similar to that story, as well as a *Secret Agent "X"* story by Fleming-Roberts:

> The Phantom nodded. "Good-bye, Anita," he said. "Take care of your father."
>
> The girl was trying to smile. "But cannot I ever see you anymore?" she murmured.
>
> "If you should need me," he said, "get in touch with Mr. Havens, publisher of the *Clarion* in New York City. I will come wherever you are."

Availability: *Phantom Detective #10* (published by Corinth Regency, 1965).

86. THE PHANTOM AND THE DAGGERS OF KALI
V30 #3—April 1940
Written by E. Hoffmann Price

Place: New York City

Main characters: The Tiger, The Baron, Charley Peters, E. Knowlton Lucas, Detective-First Class Thomes Balban, Inspector Thomas Gregg, Mary, Grimes, Richard Curtis Van Loan/the Phantom, Mr. Drake, Perrin Calder, Patricia Hastings, Yogi Bandranath Das, William Ennisley, Dr. Paul Bendix, Mitchell Hamberly, Colton Fairlee, Hilden Barret, Harrington Dowd, Dorkley Evans, Al, Lefty Miller, Satcha Inoye, Frank Havens, Steve Huston, Miss Willins, Goldie, Alf, Shorty, Anya Doubrousky, Toda Inoye, Henry Sutton Hastings, Tony, Baldy, Saddho Lal, Bill

Seven religious knives of the Indian cult of Kali are stolen from a museum, then, suddenly, certain men—all part owners of a chemical company—are murdered, supposedly by the stolen knives.

The Phantom believes that the daggers of Kali are merely being used as red herrings, and finds that the murders had actually been performed by shooting rock salt bullets from an air gun, which would cause a similar wound as that of a knife, then the rock-salt would melt leaving no trace of a bullet. The dagger would then be tossed into the death room of the victims. While the police would be searching for Hindu killers, the real murderer would not be suspected.

What it was all about was international intrigue as foreign governments tried to obtain a new invention for war, keeping the invention from the allies hands.

Notes: Added piquancy; he snorted; no *Clarion* call; "Hell's Bells!"; sardonic eyes; ferretlike; fellow; heal of his shoe has a sharp steel edge for cutting rope or other bindings; hue and cry; will-o'-the-wisp; apropos; a blue funk, blue willies; the Phantom calls Inspector Gregg, "Tom"; the Phantom allows suspects to scribble on paper as he talks with them; crooks drive a station wagon—this has been used before, too; equipage; ye-a-h; ergo, the Phantom has a short wave radio hooked up in his car; okay; Harkness Drive; hard, baleful eyes; the Baron, a super spy of a foreign government, is never identified; several clues point to this being by the same author as "The Phantom's Murder Trail" (March 1940).

Availability: *Phantom Detective* #6 (published by Corinth Regency, 1965), *The Phantom and the Daggers of Kali* (published by Jim Hanos, 1986).

87. THE PHANTOM AND THE UNIFORMED KILLERS

V31 #1—May 1940
Written by unknown; possibly George Fielding Eliot or Emile C. Tepperman

Place: El Paso, TX; Miami, FL; Juarez, Mexico

Main characters: The Boss, Number One, Alfredo Romez, Mayor Thurston, Police Commissioner Grainger (El Paso), Bink, Heavy, General Arthur, Marvin Hyslop, Frank Havens, General Miguel Martino, George Crowley, Leroy Pearson, Emanuel Zardoff, Peter Greenwald, Richard Curtis Van Loan/the Phantom, Dolly, Mr. Mercer, Phelan, Pitts, Margaret Mathews, Jerrold, David Wells, Grady, Juliano Mendoza, Tanya, Steve Russell, Professor Samuel Pettigrew (mentioned), Jenkins

Men in uniforms—American policemen and soldiers—kill Mexican women and children, as well as assassinate one of Mexico's most popular individuals. The

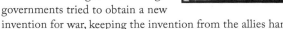

THE
PHANTOM
AND THE
DAGGERS
OF KALI
A FULL-LENGTH NOVEL
FEATURING THE WORLD'S
GREATEST SLEUTH

1933

1934

1935

1936

1937

1938

1939

1940

1941

1942

1943

1944

1945

1946

1947

1948

1949

1950

1951

1952

1953

1933

1934

1935

1936

1937

1938

1939

1940

1941

1942

1943

1944

1945

1946

1947

1948

1949

1950

1951

1952

1953

case appears to surround international trade pacts between America and Mexico. The mastermind was involved in smuggling goods across to Mexico, and the trade pacts meant that the illegal goods could not undersell the legal trade with the agreement in force. He wanted to sabotage that agreement!

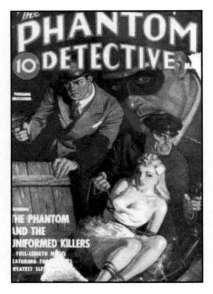

Notes: This author has, indeed, written others, and the is almost a carbon copy (in some scenes) of the previous story, only with a change of plot and characters; gimlet-eyed; he expostulated; signal light is mentioned, but Van is in Miami playing golf when he receives the call for the Phantom; Van is Havens' protégé; "S-o-o?"; a gas gun is used; "Don't be such a sphinx"; an unholy crew; a man is effeminate; the White Death; Order X; shoe-button eyes; he wears a utility belt; mastermind has plans for Number One to kill off all the men, plus Number One gets it, too—this is also a re-used plot device in a previous story!

At one point, the Phantom must enter the Red Light District of Juarez:

> Van entered the evil district of Juarez. Faces peered at him from shrouded doorways, and many of the habitués of the evil section called out bold invitations.

> ...has passed on into the heart of the un-policed district, where unimaginable iniquity was offered to those who sought it out.

> The girl, Tanya: her evening gown, cut daringly low, revealed creamy shoulders and alluring cleavage.

> Her heavily rouged lips were full and invitingly pouted. He realized at once that she was a most unusual woman; strikingly beautiful, yet with something evil about her beauty. Her slanted tawny eyes had a feline quality, while they had the rich promise and allure of full-blooded womanhood. She was not old, he judged; yet certainly she was not young.

> Her gaze spoke of intelligence, while a well-formed mouth and jaw were evidence of a ruthless strength of character. A mixture of exotic Oriental and tempestuous Latin temperament, he decided, and doubly dangerous in possessing the strongest attributes of both.

> The implications of depravity and evil along the route were almost inviting because they were cloaked in darkness.

> "You have done well, Steve Russell. You shall have the reward I promised you as soon as we can be alone."

It's perhaps a little racy for a *Phantom* novel, but a good story, nevertheless. A lot of similarities to the previous novel, yet quite different too!

Availability: *Phantom Detective* #19 (published by Corinth Regency, 1966).

88. THE PHANTOM HITS MURDER STEEL

V31 #2—June 1940
Written by Laurence Donovan

Place: Republic, PA

Main characters: Joler, Walker, Kay Brickley, Jason Sterne, Luke Smiley, Larry Colter, John Larch, Curtis Stevens, Fritz Krantz, Charles Thurman, Homer Catts, Blanton, Malcolm, Burke, Garth, Richard Curtis Van Loan/the Phantom, August Manton, Reed, Frank Havens (telephone), Pete Stanowicz, Chip Dorlan, Sgt. Rumpel (PA), Tony, Callahan, Mark, Jap, Joselyn, Police Chief Kramer (Republic), Jenkins

During a scheme to take over iron mills, the owner of the largest mill is in a sanitarium—supposedly insane—while his company has government contracts to fill. More than they can handle. A cooperation between all of the mills looks to be the only solution to the problem.

However, someone appears to want complete control, as well as a secret formula known only to the insane owner. Crooks take the owner from the sanitarium and go about killing other mill owners in the steel industry.

Notes: Slewed; okay; Adam's apple was doing acrobatics; the Phantom carries a .45; Phantom uses nerve centers and pressure points to subdue men; Havens and Phantom speak in code over the phone; the Phantom uses gas capsules; very such like Doc Savage at times.

89. THE PHANTOM AND THE VAMPIRE MURDERS

V32 #1—July 1940
Written by unknown; possibly Don Tracy

Place: Glen Valley

Main characters: George Lewis, Arnold Simms, Clyde Fiske, Ben Gray, James Tsan Yu, Frank Havens, Richard Curtis Van Loan/the Phantom, Grant Lamson, Wang, Tracy, Barney, Dr. Horace Alvord, Count Mera Mattopiky—the Vampire, Big Otto Ludorf, Charlie, Eddie, Joe

Five men at a hunting lodge believe a vampire is going to kill them. When one is murdered, his throat ripped out, one of the remaining men calls Frank Havens and request the help of the Phantom.

1933
1934
1935
1936
1937
1938
1939
1940
1941
1942
1943
1944
1945
1946
1947
1948
1949
1950
1951
1952
1953

1933

1934

1935

1936

1937

1938

1939

1940

1941

1942

1943

1944

1945

1946

1947

1948

1949

1950

1951

1952

1953

At the bottom of the mystery is a rich deposit of pitchblende, located on the mountain where the lodge is set. One man wanted it all. He invented the legend of the vampire, dressed in robe and wore a weird mask; he wanted the murders of his partners to be blamed on the vampire.

Notes: This story had a lot of similarities to the Black Bat novel, "Without Blood They Die" (Summer 1943). Some of the same plot devices in Charles Greenberg's stories, in particular "The Yacht Club Murders," but none of Greenberg's writing style. Tracy is Havens' chauffeur; lambent eyes; the rifle whanged once, twice, three times; one gang has a hideout in a cave located in the area; a baleful glare; after being held a prisoner, stripped to the waist, the Phantom still comes up with his hidden "sleeve" gun.

Availability: *Phantom Detective* #1 (published by Corinth Regency, 1965).

90. THE PHANTOM'S MURDER MONEY

V32 #2—August 1940
Written by Laurence Donovan

Place: New York City

Main characters: The Dolphin, Lester Cowdray, Lon Thurston, Luke Sparks, "Fuzzy" Wilkes, Thomas Bulkley, Ondra Sparks, Lanner Haviland, Frank Havens, Richard Curtis Van Loan/ the Phantom, Ralph Ferguson, Ruggers, Martha Reaper, Artemus Grimm, Giles, Harry Reaper, Earl of Gormley, Simon Travers, Mr. Horton, Chip Dorlan, Birch, Blackie, Larson, "Slick" Salter, Howland Wilkins, Steve Huston (mentioned), Dr. Paul Bendix, Tom Marble, Mr. Young

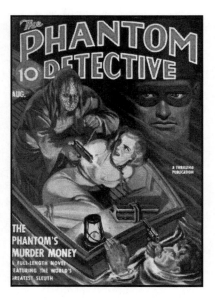

Years previously, a ship carrying gold sunk in eight fathoms of water. The crew was killed except for one seaman who was badly injured. Another ship, the *Dolphin*, rescued the seaman and learned his secret about the sunken ship with the gold. Seven men

were aboard the *Dolphin* and heard the story. The seaman drew its location in eight segments on eight one-dollar bills, so that it would take all eight bills to piece together the location.

But shortly, the *Dolphin* explodes and sinks also. The original men aboard ship escape, but leave the injured seaman aboard to die. Now, it appears someone is killing the survivors off, and the killer calls himself the Dolphin to let the victims know he comes from that ship, and they believe it is the injured seaman they left to die when the ship went down.

Notes: Has some similarities to "The Broadway Murders" (August 1938); the Phantom has brown eyes; the Phantom uses knowledge of nerve centers; vamp has green eyes; tugged at the lobe of his left ear; people are killed by a ship's harpoon; a clue is a sailor's knife; "Holy smoke!"; "Great glory!"

91. THE PHANTOM AND THE MELODY MURDERS

V32 #3—September 1940
Written by Charles Greenberg

Place: New York City

Main characters: Nickie, Harry Webber, Pat Sweeney, Richard Curtis Van Loan/the Phantom, Mr. Gray, Frank Havens, Donald Crain, Edward Foster, Emil Lundquist, Parrish, Chick, Miss Snyder, Red, Inspector Gregg, Claire Lamont, Duke Stahl, Victor Lang, Dennis Holliday, Monte Livingstone, Oscar Krause, Robert Wendell, Alex Freemen, Franz Gurka, Lou Quigley, Pat O'Neil, "Detroit" Smitty, Steve Huston, Chris Donovan, Tiny, Ikey Schultz, Dr. Bendix, Hickens, Kenneth Priestley, Lefty, Cappy, Lawrence Dayton, Anabelle Preston

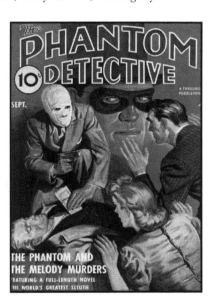

Men connected to a music studio are murdered by a maniac from an insane asylum. The Phantom has been requested by some of the board members, as they have received warnings that they will also die—the warnings are worded in such a way as to reflect on songs written or made famous by the insane man.

The Phantom learns that the maniac was supposedly cheated out of those same songs years back. He had gone mad at that time and killed several innocent people across the country, and was given the name of the Keyboard Killer. But the Phantom believes someone else is behind this current killing spree, and that the Keyboard Killer is merely a red herring.

Notes: Strange that there is a "Lawrence" as wall as a "Donovan" as characters in this story, plus the plot comes very close to Laurence Donovan's "The

1933
1934
1935
1936
1937
1938
1939
1940
1941
1942
1943
1944
1945
1946
1947
1948
1949
1950
1951
1952
1953

1933

1934

1935

1936

1937

1938

1939

1940

1941

1942

1943

1944

1945

1946

1947

1948

1949

1950

1951

1952

1953

Phantom Hits Murder Steel" (June 1940) but this story is on Greenberg's records; Kirby Institute for the Insane; once, twice, three times; Inspector Gregg mentions that he has a teenage daughter; okay; the corner of Wessley & Strand Streets—used before; balls of muscle stood out in his jaws; pregnant with significance; laden with dynamite; deaths are connected to title songs; repeats of "all right, all right"; no *Clarion* call; mastermind sets trap to destroy all his gunmen; Mammoth Pictures.

Availability: *Phantom Detective* #18 (published by Corinth Regency, 1966).

92. THE PHANTOM AND THE CRIME LEGION

V33 #1—October 1940
Written by George A. McDonald

Place: New York City

Main characters: Frank Havens, John B. Powell, Clinton Hathaway, Richard Curtis Van Loan/the Phantom, Inspector Thomas Gregg, Benjamin Thorne, Martin, Paul Bendix, Bernard Kane, George Dawson, Arthur Willett, Paul Vaughn, Sam Bancroft, Derek, Steve Huston, Vince Brummer, Alice Bayes, Lenny Franks, Whitey Williams, Pete, Louie, Max, "Limehouse" Ben, Murat, Fernand Latise, Stevens, Pierre, "Gentleman" Harry, Henri, "Apache" Laroque

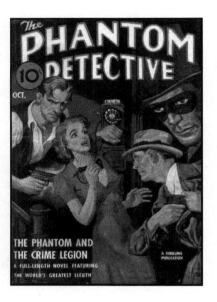

THE PHANTOM AND THE CRIME LEGION
A FULL-LENGTH NOVEL FEATURING THE WORLD'S GREATEST SLEUTH

A new gang of criminals appear to be operating in America. Men who speak few words, act in unison, and steal millions of dollars. If one of their gang is wounded at a scene, they will destroy his body with acid so it can't be identified later by the police. But when a body is saved from the acid, the police cannot identify the body from fingerprints on file.

The Phantom learns that these men are being brought over from Europe, to assist a super crook in his criminal empire. This is why their fingerprints are not on file in America. A part owner in a ship line that is losing money due to a war curtailment, the super crook figures new ways in making his millions!

A good story until the end, when within mere minutes everyone appears together when it should have actually taken hours to assemble them all. The author should have given us a better ending for such a good story.

Notes: A superfluity; mufti; did not faze them; vehicular domain; dead crooks are consumed by liquid fire, flameless; Green Circle Shiplines; signal light is mentioned but not used; tugged lobe of an ear; the Gay-Way Club; okay; *Clarion* has branch offices throughout city; pince-nez; a ship, the *Giganta;* piffle; another ship, the *Marinthe;* an evil Niagara; feller; *Clarion* has a facsimile machine which Phantom uses to fax information to Paris; agent K-12, Surete police; baptism of fire; mastermind has two identities during the story.

93. THE PHANTOM AND THE GREEN GLARE MURDERS

V33 #2—November 1940
Written by unknown; possibly Laurence Donovan

Place: New York City; Washington D.C.; Baltimore, MD

Main characters: The Green God, Richard Curtis Van Loan/the Phantom, Senator Horace McGrady, Herman Andrews, Frank Havens, Louis Albright, Dennison Greetson, Hsang Mei Liang, Fagin, Hewett Furman, James Wright, Kung Li Veng, Ch'in Kuei, Danforth Wilkes, James Kung, Curley Adams, Mike Chase, Aaron Lacey, Charles Clayborne, Homer Briggs, Thomas Tinsdale, Lawrence Flagg, Sam Jarvis, Dr. Kirby, George Archer, Carter

1933
1934
1935
1936
1937
1938
1939
1940
1941
1942
1943
1944
1945
1946
1947
1948
1949
1950
1951
1952
1953

Men fall from the sky, their crushed and broken bodies striking in a populated area. Afterwards, the sky turns green to mark the death as being by the Green God! One of the first bodies to fall from the sky actually strikes Dick Van Loan's car as it plummets to earth.

The Phantom begins his investigation by targeting an un-American group known as the Green Shirts, but he is drawn more towards the Capital, and members of congress. He learns that a treasure has been hidden in Formosa, and the map drawn on seven pieces of jade, then these pieces of jade sold to seven leading congressman—now someone appears to want all the maps, and the men dead!

Notes: He quavered; the *Clarion* call; Phantom changes his disguise in a phone booth; Havens' office has a static machine to ward off eavesdropping when he and Phantom speak about the case; the Gavel Club; Havens has a recording machine to record telephone calls—also used in "The Phantom and the Vampire Murders" (July 1940); the army of darkness; the Bloody Shirts or Tan Shirts group; unholy light; Phantom gnawed his lower lip; Phantom and Havens speak in code over the telephone; Phantom thrown into pit with a nine-foot rattlesnake—he strangles it to death; gimlet eyes; the Green Shirts; the Phantom falls asleep at end of story while talking with Havens—again, this incident, and at least three different authors may have used it—could be a joke among the *Phantom* writers. My guess is that this one is by Donovan. Perhaps the sleeping scene is written in by an editor.

1933

1934

1935

1936

1937

1938

1939

1940

1941

1942

1943

1944

1945

1946

1947

1948

1949

1950

1951

1952

1953

Availability: *Phantom Detective* #11 (published by Corinth Regency, 1966).

94. THE PHANTOM AND THE TELEVISION MURDERS

V33 #3—December 1940
Written by Laurence Donovan

Place: Long Island; New York City

Main characters: John Thaler Young, Diana Young, Jimmy Tralan, Frank "Silk" Ranick, Thelma Young, Anthony Tralan, Charleton, Andrus Jalater, Rodney Blount, Steve Huston, Archer, Sanderson, Richard Curtis Van Loan/the Phantom, Myron Carter, Rita, Simon Graves, Arthur Thurman, Frank Havens, Aturas Romalo, Harry "Knifer" Scoloni, Murphy, Dolan, Antonio Romalo, Dr. Paul Bendix, Chip Dorlan, Rocker, Sato, Dunk, Joey, Philo T. Farnsworth (mentioned), Martinez, Carlos Rodriguez

A mastermind is using television to show murders being committed. However, the Phantom knows that actors are being used to impersonate the blackmail victims.

The case concerns bonds and counterfeit bonds from a South American republic. The mastermind had been a television producer in that country, but was now a big financial leader in New York.

Notes: A man has a bony face; minor clues to a dozen past stories, including "The Phantom and the Daggers of Kali" (April 1940), "The Web of Murder" (February 1939), and several others; the Tropical Club; "By the Lord Harry"; Van is with a girl named Rita at beginning of story, then a new girl named Rita comes into the story about half way; Sanderson is Van's yacht captain; Van swims ashore from yacht, which is also similar to the previous story; *Clarion* signal is used; Van and Havens use code when on the phone; the Phantom has pale-blue eyes; tugged the lobe of left ear; "Ho!"; "Good Glory!"; the car slewed; men use bolas to ensnare their victims; special knives are used; Phantom uses nerve centers and pressure points; marble eyes; piggish eyes; baleful eyes.

Availability: *The Phantom and the Television Murders* (published by Jim Hanos, 1985).

95. THE PHANTOM'S GREATEST GAMBLE

V34 #1—January 1941
Written by Laurence Donovan

Place: New York City; Pleasant Grove, NY

Main characters: The Big Shot, Alan Greenwood, Vernon Davis, James Franklin Tate, Duane Desmond, Doris Desmond, Capt. Tom MacHugh, Frank Havens, Don Bixby, Harold Hickerson, Richard Curtis Van Loan/the Phantom, Inspector Gregg, Ole Sundsten, Mugsy, Shorty, Joe, Lop-ear, Gunner, Hank, Spike, Buttsy, John Larch, Sam Thalman, Travis Tanner, Dr. Paul Bendix, J. Franklin Griffith (Tate?), Slats, Sgt. Horan, Lois Dorset, Mr. Gravitch, Claude Napier, John Bates, Joel Bezazian, Johnson, Lucius Pindar, Manny, Joseph Barberoni, Miss Brown, Charlie, Capt. Sanderson, Capt. Dawson, Jacobs, Jimmy Ward, Elizabeth Brentwood, Maury Shaughnessy

In a very similar story to that of "The Radio Murders," a mestermind is sending out secret massages to the crooks doing his dirty work. They are told which ships to sabotage, then they recover valuable, insured cargo, and return it for profit.

Notes: Radio Station WUBC; ships the *Belle Isle, Mary Belle, Santos, Scotia,* and *Belle of Bermuda*; okay; Don Bixby is *Clarion's* advertising manager; Blimpy's Tavern; Phantom has an automatic recording device to tape radio broadcasts—will be used again in a Donovan story; fella; "Don't be an ass"; Black Maria—used in McDonald story; the *Clarion* signal is mentioned.

96. THE PHANTOM AND THE CURIO MURDERS

V34 #2—February 1941
Written by Laurence Donovan

Place: New York City; Mobile, AL

Main characters: Green Masked One, Luber, Frick, Homer Galen, Tera Loma, Robert Larkin, Donna D'Arneville, Juan D'Arneville, Yogi Krishanda, Dolores Salazar, Antone Salazar, Inspector Thomas Gregg, Frank Havens, Richard Curtis Van Loan/the Phantom, Ramon Lascalles, Theresa, Humbert, Maria, Charles Mott, Tumaco, Bara, Travala, Henry Colter, James Randall, Chip Dorlan, Luke Hammond, Jessup, Leta, Dr. Paul Bendix, Tinker

Another good story, in which a

1933
1934
1935
1936
1937
1938
1939
1940
1941
1942
1943
1944
1945
1946
1947
1948
1949
1950
1951
1952
1953

1933

1934

1935

1936

1937

1938

1939

1940

1941

1942

1943

1944

1945

1946

1947

1948

1949

1950

1951

1952

1953

mastermind hopes to make millions from stolen Spanish jewels that he intends to claim were part of a family treasure already in America.

People fall from a doomed airplane similar to "The Phantom and the Green Glare Murders" (November 1940), while there are also throwbacks to the novel, "Double-Stamped Doom" (October 1937), which could have been Donovan's first Phantom story. But I still think that one was by Robert Sydney Bowen.

Notes: Could be a new author, but reads too much like Donovan; the Phantom has brown eyes; tugged lobe of his left ear; "Good Glory!"; uses a sleeve gun; baleful eyes; a man is bony faced; a killer with a white mouse, also munches on popcorn all the time; antique collector/dealer likes stamps, which reminded me a lot of the October 1937 story; mastermind wears a glowing green mask; the Phantom shoots the hooded head of a cobra as it prepares to strike a woman; the Phantom disguises himself in gray clothes and gray complexion as well—the Whisperer?; the Phantom uses the nerve centers and pressure points; the Phantom uses ventriloquist trick to make his voice appear near someone else, which will be used over and over in these coming stories.

Availability: *Phantom Detective* #13 (published by Corinth Regency, 1966).

97. MURDER CALLS THE PHANTOM

V34 #3—March 1941
Written by Ralph Oppenheim

Place: Portland, OR; Astoria, OR

Main characters: Skipper, Howard Roth, Michael, Burgess Brand, Charles "Red" McMurtry, Mackling, Charles Minturn, Mary Minturn, Sacker, Robert Deming, Chip Dorlan, Steve Huston, Muriel Havens, Richard Curtis Van Loan/the Phantom, John Prosser, J. Thurston Hamm, John Jacob Astor (mentioned), Croaker, Lionel Shotwell, Burton Thayer, Larch South, Police Chief Newell (Astoria), Dr. Toler, Miss Davis, Dr. Barton, Jane Horton, Inspector Cardigan (Portland), Frank Havens (mentioned)

Engine plants are being sabotaged in Oregon, and the federal people on staff request the aid of the Phantom. He arrives with Chip Dorlan, Steve Huston, and Muriel Havens, and they jump right into the investigation. In non-stop action, the reader has trouble keeping tabs on anyone, so it's not surprising that the author can't either! Immediately, there is a fire at a mansion, and the Phantom is thrown into the action. Each of his aides will have their work cut out for them, too.

Notes: I read this one years ago and didn't like it. On a second reading, it was better. But still nothing to win any awards; actually, this is the first case in which Muriel has a true active part in the case, and is not just mentioned as a pretty girl; there is a Fer-de-Lance snake; Chip has blue eyes; Green Spruce Club; okay; the Phantom uses ju-jitsu and nerve centers; a vibraphone—used in "The Sampan Murders" (November 1939); man has a bony face; Skipper has a giant police dog as a pet; Muriel is blonde, with an oval face and blue eyes; the Phantom changes his disguise in a phone booth again; "Great Glory!"; "Great Scott!"; story centers around the fire at the mansion; the Phantom visits the home of a suspect—without telling the reader who it is—towards the end of the story to prove to himself who the mastermind is, then comes up with the clues at the end of the story; story moves at break-neck speed; the Phantom has deep, all-seeing eyes; Muriel uses aliases of Miss Davis and Jane Horton; people appear when and where they shouldn't be; one battle is taking place hot and heavy when Steve shows, up and the Phantom stops everything to talk to him as if nothing is going on around them; in one scene, a man and woman are tied to some kind of a frame over the water, with crooks threatening to blow the structure up. They do, and the structure falls into the sea, with the two still tied. The Phantom is in the water fighting with the mastermind, when suddenly the man who had been tied to the frame appears in a diving bell to rescue him! I don't understand the clues to Donovan, though.

98. THE MURDER BUND

V35 #1—April 1941
Written by unknown; possibly
Laurence Donovan or Ralph Oppenheim

Place: Detroit, MI

Main characters: The Murder Prophet, The Little Fuehrer, Freda, Herman Slater, Fritz, McCable, Roger Latham, Janet McGregor, Karl, Amos Stout, Paul Latham, Randolph Merkle, Horace Craft, Lela Latham, Grayson, Richard Curtis Van Loan/the Phantom, Dr. Bendix, Capt. Reagan, Chip Dorlan, Lawson, Frank Havens, Dr. Cross, Miss Andrews, Harden, Heinrich, Harkins, Hans

Defense plants in Detroit are being sabotaged, while Nazis are after some secret (never revealed) of a torpedo bomb. They are also taking bombs into Mexico. This is a strange story, and very similar to the previous one, "Murder Calls the Phantom," as if it is merely a re-write.

Notes: As in the previous story, the Phantom visits the home of one of the suspects, knocks him cold, searches the place for clues that he can use at the end of the story to prove he's the mastermind; people have marble eyes; no

1933
1934
1935
1936
1937
1938
1939
1940
1941
1942
1943
1944
1945
1946
1947
1948
1949
1950
1951
1952
1953

Clarion call; a girl throws herself forward onto a sword point, killing herself before she is tortured; story moves at break-neck speed; one of the criminals plays a violin while his minions are engaged in killing and other activities; the old Detroit Purple Gang is mentioned in passing; a house fire plays a major part in the story, as with the previous story; the Phantom uses a ventriloquist trick to make his voice heard near someone else; the Phantom has knowledge of nerve centers and la savate; mastermind uses a television set to watch over his gang; Chip Dorlan is said to be 22 years old; a gas gun is used on the Phantom; Great Glory!

99. THE TRAIL TO DEATH

V35 #2—May 1941
Written by George A. McDonald

Place: New York City

Main characters: The Snatcher, Thomas J. Hammond, O'Brien, Benjamin Russell, James Montagu, Clyde Davies, Steve Huston, Inspector Gregg, DeLevan, Frank Havens, Muriel Havens, Richard Curtis Van Loan/the Phantom, Robert Hammond, Chip Dorlan, George Talbert, Samuel Pratt, Dr. Paul Bendix, Charles Kane, Jadpok, Boston Mayes, Fletchley, Henry Latisse, Harry, Kenneth Mallaby, Max Fenner, Hendrik Doorne, Dan Brady, Duke Peters, Donovan

Again, like the February 1940 story, "The Phantom's Gamble With Death" (February 1940), men are buried alive in coffins and their families must pay ransom or they will die. Men of wealth are being kidnapped and held for ransom. The reason? Gems. Mostly diamonds that are wanted by the mastermind. Even the Phantom, Muriel and Steve are put into coffins and supposedly buried alive. They escape, fortunately.

The diamonds are wanted for two reasons: some are being sold to finance the operations—and pay the gang members. Second, the stolen diamonds are cut down to be used in industrial tools, which just happen to be made by the company controlled by the mastermind.

Again, at the end of the story, the Phantom falls asleep while riding back to New York City with Frank Havens, Steve Huston and Chip Dorlan.

Notes: Lynx-eyed; his heart did a flip-flop; Chip says, "Chee!"; okay; finger touched the lobe of his left ear; Amalgamated Machine Tool Corporation; the Hesyler Building; the Phantom carries a Colt .45; the Phantom has a dead gangster secretly removed by police; the Phantom's hair is chestnut colored; speaks crisply; Verdon Hotel; the Star of Isha, a large diamond; again, a missing finger gives the Phantom away; twin large diamonds, the "Kimberly

Twins"; Havens used to own the Paradise Diamond, we are told—however, in a previous McDonald story, Havens owned the Kimberly Star; Dan Brady was a detective for an insurance company; so many similarities to McDonald and Robert Sydney Bowen.

Availability: *Phantom Detective* #8 (published by Corinth Regency, 1965), *The Trail of Death* (published by Jim Hanos, 1985).

100. THE GRIM SHADOW OF HATE

V35 #3—June 1941
Written by Laurence Donovan

Place: Manhattan; New York City

Main characters: The Doctor, Doctor of Death, Jimmy Rice, Billy Rice, Thelma Evans, Harvey Rice, Loren Hart, Horace Doremus, Randoloph Hawley, Peter Ramsbell, Thurston Young, Andrew Crouch, James Howard, Richard Curtis Van Loan/ the Phantom, Professor Jeremy, Dr. Paul Bendix, Charles Turner, Jason Jones, Aimee Corre, Chip Dorlan, Frank Havens, Tony Marino, Kiel, Joey Marino, Loretta, Leonidas Abner, Truman Abner, Olivia Hartwell, Inspector Gregg, Steve Huston, Karl, Hercula, Dolan

A college is suffering from several murders, and its elderly founder calls in the Phantom. Some complicated twists, with clues that point towards members of an old circus troop. Plus, a mysterious "Doctor," and someone inheriting a fortune from the death of the college founder.

Notes: This didn't start out like Donovan. Instead, Champion's old formula is back, with "Death" looking over the scene in which someone is about to die. Story has some similarities to "Thirteen Cards of Death" (August 1933), and other Champion entries; luminous black eyes; eyes were burning lamps; clucking sound in his throat; erudite; a blow pipe is used; his Adams apple in his thin throat shuttled up and down; Havens calls Van, "Dick"; pulling at the lobe of his ear; no *Clarion* signal; the Crown Circus; "What the what?"; the Champion Corporation; "Great Glory!"; the author mentions Frank Havens, Muriel Havens, Steve Huston, and Chip Dorlan from the very beginning of the story, but with the exception of Frank Havens, each of the other characters only plays one part during the story, then that person bows out, and one of the others comes into the story for their segment, then they leave and the other one enters, then all come back for the end of the story—this was actually very nice, as it helped the author keep track of everyone in the story; the Phantom uses certain chemicals and his badge in order to make an atomic bomb to blew his way out of a trap in one scene; acrobats are involved in murder and crime—

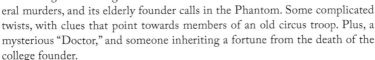

1933

1934

1935

1936

1937

1938

1939

1940

1941

1942

1943

1944

1945

1946

1947

1948

1949

1950

1951

1952

1953

1933

1934

1935

1936

1937

1938

1939

1940

1941

1942

1943

1944

1945

1946

1947

1948

1949

1950

1951

1952

1953

this was the troop attached to a famous circus before it went under.

This story is my favorite for this segment. Not the best written, but possibly the most fun. It is the hundreth story, and the Phantom even has to destroy his famous badge.

Availability: *Action Adventure Stories* #73 (published by Fading Shadows, Inc., 2000), *High Adventure* #74 (published by Adventure House, 2004).

101. THE SABOTAGE MURDERS

V36 #1—July 1941

Written by Henry Kuttner

Place: New York City; Ossining, NY

Main characters: The Fiend, Kent, Brock, Grossley, Eric Feucht, Rudolph Busch, Rudolph von Decker, Richard Curtis Van Loan/the Phantom, Frank Havens, Steve Huston, Leghorn, Denzalo, King, Jane Morrison, Blayde, Police Commissioner Inverness, Kedrick Donohue, Dr. Paul Bendix, Shorty, "Glim," Daly, Fred Ryan, Jones, Joe Carlin, Steck, Richardson, Red, Baldy

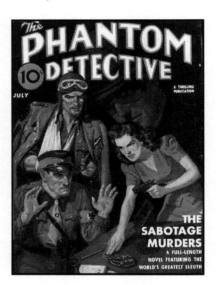

Factories are being sabotaged to delay America's armament. At the head of the saboteurs— Bundsmen within America itself! But the Phantom believes there is deeper intrigue in the schemes of the mastermind. Indeed, a super crook is merely using the Nazis in his own schemes of taking control of several armament plants. With control of the armament plants, he could sell arms to any government he wished, lining his own pockets with financial gains.

Notes: The Phantom's flat, mocking laughter rang out—though the Phantom was often criticized at Street & Smith for being a copy of The Shadow, this incident was the closest the Phantom ever came to actually copying the Street & Smith superhero; his "mocking laughter"; colloquy; the "Trojan Horse," a plot used many times within the Black Bat series; his feet want sh-sh through the dry grass; there was the *Clarion* call; police thought of the Phantom as a law-breaker, but always wished him luck—this was actually the first time we see any hint that the Phantom wasn't sanctioned by the high officials of the police department, he was merely tolerated because of the good that he ultimately accomplished; business was their shibboleth; okay; Police Commissioner Inverness (should have been Iverness) was last heard from in the May 1937 issue, and he was merely an inspector at that time—his name was sometimes spelled Iverness, and at other times, Inverness; Holy smoke; Huston uses the alias of Fred Ryan; the Phantom gives a patriotic speech to defense workers; for a change of pace, the author lets the reader hear the thoughts of others, including the mastermind, instead of just the Phantom; he goes into a trap unarmed, leaving a gun on the outside windowsill where the trap awaits him—he is thus able to retrieve the gun when the crooks are not expecting it; later, with his guns holstered, the mastermind gets the drop on him, and he must use his sleeve gun—the sleeve gun is in most of the stories from now on, and is always overlooked when the crooks search him for weapons.

Availability: *Action Adventure Stories* #85 (published by Fading Shadows, Inc., 2000).

102. THE THOUSAND ISLANDS MURDERS

V36 #2—August 1941
Written by Laurence Donovan

Place: St. Lawrence Thousand Islands; Alexandria Bay

Main characters: Injun Joe, Jerry Smith, Bruce Lerner, Jim Harley, Mary Sanford, Richard Curtis Van Loan/the Phantom, Muriel Havens, Chip Dorlan, Jerome Sanford, "Long John" Smith, Charles MacDonald, Luke, Curt, Buck, Tom, Red Bill, Landon, Ray Lukens, Blacky, Frank Havens, Danny, Lennie, Otto Schemer, Kelly, Hal, Myrna Lambert, George.

On Smith Island, one island in a chain of islands, all residents are named "Smith." Which probably isn't their real name. But it isn't known if any of them are running from the law, or merely looking to escape from civilization and the big cities. Something called "The Devil's Fire", a blinding flash of light that leaves no trace of bodies or buildings when it strikes, is preceded by the sound of drums.

When Mary Sanford, through a detective agency, learns that her missing uncle is one of the Smiths, she tells her friend Muriel, who in turn tells her father, Frank Havens, about the mysterious Smith Island. This information is enough to interest the Phantom.

The Phantom, accompanied by Mary Sanford, Chip Dorlan and Muriel Havens, heads for Smith Island secretly to investigate and bring out the uncle if possible. This would have made a great Doc Savage adventure, and at times the Phantom sounds more like Doc than he should have.

Notes: The "Find Them Detective Agency"; Frank Havens doesn't show up until the very end; okay; Muriel is dark haired, dark eyed; Injun Joe throws bird seed around the area where the Devil's Fire claims a victim; bullets are angry bees; a place known as the "Devil's Oven"; Good Glory; sloe-eyed; the Devil's Fire is a thermite bomb usually carried inside a fountain pen; no *Clarion* call, but the signal light is mentioned. Doc Savage fans should read this one!

1933
1934
1935
1936
1937
1938
1939
1940
1941
1942
1943
1944
1945
1946
1947
1948
1949
1950
1951
1952
1953

103. DEATH OVER PUGET SOUND

V36 #3—September 1941
Written by Laurence Donovan

Place: Seattle, WA

Main characters: The Black Wolf, Cyrus Starke, Lela Stark, Tom Randall, Thurman Trulow, Ralph Larch, Slim Layton, Frank Havens, Richard Curtis Van Loan/the Phantom, Anton Cushman, "Old Proverb," Bill Summers, John Hart, Steve Huston, Chip Dorlan, Mantha Strong, Burler, Harry Lant, Capt. Harvey, Rucker

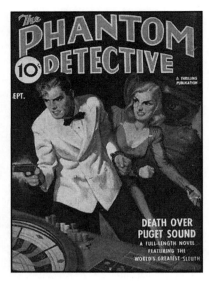

In the timber tract land around Seattle, a giant hairy man called the Black Wolf is killing men connected to the logging industry. It appears that this killer works for a strange man known only as the Echo Voice. It would appear that there are two opposing groups concerned about the building of a dam in the area.

The Phantom, accompanied by Frank Havens, Chip Dorlan, and Steve Huston, come to Seattle and the Phantom is instantly thrown into the fray when he meets the giant woman, Mantha Strong, and they are attacked by the giant hairy Black Wolf and a Siwash Indian—the Siwash Indians hunt with tongueless dogs.

This was another good action adventure, and I couldn't help wondering how it would have been as a Doc Savage adventure, with his aides. The Siwash Indians and Black Wolf would have made great Bigfoot monsters, and it would have been a rollicking adventure.

Notes: Okay; Havens owns the *Northwest Clarion* in Seattle; a saloon called the Bright Spot; Good Glory; Phantom weighs 170 pounds; the Phantom uses nerve centers and ju-jitsu; fella; woman has green eyes. Doc Savage fans should read this one.

104. RACE HORSES OF DEATH

V37 #1—October 1941
Written by Laurence Donovan

Place: San Diego, CA

Main characters: The Masker, Simm Archer, Señora Leona, Sela Kane, Doc Craig, Ling Su, "Buddy" Durkin, "Banty" Doyle, Richard Curtis Van Loan/the Phantom, Chip Dorlan, Farrell, McDermott, "Zing" Dover, Thomas Chester, Muriel Havens, Merkle Harden, Luke Owler, Arthur Conroy, Jimson, Joel Seward, "Smiles" Dawner, Silas Rudd, Señor Ruiz, "Skipper," Jack Armstrong, Jim Saunders, Crater, Hobart, Croker, Bales, Frank Havens (mentioned)

A killer known only as the Masker is killing people connected to a racetrack. One of Muriel's girl friends owns a stable and several horses at the track and asks the Phantom to investigate. Muriel and Chip Dorlan accompany the Phantom to San Diego and help out in his investigation.

At the bottom of the mystery is the ownership of the five million dollar race track, as well as hidden Spanish treasure below the race-track grounds.

Notes: Tugged the lobe of his left ear; Muriel is dark haired; movie column, "The Owl Blinks"; yacht, the *Sea Queen;* okay; one crook likes to toss pennies into the street to cause Mexican children to dash in front of on-coming cars as they try to get the coins; a man is bony faced; a man is effeminate; killers drive a station wagon, which is a throwback to some of those early 1937 stories.

105. THE BLACK GOLD KILLERS

V37 #2—November 1941
Written by Laurence Donovan

Place: New York City; El Paso, TX

Main characters: Joel March, Charles Young, Tarantula Luzon, Kay Seibert, Clyde Seibert, Carl Kraft, Stevens, Steve Huston, Richard Curtis Van Loan/Phantom, Ward Thayer, Horton Talley, Sidney Lester, Miss Stanton, John Landon, Carlos Martinez, Slim Smith, Pancho, Ramona, Chip Dorlan, Juan Lopez, Hell-For-Leather Doyle, Jose, Anthony Barton, Crowell, Harler, Frank Havens (mentioned), Muriel Havens (mentioned)

A good story in which the Phantom follows a murder case from New York City to a ranch somewhere 206 miles from El Paso, Texas, where the crooks are after a big oil deposit that will be worth millions of dollars.

A lot of action, and is actually the basic story and plot for Daniels' *Masked Detective* story, "Candles of Murder" (Spring 1943).

1933
1934
1935
1936
1937
1938
1939
1940
1941
1942
1943
1944
1945
1946
1947
1948
1949
1950
1951
1952
1953

1933

1934

1935

1936

1937

1938

1939

1940

1941

1942

1943

1944

1945

1946

1947

1948

1949

1950

1951

1952

1953

Notes: Sloe-black eyes; the Phantom has brown, humorous eyes; extant; Randolph Building; one killer uses a needle-pointed stiletto to murder his victims; killer also keeps tarantulas and scorpions in his pocket!; the BB Ranch; the Box-J Ranch; the Hells Bells Saloon in Juarez, some similarity to "The Phantom and the Uniformed Killers" (June 1940), but this isn't the same author; tugged the lobe of his left ear; Great Scott!

106. MURDER STALKS A BILLION

V37 #3—December 1941
Written by Laurence Donovan

Place: New York City

Main characters: Capt. Latore, Lecoque, Capt. Jardine, Pierre Lamont, Anton Dupre, Chauman, Ina Lou, Homer Kent, Fred Kent, "Diamond" Ronder, Pete, Dude, Martha, "Slowboy", "Old Whickers", Frank Havens, Richard Curtis Van Loan/Phantom, Steve Huston, Penny Lake, Jewel Madison, Spud, Ackers, Leonard, Traynor, "Big" Dan Spade, Capt. Rogers, Inspector Thomas Gregg, Rodney Sherman, Dr. Paul Bendix, Chip Dorlan, Muriel Havens, Marianna, Rudolph Schermell, Hauler, Capt. Bascom

A complicated plot, in which a billion dollars in gold is heading for America, presumably in exchange for oil. Meantime, a big oilman—who is almost broke—is also financing a stage show. And he has something to do with the incoming gold shipment. There are a lot of Frenchmen involved, so it's possible the ship is coming from France. Also involved is a crooked politician and a club owner who wears a lot of diamonds on his hands, who also appears to be after the billion dollars worth of gold. And not to forget an international crook that had escaped from a federal prison not long back, and who now owns a two hundred thousand dollar yacht, and who also wants the gold shipment. Presumably, all of the no-goods heard about the gold shipment through the actors in the stage play. All they seem to be waiting on is the date and place the ship will come in.

Notes: A man is funeral faced—in keeping with bony faced and horse faced; Chip Dorlan knows of and visits Dr. Bendix's warehouse hideout of the Phantom; Inspector Gregg also knows of the tugged ear lobe signal; the stage play is "Cotton Road"; okay; slaty eyes; "Good Glory!"; Steve and his girl friend, Penny Lake, are on a plane that crashes as it comes into New York, but they survive; the Phantom uses a face mask to impersonate a crook; a yacht, the *Barracuda*; "Too bad, too bad," he repeated; zircon eyes; a strange weapon that emits a paralyzing gas is used on victims.

Availability: *Phantom Detective* #14 (published by Corinth Regency, 1966).

CHAPTER III, SECTION G

CLOSING OUT
THE FIRST TEN
YEARS: 1942-1943

T HE PERIOD IN which we are now entering appears to be two-fold: first, we begin with several of the previous authors, but a little over half way we get a solid writer whom I believe is Charles Greenberg—but his writing has taken leaps for the better. When I first read some of his stories, I naturally assigned the stories to Charles Greenberg, but Will Murray told me Greenberg had ceased writing for the *Phantom* by this point, so I tried to find a new writer. These are re-written Charles Greenberg stories, or at least they are Greenberg's plot devices, along with many similar scenes from his stories. Will eventually discovered that Greenberg had, indeed, returned to the series, so these were his stories after all. He appears to be a better writer now.

The second part of this two-fold period is that we are about to enter a whole new phase of *The Phantom Detective*. If we look at the period that will end this segment, those six novels by Greenberg, then look at the next period (at least the first six stories in the next segment), we will find only two authors involved in writing the series: first is Greenberg, with six stories, then Norman Daniels with the next six. Lawrence Donovan appears to end his big involvement with this segment. Unfortunately, he won't return. This means that Chip Dorlan will not be as active now, and in the next segment a new author will bring in a new character.

After December 1942, I think we will see less of the old *Phantom Detective* writers, with the exception of Norman Daniels, who will write the series off and on until its demise in 1953. However, with Charles Greenberg, I think the editor-in-charge, Leo Margulies, was getting rid of the old, and bringing in the new. This period actually ends the first ten years of the series. Maybe that is why the sudden change in authorship of the series. Who knows? One other important change comes about after this segment; the last of the great villains will cease. Over the first ten years, the Phantom Detective faced hordes of evil masterminds, usually grotesque visages of masked or hooded demons. The second ten years will see more normal villains, mob bosses, crime lords, and their kind; plus, the stories will also be less violent, while the Phantom Detective becomes more of a detective, and less a super hero. Sad, but the stories are good, so stay with us.

1948

1949

1950

1951

1952

1953

1933

1934

1935

1936

1937

1938

1939

1940

1941

1942

1943

1944

1945

1946

1947

1948

1949

1950

1951

1952

1953

107. MURDER MOON OVER MIAMI

V38 #1—January 1942
Written by Laurence Donovan

Place: Miami, FL; Corpse Cay, FL

Main characters: The Skipper, "Singer" Durkin, Laka, Tommy Crane, Lance Grover, Howard Templeton, "Blacky" Burch, Marna Macklin, Cyrus Starke, Capt. Peters, Capt. Conners, Richard Curtis Van Loan/the Phantom, "Iron Judge" William Macklin, Frank Havens, Steve Huston, Chip Dorlan, Jams Layton, Janyx, Thad Burton, Angel Smith, "Cypress" Smith, Botts, Bat Spalan

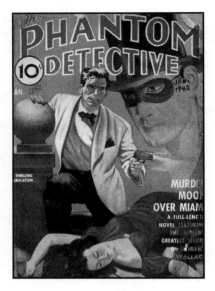

Another fairly good adventure that would have made a terrific Doc Savage story in which modern-day pirates are smuggling illegal aliens, dope, and jewels into America through an island cay off Florida shores. Actually, the smuggled items would be released while still at sea, but the water currents were naturally strongly attracted towards the cay, so everything ended up on the island—including murdered illegal aliens.

Besides the smuggling business, the mastermind also wanted a certain convict released from prison, so that he could uncover a hidden treasure that the convict hid in the area. By framing the Iron Judge's son, he hoped to ensure the early release of the convict.

Living among the swamp people is a white man who is also hiding from civilization—a man who has escaped from prison and is now treating the sick and injured among the swamp angels—natives who live off the cays.

Notes: This story had a lot of similarities to "Dealers in Death" (July 1936), but I believe that Donovan only borrowed some of the previous plot devices from that story. In one scene, everyone ends up in the swamps with the gators and snakes, taken almost straight from the earlier novel; cruisers the *Pelican* and the *Tempest;* people have fish-belly eyes; okay; his fists beat a tattoo; author lets us hear what others are thinking, not just the Phantom; "pony up for protection"; the Phantom uses ventriloquism to make his voice appear to come from near someone else; bony featured; tugged the lobe of his left ear; small spring-operated torpedos filled with thermite; marblelike eyes; a man has a bony face; one man uses a blow pipe; angry vituperation; a lot of similarities to the stories "Money Mad Murders" (November 1939) and "Murder Calls the Phantom" (March 1941).

108. STREAMLINED MURDER

V38 #2—February 1942
Written by Laurence Donovan

Place: New York City; Oldsville,NJ

Main characters: Jacklin Armstead, Claudia Ramer, Lara Neva Armstead, Curtis Lesher, Andrew Hamm, Adrian Parsons, Richard Curtis Van Loan/the Phantom, Frank Havens, Inspector Thomas Gregg, Muriel Havens, Chip Dorlan, Sam Thomas, Steve Huston, Abdul Abasha, Jasper Briggs, Stevens, Jennings, Martha, Sgt. Ripley (New Jersey), Judge Thurston Jones, Gorman Jones, Harry Stivers, Tanuko, Tom Wilkins, Kono, Aunt Dora—Dorothy Macklin Armstead

Apes guarding a silk magnate's mansion, carrying machine guns and acting almost human! The silk magnate is murdered on a train heading for New York City and a date with Frank Havens, but he had wired ahead, asking to have the Phantom Detective meet him as quickly as possible. The Phantom actually meets the train and boards it while still in route, but too late to save the silk magnate from being murdered. The Phantom reminded me a lot of Doc Savage as he entered the murder scene on the train!

From the train the scene swiftly switches to the mill town, and the large estate patrolled by the armed apes.

Millions are at stake, as a phony will leaves the fortune in the hands of a mysterious woman. It is up to the Phantom to prove the crime and unmask the super murderer. In a fierce battle at the end, the mansion is burned to the ground while the apes battle the mobsters, and the Phantom chases the mastermind to a showdown.

Notes: Again, the similarities to the Ralph Oppenheim story as well as Donovan; a green-eyed vamp; marblelike eyes; tugged the lobe of his left ear; the Phantom calls Frank, "Mr. Havens"; the automatic jetted flame; the rod rocketed; a newspaper, the *Comet;* the car slowed; "Holy cow!"; thermite used; Great glory; orangutan and other apes; the Phantom visits the office of one suspect, knocks him out and searches the office for clues—again, the throwback to Oppenheim.

109. ARSENALS OF DEATH

V38 #3—April 1942
Written by unknown; possibly George A. McDonald

Place: Adamsburg, New England; New York City; Henger, ME; Diana Springs, NY

Main characters: The Stopper, Police Commissioner Iverness, Mayor Lambert, Simeon Stillson, Cy Bisbee, "Big Tony" Alberto, Richard Curtis Van Loan/the Phantom, Major Pickford, Frank Havens, Harold Hickerson, Steve Huston, "Battling" Bob Walling, Daniel Rouse, Major Robert Sheridan Walling (same as "Battling" Bob Walling), Dr. Paul Bendix, Capt. Talbot (state police), John Sheldon, Scanlon, Alfred Sanderson, Tom Lennox, Zeb Adams, "Rubber" Rizzi, "Smiling" Tim O'Dowd, Gallo, Muriel Havens, Lefty, Pritchard, Crow, J. Hamilton Enders, Perkins, Valerie Enders Rouse, Striecker, John B. Halburtson, Pete, Sammy, Bill, Albert Cunningham, Mike, E. J. Birney, Thomas Edward Rouse, Pinky Arnst, Joe, Alexander MacLeish, Brabb, Thorson, Inspector Gregg, Titurka, Buttsy, Tony, Jowett, Mary Hobbs, Reginald Koritz, Kirk Latham, Gladstone, Hughes, Spider, Costello

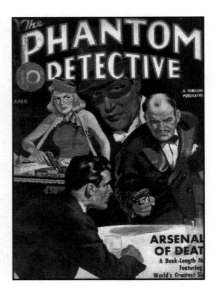

Defense plants are being sabotaged. The Phantom is called into the case and assumes the identity of Major Walling, which he uses throughout the case. In fact, the story is almost over (only 20 pages remaining) before the crooks learn that they are fighting the Phantom.

Notes: A strange story, in that it could have been originally intended as a Dan Fowler adventure. For instance, Frank Havens, the Phantom, Muriel and Steve all acted a little too such like the Director, Dan Fowler, Sally Vane and Larry Kendal. It is very possible that this author was turning out Dan Fowler stories during this time, or had in the past. Only Frank Havens knows about Dr. Bendix and the secret warehouse—but Steve Huston also knew this in the last story; the Riverside Chemical Company; guns played a rat-a-tat-tat; okay; trebly menacing; Van owns hunting lodges as well as a country estate where he keeps a string of championship polo ponies; red signal light summons the Phantom—first time this is used in over a year as part of the story; Dr. Bendix's warehouse door automatically opens at particular sound of the Phantom's car horn; fella; he said a loud "Oof!"; Grand Hotel; spells socks as "sox"; blown to perdition; the Standard Nautical Instruments Company; Murray Plaza Hotel; tugged the lobe of his left ear; stamp collecting is mentioned; the Phantom calls Frank, "Mr. Havens"; Muriel saves Steve and the Phantom; while the mastermind is in local area, he leaves record of his message in another area, and has a henchman there contact the Phantom from out of town; this story is very likely by the same author who wrote the "The Phantom's Greatest Gamble" (January 1941). I have a strong feeling that this author was probably writing Dan Fowler between January 1941 and April 1942. There are several possibilities, if this is correct.

Availability: *Arsenals of Death* (published by Jim Hanos, 1985).

110. MURDER MAKES A MOVIE

V39 #1—June 1942
Written by unknown; possibly Whitney Ellsworth

Place: New York City; Hollywood, CA

Main characters: The Masks, Sam Garden, Dr. Morton Haycraft, "Sonny" Michael Shawn, Lenny Mitchell, Frank Havens, Mr. Neery, Lupo, Richard Curtis Van Loan/the Phantom, Adrian Welch, Pierre Montat, Herb Lloyd, Henry Engle, Rita Craig, Don Marchand, Capt. Lewes, Doc Hones, Teddy Byron, Mick Crocker, Steve Huston, Chip Dorlan, Rauss, Teller, Winken, Lefty, Shag, Pierre Andrus, Carter Masefield, Anton Derek, Murphy, Opal, A. Adamson, Miles Shafton, George Convers, Samuel Grant, Muggs, Angus McDonald

1933
1934
1935
1936
1937
1938
1939
1940
1941
1942
1943
1944
1945
1946
1947
1948
1949
1950
1951
1952
1953

The upcoming filming of a fact-based movie concerning the theft of two million dollars in gold four years in the past brings on a wave of murder and torture. The Phantom learns that five men had actually taken part in the robbery, but one of them was unknown to the other four. After the robbery, the unknown man got away with all of the gold, and the other four were left with nothing.

Now, clues appear that lead the four men to believe that their unknown leader of four years' previous was a member of the team putting the planned film together. They head for Hollywood where the filming is in process, and hope to find the fifth man on the set of the movie. But now it appears that there may be a sixth man involved, pitting the other five men against each other.

Notes: I sure wanted to assign this one to Wayne Rogers, as it contained a very similar scene to another of his novels, but I just couldn't detect his writing style from the earlier story. It appears that this is a new author to the series. If it is a previous author, I could not recognize the style. One suspect is a *Hollywood Reporter* columnist; Superpix Films; Golconda Theater, "March of Crime" series of films, the current one being titled "Drake's Treasure"; their latest film is titled, "King Solomon's Gold"; the Metropolitan Museum of Antiquities; a yacht, the *Metromu;* the car ghosted to the curb; "is-it, ain't-it stuff"; ballyhoo; okay; the *Clarion* Tower is the building where the *Clarion* newspaper office is located; "all right, all right"; Lynx-eyed; Baron Munchhausen is mentioned—seems I do recall this character coming up once before; "Um-m-m"; the Purple Topper; ferret eyes; Havens has a secret apartment (page 48 of story); there's a "lop-eared" character in the story; "Holy Smoke!"; the *Los Angeles Blade, Clarion's* West Coast paper; the Phantom socks a cop on the jaw, then is allowed to meet the cop later and apologize; fellow; "Who was he, heh?" At first I wanted to assign this to Greenberg, but it just didn't fit his writing.

1933

1934

1935

1936

1937

1938

1939

1940

1941

1942

1943

1944

1945

1946

1947

1948

1949

1950

1951

1952

1953

Availability: *Murder Makes a Movie* (published by Jim Hanos, 1985).

111. THE MEDIEVAL MURDERS

V39 #2—July 1942
Written by Henry Kuttner

Place: Near New York City

Main characters: The Jester, Alex Zenarion, Hilary Zenarion, Dirk Haggard, Giles Sadler, Norwood Decker, Austin Cameron, Jock Wister, Arn Svendson, Philip Rugg, Diana Rugg, Frank Havens, Richard Curtis Van Loan/the Phantom, Police Commissioner Inverness, Deacon, Gomez, Limey, Pierre, Blackie, Martha, Capt. Morrissey (Cape Cod), O'Brien, Steve Huston (telephone only), Dr. Paul Bendix, Wu Shun, Bull, Wilkins, Inspector Underhill, Steven Courtley

A vengeful old man bequeaths a castle and ancient torture devices to a group of men that he holds a grudge against. It is a worthless old castle, but somewhere a king's ransom in diamonds is hidden away, and whoever eventually ends up with the castle will inherit the fortune in gems.

Notes: One man is a hunchback; the Sun King's diamonds; the *Clarion* signal light is mentioned; forewarned is forearmed; motion picture, with sound, is left by the dead man to give instructions about his will, so that the heirs will hear it from his own voice; Poitiers Tapestry; one man is killed in a moat, another by crossbow, and one on a torture rack; Jumping Jehosephat!; okay; he put his hand on the Phantom's knee; a man has a horse-like face; unctuously; "I'll push off"; one minute sounds western, the next science fiction—with a touch of adventure; Van has blue eyes, light hair; the Phantom's disguise is penetrated because his shoes were black instead of brown—the man he was impersonating wore brown shoes; extempore knife; cigarette case contains a make-up kit; cacophony of sound; a nyctalops, a person who can see in the dark; crook's watch fires a mercy bullet. This story appeared to be more a Kuttner story than did his first *Phantom* story, "The Sabotage Murders" (July 1941) but was not quite as good as his previous entry.

Availability: *Action Adventure Stories* #134 (published by Fading Shadows, Inc., 2004).

112. MURDER CUTS DIAMONDS

V39 #3—September 1942
Written by Laurence Donovan

Place: New York City

Main characters: Mike Ryan, Harry Young, Rufus Lemore, Lafe Grimes, Kenneth Wilson, Martha, Ronald Donaldson, Inspector Thomas Gregg, Richard Curtis Van Loan/the Phantom, Cort Hanlon, Douglas Harvey, Montgomery Tremont Lathan, Mary, Chip Dorlan, Marshall Green, McCarthy, Danny, Sonny Blade, Katy, Bingham, Jones, Pat O'Hara, Frank Havens (telephone only), Steve Huston, Ann Brinkley, Scabrow, Patterson, "Easy Money" Hogan, Briggs, Alfredo, Sands Riker, Sally Thorpe, Butch Mason, Tappy, Rod Clark, Slug Bolton, Burney, Jay Rockham, Hal Drake, Wilton Andrews, Spike, Dr. Paul Bendix, Arthur Grimes, Clifton Randall

A crime takes place, a suspect is captured, he goes on trial, and is finally convicted of murder. Several months pass while the Phantom closely watches the case. He believes the suspect is innocent and is investigating when he's not on other cases.

This could very easily have originated as a Black Bat adventure, with Tony Quinn involved in the trial where is must prove the suspect guilty while the Black Bat tries to prove him innocent. The oddity is that this novel appears at the same time as Donovan's first Black Bat story is published. (It appears that Donovan is about to be dropped from the *Phantom Detective* stories, and may have been turning his attention to the Black Bat series in hopes of writing those adventures full time.)

This case revolves around a large department store, and in particular the jewelry section. Diamonds are being stolen elsewhere and then are sold through the department store as honest gems. The owner is kept drugged while an impostor takes his place.

Meanwhile, the owner's adopted daughter thinks someone has framed her real father for a murder and moves out of her home. The head of store security is in love with her and also investigates the crimes that have sent her real father to jail.

Notes: This is probably by Donovan, but seems like a new author at times. Maybe due to the oddity of the Black Bat similarities. Okay; jewels, the "Necklace of Stars"; sunfish eyes; wheat-colored hair; a killer uses an air gun to shoot deadly darts; one killer uses a cane to dope victims through a poisoned tip; he has "a date with a colleen"; woman has green eyes; the Easy Money Club; the Glitter Gang; baleful glances; tugged the lobe of his left ear; "Great Glory!"

Availability: *Murder Cuts Diamonds* (published by Jim Hanos, 1985).

1933
1934
1935
1936
1937
1938
1939
1940
1941
1942
1943
1944
1945
1946
1947
1948
1949
1950
1951
1952
1953

113. DEATH TO THE LAUGHING CLOWN

V40 #1—October 1942
Written by Laurence Donovan

Place: New York City; Mid City

Main characters: The Laughing Clown, Mark Raines, Charlie Monson, Digby Jains, Winkilmer, John Godfrey, Fancy Pants, Jules Crinon, Bromley Kent, Forrest Sawyer, Boxer, Frank Havens, Muriel Havens, Richard Curtis Van Loan/the Phantom, Steve Huston, Chip Dorlan, Jack Haggerty, Johnny Merrick, Chuck, Jake Parsell, Harry, Blackie, Burt Myers, Capt. Neilson, Anderson, Ben Harris, Logan Reid, Mack Howard, Julian Embonet, Peter Simms, Mitta, Otto Lacher, Colonel Brett, Nels, Hank Stevenson, Bert Jennings, Sam Howly, Tiny, Shack, Lou, Rig, Pete

DEATH TO THE LAUGHING CLOWN
A FULL-LENGTH NOVEL FEATURING THE WORLD'S GREATEST SLEUTH
BY ROBERT WALLACE

In a story with the same plot as "The Phantom and the Melody Murders" (September 1940), the scene is changed from the music industry to the scene of a large fair. Supposedly, a madman is wearing the costume of a clown to commit murder and thefts.

At the bottom of the case is a Nazi plot to smuggle real jewels and art masterpieces into America and sell them for riches. On the display at the fair, they appear to be mere fakes of the originals, but they are real.

There are two clowns, one who is really insane, and they are after extortion money. But the mastermind takes over his role as clown for his own schemes.

Notes: Here we have yet another strange oddity. This story has strong similarities to the Charles Greenberg story, "The Phantom and the Melody Murders," yet this one isn't on his records. A silly ass; the Phantom calls Frank, "Mr. Havens"; Frank, even when alone, calls him "Phantom"; "Carnival of Murder"; Errol-Duffy Fireworks Co.; "Wha-a-at?"; fellow; one man is dressed all in gray, with gray complexion, etc—The Whisperer?; piggy eyes; tugged the lobe of his left ear; has a knife blade hidden in heel of shoe; uses nerve center pressure; and "Carnival of Melody"; wild cacophony; a debacle; clown uses poison darts to kill his victims.

114. BILLION DOLLAR BLITZ

V40 #2—December 1942
Written by unknown; possibly Joe Archibald or George A. McDonald

Place: New York City

Main characters: Mr. A, Thomas Kenney, Frank Testor, "Dingo" Mack, Steve Huston, Frank Havens, Billy Brophy, Dave Delancey, Leonard Barton, S. J. Manning, Slinky, Inspector Gregg, Maurice Thorberg, Richard

Curtis Van Loan/the Phantom, Herbert J. Walsh, Tony Lugiano, Linda Drake, Pete Dominick, Lefty Ricci, Muriel Havens, Dr. Bendix, Gunner McGlone, "Mousy" Bliven, Ralphy Mack, Joe, Gaffy Halloran, Mr. Martin, John Carmichael, Sully, Quincy Veblen, Matthews Hargraves, Alice Dyer Putnam, Stahmer, O'Shea, Ike, Sam Faversham, Esterbrook, MacGowan, Carr, Kulak, Mathilda Dwyer, Sally Sherman, Rosa Walden Smith, Grover Cleveland Adler, Christopher Smith, Lauderbach, Police Commissioner Iverness (mentioned)

One of the best stories during this period, there is a deep scheme to counterfeit money, rare stamps and bonds in a plan to rake in millions in profit!

Strangely, a stage play is involved, as well as people associated with the stage production. The story uses the same plot as that of "Murder Stalks a Billion" (December 1941) as well as brings to mind two other stories, "Double-Stamped Doom" (October 1937), because of the rare stamp counterfeiting, and "Cavalcade of Death" (August 1937), in which the alias of Gunner McGlone is once again used as a disguise instead of merely mentioned. I'm guessing this is a new author, and that he merely read previous stories for ideas. It doesn't sound like Laurence Donovan's writing.

Notes: The Bernhardt Building; okay; red-lipped chorines; Lucky 13 Club; stage show, "Heads High"; stamp collecting; "You've got maxie"; the Blue Island mob; the Gunner McGlone disguise was last used in "Cavalcade of Death"; fella; the *Clarion* signal light is used to call the Phantom; Huston knows the Bendix warehouse; the *Washington Globe*; Phantom calls Frank, "Mr. Havens"; the Hunterdon Theater.

115. MURDER MAKES THE BETS

V40 #3—January 1943
Written by Charles Greenberg

Place: New York City

Main characters: The Dealer, Dean Powell, "Trigger" Lawton, Joe Nutley, "Tex" Martin, Ed Kelly, "Rocky" Brett, "Big Money" Harper, Bill Kruger, Frank Havens, Richard Curtis Van Loan/the Phantom, Len Jarret, Martin Brawley, General William Phillips, Slim, Chick Foley, Bill, Jeff Kelly, Jimmy, Henry Drake, Fred Torrence, Norwood Palmer, Calvin Trent, Paddy Burke, Doc Harmond, O'Brien, Lambert, Mr. Gray, Tierney, Murphy, Jimmy Doyle, Hurley, Red, Gerry, Hugo

A mastermind is after profit in the sports world by fixing races, boxing matches, etc. The Phantom is called when Dean Powell, sports columnist

1933
1934
1935
1936
1937
1938
1939
1940
1941
1942
1943
1944
1945
1946
1947
1948
1949
1950
1951
1952
1953

1933

1934

1935

1936

1937

1938

1939

1940

1941

1942

1943

1944

1945

1946

1947

1948

1949

1950

1951

1952

1953

for the *Clarion,* uncovers the hint about the mysterious "Dealer."

A fairly good story, with the exception of most of the main characters being left out. Also, the alias of "Mr. Gray" is used again, the first time since "The Phantom and the Melody Murders" (September 1940), a story written by Charles Greenberg. However, the character of Dean Powell actually takes the place of Steve Huston. In a later story by this same author, Steve Huston is in a similar storyline that had been used for Dean Powell.

Notes: This is probably the first in a new run of stories by Charles Greenberg, though there is a possibility that the author wrote a couple just prior to this entry, as there are similarities and a few question marks. But it's a certainty that the next five entries are his; it strangely sounds familiar one minute, and not the next minute; none of the regulars are in this story, which is odd in itself; okay; paradoxically; right there and then; once, twice; Holy smoke; gimlet eyes; this author uses the word "affectation" a lot; a bitter pill to swallow; Apartment 2D; his Adam apple bobbed crazily; uses some religious quotes; a crook becomes a beastlike thing on hands and knees—which will be used often by this author, as one of the crooks is shot by the Phantom, he will go down to all fours, bringing about this quote.

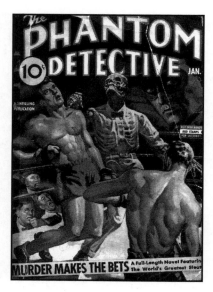

116. STONES OF SATAN

V41 #1—March 1943
Written by Charles Greenberg

Place: New York City

Main characters: The Satan, Karl Schiller, Lippy Gilman, Steve Huston, Thomas Eldridge, Flo Jarbeau, Florence Jarbouski, Frank Havens, Muriel Havens, Richard Curtis Van Loan/the Phantom, Pete, Jerry, Red, Pat, "Loony" Mary, Jimmy, Chick, Emil Kroft, George Donovan, Mr. Gray, Lionel Davenport, George Hardy, Kelly, Harrigan, Horace Thayer, Jackson Brennan, Ralph Foley, Oscar Hammet, Edmund Chaney, Pat Shelby, Eddie, Inspector Gregg, Haggerty, Robert, Nick, Otto, Ken Brady, Slim, Charley, Bill, Lefty, Tony

African diamonds have been brought into America. Now a super crook plans on taking control of a useless diamond mine in Arkansas, then salt the stolen diamonds into this mine. He will make millions.

But one man discovers the African diamonds and knows the jewels did not come from the Arkansas mine. The mastermind has him killed, but Steve Huston is a witness to the murder and discovers the strange diamonds. He contacts the Phantom with his discovery.

Notes: Many of the incidents from this novel appeared in Greenberg's "The Yacht Club Murders" (January 1939); okay; green eyes; man has a bony face; crime's hydra head; Leaping Lena; the Angel of Death; tugged the lobe of his left ear; Woodward Cemetery; baleful eyes; a crook becomes a beastlike thing on hands and knees; *S.S. Daniel Clyden*; bony, elongated face; the Sandra Mine; gunfight in a cemetery; a death by viper—actually, an African pit, or Gaboon viper; right there and then; Muriel is kidnapped to curtail the Phantom's investigation; the Phantom calls Frank, "Mr. Havens"; the Phantom uses the identity of Steve Huston—had also done that with Dean Powell in last story; crook has a knife he calls "Nellie" inside his tie; mastermind is dressed like a giant bat.

Availability: *Phantom Detective* #17 (published by Corinth Regency, 1966), *Wildside Pulp Classics: Phantom Detective #116* (published by Wildside Press, 2005).

117. MURDER MONEY

V41 #2—April 1943
Written by Charles Greenberg

Place: New York City; North City, NY

Main characters: The Lynx, Otto Warner, Lola Forrester, Richard Curtis Van Loan/the Phantom, Frank Havens, Police Chief Pat Morris, Steve Huston, Chris Luding, Tony, Red, Fritz, Rosie, Joe, Smitty, Anson Burr, Ronnie Morris, Jeffery Clark, Fred Mason, Judge Horace G. Bentley, Whitey, Martin Whittier, Harvey Trummer, Edmund Scott, Tom Craig, Arch Riley, Hubert Greeley, Wallace Colby, Nickie, Grace, Ethel Warren Bentley, Joan Ryder, Edith Warren, Madame de Sylva, Chick, Nick

A political race in North City, plus a new crime wave, involves

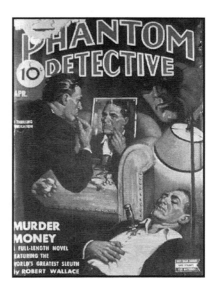

1933
1934
1935
1936
1937
1938
1939
1940
1941
1942
1943
1944
1945
1946
1947
1948
1949
1950
1951
1952
1953

1933

1934

1935

1936

1937

1938

1939

1940

1941

1942

1943

1944

1945

1946

1947

1948

1949

1950

1951

1952

1953

murder and counterfeiting. There is a love triangle, and the mastermind hopes to double-cross everyone.

At the bottom of the mess, two local leaders are being blackmailed to keep them under control, but the mastermind wants the evidence the blackmailer holds against the political bosses for his own purposes of control. The evidence turns out to be signed confessions.

Notes: A trap in which the Phantom is locked in a cistern, filling with water, is straight out of Greenberg's trap used in "Murder at the Circus" (May 1939), in which a water tower was used instead of a cistern; Van calls Frank, "Mr. Havens"; okay; vehicle parked next to a wall is really a secret entrance to the crooks' hideout—often used in Greenberg's novels; the Alhambra Club; carries a .45; people clip when they speak; tugs the lobe of his left ear; political party called the Progressive Party; no *Clarion* call; Play Land; he made a sibilant sound through his teeth; knowledge of nerve centers; Apartment 3F; green-eyed vamp; "It looks like I rang the bell"—meaning he was right in something; once, twice, three times.

Availability: *Phantom Detective #15* (published by Corinth Regency, 1966).

118. DEATH IN THE DESERT
V41 #3—June 1943
Written by Charles Greenberg

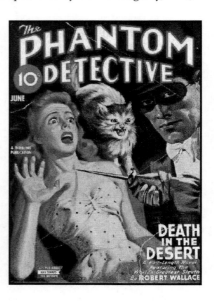

Place: New York City; Yuma, AZ; Arizona desert area; Hammond, AZ (ghost town)

Main characters: The Oracle, Tim "Pay Strike" Hardy, Big Jake Hollander, Chris Mitchell, Eva Koroski Correl, Harkness, Barton Baxter, Warner, Warren Taylor, Martha Marshall, Floyd Stewart, Roy Montague, Kay Bronson, Hugo Chenery, Claude Withering, Richard Curtis Van Loan/the Phantom, Frank Havens, Andy Shaw, Igor Kroft, Hugh Fontaine, Scotty, Mr. Gray, Lin, Inspector Gregg, Horace Hobson, Bill Hanley, Laughing Wolf, Lefty, Mike Brennan, Jeff, Duffy, Herman, Oscar "the Ape," "Denver" Charley Mannix, Sheriff McVane (Yuma), Police Chief Bill Lambert (Yuma), Ferguson

In a story strictly a re-write of Charles Greenberg's "The Movie Lot Murders" (May 1938), only much better, the Phantom accompanies a movie crew to the Arizona desert where the filming of a new movie is to be set.

Love triangles, millions in jewels, hidden caves beneath the hot desert, a weather-hardened old man, a team of dogs, fighting Apaches, plus the Phantom, all fight against prisoners who have escaped from an area prison. All that, and he must also uncover the secret identity of the Oracle.

Notes: The Apollo Productions; Van calls Frank, "Mr. Havens"; green-eyed vamp, pantherish with nine pet cats; carried a .45; okay; he whispered sibilantly; Jeepers!; crook calls his gun, "Pete"; people speak in clips; movie studio is filming "Arizona Flo"; a bitter pill to swallow; one man is a small dwarf; so many similarities to Charles Greenberg, no one else.

Availability: *Action Adventure Stories* #140 (published by Fading Shadows, Inc., 2004).

119. THE RED BISHOP MURDERS

V42 #1—August 1943
Written by Charles Greenberg

Place: New York City; Kent, PA

Main characters: The Black Bishop of Toulon, the Bishop, or the Red Bishop, Matt Tasker, Andy Malloy, Chick O'Keefe, Ramon Gonzales, Johnny Kane, Dr. John Gerry, Tommy Gerry, Margaret, Richard Curtis Van Loan/the Phantom, Frank Havens, Judson, Steve Huston, Mike Finnegan, Norman Parrish, Berger, Jonathan Lathrop, Dan Boylen, Hugh Markham, Joe, Doc Hugh Ferguson, Mr. Gray, Police Chief Gilbert (Kent, PA), Sam Dickson, Henry Bevins, Harvey Flynn, Ed Haley, Philip Morley, Hennessy, Bill Jamison, Jerry, Anita, Oscar "the Ape" Weimar

Another good story, this one deals with government contracts in factories. But one man wants it all. However, he needs money to obtain control over the factories. He hires gangsters who are hiding out in his area, with promises to change their faces through plastic surgery.

When he kidnaps the plastic surgeon in New York City, it brings the Phantom onto the scene. Clues point him to another town, where the Phantom and Steve Huston unravel the latest mystery.

The mastermind has a gun phobia that eventually points to him as the mastermind. All of Greenberg's clues are in the story, the romantic interest of a married woman for the mastermind, as well as many others.

Notes: Here and now; likes to use "affectation" a lot; Apartment 2B; once, twice, three times; okay; a man is bony faced; a green eyed vamp.

120. THE BLACK MARKET MURDERS

V42 #2—October 1943
Written by Charles Greenberg

Place: New York City

1933
1934
1935
1936
1937
1938
1939
1940
1941
1942
1943
1944
1945
1946
1947
1948
1949
1950
1951
1952
1953

1933

1934

1935

1936

1937

1938

1939

1940

1941

1942

1943

1944

1945

1946

1947

1948

1949

1950

1951

1952

1953

Main characters: The Black Trader, Steve Huston, Frank Havens (telephone), Jensen, Keller, Harry Randall, Candy, Forrestor, McPhail, Patricia Wiley, Richard Curtis Van Loan/the Phantom, George, Mr. Gray, Tony Matteo, Wally Regan, Lt. Harkness, Pat Connoly, Weimar, Jeremiah Regan, Christopher Burnett, Stephen Baxter, Edwards, Pat Gleason, Paul Millard, Hugo Zimmer, Emily, Doc, Gunner Malone (mentioned, but author mixes up the name—it should have been Gunner McGlone), Dave Fletcher, Kelly, Kent, Andy

Charles Greenberg closes out this segment. All good entries, and he will be back. In this one, a masked mastermind is running black market merchandise across America.

When Steve Huston stumbles on clues that point to an unknown person known only as the Black Trader, he runs a series of articles in the *Clarion* about the mysterious individual. The Black Trader sends his goons who beat Steve up pretty badly. When he comes to, he phones his boss, Frank Havens, and asks for help from the Phantom. The story is almost a complete re-write of "Murder Makes the Bets" (January 1943) only with Steve Huston replacing Dean Powell from that story.

Notes: Steve's newspaper column, "You Should Know This, Mr. Citizen"; okay; Club Lido; the word "affectation" again; tugged the lobe of his left ear; the Phantom has a hideout at 139 Charles Street; girl has green, slanted eyes; "She was whistling in the dark," figuratively speaking; here and there; gimlet-like, angry eyes; Steve Huston has a punctured ear drum that kept him out of uniformed service; Washington had refused to allow the Phantom to enter the service, telling him to notify Washington if his name ever came up in selective service; a man has a bony face.

1933

1934

1935

1936

1937

1938

1939

1940

1941

1942

1943

1944

1945

1946

1947

1948

1949

1950

1951

1952

1953

CHAPTER III, SECTION H

THE FINAL TEN YEARS: 1943-1953

A CTUALLY, THE BEGINNING of the last ten years was covered
in the last segment, with the January 1943 issue, "Murder Makes the
Bets," written by Charles Greenberg. He was a good writer, but his first six stories (January, March, April, June, August & October 1943) were really nothing
more than re-writes of earlier stories—or at least story plots. The author has
a favorite scene in his novels where a gangster will go down (after being shot,
usually) to hands and knees, and became "animal-like."

Beginning with this current segment, Norman Daniels turns in seven of
the first eight stories, then we have a new entry by Charles Greenberg, and the
next author in line begins with the December 1944 story, "Murder of a Marionette." Norman Daniels' stories are very important at this junction because
his stories, and those of Charles Greenberg, will be big influences on this new
author! This new author's stories will run so close to Daniels' own work, and
those of Greenberg, that at times it is hard to separate the three. The same plot
devices suddenly appear, with similar stories. And to add more confusion, the
editors at Standard Magazines forced some new gimmicks into the series; this
was done for continuity, and worked very well. So we have three authors using the same plot devices, while working in the new continuity. It fleshed out
The Phantom Detective, kept the plots balanced, created some good stories, but
made it terribly hard to separate the authors at times.

For a long time I thought the new author was R. T. M. Scott (due to certain clues), but after getting further into the final stories in which author C.S.
Montayne was involved, I read the Fall 1949 story, "The Black Ball of Death,"
in which Montayne wrote the first half of the story before falling dead over
his typewriter, and was completed by Daniels. This gave me the clue that I
needed to identify the author in question as Montayne. The author liked to use
the phrase "shape of shadow" in his story. He would insert this phrase, even
to using it in the chapter headings! Other forms of this phrase he used were
"dancing shadows," and "weaving shadows." C.S. Montayne also added initials
to "Mr. Grey," an alias of the Phantom—he added the initials of "C. S." and
"C. W." for Charles W. Grey.

For a while I thought that maybe C.S. Montayne could have been rewriting

1933

1934

1935

1936

1937

1938

1939

1940

1941

1942

1943

1944

1945

1946

1947

1948

1949

1950

1951

1952

1953

those Charles Greenberg stories, too. But he isn't, I don't think. In fact, after Montayne's death—his last complete novel was "Servant of Satan" (March 1949) (remember Greenberg's "Stones of Satan," March 1943?)—I think Greenberg returns with the Fall 1950 entry of "Homicide Town." This was his last story, as well. The story, "Murder Set to Music" (Summer 1949), was also taken from a plot by Montayne, but completed by someone else—maybe an editor at Standard. I would strongly suspect Sam Merwin Jr., but I have no proof of this.

A final curiosity concerning Greenberg. He liked to give names to gangster's weapons; knives would be named Mike or something similar, and guns names Nellie, or something else. Because of this oddity, I was immediately reminded of Paul Ernst's *Avenger* series, where that character carried Ike and Mike, a gun and a knife. However, I've been reading *The Avenger* series off and on, and have yet to encounter gangsters becoming "animal-like, on hands and knees."

The last mystery author in 1952 and 1953 is easily identified. He is Stewart Sterling (real name Prentice Winchell), who also wrote the last published Black Bat and Spider novels. The new editor for the Phantom and Black Bat stories at Standard—Norman Daniels told me it was a woman—wanted sex in the stories, and Stewart Sterling was happy to oblige. For a while I was a little confused because of one important incident (I had already picked Sterling for several reasons, but couldn't understand this one reference), in which the Phantom for one minute was called "the Shadow!" I had to wonder if my clues were wrong, and maybe this author was one of the *Shadow* authors—like Bruce Elliott or Ted Tinsley. I remained confused until I found out that Stewart Sterling was also writing *Shadow* scripts for the radio! Another thing that had me pulling my hair was the fact that Sterling created a character named Andy, and Greenberg used a character named Andy a lot!

One last comment before we look at the last ten years of stories. If the reader will refer to the novels, "The Tidewater Murders" (November 1946), who I have designated Greenberg, and to "Murder for Millions" (June 1945), who I have designated as by C.S. Montayne, in the first, we have a gangster going down to hands and knees, animal-like, and in the second we have the phrase, "shape of shadow." Pretty obvious, isn't it? Well, now look at the names of the characters in the two stories. See the repeat in names? Not so conclusive now. Wouldn't you think—because of the same character names—that they were written by the same author? I would. But I can't. Not if I keep in mind the different clues to the two authors in question, Montayne and Greenberg. I don't have the answer.

Now, let's look at the final novels:

121. MURDER UNDER THE BIG TOP
V42 #3—December 1943
Written by Norman A. Daniels

Place: New York City; Fairmont, NY

Main characters: Leon Masterson, Joe, Lt. Bradley (Fairmont), Conner, Frank Havens, Richard Curtis Van Loan/the Phantom, Joe Smith, Tiny, "Lucky" Sayles, Mike Tanner, Joe Cortazar, Pop Leeds, Ann Newton, Billy Huber, Clancy, Pamela Clark, Armando (Phantom alias), Dutch Nevard, Santora, Ray Stossel, Steve Huston, Zorita, Elizabeth Clark

Gambling houses open up around a circus town. When there are several strange murders, the Phantom enters the case, disguised as a circus roustabout. But when the character he is playing is suspected of one of the murders, he is forced to take on a new identity. Becoming Armando, a ventriloquist, he continues his investigation within the circus.

It appears that freaks are doing the killing—a midget, an incredibly thin man, and a circus strong man. Plus, most murders are done with throwing knives, another clue to circus people, as there is a famous knife thrower connected to the big top.

But it turns out that the killer, besides controlling the gambling in town, also hates the circus for the deaths of his parents many years in the past.

Notes: This is pretty mach a re-write of Daniels' "The Circus Murders" (March 1936); the Phantom and the killer swing on trapeze above the floor—similar to the incident in "The Circus Murders," where the Phantom fought with the Crimson Clown high above the floor on trapeze swings; Frank Havens even calls the case, "the circus murders"; Carmody Street; Blackie, a black panther; the killer wears all black, including a hood, and appears to be an acrobat; the Phantom and the killer have a knife fight at one point, using throwing knives as rapiers; the Cabelus-Peters Circus; "Great glory!"; he spoke tartly; Huston comes into the action towards the end.

Availability: *Phantom Detective* #7 (published by Corinth Regency, 1965).

122. MURDER OF A PLASTER SAINT

V43 #1—February 1944
Written by Norman A. Daniels

Place: New York City; Bradford, CT; Toledo, OH

Main characters: Frank Havens, Muriel Havens, Tom Sayre, Rufus Rutledge, Constable Jim Kearny, Andrew Rutledge, Richard Curtis Van Loan/the Phantom, Dr. A. Blanding, Dr. Clay, Dr. Bendix, Mrs. Curtin, Moose, Otto Oberthaler, Lt. Brady (State Police), Peter Lakeland, Steve Huston (telephone), Max MacLeland, Samuel Martin,

1933
1934
1935
1936
1937
1938
1939
1940
1941
1942
1943
1944
1945
1946
1947
1948
1949
1950
1951
1952
1953

1933

1934

1935

1936

1937

1938

1939

1940

1941

1942

1943

1944

1945

1946

1947

1948

1949

1950

1951

1952

1953

Mrs. O'Connor, William Crane, Capt. Johnson (Toledo detective), George Nash, Mr. Brown, Lloyd Harrison

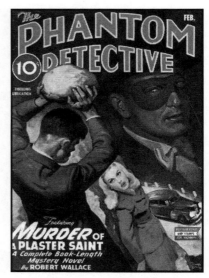

Frank Havens and his daughter Muriel are walking around town (Bradford) when they see a night watchman lying on the floor of a foundry. They break in and find the man is dead. Frank searches the body and finds a small plastic saint in a pocket. He recognizes the saint as the work of a famous sculptor in town and visits his heir to find out from the man's son that his father had been missing for several days.

When Frank Havens is attacked and severely beaten, and the plaster saint stolen, Muriel calls for the Phantom's help. When the Phantom arrives in Bradford, he finds yet another plaster saint, this one life-size, with a bullet hole where the heart would normally be on a living man.

A giant scam is at work, and is at the bottom of the case.

Notes: A man monitors a radio in the top of the *Clarion* Building, and calls the Phantom over the radio when he is needed—the Phantom has a receiving set in his car; okay; Frank Havens has a country home in Bradford; Muriel had played at the country home when she was a child; Muriel and the Phantom admit their attraction to each other during this case; Muriel is very active in the investigation.

123. THE RUBBER KNIFE MURDERS

V43 #2—April 1944
Written by Norman A. Daniels

Place: New York City

Main characters: Jim Henderson, Torchy Collins, Frank Havens, Richard Curtis Van Loan/the Phantom, Det. Lt. Brady (New York City), Dr. Bendix, Gene Atkins (F.B.I.), Suki, Jacoby, Edgar Ives, Claude Channings, Steve Huston, Jack Powell, Capt. Otto Ritt, Dooley, Rolin Hayes, Ben Foster, Kurt, Groot, Martha Channing, Van den Geer, Hans

Nazi spies and an American businessman with big plans. Price fixing within an American company brings a blackmail scheme into the affair, but this was little more than a red herring to draw the investigation away from a giant plot to bring art treasure from Europe into the USA, for sale at the highest price, to make money for Germany—and the American businessman.

The rubber knives that were used for killing? Actually, there was only one—

filled with pure mercury and frozen to solid metal. Once the knife was inside the warm body it would thaw out and become flexible once more. Other murders were committed by knives—real ones—then substituted with the rubber knives.

Notes: The red signal light is mentioned; tugged the lobe of his left ear; motion picture film used to show torture victims to their relatives.

124. THE HI-JACK MURDERS

V43 #3—June 1944
Written by Norman A. Daniels

Place: New York City

Main characters: Higgins, Miller, Paul, Les Bradley, Ralph Thurmond, Jim, Inspector Bailey, Al Gifford, Joe Hadley, "Spanish" Munoz, Bill, Dr. Bendix, Richard Curtis Van Loan/the Phantom, Frank Havens, Oliver Hadley, Martha, Frank Fabray, Shilly, Steve Huston, Osgood Stevenson, Lucian Swayne, Rocks Roper, Otto, Mike, Irene, Smitty, Muriel Havens (very minor role)

Old bootlegging men appear to be gathering for a renewal of their old racket. When a ship bringing illegal whiskey into America is hijacked, the whiskey stolen, and the crew murdered, the Phantom is called into the case by the Coast Guard.

The ship murder incident was rigged to look like a Nazi submarine was to blame for the killing, but the Phantom finds a clue that leads him to a bar in New York City, and the son of an old bootlegger.

Notes: Club Regal; Bendix is given some description in the story; the Phantom accidentally calls Frank, "sir," which isn't strange, but this could have been intended as a Dan Fowler story; okay; touched lobe of his left ear; radio sending set in the top of the *Clarion* Building, and is used to call the Phantom who has a receiving set in both his car and apartment;

1933

1934

1935

1936

1937

1938

1939

1940

1941

1942

1943

1944

1945

1946

1947

1948

1949

1950

1951

1952

1953

they "shot their bolts"—meaning they were finished; Inspector Bailey is a new character—why not Inspector Gregg, instead, unless this was originally scheduled as a Dan Fowler story?

125. THE BOOBY TRAP MURDERS

V44 #1—August 1944
Written by Norman A. Daniels

Place: New York City

Main characters: Fred Taylor, Frank Havens, Richard Curtis Van Loan/the Phantom, Mrs. Kalb, Sally Taylor, Wallace Gage, Peter Arnold, Lt. Brophy (New York City), Kirk Vernon, Don Carlyle, Robert Bonham, Harry Edmund, Cyrus McKay, Dr. Bendix, Michael Lynch, Mack, Frayne

Four years ago, a man had crossed a master criminal and left with a million dollars in loot. He entrusted the money to a friend, who hid it (tied it up) in valuable metals. When the master crook caught up with the man he killed him. But now he needs to find the valuable metals that the second man had bought and hidden with the ill-gotten millions.

After torturing and killing the second man, the mastermind now only has a clue to the whereabouts of the hidden loot. It is a race between the killer and The Phantom in finding the valuable metals. Plus, the master crook uses booby traps to kill his victims, so the Phantom must always be on the alert.

Notes: A radio sending set is atop the *Clarion* Building to call the Phantom who has a radio receiving unit in his apartment and car; Carmody Road.

126. MANSIONS OF DESPAIR

V44 #2—October 1944
Written by Norman A. Daniels

Place: New York City; Luana, FL (Hollywood, FL?)

Main characters: Lance Carter, Frank Havens, Richard Curtis Van Loan/the Phantom, Lyle Jackson, Paul Ross, Perry Dixon, Don Mallory, Kurt Otley, Mike, Joe, Dr. Bendix, Capt. Anderson (New York City), Bill Harmon, Mr. Lake, Jerry Bacon, Sheriff Cotesworth (Luana), Nancy Alyn, Anne, Scotty Henderson, Fogarty, Crazy Slade, Doc Bradbury, Dr. Blake, Tommy Jordan, Dade Qualen, Steve Huston (telephone), Jeff, Nick, Leach

Twenty years ago, several people connected to the movie industry had bought homes and estates in Florida, thinking the movie industry was going to settle in that area. When the industry settled in Hollywood, California instead, it left the estates almost worthless, and the people moved to California.

But one man decided to remain in Florida, hiding millions of dollars among the old homes somewhere that had been built on the land. Then he mysteriously disappeared—for twenty years!

But now he shows up again, claiming that he had lost his mind many years ago, and only now recovered his memory and remembered who he was. He is quickly captured by a gang and a policeman is killed. The Phantom is at a party where the crime takes place in New York City. But he believes the answers lie in the Florida location of the estates bought those many years ago.

Notes: Okay; a "long ago" crime—plot device often used by Daniels.

127. MURDER OF A MARIONETTE

V44 #3—December 1944
Written by C.S. Montayne

Place: New York City; Atlas Falls, NY; Soundview, NY

Main characters: Steve Huston, Garvey Henderson, Pietro Graselli, Joe Mars, Richard Curtis Van Loan/the Phantom, Mrs. Dixon, Bob, Julie Severne, Rosalinda, Chief of Police Babson (Westchester), Nelson Brady, Frank Havens, Joel Wickett, Sawl Argiewicz, Dan Bryer (F. B. I.), Miller Sandler, Pete, Patty Dexter, Marge, Mr. Walker, Eddie Wilson, Gus, Hugo Slade, Mike, Louis Earl, Roy Kenny, "Skip" Nolan, Dave Languer, Nicky Zaloff, Helen Wright, Inspector Gregg (mentioned), Juan, Gregory Jason, Berta, Rag, Gene, Dr. Bendix, Johnny Fowler, Tim, Turner, Arturo Ventner, O'Bryan, Chief of Police Redden (Soundview)

Smuggled jewels from war-torn France are being fenced in America. When Dick Van Loan hires a puppeteer show to perform at an orphanage, the girl dressed as a marionette is murdered during the performance, and the Phantom decides to investigate. And the intrigue involves the Phantom in even more murder. A man is dressed all in gray, and the Phantom believes him to be the

1933
1934
1935
1936
1937
1938
1939
1940
1941
1942
1943
1944
1945
1946
1947
1948
1949
1950
1951
1952
1953

mastermind.

Notes: The Red Gate Tavern; a ship, the *Nymph;* his basso profundo rose in thunderous cadence; faux pas; the shadow of immediate death; the Phantom is the Avenger of Crime; red signal light is used to call the Phantom; Van calls Frank, "Mr. Havens"; his secret atelier; somber wings of death; special keys were made by a Viennese locksmith; ghosts of deceased cigars; apartment 3B; rubbery face; okay; Casa Mojada Club; canary-yellow blonde; calcium moons; he was a symphony in gray—gray hair, to gray suede shoes, gray eyes, tie, shirt, suit; etui; Acme Hotel; a dulcet, though mechanical tone; elfin echoes; Skip Nolan is an ex-prizefighter, friend of Steve Huston; blinked balefully; building is a black citadel; Throggs Neck area; Raucher's lunch room where Steve Huston and the Phantom meet; tugged lobe of left ear.

128. THE FATAL MASTERPIECES

V45 #1—February 1945
Written by Norman A. Daniels

Place: New York City

Main characters: Fred Lawson, Rocco Gorelli, Leslie Jackson, Capt. Kullamn, Dr. Wilber Keen, Richard Curtis Van Loan/the Phantom, Frank Havens, Harvey Elliot, James Gray, Felix Creham, Dr. Bendix, Jose Montero, Mike McCarthy, Dr. Cliff Davis, Alan Ayres, Henry Hubbard, Steve Huston, Joe, Mike, Pete, Whitey, Carlton, Curtis Brownlee, Arthur Walsh

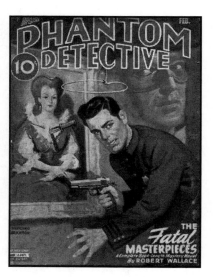

Masterpieces of art have been secretly hidden during the height of the war, in fear that German bombs might target the New York Museum where the art was displayed. When fears are lessened, the art is scheduled to be brought back to the museum. However, en route from the hidden location, the truck carrying the art treasures is forced over a cliff and bursts into flames, supposedly destroying the valuable art.

The Phantom believes that what has been destroyed were merely fakes, and that the fakes have been destroyed to hide the duplication. He believes that the real artwork have been secretly sold to collectors who would always keep the hidden masterpieces away from spying eyes. With the return of the art to the museum, the fakes would have been discovered.

Notes: Again, the radio message is sent out for the Phantom; a battle along rafters high above the floor was high drama; labored with vim; a roar like a Niagara; his words contained fire and brimstone; muffed the job; okay; shoe-button eyes; an old time gangster used to send a funeral wreath to his victim, and the current killer is copying him; Steve disobeys the Phantom and is close to being taken off the case; the Phantom referred to as a criminologist, more so than a crime fighter.

129. THE MANUSCRIPT MURDERS

V45 #2—April 1945
Written by Charles Greenberg

Place: New York City

Main characters: Armand Duval, Jeff Widmer, Emil Gurka, the Baron, Miss Marsh, Steve Huston, George Sterling, Richard Curtis Van Loan/the Phantom, Frank Havens, Pat Bowen, Paul Gerber, Mr. Gray, McLean, Judge Silas Woodrow, Matthew Griffin, Jeffrey Todd, Dr. Meredith Sloan, Marvin Sloan, Edmund Bricker, Felix, Dr. Roger Thorne, Henderson, Dave Stahl, Kurt Heinrich von Stundert, Roy Mercer, Kenneth Price, Inspector Gregg, Stella Chapman, Paddy Ryan, Hugo Hathaway

A mastermind has a scheme to obtain great manuscripts, such as those by Poe, Twain, and others, from private collectors who own them. He secretly suggests to the owners of these valuable manuscripts to offer them to the towns where the authors were from, and have Frank Havens hold the valuable manuscripts until the price is paid and the manuscripts turned over to the towns involved. But while the papers are being transferred, they are stolen, and the mastermind asks for a high ransom.

Notes: Muriel is mentioned (not by name) as owning a green convertible; a boat, the *Albatross*—in connection to Jack London; Club 81; animal-like, on hands and knees—this is certainly a clue to Charles Greenberg, but it won't always be present by this author; a man has a bony face; the golden harvest of riches; a girl has greenish eyes; his breath made a whistling, sibilant sound; Miss Marsh is the severe-faced and super efficient secretary to Frank Havens; blue, agate eyes; paradoxically; okay; crime reared its ugly head; contains good information on beginning of the Phantom; the author uses "World's Greatest Sleuth" and "Man With a Thousand Faces"; affectation; blithe manner; wild and wooly imagination; "And yet—and yet—"; a man is a barrel-chested giant on dwarf legs—from Charles Greenberg, again; "Good glory!"; Croyden Hotel; Mr. Gray from Denver; a roadhouse, the Golden Galleon; Dave Stahl is a *Clarion* photographer.

1935

1936

1937

1938

1939

1940

1941

1942

1943

1944

1945

1946

1947

1948

1949

1950

1951

1952

1953

130. MURDER FOR MILLIONS

V45 #3—June 1945
Written by C.S. Montayne

Place: New York City; Washington, D.C.

Main characters: The Big Boss, Frank Havens, Senator Joe Whelan, Arthur Welden, Sgt. Shea (D.C.), Cummings, Mrs. Morrison, Richard Curtis Van Loan/the Phantom, Rowley Tilden, Leonard Craymore, Dorothea Winship, Dr. Paul Bendix, David Raynor, Hal Garren (F.B.I.), Tom Smith, Steve Huston, Dr. John Parker, Glenda Ensley, Robert "Happy" Miller, Mathilda, Harvey Bell, Dan, Joe Chandler, Danny Weber, Louis, Martin Hildreth, Mac, Pete, Hokey, Eddie, Charlie, Pierre, Caesar Manion, Arnold Kempner, Nathaniel Brister, Chalmers Thayer, Lawson March, Lopez, Inspector Thomas Gregg, Miss Atwood, Neal, Mike, Henry, McCabe (policeman), Williams

Financial plans are stolen and six leading financial geniuses are suspected. When Senator Whelan asks Frank Havens to accompany him to a crime scene, the senator explains the danger of the American government facing financial ruin if the plans are known and used by someone who understands them. It is decided to bring the Phantom into the investigation.

In a very good story, the Phantom works with an F.B.I. agent to uncover the local criminals involved in the case. But at the end, it's the Phantom who moves in on the master crook.

Notes: To do—what?; okay; Van is a house guest of the Tilden's at their mansion; red signal light atop the *Clarion* calls for the Phantom; records of the Special Finance Committee are stolen; Rana, an Afghan dog; his Adam's apple bobbed up and down; "Tempered in the crucible of crime"; Monte Carlo Club; the Clinton Hotel; moon silvered landscape; web of minutes; Crystal Swan; banal exchange; meets Steve Huston at a bowling alley; her eyes were sparkling tourmalines, heavy-lidded and provocative; Inspector Gregg called in at last minute of the story; crime would raise its ugly head.

131. KILLER PORTFOLIO

V46 #1—August 1945
Written by Charles Greenberg

Place: New York City

Main characters: Dr. Zachary, Eunice Wayne, Muriel Havens, Mario de Sylva, Bettina, Freddy, Roberts, Harvey Dunn, Richard Curtis Van Loan/the Phantom, Patrick McKluskey, Jan Olsen, Steve Huston, Andy Foreman, Mr. Gray, Inspector Gregg, Gaston Dubios, Mark Tyson, Dr. Jackson Wayne, Floyd Stilman, Horace Prentice, Paddy "Tiger" Molloy, James Gregory, Chester Mead, Jonathan Hewitt, Jeff Lingle, Chick, Adams, Davis, Dr. Philip Randall,

Nancy, Scotty McLane, Nick Darnell, Paddy Ryan, Arthur Landis, Joe, Elaine Wayne, Slim, Poncho, McCarthy, Frank Havens (telephone)

Muriel is kidnapped for ransom to pay crooks that work for the mastermind. The super crook is actually after records from a doctor's office revealing the mental illnesses of several people in high places that he wants to blackmail for profit.

Certainly the same author as "Murder for Millions" (June 1945) and still using some plot devices of Charles Greenberg leads me to believe it is his.

Notes: In one clue, I was struck to the similarity to the June 1942 story, "Murder Makes a Movie," but I could be wrong on this; animal-like on hands and knees; a green convertible belongs to Muriel's friend; to do—what?; Muriel's girlfriend, Eunice Wayne, is murdered in front of her; in 1936, a girl named Wayne appeared in several stories, with the first name of Nita, but this is not the same author; the Silver Swan Club; Roberts is Havens' butler; okay; blithe manner; do a Barney Oldfield; affectation; column, "What Else Would You Like to Know?"; Hanover's cafe; political Labor Party, the Progressive Party; once, twice, three times; Great glory; fella; the Mercury Club; towards the end of the story, some names get switched—Paddy Molloy becomes Paddy Ryan, which connects this one with "The Manuscript Murders," and Eunice Wayne becomes Elaine Wayne; a man is a dwarf, which was used a lot by Charles Greenberg.

132. DEATH TO A DIPLOMAT

V46 #2—October 1945
Written by unknown; possibly Charles Greenberg or C.S. Montayne

Place: New York City

Main characters: Steve Huston, Juan Roberto, Carlos Esteban, Nelson Millard, Emily Portal, Charles Webster, Richard Curtis Van Loan/the Phantom, Cassidy, Gerald Longstreet, Elodie Longstreet, Lanny Hildreath, Frank Havens, Dr. Bendix, Andrew Crawford, Smith, Inspector Gregg, Joyce McCabe, Wilkins, Sig Sorensen, Bart Egan, "Chalky" Bush, "Doc" Garney, Roger Kuren, Conrad Bigelow, Lyon Howland, Jones, Dr. Blauvelt, Alfred Ritchie, Marion Flagg, Morley Patrick, Ed Cooper, "Skip" Nolan, Frankie Kane, Sanchez, Andy, Harry Gent

A Honduran diplomat is murdered and Washington wants the Phantom to investigate. However, the Phantom finds no political intrigue, but rather a Central American mine in the offing. Actually, the mastermind needs money to buy the stockholders out so he can control the profit of the mine ownership.

1933
1934
1935
1936
1937
1938
1939
1940
1941
1942
1943
1944
1945
1946
1947
1948
1949
1950
1951
1952
1953

1933

1934

1935

1936

1937

1938

1939

1940

1941

1942

1943

1944

1945

1946

1947

1948

1949

1950

1951

1952

1953

He hires a New York City gang to help him blackmail a young married woman. With the blackmail money, he can pay his gang members plus buy the stockholders out.

Notes: Reads like "Murder for Millions" (June 1945), so is connected to that story; a character named McCabe appeared in "Murder for Milions" as well; Rosita Gold Mine; red signal light atop the *Clarion*—now we are told that criminals everywhere knew the meaning of that light, the beacon that calls the Phantom to a case; a radio massage also is sent for the Phantom; "Stick out your ears and I'll load 'em"; Apartment

6B; Havens has a private dinning room at Toni's—although in this period, Havens will have private rooms in a number of clubs; it is at these clubs that Havens, the Phantom, Steve Huston and, later, Chip Dorlan will meet at one time or another; the Magyar, a club catering to Hungarian people—this club has been used in other stories, too; with vim; tugged the lobe of his left ear.

133. THE CASE OF THE POISON FORMULA

V46 #3—December 1945
Written by C.S. Montayne

Place: New York City

Main characters: Dr. Lester Maitland, Dr. Rodney Heath, Vicki Marsh, Andrew Drake, John Stanley, Myra Thayer, Richard Curtis Van Loan/ the Phantom, Reginald Thayer, Joseph, Jepson, Muriel Havens (mentioned), Steve Huston, Frank Havens, Inspector Gregg, Dr. Bendix, Eddie, Snowball, Carrigan, Sid, Clipper, Abbott, Dr. Everly, John Worley, "Skip" Nolan, Mr. Edgren, Mayo, Tom Bullard, Fred Riley, Robert, Lew

A scientist has created a cure for the common cold, but when the medicine goes on sale many people die after taking it. Investigation reveals that the formula for the medicine has been switched, making the cure a poison. When the scientist is murdered, the Phantom is called in to find the mastermind behind the poison formula.

Notes: This reminded me of "Murder of a Marionette" (December 1944) and later, "Death Rides the Winner" (August 1946); a fluty echo; shape of shadow; call for the Phantom comes over his car radio; *Clarion* light that calls the Phantom is mentioned; Van is spending the weekend with the Thayer's; Toni's restaurant and grill; okay; pulled at the lobe of his ear; the Green Spot; Van had learned knowledge of the East Indian wrestler; sibilant voice; we're now told that Skip Nolan works for the Phantom; girl has tip-tilted nose; the Pilgrims Club; éclat; epicurean; bellicose rantings; *Clarion* signal light is used towards the end of the story. This appears to be C.S. Montayne's story. When I first read it, I wanted to assign it to R. T. M. Scott because of the Maitland clue, but that wasn't enough to go on. The Skip Nolan character appears to have been brought over from Greenberg's stories, but his position is slightly changed.

Availability: *Action Adventure Stories* #137 (published by Fading Shadows, Inc., 2004).

134. DOOM ON SCHEDULE

V47 #1—February 1946
Written by Charles Greenberg

Place: New York City; Bedlow Green, VT

Main characters: Steve Huston, Nancy Porter, Richard Curtis Van Loan/the Phantom, "Frenchy" Atlee, Frank Havens, Dr. Bendix, Inspector Thomas Gregg (mentioned), Mike Garrity, Archer Gallup, John Watson, Miss Vincent, Ruth, Roberts, Sheriff Allen, John MacComber, Rogers, Gypsy Savage, Gil Swain, Charlie, Lem Tucker, Malcolm Reed, Jessup, Henry Franklin, Zeke, Landon Borden, Dave Thayer, Raff, Johnny, Ed, Kelton, "Gabby" Henderson

Steve Huston, taking two weeks for a fishing vacation, is traveling by train when it is derailed, and many passengers are killed and injured. Steve is thrown from the wreck, and while half conscious under a bush, he hears men around the wrecked train talking about their part in the derailment.

Steve contacts Frank Havens, requesting the Phantom. And due to the many deaths in the train wreck, the Phantom feels an obligation to find the killers and uncover the criminal plot behind the terrible train wreck.

A mastermind wanted to buy the railroad, along with a new patented device that he feels will be worth millions to other railroads.

1933
1934
1935
1936
1937
1938
1939
1940
1941
1942
1943
1944
1945
1946
1947
1948
1949
1950
1951
1952
1953

1933

1934

1935

1936

1937

1938

1939

1940

1941

1942

1943

1944

1945

1946

1947

1948

1949

1950

1951

1952

1953

Notes: His sibilant order; one minute, two, three; Hathaway fishing rods; Roc-A-Co Club; the Sky High Club; she had a tip-tilted nose; red signal light atop the *Clarion* calls the Phantom; the Pilgrims Club; Huston is a protégé of Frank Havens; criminal underworld knows that when the light atop the *Clarion* signals, the Phantom is on another case; has psychic premonitions; Rogers is the name of the man who owns the garage where the Phantom's three black beauties—his crime fighting cars—are stored; Rogers also knows the signal of tugging his left ear lobe for identification; atelier; the Triple Crown pub is rendezvous for Steve Huston and the Phantom; banal remarks; Queer Street.

135. MODEL FOR MURDER

V47 #2—April 1946
Written by C.S. Montayne

Place: New York City

Main characters: Frank Havens, Steve Huston, Inspector Gregg, Max, Richard Curtis Van Loan/the Phantom, Dr. Paul Bendix, Jennings, Timothy, Haskell Duane, Barry Murdock, Elaine Riker, Dan Murdock, Madame Clothilde Lamonte, Chester Brown, Toni Chicosola, Charles Gorham, Carney, Sherman Black, Larry Davison, Roland Sprague, Tim, Charley, Theodore Marsh, Della Conte, Andrew, Martin

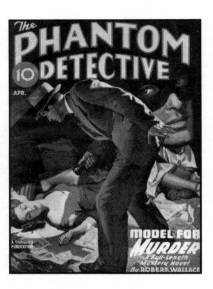

A shipment of art treasure is stolen and disappears completely, until Frank Havens finds a small figurine in a little shop near the *Clarion* Building. When he has Steve Huston pick it up for him, it begins another case for the Phantom. For the figurine is part of the missing art treasure, and within the figurine itself are two one thousand dollar bills!

The Phantom uncovers a giant blackmail scheme, along with the stolen art treasure.

Notes: A throwback to "Murder of a Marionette" (December 1944) and "Killer Portfolio" (August 1945); has psychic premonition; Havens and Van dine at Margay's; Max is head waiter at Margay's; whispering obligato; we're told that Van never calls Frank Havens by his first name, out of respect for his older friend; pulled a boner; the Surf and Sand Club; a boat, the *Nymph;* Toni's Chop House; tugged left ear lobe; Black Horse Tavern; fluty voice; okay; red signal light is used; a sibilant hiss; a baleful threat; the Phantom is the Destroyer of Crime; on tenterhooks; garage owner knows signal of ear lobe tug; atelier.

136. THE CASE OF THE MURDERED MENDICANT

V47 #3—June 1946
Written by C.S. Montayne

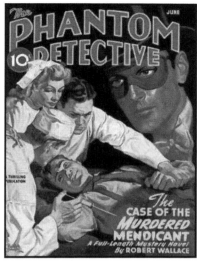

Place: New York City

Main characters: Pulaski, Ludwig Krantz, Matt Murphy, Nola Murphy, Lynda Demarest, Murdock Demarest, Red Decker, Richard Curtis Van Loan/the Phantom, Mr. Wayne, Frank Havens, Steve Huston, Anson Howard, Scanlon, Inspector Gregg, Dr. Frederick Allison, Dr. Blauvelt, Dr. Bendix, Ed Small, Harry Small, Allen Webb, Cliff Howard, Anita, Millington, Dr. Dempster, Ridgeway, Dr. Edward Lampton, Mr. Lamont, King Ryan, Amos Payton, Albright, Danny, Joe, Bart, Sabine, Pasternak, Dr. Noble, Professor Edwin Hurd, Chester Worden, Lt. Farrell (New York City), Julius Wexler, Miss Wilson, Muriel (mentioned)

A super crook back in town is recognized by a retired police detective. The crook murders the elderly cop, and this brings the Phantom in. Later, another body is discovered that has been killed the same way as the policeman.

The Phantom believes that a giant plot is in the works and soon discovers that it all surrounds a dying millionaire who has been kept in a mental hospital. Easy to guess, the man isn't really in bad health. The super crook—and a doctor—are keeping him doped up.

Notes: A shape of shadow; White Crown Cafe; the Pilgrims Club; tugged lobe of left ear; Bowen-Kent glass; the Golden Horn; the Oasis Club; okay; Toni's; Havens owns the magazine publication, *House, Home and Garden*; King Ryan, an ex-Secret Service agent, now runs the Creston Agency; Green Horse Tavern; he said, sibilantly; the Publisher's Club; Happy's Shanty Tavern; Dr. Noble is Havens' personal physician.

137. DEATH RIDES THE WINNER

V48 #1—August 1946
Written by C.S. Montayne

Place: New York City

Main characters: The Blue Fox, Roger Lacounte, Barney, Steve Huston, Ranny Zucco, Benny Cole, Richard Curtis Van Loan/the Phantom, Martha Mallinson, Malcolm Mallinson, Spencer Laidlaw, Freck, Babson, Frank Havens, Inspector Thomas Gregg, Dr. Bendix, Ruiz Mendoza, Mildred Gale, Stephen Foster, Poker, Froggy, Clip, Al Brayden, Jeff, Mike Stefano, Mona Harvey, Joseph Garr, Jack McVane, "Skip" Nolan, Rosalie Stevens, Agnes Harding, Shorty

Crooked activity at the race track prompts the governor to ask Frank Havens to run a campaign in his newspaper against the illegal activity. When

1933
1934
1935
1936
1937
1938
1939
1940
1941
1942
1943
1944
1945
1946
1947
1948
1949
1950
1951
1952
1953

murder is added to the gaffe, the Phantom is called in.

Gambling, the race track, and Wall Street investments are at the bottom of the crimes.

Notes: Applegate Building; Van is spending the weekend with a family he knows; a symphony in blue—dressed all in blue; Barney's Tavern; russet-brown hair; he clicked his teeth; girl makes a comment about the "Samba" dance being thought of as a Pullman porter; the red signal *Clarion* call, as well as a call on the TV set; atelier; Marquette Building; copper-shaded lights glimmered like tethered moons; Golden Drum night club; Van is protégé of Havens; insigne; equipment in waistband of trousers; Nile green; escritoire; the Green Spot; pulled lobe of his ear; matutinal brew; the gay garroteer; Dolly Varden Cosmetic Company; Peter Pan Beauty Shop; the Phantom drinks lime and seltzer; magenta; fuchsia; Van calls Frank, "Mr. Havens"; Briarwood Farm; Apt. 3B; Barn door mouth; okay; killer uses a garrote to strangle his victims.

Availability: *Action Adventure Stories* #145 (published by Fading Shadows, Inc., 2005).

138. THE TIDEWATER MURDERS

V48 #2—November 1946
Written by Charles Greenberg

Place: Clifton, NY; New York City

Main characters: Dave Jonas, William Decker, Dan Whelan, Johnny Lynch, Mrs. Thurlow, Police Chief Bill Eaton (Clifton), Dr. Porter, Mrs. Nesbitt, Will Brock, Tom, Russel Markham, Joseph Whelan, Mark Hale, Dr. Emmet Raine, Clyde Fowler, Larry Nason, Ed, Jackson, Richard Curtis Van Loan/the Phantom, Ezra Phelps, Steve Huston, Gus Keller, Louise Perry, Chester Perry, Carp, Peggy, Edith Tilton, Chandler, Haley, Mary, Aggie Barnes, Chuck Evans, Mr. Gray, Inspector Gregg, Pete & Lola Harrigan, Nick Moran, Lefty, Ryan, Frank Havens

A mastermind plans a big scheme to obtain millions. The case begins in the small town of Clifton, where an old fisherman is mysteriously murdered. A cub reporter on the local newspaper contacts Steve Huston with a message that he has learned something important, and when Steve returns his call, a false report has the cub reporter being killed, too. Steve asks Frank Havens to contact the Phantom for help.

The mastermind promised the gangsters that he would give them new faces for their help in his plans. It is a twisted plot, and a fairly good one. Steve gets the cub reporter a job on the *Clarion* at the end of the story.

Notes: This one goes back to "The Red Bishop Murders" (August 1943) as well as others; also falls back on some of Greenberg's plot devices; triangle love affair between a woman and the master crook; a ship, the *Helena;* okay; he made a sibilant sound; a man is effeminate; a pregnant silence; Jackson is city editor of the *Clarion;* the *Clifton Gazette;* Johnny Lynch is a cub reporter on the *Gazette;* blithe manner; affectation; tugged lobe of his left ear; Good glory!; "Looking—where?"; the Yacht Club; a bony face, hatchet-faced man; "Jeepers!"; Mr. Gray from Denver; Gregg brought in at end of story; Pete's Bar & Grill; "By Jupiter!"; animal-like on hands and knees.

139. THE CHINESE PUZZLE

V48 #3—January 1947
Written by C.S. Montayne

Place: New York City

Main characters: Dr. Weng Cho, Eve Sanford, Chang Wei, Major Roland Sanford, Weng Hau, Richard Curtis Van Loan/the Phantom, Inspector Gregg, Sammy, Armitage, Frank Havens, Smythe, Taylor, Wheeler, Fred Brady, Dr. Bendix, David Hawley, Robert, Harry Cheng Lin, Colin Klaffer, Lee Walt, Frank Morra, Yang, Archie Carter, Slim, Harvey Slade

The Phantom has been working on a case involving the Red Tears, three red gems smuggled out of China. Working with the Phantom is Eve Sanford, who has spent many years in China, as well as being an actress. Her voice instructor is Weng Hau.

When Weng Hau's brother returns from a trip into China, he is murdered and the bag he has carried with him is stolen. The Phantom feels that the murder is connected with the case he is already working on, just another area of the smuggled gem crime—the Red Tears!

Notes: The magazine becomes 15¢; the Hotel Malvern; okay; a Greenough microscope; the Green Spot; Red Tears; the Patroons Club; a stage play, "The

1933
1934
1935
1936
1937
1938
1939
1940
1941
1942
1943
1944
1945
1946
1947
1948
1949
1950
1951
1952
1953

1933
1934
1935
1936
1937
1938
1939
1940
1941
1942
1943
1944
1945
1946
1947
1948
1949
1950
1951
1952
1953

Bridge of Rapture"; shapes of shadow; sibilant commands; Crystal Glade Club; the Conover Building; Pilgrims Club; Ace-High Parking Lot.

140. CARTEL OF CRIME

V49 #1—March 1947
Written by C.S. Montayne

Place: New York City; Sound Cliff, NY

Main characters: The Professor, Steve Huston, Dimitri Rostand, Brady, Inspector Gregg, Eddie, James Saunderson, Frank Havens, Richard Curtis Van Loan/the Phantom, Mr. Blake, Robert, Judge Joel Marshall, Samuel Hoag, Lee Ashland, Clancy, Dave, Johnson, Dr. Bendix, Miss Walker, Arthur Conant, Dr. Robert Lannon, Miss Martin, Ed Sharp, Joe Deming, Mrs. Aubrey, Mrs. Whitaker, Mr. Shrive, Mac, George, Barlow, Police Chief Ted Murray (Sound Cliff)

A super criminal has plied his trade across Europe, leaving each area just a step before the police can catch up with him. Now he's in New York City and Washington D.C. authorities ask for the Phantom's help in finding enough on the man for an arrest before he can bilk American citizens.

However, before the Phantom can get any evidence against him, the super crook is murdered, and valuable records are missing from his home. Now the Phantom needs to locate the missing records and find out who killed the super crook.

At the bottom of the case is control over a crime cartel, stretching from America to Europe. Is the wife, separated from her husband for six months, involved in his murder? Or her current boyfriend? And who is the mysterious "Professor?" What does a dog that can't bark have to do with the case? The Phantom must find out.

Notes: Tilden Towers; okay; tugged lobe of ear; a green-shaded Bowman light; peregrinations; Club 600; the Phantom visits Inspector Gregg's home in an elderly section of Manhattan, a stately old house, with time-worn brownstone steps; vim and vigor; a barkless dog; Throggs Neck area; Apartment 2B; dog's name is Sandy; Lone Star Garage; the Pilgrims Club; checked his tongue; a clue of nitro pills left at scene.

141. THE ANGEL OF DEATH

V49 #2—May 1947
Written by C.S. Montayne

Place: New York City; Wayville, CT; Sand Island, GA

Main characters: Jerry Madigan, Richard Curtis Van Loan/the Phantom, Blake, Delmar Palmer, Marcia Rickand, Amanda Palmer, Frank Havens, Miss Sawyer, Hamilton Crosby, Amos Hayden, Arthur Rickand, Tom Hubbard, Inspector Gregg, Dr. Bendix, Steve Huston, Malcolm Kent, Cassidy, Garvey, Barney Raff, Mr. Black, Abe Shandelle, Beefy Doyle, Masterson, Riker, White, Jessie, Mr. Defoe, Sandberg, Stokes, Robert Anderton, Ralph Godfrey, Nick, Bodie, Cliff Rowley, Police Chief Harron (Wayville), Charles Warner, Perry Martin, Otto Framm, Hugo Framm, Jed, Jose Sandera, Patricia Driscoll, Berkeley Driscoll, Dr. Scribner

Van Loan, while passing a curio shop, notices a tarnished snuffbox. Entering the shop, he discovers the snuffbox to be solid silver and quite valuable. He also knows where the silver collection it goes with belongs. The owner of the shop refuses to sell the snuffbox.

Van Loan attempts to contact the original owners of the silver, but when the owner is found murdered, the Phantom enters the case with his own investigation. The case has several elements; one, a beautiful woman who is nicknamed "The Angel of Death," because her marriages are short, ending with the deaths of her rich husbands. She is scheduled to receive the bulk of the fortune, which includes the silver collection as soon as the will has been settled. The Phantom must now find out if she killed her latest husband, and what is behind the silver turning up in the curio shop.

Notes: This one is similar to "Murder of a Marionette" (December 1944), "Killer Portfolio" (August 1945) and "Model for Murder" (April 1946); a yacht, the *Triton;* the Pilgrims Club; Miss Sawyer is Havens' secretary; tugged lobe of ear; a Greenough microscope; Durand's the Three Deer Farm; the Eagle's Claw bar; sloe eyes; Room 300; shape of shadow; a sibilant voice; apartment 2B; Club Carousel.

Availability: *The Angel of Death* (published by Jim Hanos, 1989).

142. MASTERPIECE OF MURDER

V49 #3—July 1947
Written by C.S. Montayne

Place: New York City

Main characters: John Mattling, Martin Mattling, Cyrus, Capt. Olaf Swenson, Harry, Mac, Thomas, Stephen Courtney, Flora Ferguson, Richard Curtis Van Loan/the Phantom, Lynton Garner, Frank Havens, Inspector Gregg, Mr. C. S. Gray, Mr. Lang, Frank Miller, Ernie Berg, Sgt. Shea, Harry Murdock, Barry Carter, Ward Barlow, Joe Normany, Tony Rocci, Fred Lavery, Steve Huston, Clinton Robertson, Gleason, Dave Roy, Dr. Bendix, Mr. Belford,

1933
1934
1935
1936
1937
1938
1939
1940
1941
1942
1943
1944
1945
1946
1947
1948
1949
1950
1951
1952
1953

1933

1934

1935

1936

1937

1938

1939

1940

1941

1942

1943

1944

1945

1946

1947

1948

1949

1950

1951

1952

1953

Rafford Saturn, Eddie Grogan, Mike, Charlie, "Brownie" Hack, Mrs. Stone, Anthony Rodgers, Rita, Dona Whelan, Robert

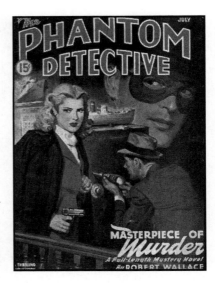

A super crook from California has set up shop in New York City, where he's trying to obtain a shipping line. When the owner won't sell, accidents begin to happen on the ships belonging to the line, causing great financial loss to the shipping line's owners.

An owner's son starts his own investigation and uncovers a lot of evidence, including the possible identity of the super crook. The mastermind has the son killed, and the safe containing the evidence broken into. But when the safecracker gets the evidence out of the safe, he is killed and yet another party now has the evidence in which to blackmail the super crook.

Notes: Usually, the alias of Mr. Gray is just that, but in this case, we are given the initials of C. S. We know that C.S. Montayne should be writing the stories by this period. If the C. S. was a clue to Montayne, then his writing is a lot like Charles Greenberg. A freighter, the *Star of Brazil;* the Coastwise Lines; the Mary Wattling ship; Querido Mio; Patroons Club; Baptiste, a French restaurant; the *Santa Cruz,* a ship; the *Rio City,* a ship; Elkhorn Tavern; the Black Star Mine; the Green Spot; a Lecroix microscope; tugged lobe of his ear; shape of shadow; okay; he had a lot of face, jowls, and a full-lipped mouth; Elite Bowling Alley; Mrs. Stone is Steve's landlady; Queer Street; sibilant whisper. I can't pass up the C. S. clue, which points to Montayne. There are similarities to the story, "Cartel of Crime" (March 1947), and several others that I have identified as Greenberg entries. Very difficult to pinpoint this author.

143. THE CASE OF THE MURDERED WITNESS

V50 #1—September 1947
Written by C.S. Montayne

Place: New York City; Wellington, DE

Main characters: Ernest Shaler, Steve Huston, Richard Curtis Van Loan/the Phantom, Wendy Malcolm, Clayton Sherman, Olga Tanner, Dulaney, Senator Lawton Larue, Frank Havens, Inspector Gregg, Dr. Bendix, James Carney, Buck Rooney, Colonel Tanner, Chet Harrington, Miles Carter, Charles Smith, White Arrow, Sheriff Seth Higby (Wellington), Chuck Dodson, Stanton Wilcox, Menlo Gates, Norman Thayer, Harry Benson, Wally, Ted, Pendleton, Dr. Edith Rand, Julian Bender, Reginald Beresford, Miss Marsh, Myles Bennett, Charley, Shorty, Joe, Bob, Julia, Tom, Detective Tim Rowley (New York City)

Oil people from Oklahoma are involved. One man, ordered to testify before the senate, mysteriously disappears, then a body is found—a man, murdered, with his face eaten away by acid. Washington has already requested the Phantom in tracking down the vanished oil-man, and with the murder pointing towards the missing man, the Phantom must uncover the identity of the body, as well as solve the murder.

Notes: The Charles Greenberg influence is felt again in this story, as several of Greenberg's stories had similar plot devices; okay; Diamond Point Yacht Club; the Patroons Club; Tony's Tavern (same as Toni's?), the Green Spot; the Fowler House; a man has a bony face; Greenough microscope; a sibilant exclamation; Pendleton is Van Loan's stockbroker; a ship, the *Queen Elizabeth;* Miss Marsh is Havens' secretary; shape of shadow; red signal light used to call the Phantom; Frank Havens is kidnapped.

144. THE CASE OF THE BURNING ROCKS

V50 #2—November 1947
Written by C.S. Montayne

Place: New York City; Washington D.C.

Main characters: Jim Darrel, Senator Future Selden, Bob Clancy, Tucker, Neal Waterman, Phillip Johnson, Steve Huston, Frank Havens, Richard Curtis Van Loan/the Phantom, Craig Blakely, Dolly Gotham, Henry Jessup Taylor, Peterson, Miss Marsh, Arthur Selden, Carson Blake, Peggy Lamant, Martha, Ed Winston, Inspector Gregg, Molly, Joe Mitchell, Bill Everly, Mike Harry Carter, George Brewster-Peckham, Hugh Vernon, Mrs. Jackson, Charley, Walker, Bill Eaten, "Lefty" Crawford, Dr. Bendix, Lyman Buck, Ashley Venning, Roger, Rutledge, Miss Wilson

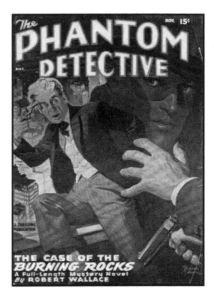

A photographer friend of Steve Huston's, returning from an assignment, is murdered in his apartment. Because Steve is so upset over the murder, Frank Havens asks the Phantom to investigate the death and find the killer.

1933
1934
1935
1936
1937
1938
1939
1940
1941
1942
1943
1944
1945
1946
1947
1948
1949
1950
1951
1952
1953

Before the case is closed, the Phantom encounters the family of a senator, a large tract of virgin land owned by the senator, and blackmail!

A super crook is blackmailing the senator's wife. With the money he plans on buying a virgin tract of land owned by the senator. This land is sitting over a large deposit of oil. Not only must the senator's wife pay the blackmail money, but she must convince her husband that he should sell the worthless land in question.

Notes: Dolly Gotham is the social columnist for the *Clarion;* shape of shadow; has psychic premonition; Miss Marsh is Havens' secretary; tugged lobe of his ear; the White Star Cafeteria; Armand's Restaurant; the Green Spot; the Blue Lagoon; Jack Gaynor's 36 Club; the Haymow Club; Little Paris Club; Mike & Ike's Club; sentences end like "I told you—"; Spangler Detective Agency; girl has a tip-tilted nose; Patroons Club; clue of insulin kit left at scene; similarities to "Cartel of Crime" (March 1947) and "Masterpiece of Murder" (July 1947).

145. THE CROCKED MILE RIVER MURDERS

V50 #3—January 1948
Written by C.S. Montayne

Place: Catskills, Crooked Mile River Village; New York City

Main characters: Muriel Havens, Frank Havens, Danny Brayden, Richard Curtis Van Loan/the Phantom, Hubbard Craig, Martha, Professor Ernst Selgard, Dr. Amos Lambert, Sheriff Ben Thatcher (Catskills), Jed, Harv, Mac, Steve Huston, Barry McClain, Pierre Faubrey, Adele Selgard, Mr. Martin, Addison, Conrad Schiller, Libby Rogers, Chip Dorlan, Thomas Blake, Inspector Gregg, Louis Ravac, Ezzra Cole, Murphy, Wilmerding, Mr. Gray, Patton, Johnson, Ledyard, Thompson, Leonard M. Spencer, Peter, Martha Davin, Carlo, Franz Wisner, Larson, Mayhew, Simone, Jarman, Edouard, Clyde Miller

THE CROOKED MILE RIVER MURDERS
A Full-Length Mystery Novel by ROBERT WALLACE

The strange murder of a Swiss scientist near the Havens' vacation home on Crooked Mile River brings the government into the case, as the scientist had been working on important experiments for America.

They ask Frank Havens to bring the Phantom into the case, and he quickly decides there are no government secrets involved. Instead, the mystery seems to surround a Swiss watch. The Phantom discovers the watch had contained five hidden black pearls, which an international crook was after.

Notes: Okay; Satin Slipper Club; psychic premonition; I felt that the author was not happy with the Chip Dorlan character, so his return may have been at the request of the editors; Rockledge Cape; gimlet-eyed; shape of shadow; "Then—what?"; Logan's Tavern; a man has a young-old face (not seen since 1938, but this isn't the same author); sloe-eyed; tugged lobe of ear; Greenough microscope; the Green Spot; Chip Dorlan had recently returned from the military—he had served in Military Intelligence during the war, and was responsible for capturing many spies and saboteurs—now he brings maturity and experience in his assignments for the Phantom; the Blue Star Ship Lines; Patroons Club; making his Adam's apple bob up and down; Muriel feels that she is half in love with Van Loan and the other half loves the Phantom—possibly a hint of things to come, as it won't be long now until the Phantom discloses his identity to all involved, including Muriel.

146. THE CLUE OF THE SECOND MURDER

V51 #1—March 1948
Written by C.S. Montayne

Place: New York City; Sonajo, NV

Main characters: Harley Holt, Durham Holt, Richard Curtis Van Loan/the Phantom, Joel Sanderson, Joe, Inspector Gregg, Gibbs, Muriel Havens, James Callen, Clyde Caldwell, Lt. Michael Shevlin, Frank Havens, Jackson Bagby, Harry Langley, Matthew Brady, Hugh Farney, Leslie Post, Wilson, Steve Huston, Chip Dorlan, Rowley & Grover Delafield, Mr. Gray, Lawson Thayer, Joseph Jones, White Horse, Miss Clara Sawyer, Jed C. Burke, Mrs. Symond, Joe, Loro Ayre, Conklin Courtwright, Dr. Bendix, Alfred Petrie, Olga, Andy Hubbell, Max

A small town character from Sonajo, Nevada comes to New York to publish his book about an empire ruled by two cunning brothers to control who hold an entire town in their grip. But news gets out of his intentions and killers are dispatched to intercept and kill him. However, when he stops to eat at a New York restaurant, his path crosses that of another young man, a man newly arrived in New York also. But his is a different story. He's here for an interview with Frank Havens, a close friend of his father's, who he hopes will give him a job on the *Clarion*.

When he leaves the restaurant, he is handed the wrong overcoat, an overcoat marked for the killers. He is shot down, and Frank Havens asks the Phantom to run his killers to earth.

Tracing the overcoat, which the Phantom had found was too small for the dead man, to the restaurant where the men had both stopped to eat upon their arrival in New York, the Phantom discovers the identity of the second man,

1933
1934
1935
1936
1937
1938
1939
1940
1941
1942
1943
1944
1945
1946
1947
1948
1949
1950
1951
1952
1953

1933

1934

1935

1936

1937

1938

1939

1940

1941

1942

1943

1944

1945

1946

1947

1948

1949

1950

1951

1952

1953

the man from Nevada, but before he can reach him, he becomes the second murder victim.

Notes: Myler's Chop House; Mayfair Club; Gibbs is Havens' butler; crime raised its ugly head; Pilgrim Hotel (was a Club in other stories); clue of a nasal inhaler left at scene; okay; tugged lobe of ear; sibilant voice; the Green Spot; the Belfair Club; the Red Gate House; a planned book, *The Hidden Empire;* "Tell him—what?"; Similar to several stories, especially those where strange clues are left at the scene—insulin kits, nitro pills, etc.

147. THE DIAMOND KILLERS

V51 #2—May 1948
Written by C.S. Montayne

Place: New York City

Main characters: Morton Orth, Tim Seward, Daniel Rayle, Ed, Ames Bristol, Judith Bristol, Steve Huston, Frank Havens, Muriel Havens, Richard Curtis Van Loan/the Phantom, Charles Wakeman, Dr. Armstrong, Nelson Tork, Mr. Gray, Lee Hargrave, Charlie Conlon, "Smoky", Rudie Endel, Howard Baker, Chip Dorlan, Craig Atwood, Marlo Morgan, Fanny, Brad, Langley, Eddie Marsh, Capt. Eckstrom, Ricco, Tex, Art, Mayo, Inspector Gregg

The owner of a shipping company is murdered before he can meet with a Customs Department official to give details on possible smuggling activity. At the same time, a Customs agent is also murdered, and there's no record left of the illegal smuggling operations.

The daughter of the shipping owner contacts her college friend, Muriel Havens, and asks for the help of the Phantom in running down her father's killers.

The Phantom learns that diamonds are being smuggled into America in bottles of champagne. The cases containing the diamonds are marked, and spirited away once they have passed Customs at the dock. With millions at stake, the head of the organization is killing off those who are on to him.

Notes: The White Elephant cafeteria; Van Loan's alter ego; Johnson Street; Publishers Club; Margate Hotel; Bowling Green, Keeler's Restaurant, a typical Longacre Square eating place; okay; a police launch, the *William Daly;* Greenough microscope; the 900 Club; clue left at the scene is a pair of workman's pliers with a foreign substance on it; Chantilly bar; Eagle's Hotel; dancing shadow, half in shadow.

148. THE TIMBER TRACT MURDERS

V51 #3—July 1948
Written by C.S. Montayne

Place: Lake Heron, ME; Branham, ME; Oakvale, ME

Main characters: Dale Warden, Sara Gilson, John Warden, David Carew, Morgan Moore, Sheriff Butler (Branham), Florence Wagner, Willard Wagner, Richard Curtis Van Loan/the Phantom, Muriel Havens, Joe, Brad Knowlton, Mike Kennard, Frank Havens, Frenchy Pete, Sheriff Bonner (Branham, named changed unknowingly), Steve Huston, Chip Dorlan (mentioned), Joe Irvan, C. W. Gray, Doc Wilson, Stella Warden, Inspector Gregg (telephone), Russell Tweed, Ernie Blanchard, Jeff Carter, Joel Cassidy, Bill Smith, Sarah, Dr. Grant Charlton, Dr. Bergh, Hank Slater, Miss Foster, Phil, Sid, Clem

Near Lake Heron, a large tract of timberland is up for sale. The owner had been found, a possible suicide, and the land was willed to the man's two nephews. Frank Havens and another big businessman planned on bidding for the purchase of the land, as it was a rich pulp industrial tract. However, it appears that others are also after the land, and they won't stop at murder to get it.

A very nice entry. Plenty of action and thrills. Before the Phantom can bring a killer to justice, more murders are carried out. But with the aide of Steve Huston, and a French Canadian guide, the Phantom unmasked the killer at the end.

Notes: First chapter heading is "The Shape of Shadow"; Thunder Cave; dancing shadows; shape of shadow, the Sunbriar Club; the Publishers Club; Chip Dorlan is away for a three-week vacation on the West Coast; newspaper, the *Branham Banner;* okay; vituperation; a sibilant command; Patrons Club; Antlers Club; tone was soft and dulcet; the Antlers Club is a combination roadhouse, inn, and bowling alley; sheriff's name is switched almost immediately.

149. THE LISTENING EYES

V52 #1—September 1948
Written by Norman A. Daniels

Place: New York City; Beloin, NY

Main characters: Steve Huston, Paul Cope, Frank Havens, Richard Curtis Van Loan/the Phantom, Dr. Bendix, Bernard Randall, Inspector Gregg, Sidney Earle, Toni Chicosola, Howard Ferguson, Ivan Dubin, Peter Dubin, Edward Jason, Miller, Muriel Havens, Dr. Frederick Glenn, Roger Singleton, Anderson, Hammond

1933
1934
1935
1936
1937
1938
1939
1940
1941
1942
1943
1944
1945
1946
1947
1948
1949
1950
1951
1952
1953

Steve Huston accidentally runs across a frightened man, who it appears someone wants to murder. Rescuing the man, Steve is hired as a bodyguard to protect him. But in no time, the man is murdered.

The Phantom comes into the case, but at every move, his plans are known beforehand as if the crooks were able to read his mind. Actually, that is close to the truth.

As clues are uncovered, the Phantom learns that three years previously, an accidental explosion had happened where five secreted men were employed to build a super explosive for war use. These scientists had lost their hearing in the accident, and they blamed the owner of the plant.

Their uncanny ability was really nothing more than reading lips at a distance as they watched the Phantom, thus knowing his plans as he made them.

Notes: Similar to Daniels' Black Bat story, "The Murder Prophet" (June 1947), and others with similar plots; okay; the Bentley Building; mouse-colored hair; Toni's Chop House; "So-so"; Carmody Street; Apartment 4D; Phantom calls Havens, "Sir"; Huston weighs 150 pounds; red signal light atop the *Clarion* calls the Phantom to action; Malloy Hotel & Lounge; Muriel brought in towards the end of the story as Huston's usefulness had been compromised; in a blue funk.

150. MURDER ACRES
V52 #2—November 1948
Written by C.S. Montayne

Place: New York City; Hundred Acres, near Poughkeepsie, NY

Main characters: Neal Brady, Nora Dolan, Senator Wilden Ryder, Richard Curtis Van Loan/the Phantom, Frank Havens, Jules, John Fay, Henry Davit, Charles W. Gray, Della Ryder, Muriel Havens, Conrad Lasher, Tano, Mrs. Carter, Joseph Garry, Steve Huston, Chip Dorlan, Inspector Gregg, Miss Marsh, Marvin Wanz, Olson, Dr. Bendix, Clement Morton, Harry Dancer, Bagby, Scanlon, Capt. Fred Dayton (State Police), Cyril Malcolm

An ex-senator, who had bought a famous—or infamous—piece of land, was trying to sell it. But in the meantime, his daughter had been framed in a hit and run accident in which a man was supposedly killed. The girl was being blackmailed, and the mastermind planned on using the money he took from the daughter to buy the land from her father using the senator's own money.

At the bottom of the mystery is a hidden treasure in gems that the previous owner had hidden on the land. This man had been killed in a shoot out with one of his partners, but no one knew the location of the treasure. So the land had to be bought in order for the mastermind to conduct his search in secret.

Notes: The magazine becomes 20¢; similar to such novels as "The Case of the Burning Rocks" (November 1947), "The Clue of the Second Murder" (March 1948), and "The Timber Tract Murders" (July 1948); etc. okay; split heirs; Malta Tavern; an old-young face; Patroons Club; Jules is special waiter at the Patroons Club; aroma of defunct cigars; sibilantly; shape of shadow; the Green Spot; room 1107; a restaurant, the Press Club; "this shadow drama"; Colonnade Club; *Douglas Post;* Pyramid Building; Miss Marsh is Havens' secretary; Carousel Club; Greenough microscope; Duval's French Restaurant.

151. THE CASE OF THE BIBLE MURDERS

V52 #3—January 1949
Written by C.S. Montayne

Place: New York City; San Rao, Brazil

Main characters: Dr. Haley Niblo, Steve Huston, Sheriff Jim McGinley (NY?), Leonard De Castro, Mrs. Walker, Dr. Gilson, Richard Curtis Van Loan/the Phantom, Muriel Havens, Frank Havens, Hobson, Juanita, Dr. Bendix, C. W. Gray, Inspector Gregg, Dr. Bagby, Lt. Shelvy (New York City), Marlow Julian, Eddie Garner, Barney Mack, Nick Quinto, Dave Archer, Chip Dorlan, A. D. Borden, John Crawford, Shanley, Jose, Dolores De Castro, Capt. Prado (San Rao), Juan Lestrado Barros

An old friend of Frank Havens is missing and he has Steve Huston start checking around. Shortly, Steve finds the missing man being held in a private hospital, drugged against his will. Along with the sheriff, Steve assists

1933
1934
1935
1936
1937
1938
1939
1940
1941
1942
1943
1944
1945
1946
1947
1948
1949
1950
1951
1952
1953

in removing the man from the hospital, but the doctor and his assistant have disappeared.

After the man has been put in the private care of a nurse, the crooks make entry to the home and kill him. It appears that there is a secret fortune hidden somewhere—hidden, but a clue in a Bible sends all parties in search of the enigma.

A million dollars and a license to a tract of land in South America is behind the mystery and deaths. The Phantom travels from New York to Brazil, then back to New York in search of the masterminds behind the case.

Notes: The ghost of a smile; a bony face; made a clucking sound with his tongue; a shape of shadow; the Phantom orders a ham on rye, with a Pepsi, the first time a name brand of anything is mentioned; his shadow—or shag orders a chocolate milk shake; the White Elephant Café; touched lobe of his left ear; Progressive Utilities; Stanwick Building; Greenough microscope; Miguel's eatery; off on a tangent; okay; the Green Spot; "you muffed it"; a premonition of danger; Patroons Club; folded on the floor, with an animal-like moan.

152. SERVANT OF SATAN

V53 #1—March 1949
Written by C.S. Montayne

Place: Pam, MI; New York City; Denver, CO; North Freeling, Saskatchewan, Canada

Main characters: Sartain Kurt Parish, Muriel Havens, Richard Curtis Van Loan/the Phantom, Jeremy McClintock, Toby Jones, William Parish, Yancey, Steve Huston, Miss Marsh, Frank Havens, Lyda Parish, Inspector Gregg, Smitty, McCabe, Eddie Nolan, Carver Parish, Marvin Maxon, Allison, Harry Brister, Chip Dorlan, Jake Blade, Mr. Gray, Wasson, Police Chief Cy Silsby (Pama), Hattie, Thomas Walker, Jed Tucker, Arthur Conway, Cynthia Brackett, Miss Angie Macy, Sheriff Seiter (NJ), Edward King, Clinton Gurney, Mrs. Smith, Miss Suwanee Delson, Bennett, Joe, Sam Granby, Eva Shaw, Irwin Clyde, Hobson, Mr. Armstrong, Cassidy, Jason Foster, Flo, Harry Maxon

The PHANTOM DETECTIVE
Servant OF SATAN
A Full-Length Mystery Novel By ROBERT WALLACE

Sartain had caused the death of three siblings, the children of a gold tycoon already dead. The tycoon's wife was expected to inherit the fortune in its entirety. Was the widow involved? Did she have her three stepchildren murdered, in order to obtain the complete fortune? And who was the mysterious Sartain—Satan—leading the killers in their act of murder?

At the bottom of the case is inheritance, and a plot to obtain even more millions as an old gold mine begins operation once more.

Notes: His Adam's apple bobbed up and down; similar to "The Angel of Death" (May 1947), "The Clue of the Second Murder" (March 1948), "The Case of the Burning Rocks" (November 1947); Lone Pine Inn; somniferous; Rumson Turf Club; the Purple Lantern; okay; the *S.S. Regardia,* the Blue Star ship line; pulled lobe of his left ear; the Silver Sleigh; Magnalux Gold Mine; the Green Spot; Plymough Bar & Grill; Eureka Bowling Alleys; perambulated; the Breakfast Club; the *Press* Building, crime raised its ugly head; the Eagle Inn; Silver Queen & Bison Basin Mines; Havens owns the Paragon Building; Landlubbers Club; Mrs. Smith is Chip's landlady; he ordered, sibilantly; a room number 1710 again; Sheep Creek Hotel; psychic premonition.

153. THE CITY OF DREADFUL NIGHT

V53 #2—Spring 1949
Written by Norman A. Daniels

Place: A city of 300,000 population, 500 miles from New York City; New York City

Main characters: Robert Covert, Paul Hanley, Wally Walsh, Mark Tormay, Kirk August Sloper, Police Chief George Abel (town not named), Frank Havens, Steve Huston, Mike Lathy, Richard Curtis Van Loan/the Phantom, Dr. Bendix, Sgt. Callahan, Janis Scott, Tom Wiley, Hank Mornay, Joe Proctor, Philip Covert, Muriel Havens, Paul Blannick, Tucker, Richard Gibson, Inspector Gregg, Doc Noakes, Montague

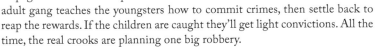

Teenage kids are being used as scapegoats in a crime spree. The adult gang teaches the youngsters how to commit crimes, then settle back to reap the rewards. If the children are caught they'll get light convictions. All the time, the real crooks are planning one big robbery.

The Phantom discovers the big crime and prepares for it. As a red herring, the adult crooks plan mass gas station and small store robberies all over town, to be committed by the teenagers, to draw the police after them, while the actual gang hits the local bank for a million dollar haul.

The Phantom has police set traps to catch the kids before they commit their crimes, and with movie cameras set up at the bank to catch the robbery on film as the police wait to capture them. With the film, the Phantom hopes to show kids around the country that crime does not pay.

Notes: Daniels turned this manuscript over on August 21st, 1948, only a week after he'd turned in the Black Bat story, "The Missing Million" (Summer 1950, which was turned in on August 14, 1948). Less than two months later, he would turn in the half completed C.S. Montayne story, "The Black Ball of Death," on October 16, 1948 (Montayne died of a heart attack on August 3,

1933
1934
1935
1936
1937
1938
1939
1940
1941
1942
1943
1944
1945
1946
1947
1948
1949
1950
1951
1952
1953

1948). This current story is very similar to Daniels' Black Bat story, "Murder's Playground," from May 1949—my guess is that Daniels had to come up with this current story to fill in a space after Montayne died; the Blue Moon nightclub; Steve goes undercover as a police officer; tugged lobe of left ear; Security Trust Bank; Club Samoa; "His reply made Muriel's eyes open wide, caused the Phantom to wince, and brought Chief Abel out of his chair with a clenched fist"—I wonder what the crook had said!; a newspaper, the *Sphere*.

154. MURDER SET TO MUSIC

V53 #3—Summer 1949
Written by unknown; possibly
Sam Merwin Jr. and based
on a C.S. Montayne plot

Place: New York City

Main characters: Bill Ryan, Johnson, Lt. Harris (New York City), Steve Huston, Jon Hugo, Claude Dean, Frank Havens, Richard Curtis Van Loan/the Phantom, Muriel Havens, Carla Hugo, Asst. D.A. Callen (New York City), Dr. Borg, Gibbs, Michael Barstow, Mark Warren, Inspector Gregg, Catherine Clark, Peter, Mr. Gray, Kirk Elliot, Quigley, Paul Stephens, Dr. Bendix, Truck, Efrem Klemper, Chip Dorlan, Jorkin, James Jones, Arkwright, Davis, Antonio Scarpini, Luigo

Three murders are committed, each victim a famous violinist. But the crimes seem to focus on the first murder, that of a violinist recently back from a tour in Italy. What had he brought back with him to cause his death, and the deaths that follow?

As Frank Havens and a few guests at his home await the arrival of the popular virtuoso with the violin, Steve Huston is at that minute investigating the murder of Havens' expected guest. With the complicated twists to the case, Havens asks the Phantom to investigate. Complicating the plot is the partnerships of one murder victim in a winery. But the Phantom learns it all centers on five valuable *Stratavarises* the first victim had recently brought back from Italy.

Notes: This story starts out with a lot of Montayne's plot devices, especially those used in "The Clue of the Second Murder" (March 1948), so either the author is completing notes started by Montayne, or possibly he had just read C.S. Montayne's previous stories before writing his own; one plot device Montayne used was to bring in a butler of a murder victim to act in a small part in the investigation—this is used in this story; okay; Claude Dean is the music critic for the *Clarion*; Gibbs is Havens' butler; one of the Phantom's cars is a gray coupe; tugged lobe of his ear; the rabbit test on human blood—used in a previous Montayne story; snaked out his automatic; pinze-nez glasses on a black cord; the Press Club; sentences end in more colons and semicolons, and reminds me of a possible editor finishing the Montayne notes; cat-like tread; the red signal light is used towards the end, and we're told it's only used now in dire emergencies; Van's alter ego of the Phantom.

155. THE BLACK BALL OF DEATH

V54 #1—Fall 1949
Written by Norman A. Daniels & C.S. Montayne

Place: New York City; Lake Crandle, NJ

Main characters: Steve Huston, Frank Havens, Matthew Arden, Arthur Arden, Luke, Clayton Marsh, Richard Curtis Van Loan/the Phantom, Hackett, Sheriff McCabe (Lake Crandle), Dr. Hugo Winterly, Sam Ruddy, Bess, Mrs. Stewart, Bernard Pennell, Hiram Grundy, Chip Dorlan, Horgan, Carter, McGregor, Marge, Victoria Selden, Miss Marsh, Mr. Gray, Daniel Fordyce, Inspector Gregg (mentioned), Mrs. Wayne, Hugh Royal, Maxine Hillary, Len Barker, Paul Jardin, Douglas Hoag, Vogel, Park Sunderland, Tom

Steve Huston and Frank Havens are returning to New York City from an outing in another town, when they experience automobile trouble. Stopping at an old friend's cabin, they discover the owner's son has been murdered.

When the Phantom enters the case, he feels that there is a deeper plot than what lies on the surface. He soon uncovers a gigantic scheme to bilk millions from unsuspecting victims.

Notes: This was definitely a strange feeling reading this story and knowing beforehand that C.S. Montayne had actually fallen dead over his typewriter while typing this story. The weird part is that you can tell at what point he was at in the story: the Phantom and Steve Huston are trailing a girl involved in the case, when they enter a bar and the Phantom takes over from Steve who had followed the girl to that point—however, Steve is almost forgotten when he should have been present. Another strange part involving this story is that Montayne's story was actually patterned after a Daniels entry. Montayne used previous stories to write his own adventures, often employing plots from previous Norman Daniels stories. This one is patterned after Daniels' "Murder of a Plaster Saint" (February 1944), and for Daniels to actually finish the Montayne manuscript was weird. Actually, Montayne wrote almost half the story, maybe a little more, while Daniels wrote the last half. The change of authors comes somewhere between chapter 13 and chapter 15, very likely in chapter 14; a baleful stare; a premonition of danger; the Lakeside Inn; the Green Spot;

1933
1934
1935
1936
1937
1938
1939
1940
1941
1942
1943
1944
1945
1946
1947
1948
1949
1950
1951
1952
1953

1933

1934

1935

1936

1937

1938

1939

1940

1941

1942

1943

1944

1945

1946

1947

1948

1949

1950

1951

1952

1953

Tom & Jerry's Carousel Club; Esplanade Club; dulcet, rococo; the National Trust Company; Hotel Trois Arts; sloe eyed; Fowler's Bar & Grill; Monarch Hotel; Club Elite; Avedon Building; Formula 8.

Availability: *Wildside Pulp Classics: Phantom Detective #155* (published by Wildside Press, 2008).

156. THE TALL TOMB

V54 #2—Winter 1950

Written by Norman A. Daniels

Place: Stratton Heights

Main characters: Alonzo Stratton, Loren Corson, Det. Capt. Porter (Stratton), Grogan, Johnson, Dr. Norton, Roy Bambrick, Dunn, Perry Whitmore, Austin Howell, Police Chief O'Shea (Stratton), Luke Mulloy, Richard Curtis Van Loan/the Phantom, Frank Havens (telephone), Steve Huston (telephone), Helen Taylor, Nancy Vail, Cecil Scott, Shill, Frank Appolo, Inspector Callahan (Chicago), Paul Stewart, Judge Turner, Muriel Havens (mentioned)

A reporter on one of Frank Havens' newspapers uncovers a strange story that he wants to investigate. Asking for a leave of absence, he disappears for a while, until he is found in Stratton Heights, wounded and dying. The Phantom is sent by Havens to investigate the reporter's case.

The Phantom learns that there is a strange history to Stratton Heights. The founder of the town, Alonzo Stratton, had built the city and factories, but after a violent encounter with the labor unions and his workers, Alonzo is driven from the town he created. But with the help of others, he had left with $15 million in cash. His own money. He was also known to like to get even with his detractors—not in a violent sense, but rather to get the last laugh.

In the meantime, another citizen appears to be constructing new buildings and offices, new hospital wings, and is a general benefactor to the city. The people love this man for all that he is doing. However, now there are a number of murders in town, Havens' reporter being one of them.

The Phantom learns that this new benefactor was actually an agent of Alonzo Stratton, and what he was doing in the town was under the direction of Alonzo. However, the benefactor decides that this was too good of an opportunity to pass up, and decided to take over all of the wealth of Alonzo who by now is actually dead—murdered by his agent.

Notes: The *Denver Sphere;* "can't muff anything"; Carmody Street.

157. THE HAPPYLAND MURDERS

V54 #3—Spring 1950
Written by Norman A. Daniels

Place: Seaview, NY; New York City

Main characters: Russ Burton, Cpt Fred Slocum (Seaview), Richard Curtis Van Loan/the Phantom, Tory Trevor, Stuart Hawkes—the Jinx, Barry Austin, Dr. Bendix, Mr. Loomis, Doris Dana, Rodney Jadin, Mary, Herb Farrel, John Wilcox, Lester Dana, Mr. Gray, Frank Havens, Muriel Havens (mentioned), Steve Huston, Teddy Blane, Ernest Palmer, Lew, Hazel, Bill, Janet, Alicia

A carnival town, full of gambling and vice, is ruled over openly by a fat crook who doesn't fear the law. The F.B.I. and Treasury agents have already gone over the town and can find nothing to pin anything on the head crook, or his gang.

When the Phantom enters the case, things start hopping, and the Phantom soon learns that a mysterious moneyman is behind the fat crook posing as the headman of the gang. After a number of murders, the Phantom closes in on the mysterious leader, and he starts burning his bridges—in this case, the carnival—as he tries to hide his evil ways and keep his respectability in the town.

Notes: The Blue Parrot bar; a young girl in bobby sox and a swing skirt; the Tower Hotel; tugged lobe of his left ear in signal.

158. THE DEADLY DIAMONDS

V55 #1—Summer 1950
Written by Norman A. Daniels

Place: New York City

Main characters: Dell Folen, Martha Omley, Richard Curtis Van Loan/the Phantom, Lt. Johnson, Kip Bartram, Inspector Gregg, Buster, Dutch, Joseph Iselin, Edmund Ward, Bert Hagen, Hank Sylvester, Mr. Gray, Frank Havens, Muriel Havens, Roger Courtney, Bill Tierney, Otto Arden, Cleo Ahern, Joe Faris, Cliff Sprague, Steve Huston, Gordon Sanborn, Ronnie, Alan Stelling, Chip Dorlan (mentioned)

Van Loan is entertaining Martha Omley, the woman who had almost married his father, as they hit the New York nightspots while she is in town. One night crooks hold them up, steal her jewels and break her jaw in the course of the robbery.

The Phantom decides to track down the crooks, and in his investigation discovers a giant jewel theft ring in operation. He immediately starts looking for clues to the identity of the leader of the gang.

1933
1934
1935
1936
1937
1938
1939
1940
1941
1942
1943
1944
1945
1946
1947
1948
1949
1950
1951
1952
1953

1933

1934

1935

1936

1937

1938

1939

1940

1941

1942

1943

1944

1945

1946

1947

1948

1949

1950

1951

1952

1953

Half of the time, Van Loan is in the action, with the other half the Phantom in the disguise of Mr. Gray. A sign of things to come—the end of the super hero was coming, with the once great Phantom reduced to a mere man.

Notes: Club Peacock; Martha is from Smith Falls, Maryland; Muriel is a brunette, with blue eyes; Club Antoine; the *Clarion* call; pulled at the lobe of his left ear; okay; the Phantom's badge is used, but Van carries a regular police sergeant's badge which he often uses; Carmody Street.

159. HOMICIDE TOWN

V55 #2—Fall 1950
Written by unknown; possibly Bruce Elliott or Charles Greenberg

Place: Wainboro, NY

Main characters: Jeff Markham, Pete Grogan, Adam Smith, Steve Huston, Edmund Parish, Burt Stevens, Gilbert Dutton, Laura Wayne, Chester Reed, Nick Vail, Stella Marshall, Larry Mason, Eunice Weatherbee, Richard Curtis Van Loan/the Phantom, Felix, Mr. Gray, Dr. Martin Young, Mrs. Elsa Olsen, Henry Bixton, Dr. Tucker, Al Farrell, Eddie Carson, Joe Doyle, Police Chief James Blackburn (Wainboro), Crabtree, Mike O'Brien, Lake, Dr. Nash, Bill, Jim, Mr. Dick Slate, Mr. Steve Clark, Gus, Big Jim Boyle, Leonard Blish, Martha, Nancy, Frank Havens (telephone)

Steve Huston, while on vacation in his hometown of Wainboro, witnesses the corruption and gambling that has taken over the town in recent years. A mysterious man, known as Adam Smith (not his true name) controls the town politics, the gambling, and the city building and contract awards.

When Steve's old pal, who works for the local newspaper, is murdered, Steve calls Frank Havens and requests the Phantom's help in the murder investigation.

Notes: I've read a fairly similar Dan Fowler story plot; the Flagship; comic-opera; the Wainboro Gazette; okay; small balls of muscles bulged the corners of his jaws; uses "keed" instead of "kid"—again, I've seen this in a Dan Fowler author; Wainboro is Steve's home town; Bentley Hotel; Sapphire Room of the Penguin Club; affectation; Mr. Gray from Denver; a bony face; Black Maria's; here and now; Phantom has chains and spikes for wall-climbing sewed in the cuffs of most of his trousers; clue of a gold coin left at scene; Reform Party, a political party in town. Oddly, this had throwback clues to Montayne, but couldn't be one of his. Perhaps a new author, and he recently read a Montayne *Phantom?* When I originally read this one, I just credited it to Greenberg, but on a second read, it doesn't read like his, either.

160. MURDER MONEY

V55 #3—Winter 1951
Written by Norman A. Daniels

Place: New York City

Main characters: Clyde Bannister, Cherokee, Eric Stanton, Grace Stanton, Mac, Lloyd Newman (T-Man), John O'Brien, Richard Curtis Van Loan/ the Phantom, Muriel Havens (minor part), Frank Havens, Mr. Porter, George Tannon, Chet Blake, Fenton, Roger Keith, Dr. Bendix, Steve Huston, Clegg, Jepson (D.A.), Stuart Landis, Joe Tormay, Clint Seymour, Monroe Clark, Paul Corey, George Blake, Marty, Jack

Organized crime is controlling gambling and other vice around New York City. The Treasury men place an agent in with the mob, but they're afraid he is suspected and can't get away. When the gang kills one man, it's felt that their agent will be next.

The Phantom is called in, opens a gambling establishment in competition with the gang. When the gang approaches him, he lets them believe he has an "in" with the politicians and can operate as many establishments as they'd like. They take the Phantom into their gang.

But they haven't forgotten the T-Man spy in their group, and kidnap the agent's wife to force his hand. However, it's the Phantom who appears to fall for their trick, so they think "he" is the T-Man spy. The gang never suspects that the Phantom is on the case throughout the story.

Notes: Cherokee's Tepee roadside gambling and dining room; Green Acre Tavern; red signal light is mentioned.

1933
1934
1935
1936
1937
1938
1939
1940
1941
1942
1943
1944
1945
1946
1947
1948
1949
1950
1951
1952
1953

1933

1934

1935

1936

1937

1938

1939

1940

1941

1942

1943

1944

1945

1946

1947

1948

1949

1950

1951

1952

1953

161. THE VIDEO
VICTIMS

V56 #1—Spring 1951
Written by Norman A. Daniels

Place: New York City; Uncas

Main characters: Chester McLean, Richard Curtis Van Loan/the Phantom, Lisa McLean, Arnold King, Dr. Bendix, Muriel Havens (mentioned), Steve Huston, Frank Havens, Alonzo Woodward, Hugo Brennan, Dr. Falkner, Gordon Pulver, Sgt. Mathers, Gerald Oliver, George Lang, Inspector Gregory (New York City), Ben Corbett Wilkins, Pete, Marty, Johnson, Joe, Tom Finley, Paul Miller, Hank Jobe

A small town TV station owner asks for the Phantom's help, but upon the arrival of the Phantom the TV station owner leaves town and will not speak with him. His partner is trying to run the station while saboteurs are trying to wreck it. Then men suddenly turn up dead.

A fairly nice entry by Daniels, and not one often used. The partners of the TV station had actually sold half interest to the station several times, but as long as the station wasn't making much money, they had nothing to worry about. But a large network cable company brought their cable line through town and suddenly the local station became a part of a larger network, which meant a lot of profit. And also meant that several half partners had to die.

Notes: Windmere Hotel; lackadaisical; touches ear lobe in signal; calls Frank, "Mr. Havens," and Havens calls him, "Dick"; "Um"; okay; forward-minded; the Phantom calls the girl, "kid"; the Phantom uses two guns; bullets are killer slugs; Hotel Wayne; a bit of a prig; the Harrison House; Ben Corbett works for the *Clarion;* Holy Smoke; "Uh-uh"; some times people speak in grunts; "Keep your shirt clean."; drummed the desk with his fingertips; Van Loan talks to Muriel on the phone, and Lisa McLean is sent to stay with her; the Phantom uses Steve on the case; everybody knows the Phantom in his present disguise.

Availability: *Wildside Pulp Classics: Phantom Detective #161* (published by Wildside Press, 2009).

162. CRIMSON HARVEST

V56 #2—Summer 1951
Written by Norman A. Daniels

Place: Washington, D.C.; Spring Falls

Main characters: Frank Havens, Richard Curtis Van Loan/the Phantom, Sidney Clement, Conrad Weldon,

1933

1934

1935

1936

1937

1938

1939

1940

1941

1942

1943

1944

1945

1946

1947

1948

1949

1950

1951

1952

1953

Muriel Havens (mentioned), Betty Clement, Mr. Gray, Det.-Lt. Matt Sanford (Spring Falls), Joe, Russell Tyler, George Bradford, Roy Hassard, Pete Dudley, Mike, "Big" Tony Rober, Capt. Grogan (Spring Falls), Alan Prentiss, Lou Paget, Fred Elliot, Marty, Rocky, Paul Reynolds, Steve Huston, Dick Mastro, Griff, John, Gilmore

A long-time businessman from a town supposedly without crime is called to testify at a congressional board of inquiry in Washington, D.C. When he has dinner with Frank Havens and Van Loan, he is suddenly murdered and Frank wants the Phantom to find out who killed him and why.

In his investigation, the Phantom finds hidden crime in the city supposedly without crime. A giant scheme is working within a trucking outfit, a farm and produce market, and controlling interest in stocks for a milk dairy seems to be the goal of a hidden mastermind.

At the bottom of the crime is a giant scheme to produce illegal whiskey: the products needed to distill the whiskey were obtained at the city farm and produce market, while the trucking company transported the illegal whiskey across country, and the dairy was needed for the hidden plant to make the whiskey.

Notes: The Phantom has a double shoulder holster for two guns; touching the ear lobe as a signal is mentioned, and used towards the end of the story; piggy little eyes; uses pressure on nerves to render a man unconscious; a tocsin call; Carmody Street; shoe-button eyes.

163. MURDER MILLIONS

V56 #3—Fall 1951
Written by Norman A. Daniels

Place: New York City

Main characters: Clint Jordan, Professor Elnor, Deacon Price, George Sharon, Dr. Wickers, Inspector Gregg, Richard Curtis Van Loan/the Phantom, Andy Grant, Joe Moore, Frank Havens, Muriel Havens (mentioned), Steve Huston, Peggy Dexter, Walter Osborne, Ted Wales, Petey Drake, Stuart Burton, Jack Sherry (Asst. D.A.), Leora Courtney, Preston (prison warden), Carl Baker, Jim Baker, Harry Gilbert, Norbert, Alan

In a story that reminded me of the Black Bat, the Phantom intervenes in a mob wipe out as they attempt to kill a man who knows too much. The Phantom rescues the man, but as the man is running away, gangster bullets strike him in the back, severely damaging his spine.

1933

1934

1935

1936

1937

1938

1939

1940

1941

1942

1943

1944

1945

1946

1947

1948

1949

1950

1951

1952

1953

The injured man tells the Phantom that he knows the identity of the mastermind but will only reveal the man's name if the Phantom will prove another man innocent of the crime he was convicted of. With the injured man under guard at the hospital, the Phantom starts out to unravel a weird case.

The man he is supposed to prove innocent cannot be innocent, and has paid for his crimes by execution. He had murdered a man out of jealousy before witnesses, and his girlfriend even admitted that he was guilty. So why had the injured man asked the Phantom to prove he was innocent?

It was merely his way in leading the Phantom towards the identity of the mastermind, without himself giving the man's name. The more the Phantom investigates the convicted killer, the closer he comes to the actual mastermind.

Notes: A good story, with quite a few twists, and a good mystery as well as action-packed; hydra headed monster; touched his ear lobe in signal; the Palisade Hotel; the Blue Jungle Club; Carmody Street.

164. THE SILENT KILLER

V57 #1—Winter 1952
Written by Norman A. Daniels

Place: New York City

Main characters: Tim Harris, Anna, Joey, Beryl, Barry Austin, Paul Bronson, Sally, Marge, Bob Warren, Richard Curtis Van Loan/the Phantom, Muriel Havens, Mr. Gray, Faulkner, Dr. Frank Galey, Frank Havens, Matt Ely, Steve Huston, Bruno Richards, Marty Bell, Ernie, Otto Hanover, Julian Dalban, Cyril Osborne, Clark, Sidney Thorne, Paul Cowley, Rocky, Inspector Gregg

Drugs are flooding New York City, and the target for drug dealers are young kids and young adults. As Muriel and Van Loan are leaving a theater they come across the murder of a young man, presumably

killed by another young man.

The Phantom enters the case, and soon uncovers some of the higher ups in the criminal organization. The gang is expecting a large shipment of drugs coming in from another country, and the Phantom hopes to stop it before they reach the streets—and the young people.

Muriel is captured by the mastermind, and held against the Phantom in case he gets too close. Fortunately, the Phantom discovers the mastermind's identity and rescues Muriel. As they await the police, Muriel catches the Phantom in a trick, thus discovering his true identity, although she was already sure of his identity prior to this.

Notes: Muriel is a blonde; Mr. Gray of Cleveland; Rocco's restaurant; Elite Cafe; touched his ear in signal; a fishing boat, the *Marigold*.

165. THE DOOMED MILLIONS

V57 #2—Spring 1952
Written by Norman A. Daniels

Place: Hungary; Vienna, Austria; New York City; Washington, D.C.; Nassau

Main characters: Feodor Danowski, Ludwig, Steve Huston, Maget, Zarnov, Muriel Havens, Richard Curtis Van Loan/the Phantom, Jim Davis, Cedric Westcott, Ann Lansing, Otto Bruger, Harry Nagel, Yvette Tafler, Bill Riley, Dr. Grenfell, Hartert, Igor Igorsky, Lt. Martinez (Nassau), Frank Havens (telephone)

One of the better stories during this period, in which the Phantom must fight against Russian spies. A Pole in Hungary has reached a high position in the Communist regime, but wants out. He obtains two briefcases full of names of men and women who have been arrested by the Communists and have disappeared, either killed or taken to work camps in Russia.

The Pole is killed during his escape, but an unknown friend gets the papers and schedules a meeting in Nassau where the papers will be turned over for broadcast over Radio Free Europe.

But Russian spies have captured Steve Huston, who was in on Danowski's escape to the West. Under drugs he gives information to the spies. Nassau is full of spies already, including a super spy known as Zarnov, and before the Phantom can obtain the papers, rescue Steve Huston, and bring the case to a close, Van Loan is nearly killed, plus he tells just about everybody he comes in contact with that he, Van Loan, is really the Phantom.

Notes: Van Loan reveals to Steve Huston that he is the Phantom in this

1933
1934
1935
1936
1937
1938
1939
1940
1941
1942
1943
1944
1945
1946
1947
1948
1949
1950
1951
1952
1953

1933

1934

1935

1936

1937

1938

1939

1940

1941

1942

1943

1944

1945

1946

1947

1948

1949

1950

1951

1952

1953

story; the Golden Fiddle Restaurant; Havens has told the State Department the Phantom's true identity; small piggish eyes; the Phantom rescues Steve Huston while he is Van Loan, so Huston now learns the real identity; Ann Lansing works for Havens' newspaper in Nassau.

166. THE MURDER MACHINE

V57 #3—Summer 1952
Written by Norman A. Daniels

Place: Leland

Main characters: Rodney Bentley, Mayor Proctor, Claude Hammond, George Mead, Matt Thurston, Lark, Steve Huston, Police Chief Anders (Leland), Laughlin, Richard Curtis Van Loan/the Phantom, Terry "Whitey" Rogers, Willie Giffen, Fred Sterling, Mike, Joe Lennox, Peter Cook, Frank Havens, Muriel Havens, Capt. Mathers (Leland), Jim Meskill, Maxie Brown

The Phantom has been in Leland for about a month, undercover, setting up an alias as a free-lance gambler, while a reporter from Havens' newspaper is concluding his investigation into corruption and crime in the city. As the reporter prepares to leave town, the murder machine catches up with him and sets an accident in which he is killed.

At this point, the Phantom brings Van Loan to town, along with Steve Huston and Muriel Havens, to help him in his investigation. As Van Loan, the Phantom can institute a frontal attack on the crooks, while as the secret alias of the gambler, he can work from within.

Notes: Steve Huston still knows the Phantom's identity, but this will change in the next three stories, as the new author doesn't know that Steve is aware of the secret identity; Club Sesame; Muriel has dark hair; everyone knows that Van Loan is the Phantom, including the crooks.

167. CANDIDATE FOR DEATH

V58 #1—Fall 1952
Written by Prentice Winchell

Place: Chicago, IL; New York City

Main characters: "Honest" John Martin Midworth, Judson, Harry, Frank Havens, Muriel Havens, Johnnie Garrett, Richard Curtis Van Loan/the Phantom, Miss Burr, Mr. Gray, Steve Huston, Inspector Gregg (telephone), Marie, Arnold Karrisson, Det. Lt. Jim Rush (Chicago), Bruno, Reilly, Lt. Broderick (Chicago), "Boy-Face" Gulick, Culp, Mary, Rudolph Bliss, Nelson, Rocky, "Runt," Ben

At a political convention, the leading candidate for presidency of the United States is murdered shortly after his party has given him the nomination. For some reason the candidate was withdrawing from the race in which he was assured an easy victory.

Frank Havens calls in the Phantom. In a curious switch, the candidate's own wife is the mastermind. She had backed her husband in his political career, all the time being an agent of a foreign power. When her husband discovered her involvement, he had decided to withdraw from the race. His wife had her lover kill her husband for her.

At first glance, you wonder why she had her husband killed instead of forcing him to continue in the race. But with the political party about to name her lover as the successor to the party's nomination, the White House would still be under her control.

Notes: This story, along with the next two, are by Stewart Sterling, who wrote the last published Black Bat story, and I found many similarities between these stories; there are no chapter headings, nor were there in Sterling's Black Bat; many sentences end mid-way, also the writing style of Sterling's Black Bat story; and Havens owns the *Chicago Enterprise*—the newspaper in the Black Bat story was the *Enterprise;* "no-o"; gimlet eyed; the thunder of Niagara; Muriel is now a blonde again; "We... don't... know"; Mr. Gray from Cleveland; okay; tells a Chicago detective that he's Richard Curtis Van Loan; perhaps this following is the Phantom's greatest disguise—"As it was, the Shadow ran along parallel to the car"—the Shadow, not the Phantom? hmmm; the Crimson Cat Club; hamitue; eyes were a baleful green; Van Loan laughed then, a short, quick laugh...; actually, there was a Chicago detective named Sam Malone running in short stories in *The Phantom Detective* by an author named Jackson Hite, and there will be another clue to this character in the future; with the clue of the Shadow, my first thought was towards Bruce Elliott, but these stories strike me more as the Spider, Wentworth, and Nita Van Sloan, instead of the Phantom, Van Loan, and Muriel.

168. THE STARING KILLER

V58 #2—Winter 1953
Written by Prentice Winchell

1933
1934
1935
1936
1937
1938
1939
1940
1941
1942
1943
1944
1945
1946
1947
1948
1949
1950
1951
1952
1953

1933

1934

1935

1936

1937

1938

1939

1940

1941

1942

1943

1944

1945

1946

1947

1948

1949

1950

1951

1952

1953

Place: New York City

Main characters: Muriel Havens, Richard Curtis Van Loan/the Phantom, Det. Lt. Bart Edson, Mike Maxon, Inspector Gregg, Dorothy Turner, McMahon, Barney Rush, Irene Russell (alias of Muriel), Andy, Jimmy, Eddie, Fat Herman, Arnold Fenwick, O'Halloran, Fenn, Noisy, Gus Banning, Frank Havens (mentioned)

The robbery of a large diamond has taken place along the water-front, in where there have been several murders, including the murder of an undercover cop. This latest one is witnessed by Muriel Havens. She calls Van Loan, as she is worried that the killer may have recognized her. Van cautions her to remain where she is until he can reach her.

Now, the Phantom must search for the killer, a staring-eyed man, before he can reach Muriel Havens.

Notes: This was a nice entry, only marred by all the sexual content. The Phantom has Muriel on his mind to such a degree that it's a wonder he ever catches the killer. Take this little play for instance:

"You mean you're afraid of getting fat!" Van Loan said.

"All right... I might get fat," she replied.

"I don't know. I like a little meat on the bone."

Muriel dug her nails into his arms and hissed softly, "You stinker! What do you think I've got?"

"I'd like to find out."

Muriel gave him a quizzical glance as they headed toward the cocktail lounge. "As if you didn't know!" she said.

Often reminded of Richard Wentworth and Nita Van Sloan instead of Richard Curtis Van Loan and Muriel Havens, including some of the scenes; Van's thoughts of sex—and Muriel—are often distracting; cussing is also more vulgar now; glinting eyes; Van calls Muriel, "Baby"; Van Loan yelped; the Crow's Nest; okay; strong hint of sex between Van Loan and Muriel; Andy worked for Van Loan, calls him "Skipper"; carries a .38; he clipped out; Van Loan owns a schooner, names it the *Barracuda* for his role in this story; Inspector Gregg is aware of the Phantom's identity in these three stories by Sterling; Steve Huston does not know Phantom's identity when he is in the stories.

Availability: *Action Adventure Stories* #123 (published by Fading Shadows,

Inc., 2003).

169. ODDS ON DEATH

V58 #3—Spring 1953
Written by Prentice Winchell

Place: New York City;
Ossining prison; Hastings, NY

Main characters: Rigo Vanetti, Tony Carvello,
Johnny Ryan, Judge Turner, Richard Curtis Van
Loan/the Phantom, Muriel Havens, Frank
Havens, Inspector Gregg, Lou, Larson (prison
warden), Capt. Burke, Hawley, Plank, Gault,
Shaky Schultz, Mae Walsh, Benson, Evans, Steve
Huston, Hannaran, McNulty, Judge Benedict, Rod
Ayres, Francis Blair, Fritz LeDuke, O'Neil, Delaney,
James J. Browning, Mr. Gray, Murphy

A big shot gambling boss is
convicted for a lesser crime, and sentenced to a short term in Sing Sing. The
Phantom, working with the police, puts a plan into operation. The convicted
crook is hidden away while the Phantom is taken to prison disguised as the
crook.

In prison, the Phantom learns several clues that point to the real mastermind who controls a powerful syndicate that deals in drugs, prostitutes, and
other criminal vices. Faking the death of the crook in prison, the Phantom re-
joins the police as they attempt to run the master crook out of his hole. Thinking the big shot has died in prison, the mastermind needs to show the rest of
his gang that the big shot had merely worked for someone higher up—and he
was that man. He calls a meeting of all of his mob, and the police, with the
Phantom, are there to round up all the crooks.

Notes: On the cover, it states, "Featuring the Phantom & Muriel Havens
in...", so Muriel gets equal billing now; Muriel's hair is color of a raven's wing;
sentences end before complete; again, strong feeling of *Spider* characters; okay;
"no-o"; the Phantom is talking, but narrative ends with "Sam said"—again,
the strange connection with Jackson Hite's short stories in the back pages of
The Phantom Detective, in which he has a story character from Chicago named
Sam Malone; all right, all right; when the inspector is talking about prostitutes,
he notices Muriel and stops—at which she says, smiling, "Go ahead, Inspector.
I know the facts of life"; Muriel knew how Van felt about not being alone with
her for a little while tonight. But the opportunity would come soon.

170. MURDER'S AGENT

V59 #1—Summer 1953
Written by Norman A. Daniels

1933
1934
1935
1936
1937
1938
1939
1940
1941
1942
1943
1944
1945
1946
1947
1948
1949
1950
1951
1952
1953

Place: New York City

Main characters: Muriel Havens, Frank Havens (mentioned), Richard Curtis Van Loan/ the Phantom, Nancy Arnold, Cathy, Walter Bowden, Rocky Spaull, Bert, Inspector Gregg, Alan Foster, Fred Finch, Janine Sims, Nick Tambo, Bill Murray, Elise Watson, Milford Watson, Mac, Petey, Kip Graham, Thelma Norris, Bennie Norris, Allington, Longman, Donier, Mickey Hayden

For the last story, the Phantom becomes nothing more than a protégé of Richard Curtis Van Loan. Although everyone knows that Van Loan is the Phantom, he tells everyone that he merely sponsors the Phantom, now and then helping him in his cases. Frank Havens no longer has any active part with the Phantom, and it's left up to Van Loan.

However, in this case, a friend of Muriel Havens asked her to contact the Phantom for her as she plans a rendezvous with her missing sister late at night in a dark park. The missing sister had been involved with gangsters prior to her coming up missing a year previously.

Muriel, unable to make contact with the Phantom, accompanies the girl—secretly—to the rendezvous in the park, and hides in the bushes as her friend makes contact with her missing sister. Muriel witnesses her friend's capture by two men, and the murder of the missing girl.

When she finally contacts the Phantom, she asks him to investigate and find her friend before she, too, is murdered. When the Phantom starts his investigation, he uncovers a weird plot in which gang lords are mysteriously hidden away while their organizations are held together by a proxy. The missing underworld heads were facing possible deportation from the United States, so they had to go into hiding and let someone else run their organizations for a while. Meanwhile, the hidden mastermind appears to be actually taking over the operation in some cases, and the mobster bosses come up dead.

The Phantom eventually rescues Muriel's friend, and finds out that her sister had been living incognito while her gangster boyfriend was hidden. She had known too much, and when she made contact with her sister, it was decided to kill her.

Notes: Story is about ten pages longer than is normal for this period, and with the sexual content, I wonder if all of the story is by Norman Daniels. Maybe an editor added some sex scenes, thus lengthening the story at the same time. Muriel is dark haired; the Phantom also has a gun in a crotch holster; Van Loan tells people he is backing the Phantom—not that he is the Phantom, however, everybody knows he's the Phantom; tugged the lobe of ear;

"You're a white guy," he said; no closing this time around, as in most stories, we're told that the Phantom will now rest until a new case appears to bring the Phantom out to battle crime again, but not this time; there is no mention at all of Steve Huston.

Thus ended the long twenty-year run of one of the most fascinating pulp heroes to have been created back in the 1930s. A strange series, in which just about everybody wrote at least one *Phantom*. Still, there was some order to the chaos, and the editors tried to maintain one author during each period, just filling in with other authors at times. Perhaps, to allow a breathing spell for the regular author, or maybe to show each author that no one had complete control over the writing of the stories. And, strangely enough, the second ten years of the stories had a strong order to them. The series became more solid, and fewer authors were involved. Though I still maintain that 1936 was possibly the best year, with "Dealers in Death" (July) and "Death Rides the Blizzard" (November) stories being the best in the complete run; the 1943 to 1953 period contained some great stories as well, though perhaps less exciting.

1933
1934
1935
1936
1937
1938
1939
1940
1941
1942
1943
1944
1945
1946
1947
1948
1949
1950
1951
1952
1953

1933

1934

1935

1936

1937

1938

1939

1940

1941

1942

1943

1944

1945

1946

1947

1948

1949

1950

1951

1952

1953

CHAPTER III, SECTION I

THE LOST STORIES

WERE ALL OF the *Phantom* stories published? No. There are undoubtedly some stories out there yet that were written for *The Phantom Detective*, but published later with all traces of the Phantom removed.

We knew all along that Norman Daniels had written a *Phantom* story in
1935 that had been rejected, and Daniels cut the story in half, removing all
traces of the Phantom. The story was "The Happiest Hour Murders." Will
Murray, during the 1993 PulpCon in Dayton, was searching the tables when
he came across an odd Daniels story in the October 1935 issue of *Thrilling
Detective*. The story was "Many Men Die," which in itself was odd. The title
sounded more like a statement than a title. Regardless, Will looked inside and
found this blurb:

> Beware of your Happiest Hour! That grim warning of impending doom pre-
> ceded the violent death of each of the Shermans!

Here it was, the missing "The Happiest Hour Murders!"

After reading the story, I was able to recognize the basic plot of a number
of Daniels' stories, as well as his *Phantom Detective* stories. Unfortunately, this
was only about half the length of the normal *Phantom* during this period, so
there was a lot missing from the story. However, let's look at it as if it had
been a *Phantom* adventure, only using the names of the characters in the final
version.

MANY MEN DIE

from *Thrilling Detective*; V16 #2—October 1935
Written by Norman A. Daniels

Place: Never said, but probably New York City

Main characters: Jasper Sherman, Ralph Sherman, Horace Penfield, Harkness, Frankie Sherman, Det. Sgt.
Barry Benedict, Billy Shane, Walter Sherman, Police Commissioner Hartly, Schultz, Jane Thorne, Kirk Landis, Ted,
Fisher, "Killer" Pinney, Spad Mosely, Jimmy the Dip, "Spanish" Garcia, Dutton, Johnson, Silk

An old family curse says that each of the Shermans will die at their happiest hour, and in the past several of the Shermans had died during such celebrations as wedding anniversaries, marriages, birthdays, etc. Well, this time one of the Sherman sons is returning after many years absence, and the family is happily awaiting his arrival. But, as to be expected, he no sooner reaches the doorstep than he is killed. Right on his heels is Det. Sgt. Barry Benedict, who had been trailing an escaped convict named Billy Shane. Sure enough, the young son was that missing murderer, who had gone to prison using another name.

1933

1934

1935

1936

1937

1938

1939

1940

1941

Barry Benedict calls in the police commissioner who tells Barry to handle the case on his own. Barry Benedict is the Phantom, with a set of master keys that he carries with him. The police commissioner takes the place of Frank Havens, and maybe the police commissioner or police inspector in the story. What is plain at the beginning is that Frank Havens and Van Loan were probably at the house waiting for the return of the son, as the family was close friends to Havens (in this case, they were close friends of the police commissioner). When the murder occurred, the Phantom probably took immediate charge of the investigation.

Most of the action takes place around the Sherman mansion, although our hero does make trips into town. I would imagine that what was cut from the original story was the Phantom's investigation away from the mansion, and only the mansion scenes were left intact.

It would have been a nice entry. As it was, "Many Men Die" was a nice story, and indeed, many men die in the story. Way too many for such a short story. In fact, at one point, the detective and another man discover two dead bodies at the bottom of a well. We are immediately led to understand that this was a major clue. However, this was immediately forgotten and there was no explanation for the bodies at the end of the story, nor who they even were. And with the police guard all around the mansion, still the crooks come and go at will. There are gun battles between the detective and crooks, yet where are the police guards around the mansion? They come up later and are told to guard the bodies or some such thing.

The case stems from the son who was killed at the beginning of the story. As Billy Shane he had run with the Silk gang, the leader never having been identified. Billy Shane had escaped the initial pursuit of the police, and had brought stolen gems and money to the mansion before he was eventually cap-

1942

1943

1944

1945

1946

1947

1948

1949

1950

1951

1952

1953

1933

1934

1935

1936

1937

1938

1939

1940

1941

1942

1943

1944

1945

1946

1947

1948

1949

1950

1951

1952

1953

tured and sent to jail. When he escapes from prison, he heads for the mansion in hopes of retrieving the loot for himself, but Silk, his old boss, is also after that missing loot. Working his way into the household, he has time to search for the missing loot after he's killed young Billy Shane.

A mystery in the story concerns the way the victims are murdered. Like Billy Shane, he is killed by a knife in the back as he steps onto the porch. Others are also killed in a similar manner. But there could have been no one behind the victim to plunge the knife into his back. The Phantom—er, excuse me, Barry Benedict, discovers on the roof of the porch (hidden in a rain gutter) a long pole with an attachment on it to hold a knife. The killer merely had to lie over the porch roof and swing the pole downward and the knife would strike its intended victim. Simple.

Notes: This story was undoubtedly rejected by Marcus Goldsmith. I've an idea he didn't care for the murder technique. I would imagine there were many stories rejected by Mr. Goldsmith. Only the records of Norman Daniels had alerted us to "The Happiest Hour Murders," so we were able to locate this one. For instance, the Winter 1952 *G-Men Detective* advertised the next Dan Fowler story as "Each Night I Die," by C. K. M. Scanlon. As we know now, the next Dan Fowler story was "The White Death" by Richard Foster. What happened to "Each Night I Die?" I bet it's out there somewhere, probably under a new title, the author's real name, and published in one of Standard's other magazines, though this isn't a necessity.

Availability: *Behind the Mask* #47 (published by Fading Shadows, Inc., 1999).

And yet another masterful disguise was the case of the Blue Ghost. I finished reading *The Phantom Detective* series several years ago, and had since despaired that I would never have the chance to read another adventure of the world's greatest detective. Like G-8, there's a certain something that pulls the reader back for more. I've got an idea that the mysterious something is the characters, not the stories. But whatever it is, let's just call it nostalgia and let it go at that. The Phantom, Frank Havens, Muriel, and Steve Huston thrilled us for many an adventure, and I hated to see the day come when there were no more of those adventures to read.

Imagine my thrill when Will Murray casually mentioned a *Phantom Detective* rip-off character, called the Blue Ghost, who appeared in *Detective Fiction Weekly* during 1940; two stories that ran in serialization. At the time, little was known about the character: Will had heard about the Blue Ghost from the late Bob Sampson. Will's information peaked my curiosity and I began searching for the two stories in question.

Will Murray is responsible for running down the true name of the author for these two stories, so I will not spend much time on him, merely to say that the author was Jack Byrne (John H. Byrne), a one time Standard re-write man, and later a Munsey editor; his re-write of Norman Daniels' "Dealers in Death" (July 1936) was a turning point in the *Phantom Detective* series, bringing in new characters and new gimmicks in the stories. Though Will believes that Byrne may have only been involved in the re-writes of some of the *Phantoms,* two in particular, "Dealers in Death" and "Death Rides the Blizzard" (November 1936), he may or may not have written *Phantoms* himself, and that he probably left Standard in mid 1936, leaving the *Phantom* series far behind him.

This brings up several questions, though; one in particular—where did the two Blue Ghost stories come from, if they were not originally written as *Phantoms?* And if they had been written as *Phantoms,* could there have been more—and were there others published as *Phantoms,* before or after 1936? My guess is, Byrne did write at least a couple *Phantom Detective* stories for Standard, and I'm even thinking that maybe they were printed after 1936. But who knows?

I'm pretty sure that Byrne did some re-write to the Dan Fowler story, "Big Shot" (February 1936). And what about the Dan Fowler story, "Gems of Jeopardy" (June 1938)? If he wasn't a re-write man at this time, could he have written the story—kind of free-lancing from Munsey at the time? There are several similarities in his writing and this story. Or maybe I'm just seeing blue ghosts and he had nothing to do with either of them. And here's something else, the name of Leopold has only been used twice in the two series, *Phantom Detective* and Dan Fowler; well, actually, the name only appeared (twice) in the Dan Fowler stories, "Devil's Playground" (April 1938), and "The Insurance Murders" (February 1939). At the time I read these stories, I thought it was an editor playing a game with Leo Margulies because of the affair he had had with Cylvia Kleinman; both the Leopolds in the stories belonged to the F. B. I. agent, Klein. But what if that wasn't the case, what if the author was Byrne, moonlighting from Munsey?

There are *Phantom Detective* suspects: "The Beast King Murders" (July 1937), and "Hammers of Doom" (September 1937), as well as "The Phantom's Gamble With Death" (February 1940). But before you start marking these on your magazines—don't! I am only saying that there are some clues, some similarities to the Blue Ghost stories written by Byrne, nothing that is conclusive, and I could be completely wrong.

Another *Phantom* story from 1939 that was giving me some fits, "The Radio Murders" (April 1939), came under scrutiny while I was investigating stories that had some semblance to Byrne. However, there is nothing to really tie the story to him.

But what about those two Blue Ghost stories? Well, here are the characters involved: Charles Dexter "Dex" Bradford (Richard Curtis "Dick" Van Loan) and Adam Wilde (Frank Havens). There is no Muriel, no Steve Huston, no Chip Dorlan, nor a Jerry Lannigan. But there is a Milo Hackett (Dr. Paul Bendix). The one alias he uses in the stories (besides Hackett) is Benedict Rogge. Adam Wilde owns the Federated Broadcasting Company, with radio networks around the world; maybe not the famous *Clarion* newspaper, but close enough. The Phantom—er, excuse me—the Blue Ghost is called to action by a flashing sign on top of the FBC building. A large globe with a flashing lightning

1933
1934
1935
1936
1937
1938
1939
1940
1941
1942
1943
1944
1945
1946
1947
1948
1949
1950
1951
1952
1953

strike is changed from yellow to blue when the Blue Ghost is needed. When this doesn't reach him, Adam Wilde uses a certain radio broadcast to call him, a program called *The Night Owl's Serenade,* by ringing a tiny bell in the background. A radio call for the Phantom was very similar in one of the questionable *Phantoms* I mentioned earlier.

One of the delightful oddities of the Blue Ghost series was Dex referring to Adam as Asinine Adam, Astute Adam, Almighty Adam, or Admirable Adam. The author had fun with this. One of the characters in one of the stories was called Great Graves. At least two other characters had double letters in their names: Willis Wallace Wagstaff and Alice Angott. I've heard a name used for this, but I can't remember what it's called. In my quick search through the *Phantom* and Fowler stories, I was unable to find an author doing this, but I didn't search all issues. Perhaps he used this in chapter headings, too? (What about A. Adamson?)

Though neither of the stories in the Blue Ghost series was of the quality of "Dealers in Death" and "Death Rides the Blizzard," they were fun, nevertheless. In "The Blue Ghost", a five part serial, from February 3, 1940 through March 2, 1940 in *Detective Fiction Weekly,* as written by Miles Hudson (Jack Byrne), we have a very complicated plot.

THE BLUE GHOST

from *Detective Fiction Weekly;* V134 #4-V135 #2—February 3-March 2, 1940

Written by Jack Byrne

Place: Tropic City, Florida; Contraband Cay, Florida, and Cragsmoor Castle, somehere in New York.

Main characters: Adam Wilde, Charles Dexter (Dex) Bradford, Micky, Augie Ferroni (mentioned), Marty Helmuth (mentioned), Otto Blandon (mentioned). Mr. Mesmer (mentioned), Madame Louise (woman of doom, mentioned), Milo Hackett (alias), George Ivanov, Magda, Colfax, Frank Randall, Louie, Davy, Paul Yerkes, Capt. George Harper-Lytton, Eitoro, Julia Ormond, Prentiss Savage, David Ormond, Tiger Kilgallen, Niles, John Warlock, Dan Gibson (name

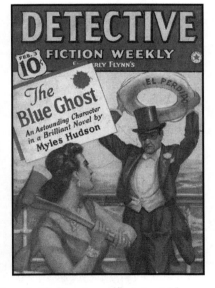

accidentally changed to Stafford once), Juliana Conroy, Dr. Felix Strang, Harvey Joliffe, Hoxton, McCullum, Jorgens, Harmon Briscoe, Dunbar, Victor Odell, Treadway, Benedict Rogge (alias), "Stub," "Buff," "Ditto" Dittmars, Hagar, Felipe, Sigmund, Ito, Bergdahl, Haggerty, Alice Angott, Dr. Oldfield.

Dex Bradford and Adam Wilde are vacationing in Florida while Dex is recovering from a bullet wound. Adam suggests that they attend a social gathering at the house of a rich family. But here they run into danger and action. An old friend, a magician, is performing at the gathering, but Adam notices that it is an impostor, not his old friend. When Dex and Adam leave the gathering, they almost get into the wrong sedan. It turns out that the magician owns a sedan exactly like that of Adam. When they leave, finally, they are attacked on the road by gangsters who had targeted their sedan instead of the one owned by the magician. From there, the story gets more complicated.

While the magician was on a world tour, the secrets of two nations were stolen. Russian agents and Japanese agents are after the return of these stolen secrets and believe the magician has them. To throw even more complication in the story, another group, known as the Third Party, is also after the stolen secrets. This Third Party is a group who is after power and money, and not associated with any nation, only their own desires.

Reminded me a lot of Cypher, the organization that battled the Shadow in the Dennis Lynds Belmont Shadow series in the 1960s.

Notes: A banal mask; a will-o'-the wisp; argus eyes; shoots a crook over the left eye; his sign of identification is a card with a gleaming blue splotch like a blot of blue ink—he also has a jeweled cigarette case, both seem to take the place of the Phantom's famous domino badge; the windigo, the night-wraith; his flashlight emits a green beam—a dim light; hue and cry; hummed a soft, tuneless refrain; Adam's Palm Beach estate is referred to as the Wildewoods establishment; Machiavellian; a ship, the *El Perdido;* the Third Party; a mask for the Furies (the Furies was mentioned in a Dan Fowler story); a previous novel is mentioned, "The Scarlet Web of Murder." In this story, supposedly, the Blue Ghost—who could read lips—failed to understand lip reading in a foreign language, which proved dangerous: There is the *Phantom Detective* story, "The Web of Murder" (February 1939), but I can't remember if there was an incident of this nature in the story. Might be interesting to find out, though.

Availability: *Action Adventure Stories* #11 (published by Fading Shadows, Inc., 1997).

BLUE GHOST BEWARE

from *Detective Fiction Weekly;* V141 #3-V142 #2—November 16-December 21, 1940
Written by Jack Byrne

Place: New York, and the college, called the Cathedral, sounds a lot like Notre Dame, but who knows?

Main characters: Leopold Ostrow, Steven Cobb, Adam Wilde, the Big Boss/Mr. X, Eliot Graves, Arthur Saks, Samuel Vicekery, Willis Wallace Wagstaff, Thomas Faith, George Thabit, John Muldoon, Luke Ballou, Charles Dexter "Dex" Bradford, Milo Hackett (alias), Augie Ferroni (mentioned), Hooks McKee (mentioned), the Frantzen brothers, Jonas Vandiver, Manuel, Benjamin Faulkner, Valentine DaCosta, Ancil Lindstrum, Quentin Spargo, Dronda Reade, Lilith Ostroy, Paul Willebrandt, Benedict Rogge (alias), Lt. Pound, Shaughnessy, Capt. L. S. Vail, Risetto, DuBerry, Withrow, Elias Coperthwaite (mentioned), Sgt. Roszizowicz, Walter C. Carscadon (mentioned), Digby.

The story involved a college that had received millions of dollars from an inheritance. Now there appears to be several factions within the college board with opinions on how the money should be used. It also appears that sev-

1933
1934
1935
1936
1937
1938
1939
1940
1941
1942
1943
1944
1945
1946
1947
1948
1949
1950
1951
1952
1953

1933

1934

1935

1936

1937

1938

1939

1940

1941

1942

1943

1944

1945

1946

1947

1948

1949

1950

1951

1952

1953

eral art masterpieces have been replaced with forgeries, as well as some stocks and bonds. When some of the board members are killed, Adam Wilde asks the Blue Ghost to investigate, and the college is his alma-mater. Not as complicated as the plot in "The Blue Ghost," but a fun story nevertheless.

Notes: The Touchdown Club; Mr. Mouse; Mr. Fingers; man uses sun lamp to tan; Adam Wilde may have graduated college in 1911, making him about 53 years old during the period; a club, the Park Union; other clubs are Stork, Morocco, Cavendish, Plaza, and Players—a lot of club names would be used in the 1945 to 1953 period of the *Phantom Detective;* author has characters calling each other "boy" a lot, which was often seen in the Dan Fowler series; Manuel is Wilde's chauffeur in both stories; "What devilment is afoot?"; a young-old face; the Medici daggers; another story, "Killers, Incorporated" is mentioned, with a Dr. Keyne involved; "You muffed it"; a wan smile; Dex uses contact lenses to change the color of his eyes.

Availability: *Action Adventure Stories* #12 (published by Fading Shadows, Inc., 1997).

Well, there you have it. Forget the Blue Ghost, this was our old friend, the Phantom. And I've got an idea Byrne was writing a few *Phantoms* (maybe Dan Fowlers, as well) during his stint as editorial director of the Munsey line. But was he responsible for bringing in Steve Huston and the *Clarion* signal light to the *Phantom* series, or was this suggested through editorial? Seems to me a rewrite man would not have that authority. However, some of the 1936 changes that appeared in the July issue of *The Phantom Detective* did appear in the two 1940 Blue Ghost serials; so either Byrne is the creator of those devices, or he brought them over to *Detective Fiction Weekly* when he crossed over to them. Whatever the case, the two Blue Ghost stories were fun reading, and I just pretended I was once more reading a thrilling mystery from the case book of Richard Curtis Van Loan, the Phantom.

Let's look at the one story promised for Fall 1953, titled "The Merry Widow Murders." Here is the synopsis of that story:

It was a tune such as might be whistled idly in the darkness of night... or heard issuing from the speaker of a garish, flashing juke box... a melody ordinarily gay and lilting, but now bearing a message of death and, mystery, setting the pace for a macabre dance executed by the minions of a modern empire of crime!

It was—the Merry Widow Waltz. And it became the theme song of the case known as "The Merry Widow Murders," next issue's suspense-packed novel taken from the strange annals of one of the most exciting manhunts in my entire career!

"The Merry Widow Murders," as fictionalized by Robert Wallace, is a smashing novel that plunges you into a new kind of racket of blaring jukeboxes, blazing guns and sinister death. From teeming Chicago's crime-controlled underworld to the lonely reaches of sprawling Cook County, you'll have a table right next to the dance floor as death waltzes past!

It's a novel of gambling—with busy slot machines pouring out blood instead of jangling quarters. First—a top reporter vanishes, is found slain. Then a dance spot owner is killed, a cop is almost beaten to death, and a beautiful blonde vocalist is mercilessly strangled.

They seemed like disconnected crimes—but they had one thing in common. All those who were slain were suspicious of the new jukeboxes that were being used around town—and had expressed their suspicions openly. In fact, the blonde songstress had a definite hunch and had called the newspapers—but she was a corpse before she could be reached. And corpses don't talk.

Because Frank Havens had received fragments of private information and was eager to get to the bottom of it, Muriel Havens and myself were suddenly drawn into this sinister web of crime. We knew that ordinarily the trail of a new gang lord is marked by spewing lead and a big-money fix. Without a doubt an all-powerful syndicate was behind it all, dealing out murder to those who wouldn't pay off. But who was the Mr. Big nobody could isolate?

You'll think twice before whistling in the dark again after you read "The Merry Widow Murders." You'll thrill to this timely novel of a million-dollar shakedown—packed with action, novelty, surprises and suspense from start to finish.

I would be very surprised if this novel did not appear somewhere. I'm guessing that it was probably published later in either *Triple Detective* or *Five Detective Novels*. And, if I'm not surprised, from the Chicago clue at least, this is probably Stewart Sterling once again. However, in searching for this story, don't pay any attention to my guesses. Look for the plot. You might check stories by Sterling, but the plot is what counts here. The title would have been changed, as well, so don't look for "The Merry Widow Murders." Again, the plot will identify this lost story for us.

1933
1934
1935
1936
1937
1938
1939
1940
1941
1942
1943
1944
1945
1946
1947
1948
1949
1950
1951
1952
1953

CHAPTER IV

SOME FINAL NOTES

A T THE TIME I was reading these novels I listed several stories as by
Author O. Meanwhile, I was in contact with Will Murray, and I told
him that these novels were rewritten Charles Greenberg stories. I suggested
that maybe Greenberg had loaned his novels to a friend, who was rewriting
them as his own, or else an editor had given a new writer Greenberg's stories
to read as a sample. We only knew of Greenberg's initial *Phantom* period, and
were not aware he had returned later. Will Murray had no suggestion as to why
these novels read like Greenberg's stories, until he later talked with someone
that knew Greenberg, and was told that he had returned for a second period of
Phantom Detective novels. Unfortunately, we did not have a list of the titles. Let
me also say that I thought the later stories were much better than his original
entries. Better written and more enjoyable.

To add to my problem, when C.S. Montayne came into the series, he must
have read Greenberg's later novels for reference, and his stories have a lot of
similarities to Greenberg's (as well as Daniels')! So at one point it was impossible to say this one is by Greenberg and this one by Montayne, they were just
too close! I was worried that maybe Montayne was rewriting those Greenberg
stories I had listed as Author O. But we are pretty sure Greenberg returned
to the series at this time, so we have dropped the designation of Author O for
Greenberg in this index.

And there appears to be a *Secret Agent "X"* connection to the *Phantom*.
We can go back to "Death Rides the Blizzard" (November 1936), which Will
Murray believes was written by Ray Cummings, but heavily edited by Jack
Byrne, yet has strong similarities to *"X."* Another that appears to be by this
same author, "The Phantom's Murder Trail" (March 1940), also has strong
similarities. But they aren't the only ones. "The Front Page Murders" (June
1938) and "Death Glow" (November 1938) made me think of the *Secret Agent
"X"* story, "Kingdom of Blue Corpses" (December 1935), which Will believes
was written by Paul Chadwick. Could it be? But another mystery pops up over
at *G-Men Detective*, when a Dan Fowler story appears right after the *"X"* series
folds, with a story titled "Crimson Crusade" (April 1939). Dan Fowler sounds
more like "X" than Fowler, even with a wound in his side (remember the "X"

wound?). But the mystery concerns the plot; there are at least half a dozen similar plots as this one over at *The Phantom Detective*. So I've got an idea our mystery author was knocking out *Phantoms,* with an occasional *Secret Agent "X"* yarn ("Kingdom of Blue Corpses"), and had attempted one more just before *"X"* folded ("Crimson Crusade"), which he turned into a Dan Fowler. Was this Paul Chadwick or someone else? Either the Phantom was masquerading as Secret Agent "X," or Secret Agent "X" was masquerading as the Phantom!

Donald E. Keyhoe is a name we have never associated with the *Phantom Detective* stories, but Keyhoe may have been writing *Lone Eagle* and Captain Danger stories and could have turned to *The Phantom Detective* at any point. Just look at the names on the Dan Fowler yarns, any of these could have written *Phantom* stories. I am sure that Stewart Sterling wrote *Phantoms* prior to the final issues. He was also writing Dan Fowlers at the time. But without the records, we will never know for sure just who wrote what. We can only guess at their identities. Speaking of Sterling, I should mention that I recently picked up a hardback novel by him, *Too Hot to Handle,* a Fire Marshal Pedley novel, copyright 1961 by Random House. Remember my notes wherein the Phantom oddly falls asleep at the end of several novels? This was likely a running joke among the *Phantom* authors. They must have asked, "When does this guy ever sleep?" But strangely, at the very end of *Too Hot to Handle,* Pedley falls asleep while explaining the case—just like the Phantom in those earlier novels!

CHAPTER V

LORDS OF
THE PHANTOM

IT'S PROBABLY NO coincidence that the earliest and most significant
writers behind the *Phantom Detective* series came out of the gangster pulps.

Prior to the Depression, pulps celebrating the Prohibition-era gangster and
bootlegger were all the rage and lingered into its early years. Like most genres,
they were clobbered in 1930 and '31 when Americans realized the Depression
was here to stay and cut back on their magazine buying. Luckily for the pulp
field, *The Shadow* was launched early in 1931. It went on to become the sole
pulp success story in that dismal year. By the fall of 1932, with pulps dropping
like dead bootleggers everywhere, Street & Smith had unexpectedly upped
The Shadow's frequency to twice a month and began laying secret plans for *Doc
Savage* and a revival of *Nick Carter.*

The secret was soon out. *The Shadow* was selling. Leo Margulies' Thrilling
Publications was the next house to dip into the pulp-hero pool with *The Phantom Detective.* Launched with a February 1933 cover date, the first issue was
entered into copyright in November 1932. Possibly that was simply an "ashcan"
dummy issue sent to the Library of Congress to protect the trademark until
they would get the real premier issue out.

The first writer tapped to ghost the *Phantom* was D'Arcy Lyndon Champion who committed his pulp sins under the names Jack D'Arcy and Tom
Champion. A veteran of the gangster pulps edited by Harold Hersey, Champion also had an interesting connection to Walter B. Gibson of *Shadow* fame.
He had worked under Gibson editing *Tales of Magic and Mystery* in 1928.
Champion was also a proficient writer of true crime stories, though how much
practical use that might have been on the exaggerated exploits of the Phantom
is difficult to say.

It wasn't long before Champion dragged in a backup ghost. Anatole France
Feldman was a major star of *Gangster Stories* and like magazines, and was
the creator of the notorious Big Nose Serrano character who blazed his way
through its pages in the years leading up to the advent of the Phantom. The
fifth *Phantom* novel, "The Jewels of Doom" (July 1933), seems to be a collaboration between Champion and Feldman, who also wrote as Anthony Field.

It's questionable whether or not first *Phantom* editor Alexander Samalman knew that Feldman was working with Champion. The first true ghost comes in with "Cities for Ransom" (September 1933). Arthur J. Burks, the so-called Speed Merchant of the Pulps, did that one.

Champion and Feldman continued Phantoming along, constantly repeating plots and themes until doubtless everyone was sick of the vicious cycle of mayhem and murder.

Then abruptly, *The Phantom Detective* hiccuped.

The January, 1934 issue announced G. Wayman Jones' "The Tick-Tack-Toe Murders" for February. But when that issue rolled around, in its place was "Death's Diary" and a new byline, Robert Wallace, a house name that had been introduced in *Thrilling Detective* at the same time the *Phantom* debuted. A lame apology promised the missing novel for the next issue.

When it duly but belatedly appeared, the story was obviously the work of Anatole Feldman. "Death's Diary" had been a Champion production. Clearly Feldman missed his deadline or turned in an unsatisfactory manuscript. (Signs of a Champion rewrite are evident in "The Tick-Tack-Toe Murders.") Feldman's style promptly disappears from the pages of *The Phantom Detective,* as does the mythical G. Wayman Jones.

Champion soldiered on as Robert Wallace for five more novels until "Spawn of Death" in September 1934. This work might be Art Burks returning to the fray. But the frequent use of the word "ere" throughout this tale points to George Fielding Eliot, soon to assume the mantle of C. K. M. Scanlon to chronicle the exploits of crack F.B.I. agent Dan Fowler in *G-Men.*

This writer is gone as soon as he appears, for the next issue debuts Norman A. Daniels. A relative newcomer to the field, Daniels broke into the field selling to *Gangster Stories* in 1931. A solid, workmanlike pulpster, Daniels immediately began alternating with Champion and another newcomer, George A. McDonald, who made his pulp debut in *The Underworld Magazine* in 1931, and had been prolific for Street & Smith's *Detective Story Magazine.*

With "Written in Blood" (May 1935), Champion seems to drop out, leaving Daniels to carry the series solo for a while. McDonald also vanishes, but he has gone over to Dell, where he writes the Lynn Vickers novels as Bryan James Kelley for *Public Enemy.*

One Daniels effort, "Island of Sudden Death" (October 1935), may have been written for a Thrilling pulp first announced as *Secret Service Detective Stories.* In this story, the Phantom works with the Secret Service, but the plot mirrors that of the first Dan Fowler novel in *G-Man,* which was released the same month as "Island of Sudden Death." It's possible that *Secret Service Detective Stories* was abandoned in favor of *G-Man,* and the Daniels novel recast as a *Phantom* to salvage it.

The year of 1936 seems to mark a crucial turning point for the series. April's "The Criminal Caesar" bears the fingerprints of a returning Feldman, although he might only be revising someone else's novel. (It's suspected that he was doing this to Daniels' and McDonald's earliest efforts.)

A new author seems to surface in "The Death-Skull Murders" (May 1936). One suspect is Edwin V. Burkholder, who also wrote as George Allan Moffatt for Thrilling and Street & Smith. Like Champion and Feldman, he was a prolific contributor to *Gangster Stories,* and was remembered by Thrilling editor-in-chief Leo Margulies many years later as ghosting early *Phantoms.*

Daniels seems to have fallen out of editorial favor at this time. His "Dealers in Death" (July 1936) and "Specter of Death" (August 1936) were both revised by a more powerful hand, which research indicates is legendary Fiction House editor Jack Byrne. Byrne was moving over from Fiction House to *Argosy* in 1936, but along the way he seems to have stopped at Standard to revise these novels, the first of which introduces the Phantom's signal light and other important long-running elements like Phantom aliases Gunner McGlone and Dr. Bendix, as well as the recurring character of crime reporter Steve Huston.

From this point on, the tone of the series grows increasingly hard-boiled and tough. Gone is Champion and his light touch to the escapades of various masters of mayhem. Indeed, the byline of Jack D'Arcy virtually vanishes from all Thrilling pulps in 1936.

Some very interesting people pop up after this. Science Fiction legend Ray Cummings writes "Death Rides the Blizzard" (November 1936) and "Harvest of Death" (May 1937). *Doc Savage* ghost W. Ryerson Johnson turns in his only *Phantom* entry, "The Silent Death" (December 1936), and a month later his friend Charles Greenberg turns in his first *Phantom,* "The Murder Caravan" (January 1937). Greenberg has been an invisible presence before this. Working as an editor and rewrite man, he has revised several *Phantoms* before quitting to freelance. He probably had a hand in Daniels' "The Diamond Murders" (January 1936) and "The Circus Murders" (March 1936). A *Black Mask* writer under the name C. G. Tahney, Greenberg will turn out many top-shelf *Phantoms* in the years to come.

With the cancellation of *Public Enemy,* George McDonald returns to the series with a vengeance, beginning with "The Sign of the Scar" (September 1936) which introduces the short-lived *Phantom* assistant, Jerry Lannigan. Perhaps "Empire of Terror" (October 1936) is also McDonald's work too.

"The Golden Killer" (April 1937) is the work of "The Death-Skull Murders" author. Who is he? Suspects range from Ed Burkholder to one of Thrilling's anonymous house hacks like Donald Bayne Hobart or Charles S. Strong. Since "Double-Stamped Doom" (October 1937) has virtually the same opening as "The Death-Skull Murders," it too may belong to this unknown.

Paul Chadwick, having recently left *Secret Agent "X,"* pens "The Dancing Doll Murders" (June 1937) and "Cavalcade of Death" (August 1937). It's possible he was involved with "The Golden Killer," and other stylistically connected novels.

For a while, McDonald and Greenberg carry the load. Plots and scenes repeat and repeat and it looks like MacDonald has a ghost, or there's a lot of loose copying going on.

Joe Archibald, a frequent early contributor to the back pages of *The Phan-*

tom Detective under his own name, can be suspected of having a hand in novels like "The Corpse Parade" (December 1937) and "Fangs of Murder" (January 1938) where scenes repeat and recycle with only the character names and locales changing.

"Minions of Murder" (November 1937) seems to be written in the same style as a short story by Lloyd Lewell in that same 1937 issue, But who was Lewell? A pen name? A house name—or a real writer? Stylistically, evidence points to George McDonald.

In 1938, Thrilling announced they were opening the *Phantom* series to any seasoned pro who wanted to take a whack at one. All of a sudden guys are sneaking into the Thrilling offices looking for a fast check in return for a quick *Phantom*.

"The Front Page Murders" (June 1938) may be the first of these books. It has some earmarks of Paul Chadwick, but this is not conclusive.

Seasoned pro Laurence Donovan pops up with "The Broadway Murders" (August 1938). Paul Chadwick is back for "The Counterfeit Killers" (September 1938). A year away from starting *The Avenger,* Paul Ernst does "Graduates of Murder" (October 1938). *Spider* author Norvell W. Page turns in "Death Glow" (November 1938). Page may have also written "The Murder Syndicate" (December 1938), but this is not certain.

I want to say "The Web of Murder" (February 1939) is Page too, but I also see faint tracks suggesting his fellow *Spider* ghostwriter Emile C. Tepperman. "The Radio Murders" (April 1939) might also be Tepperman, but Edwin Burkholder can't be ruled out.

Fresh from assisting George Fielding Eliot on the Dan Fowler novels in *G-Man,* Whitney Ellsworth pens the only recurring villain novels in the entire series, "Murder at the World's Fair" (June 1939) and "The Forty Thieves" (July 1939). He is probably the author of a third effort, "The Phantom and the Uniformed Killers" (May 1940).

In apparent imitation of the new titling style over at *The Spider,* starting at the end of 1939, the novels will all be stereotyped "The Phantom and the...." This practice will continue into 1941.

Over time, the hero's nom de guerre officially becomes the Phantom Detective. This is probably to differentiate him from the growing fame of Lee Falk's newspaper strip crimefighter, the Phantom. The magazine was originally called *The Phantom Detective* in imitation of *The Shadow Detective Magazine,* which was its original title.

W. T. Ballard does "The Phantom Strikes Back" (October 1939). Norman Daniels produces a single fill-in novel, "Murder Rides the Skies" (December 1939). In 1939, Don Cameron turns in a *Phantom* that's never been identified. Western pulpateer William L. Hopson takes a shot at one and in his own words, "flopped miserably." If it saw print, it would have been published around 1939-41. "The Phantom Comes Through" (June 1940) might be Hopson's work, although Cameron could have written it. Since Hopson claimed to have written at least one novel for *Black Book Detective,* it is possible his *Phantom* was salvaged for *Black Book,* where it appeared as "The Spy-Ring Murders" by C. K. M. Scanlon in August 1938. (It's also possible Hopson ghosted a Black Bat novel for that title instead.)

I suspect E. Hoffmann Price of committing "The Phantom and the Daggers of Kali" in April 1940. He was probably writing some of the Eagle novelettes for *Thrilling Spy Stories,* and can't be ruled out for more *Phantoms.* Nor can Manly Wade Wellman, who wrote the odd Dan Fowler novel at this time. Edmond Hamilton, author of *Captain Future,* could also be an unsuspected *Phantom* scribe. Aviation writer Ralph Oppenheim wrote "Murder Calls the Phantom" (March 1941), his only known entry in the series.

One of the up-and-coming Thrilling writers of this time was Don Tracy. He may be the guy behind "The Phantom and the Vampire Murders" (July 1940) and a few others. Likewise Sam Merwin, Jr., who ghosted at least one *Masked Detective* in 1941. He is suspected of doing *Phantoms* in this period. One possible Merwin *Phantom* may be "Murder Makes a Movie" (June 1942).

For some reason, probably because he became persona non grata over at Street & Smith, Laurence Donovan is back with a vengeance after introducing young Phantom aide Chip Dorlan in "The Sampan Murders" (September 1939). Greenberg and McDonald begin phasing out, and Donovan is suddenly the sole identifiable *Phantom* ghost.

In 1940, Thrilling announces that they are abandoning their house names, and a great opportunity to see the writers unmasked comes and goes. The C.K.M. Scanlon house name is dropped on the Dan Fowler novels in *G-Men* with the March, 1940 issue. But on *The Phantom,* the editors had a change of heart. Robert Wallace remains an impenetrable mask.

This decision may be laid to the defections of the series' primary authors. By 1940, George Fielding Eliot had left Dan Fowler. Thrilling editor Jack Schiff has claimed that D'Arcy Champion remained with the series until 1938. This is possible. Champion seems to have dropped out of the field as Jack D'Arcy, and resurfaced in 1938 writing for *Dime Detective* under the byline of D. L. Champion.

If Champion is still present, his style has changed, and he's difficult to spot. "The Phantom's Gamble with Death" in February 1940 could be his work. If so, then "The Beast King Murders" (July 1937, which introduced Inspector Tom Gregg) and "Milestones of Murder" (April 1938), among others, should be credited to him.

Laurence Donovan conks out in 1942, a year in which literary chameleon Henry Kutter turns in the first of two *Phantoms,* "The Sabotage Murders" (July 1941) and "The Medieval Murders" (July 1942).

Early in 1942 paper shortages hit the field. *The Phantom Detective* shifts to bi-monthly frequency. Further, to conserve paper, the lead novel is cut. Laurence Donovan drops out with "Death to the Laughing Clown" (October 1942). So does George McDonald. At least one novel, McDonald's final known effort, "Billion Dollar Blitz" (December 1942), shows evidence of having been severely pruned to accommodate the new abbreviated length.

With this novel a shift away from the fast-action pulp approach toward more realistic down-to-earth *Phantoms* is finally solidified. The super villain, masked menaces and outlandish death traps are gone, never to return. The Phantom no longer whirls in and out of disguise, at the turn of a page.

Charles Greenberg is back with a vengeance starting with the January 1942 novel "Murder Makes the Bets." He would write the next eight novels in a row while waiting to go into the service.

With the war, writers were at a premium. Perhaps for this reason, Norman Daniels returns with "Murder Under the Big Top" (December 1943).

Carlton S. Montayne was an old-time pulp writer when he started writing his *Phantoms* in 1944 with "Murder of a Marionette" (December 1944). For the remainder of the magazine's run, he and Norman Daniels would carry the series until 1945, when a returning Charles Greenberg (starting with "The Manuscript Murders," April 1945) replaces Daniels during the immediate post-war period. Montayne had been writing for *Black Mask* on and off, and brings a new sophistication to the series.

Few *Phantoms* after 1943 can be honestly said to be the work of any specific writer. The series settles into a comfortable groove reminiscent of the kinds of stories being told on the *Shadow* radio program and in *The Shadow Magazine*. Instead of Lamont Cranston and Margo Lane hob-nobbing at the Cobalt Club and other such posh environs, it's Dick Van Loan and Muriel Havens in a bewildering succession of cafe society haunts.

After steadily producing some dozen *Phantoms,* C.S. Montayne falls over his typewriter dead of a heart attack while writing a story that would bear the ominous title, "The Black Ball of Death" (Fall 1949). Daniels was called in to complete the tale and carry on the series, which had just gone quarterly. The year was 1949, the beginning of the end of the pulps as a publishing force.

One 1949 effort, "Murder Set to Music" (Summer 1949), seems to be the work of a wild-card writer still not identified. Robert Sydney Bowen is a possibility.

In its last year, attempts were made to spice up the series to compete with the proliferating paperback novels with their racy covers. Prentice Winchell is brought in for this purpose. He is better known as Stewart Sterling, and by some freak accident had managed to write the final published Black Bat novel before that series too died. It's possible that Bruce Elliott of *Shadow* fame also had a hand in *The Phantom's* declining days.

A final Norman Daniels effort, "Murder Agent" (Summer 1953), concluded the series, twenty years after it began. "The Merry Widow Murders" promised for the never-published Fall 1953 issue, never appeared. It's suspected to be the work of Prentice Winchell, and may have appeared in another Thrilling magazine under a different title, with all Phantom references removed.

For a series in which no publisher payment records exist, we can credit an amazing number of novels to specific writers. But some authors' names hang in the air, their contributions to the series the stuff of legend, or rumor or mistaken identity.

One crime pulp alum, Margie Harris, might have had a role in the series. Hector Gavin Gray too is a possibility, as is Tom Curry. *Doctor Death* writer Harold Ward took a crack at a *Phantom* circa 1935. His sample chapters for "Framed for Murder" were rejected and he never tried again.

Science fiction historian Sam Moskowitz once claimed that he had read somewhere that *Wonder Stories* contributor Arthur G. Strangland ghosted several *Phantoms*. Unfortunately, Moskowitz never cited his source. Strangland's name does not appear in the back pages of *The Phantom*, unless he is writing under a house or other name. It's entirely possible Moskowitz was mistaken.

Oscar Schisgall has been mentioned as a *Phantom* writer by editors associated with Thrilling, but any work by him remains unidentified and speculative. Robert Sydney Bowen has also been linked to *The Phantom*, but denied it before his death.

As for D.L. Champion, the writer who started it all, he ended his writing days back where they began, writing for the true crime magazines, along with Edwin Burkholder. Ironically, Walter B. Gibson was also doing a lot of that work in the 1950s.

CHAPTER VI

FOE OF
THE PHANTOM

THE PHANTOM DETECTIVE is something of an enigma among single-character pulps. It was the longest-running magazine of its type, just over twenty years, from February, 1933 to Summer, 1953. It ran longer than even *The Shadow* and *Doc Savage* although it racked up fewer issues than either of those runs. It was a static series by and large. Its hero, Richard Curtis Van Loan, your standard wealthy-young-man-about-town, was a bored playboy who fought crime in secret as the Phantom. (He was only rarely called the Phantom Detective in the novels—that was the name of the magazine.) He remained about the same throughout the magazine's life; only his supporting cast changed, and even that only a little.

Van Loan became a crime fighter because he found his post-World War I life of idleness to be distasteful. His mentor, *Clarion* newspaper publisher Frank Havens, talked Van into becoming the Phantom in the first place, and Van discovered he had a distinct taste for sleuthing, as well as disguise—which was his forté. Murial Havens supplies the watered-down love interest. The rest of the cast includes Steve Huston, brash *Clarion* reporter, and streetwise Chip Dorlan, a kid who grows up in the course of the series.

Throughout his career, the Phantom, summoned by the red signal light atop the *Clarion* Building, vaults into action in some of the most formula writing ever to mark a pulp series. A series of murders by an unknown supercriminal, its motivation buried deep in the murky past, is frequent *Phantom* fare. The supercriminal, during the thirties, usually sports a snazzy nom de guerre and appropriate modus operandi. Over the years, the Phantom tackled such desperados as the Fang, the Dolphin, the Satan, the Snatcher, the Green God, the Blue Light, the Murder Merchant, the Tycoon of Crime—the list goes on and on. By the war, the fancy names and hoods and masks are gone, but the basic formula of multiple murders and multiple suspects (whom the Phantom rounds up in the finale in order to expose the guilty one) remain almost sacrosanct.

Only once—in 1939—did one of these masterminds ever return to do battle. His name was Clifford Boniface, and his is a strange, strange story.

One of the reasons for the lack of continuity in *The Phantom* was the reported legion of writers who were supposed to have written the novels under its two house names, G. Wayman Jones and Robert Wallace. (The Jones name was dropped after the first year in favor of the Wallace byline, for reasons that are unknown but may have something to do with the need for a stronger-sounding house name.) Reports have it that everyone and his brother did *Phantoms* at one time or another. This is exaggerated, perhaps. The series was originated by Jack D'Arcy. D'Arcy was to *The Phantom* what Lester Dent was to *Doc Savage.* He started the series and apparently wrote a goodly number of the yearly output for most (perhaps all) of the run. However, he did not have exclusive control over the series, and many are the names of the other Robert Wallaces, who include Charles Greenberg, Laurence Donovan, Anatole France Feldman, Ed Burkholder, Norman A. Daniels, W. T. Ballard, Ryerson Johnson, George A. McDonald, Robert Sydney Bowen, Emile C. Tepperman—you get the idea.

The point is that with pulpsters coming and going, some writing scores of *Phantoms* (like D'Arcy) or just one (like Ryerson Johnson) it's all an editor can do to keep these guys from mixing up the characters and repeating plots. But somewhere along the way, someone came up with the idea of a recurring villain.

Thus, Clifford Boniface, superspy, and star of "Murder at the World's Fair" (June 1939) and "The Forty Thieves" (July 1939).

I don't know who wrote these novels or why a recurring villain came about after so long, but I can take a stab at those questions.[1] One of the editors at Standard Magazines—who published Van Loan's exploits—was Mort Weisinger, friend of Lester Dent and *Doc Savage* reader. This was not long after John Sunlight ran through two *Doc* novels, and Sunlight may have given Weisinger, or someone, the idea of a similar villain in *The Phantom Detective.* The author who perpetrated these novels is less easy to establish. I don't think it's D'Arcy. His style most reminds me of William O'Sullivan, author of many sports pulp stories and the short-lived *Captain Satan.* But this is hardly conclusive, so let's just call him Robert Wallace.

There was one technical problem with doing a recurring villain in *The Phantom Detective:* the villain had to remain a mystery until the final scene in which he's exposed and disposed of (by jail or death, usually). How can you bring him back once his face and real name are exposed—especially for that all-important final confrontation scene? There are ways, and Robert Wallace found a fascinating one.

It all began at the 1939 New York World's Fair (where just about every major pulp hero managed to have an adventure) where law enforcement officials from all over the globe have gathered to honor no less than the Phantom. During the banquet, two scientists, Dr. Clement Hersch and Professor Arnold Dane, demonstrate their wonderful Herschographer, which projects a ray that can turn a person temporarily invisible. And it seems to do just that.

---

1. Since writing this article, I learned from Bruce Ellsworth, a relative of Whitney Ellsworth, that he wrote these novels.

Then—just as Hersch announces that he intends to turn a portable version of the Herschographer over to the U. S. Government—he is shot to death and his invention stolen.

Next thing anyone knows, the Churchill-Dunlap armaments company starts receiving threatening notes from a blackmailer who signs himself "the Unseen." Conveniently, this firm's architectural wonder of a headquarters is part of the World's Fair, thus enabling most of the action to remain there. The Unseen wants the company's formula for super-H. E. cordite, but company president Horace M. Caldwell doesn't believe in either invisible men or capitulation, and he refuses.

While the Phantom—in one of his many disguises—is interviewing Caldwell, Caldwell is shot at point blank range—by no one!

There are plenty of suspects and cross-motivations, but as the Phantom haunts the fair, he comes across evidence of a group of spies operating near Churchill-Dunlap, and he trails one of them to a mysterious house where he meets "the Chief," who just happens to be in possession of the freshly-kidnapped Arnold Dane.

The Chief is an incredibly handsome gentleman, full of smiles, blue-eyed, and sporting wavy blonde hair. Sunny-haired, the author calls him repeatedly. His name is Clifford Boniface, super-spy, nationality unknown. His last name, I would assume, is a pun on "bonney face."

A prisoner of Boniface, the Phantom is astonished to learn that Boniface has been hired by a foreign power to acquire the Herschographer, not the super-H. E. cordite formula. Boniface is not connected with the Unseen. He's got two separate villains to contend with—an unsettling new experience for the Nemesis of Crime, especially after 75 issues.

Once that sinks in, the Phantom manages to escape with Dane over his shoulder. Back at the World's Fair, there is continued confusion, suspects, and threatening notes from the Unseen. More suspects die by invisible hands. The Phantom and Boniface cross paths again, and Boniface takes a bullet, slinking off into the night trailing blood.

Eventually, the Phantom wraps the matter up and unmasks the Unseen and his tricks (in a manner practically lifted from the 1934 *Shadow* novel, "The Unseen Killer"), all in a nice neat package.

Except for sunny Clifford Boniface, who was gentleman enough to leave a note:

> Please excuse the abominable writing, but I'm carrying one of your souveniers in my right hand, and it's a bit difficult writing this note.
>
> That second shot of yours, incidentally, didn't do much but tear a hole in my perfectly good jacket and rip some flesh from my shoulder. Did you like my death agonies? I should have been an actor, eh?
>
> Sorry to have run off like this, but it seems I have made an unholy mess of this job. Oh, well, we all mess up sometime. Maybe the next time it'll be you.

And there's going to be a next time, my dear Phantom. Depend on that!

CLIFFORD BONIFACE

Not your average snarling Phantom villain, that Clifford Boniface. When he returns in "The Forty Thieves" you wouldn't suspect his presence in the novel to begin with.

The Phantom is called in by Frank Havens to investigate a nationwide epidemic of well-coordinated thefts, the work of the so-called Forty Thieves. The matter begins with ordinary thefts, then shifts to include the wholesale hijacking of new cars. It all links up with the owners of America's major auto factories, who are up to their ears in insurance skullduggery and dying members.

When a caravan of new cars is strafed by planes, the Phantom discovers that foreign agents are involved and inpersonates one who leads him to another mysterious house and—surprise!—Clifford Boniface, sunny personality and all.

Well, actually Boniface is in a foul mood. His plans are not going smoothly, his followers are bungling left and right, and he discovers one of them is the Phantom. Just then the police, tipped by the Phantom, surround the headquarters of Boniface's Forty Thieves.

In a scene that's very similar to one from "Murder at the World's Fair," Boniface grants his enemy a last cigarette and the Phantom escapes neatly. Confusion. Boniface beats a hasty retreat. Back to square one for everybody.

Except that the Phantom has picked up a clue. One of the passwords of the Forty Thieves is the title of the South American republic of Tralojas' national anthem. Tralojas recently had some political trouble and exiled a pack of rebels, some of which have reformed in America under the leadership of a fair-haired man of mystery known as General Gomerra, el Liberator.

Sounds like Clifford Boniface and his Forty Thieves, doesn't it?

But then the Phantom develops some links between the Tralojan government and some members of America's auto makers.

The novel climaxes in a complicated unraveling in which the Phantom nicely befuddles all of the villains. Naturally, Boniface catches another bullet, this one fatal. As he lies dying, he manages one of the more memorable exits of any villain in the Phantom's experience:

> The Phantom crossed the room and knelt beside Clifford Boniface. The superspy, hireling of a dozen governments, relentless killer, bon vivant and loser in this final game, smiled up at Van Loan with all the sunny brilliance of his old grin.
>
> "Ought—to—have—stuck to—stamp collecting," he gasped. "Bet—I could have—beaten you—at that."
>
> "Doubtless you could have," agreed the Phantom pityingly.
>
> (...) Clifford Boniface sighed. "Thought I was—good," he whispered, "but— you're—the best. Maybe all crooks—are fools—after all. Anyway, I let—a dirty rat—fool me. If only—"

His voice trailed off. His mouth opened wider to gasp for breath. He shuddered slightly, and his head rolled. Van Loan felt for his pulse and then got slowly to his feet.

"Yes," he said, and his voice fell upon Inspector Cassidy's ears, but he was speaking to Boniface, "crooks are fools. They are such damn fools!"

Unlike Most *Phantom* villains, Clifford Boniface was presented in something akin to a sympathetic light. Again, here he resembles John Sunlight from the *Doc Savage* novels. (Notice the similarity in their last names, "bonney face" and "sun light.") Because this superspy appeared in two novels, he is unique among *Phantom* adversaries, but he was not the main villain in "Murder at the World's Fair," and whether you could say he was the main foe in "The Forty Thieves" is perhaps open to interpretation. I like to think he was, as he certainly played a larger role in the second novel than he did in the first, and wasn't merely another skulker in the shadows in that second novel.

We never do find out much about Boniface. His nationality remains unknown. Just another pre-World War II superspy, I suppose. But he's fascinating. The only foe to challenge the Phantom twice, he wasn't really much more than a hired gun. But he was an interesting hired gun, and drawn so sharply by the unknown Robert Wallace that he sticks in one's memory far longer than those lesser lights like the Beast King, the Keyboard Killer, the Tiger, etc., who plagued Richard Curtis Van Loan for better than twenty long, long years.

I guess we'll never really know Clifford Boniface's real story.

CHAPTER VII

THE LAST
PHANTOM
ROUNDUP

IN MY OPINION, among the best articles that ever appeared during *Echoes'* mighty run were Tom Johnson's multi-part analysis of the *Phantom Detective* series, ultimately collected in book form. As someone almost obsessively interested in authorship, I was particularly enthralled by Tom's attempts to figure out the true identities of the various and sundry Robert Wallaces.

We've come a long way since January of 1971, when fan Alan Grossman wrote former Standard/Thrilling editor Leo Margulies, asking for the identities of the writers behind *The Phantom Detective* and other Thrilling housename series, and was told:

> The early *Phantom Detective* novels were by Jack D'Arcy (D.L. Champion). Anatole France Feldman, Edwin V. Burkholder and Norman A. Daniels also wrote some of them. These four authors wrote about ninety percent of the *Phantoms*.

Subsequent research turned up only a sprinkling of Feldman *Phantoms*, all in the first year of the series. In fact, Feldman seems to disappear from Standard circa 1934. Likewise, Edwin V. Burkholder. I once theorized that, since I found an Arthur J. Burks *Phantom* from 1933 ("Cities for Ransom"), perhaps Margulies confused Burkholder with Burks. I've learned since that Burkholder was Margulies' landlord during the latter's agenting days. I doubt the passing of time would create that kind of memory confusion. At any rate, I have identified only one Burkholder *Phantom*, "Spawn of Death" (September 1934), and sometimes wonder if others even exist.

But he cannot be discounted. Champion, Feldman and Burkholder were all, as I understand it, good friends. In fact, all three were regular contributors to *Gangster Stories* and similar gang pulps in the period before *The Phantom Detective* came on the scene. For the record, Burkholder—under his preferred pen name of George Allan Moffatt—disappears from the Thrilling stable early in 1935, so any other Burkholder *Phantoms* would likely have been published prior to the May, 1935 issue.

There's no question that Margulies' memory was off. In the same letter, he claimed: "Nearly all of the *G-Men* Dan Fowler stories were by Major George Fielding Eliot." That might have been true during the earliest years of that series, but as Tom Johnson's research into that series has showed, Eliot soon tapered off his involvement. After 1940, none of the Dan Fowlers were by Eliot.

Tom did a great job of ice-breaking—or should I say ghost breaking?—but since publication of his own findings, other illuminations have been made, among them articles of my own.

I thought I'd gather up the loose threads of my own recent Phantom researches so readers could add them to their collections. I won't go into a lot of detail or try to prove my case through style or intuition, but simply present my findings with the same caveat Tom gave when presenting his: namely, these identifications are not gospel.

Tom's findings show that the original *Phantom* scribe, D.L. Champion a.k.a. Jack D'Arcy, bailed out of the series with "Written in Blood" in May 1935. I don't disagree with Tom. But editor Jack Schiff remembered Champion staying with he series until 1937 or so. This is possible. Champion seemed to retool his writing after 1936, for the first time emerging as D.L. Champion. If he did come back, his work markedly improved. But neither Tom nor I could find him again with certainty. I had sometimes thought "The Beast King Murders" (July 1937) might have been the returning Champion. But these days I lean toward George Fielding Eliot, or someone else.

"The Criminal Caesar" (April 1936) was one later story Tom thought had Champion touches in it. Perhaps. But this novel was named in advertisements by agent August Lenninger as being sold by him. Lenninger was Norman Daniels' agent, but Daniels records do not list this story. That leaves other Lenninger clients. I have no firm opinions, but here are the most likely suspects: E. Hoffmann Price, Claude Rister, Margie Harris, G.T. Fleming-Roberts and Charles S. Strong. Take your pick. All of them were writing for Standard at that time. Some stylistics point to Anatole France Feldman. (By the way, Harris was another prolific *Gangster Stories* alum.)

Both Tom and Bob Sampson fingered a couple of Daniels' *Phantoms* as reading more like other writers than Daniels himself. "Murder Empire" (December 1935) seems to be a George McDonald rewrite. It's not clear who revised Daniels' "The Circus Murders" (March 1936), but someone did. And heavily. Bob Sampson was certain it was George McDonald, noting many phrases that "equate word for word" with McDonald's *Federal Agent* novels. Bob also believed "Notes of Doom" (June 1935) was a Champion rewrite of Daniels, and Daniels' "Island of Sudden Death" (October 1935) read like Daniels, McDonald and Champion.

Years later, the hundredth *Phantom*, "The Grim Shadow of Hate" (June 1941), struck Tom as Champion's work. But I'm pretty confident this is none other than Laurence Donovan.

Ray Cummings has long been said to be a *Phantom* ghost. After long hours of stylistic comparison, I am confident the following are by him: "Death Rides the Blizzard" (November 1936), "Harvest of Death" (May 1937) and "The

Phantom's Murder Trail" (March 1940). Tom thinks "The Phantom and the Daggers of Kali" (April 1940) is by the same author as "The Phantom's Murder Trail." I'm not yet convinced of that, but I'm not sure who this author is. I have sometimes wondered if E. Hoffmann Price, or even Manly Wade Wellman— who did a few Dan Fowlers and was rumored to have ghosted *The Phantom*— might not be our man. Paul Chadwick has also crossed my mind for that one. Not to mention C.S. Montayne.

Speaking of Chadwick, I am convinced these are his work: "The Dancing Doll Murders" (June 1937), "Cavalcade of Death" (August 1937) and "The Counterfeit Killers" (August 1938). I haven't read "The Death-Skull Murders" (May 1936), but that title reminds me of Chadwick's *Secret Agent "X"* novel, "The Death-Torch Terror" (April 1934), so that I keep hoping it will turn out to be his—although the betting money seems to be on George McDonald. "The Front Page Murders" (June 1938) smacks of Chadwick, too, but I haven't determined the authorship of that one to my satisfaction.

The problem of Robert Sydney Bowen is a puzzling one. He claimed to have ghosted *Phantoms,* but the only one I feel halfway certain is his is "Double-Stamped Doom" (Octobr 1937). I have suspected "The Corpse Parade" (December 1937), "Fangs of Doom" (January 1938) and "Tycoon of Crime" (February 1938) and since he was still kicking around the pages of *Thrilling Detective* and *Popular Detective* well into the post-war period, he's a logical candidate for having ghosted some of the borderline stories Tom isn't positive are by C.S. Montayne, like "Murder for Millions" (June 1945) and "Killer Portfolio" (August 1945). But with all the in-house editorial revisions (not to mention writers rewriting other writers) going on at Standard, unless the text screams a name, it's best to whisper one's theories, not shout them.

We're all pretty certain George McDonald was a pretty large presence in the series, but after his first couple of stories, it's hard to say how long he stays. Tom thought "The Sign of the Scar" (September 1936) and the next novel, "The Empire of Terror" (October 1936) were McDonald's work. So did Sampson. But the two have as many dissimilarities as concurrences. And "The Golden Killer" (April 1937) really reads like an older, more affected writer, like a Ray Cummings, rather than the guy who had been writing the hard-boiled Lynn Vickers G-Man novels in *Public Enemy/Federal Agent.* Still, writers do evolve over time. McDonald might have continued with *The Phantom* all the way into the 40s. "The Phantom and the Crime Legion" in October 1940 may have been his swan song. On the other hand, if "Billion Dollar Blitz" (December 1942) wasn't by Joe Archibald, maybe that too was McDonald.

Archibald is another of my favorite suspects. For a long time, I toyed with "The Phantom's Gamble with Death" (February 1940) as being his. I haven't completely let go of that suspicion. The trouble is, his work can be confused at times with Robert Sydney Bowen's. And Bowen's work can sometimes sound like George McDonald's.

Other names have frequently surfaced as *Phantom* ghosts. Two former Standard editors mentioned to me Paul Ernst and Oscar Schisgall as definite contributors. But where are their works? Do they even exist? I once went through Schisgall's papers at Boston University, but found no evidence of *Phantoms*. Still, I came away thinking his files weren't complete. As for Ernst, I can certainly see him ghosting *Phantoms*. "Graduates of Murder" (October 1938) had some of the flavor of an Ernst story. But that's as far as I care to go with Ernst.

Norvell W. Page and Emile C. Tepperman were also named by *Phantom* editors. When I reread "Death Glow" (November 1938) recently, I said to myself: "Oh my God, this reads like Norvell Page!" So I went looking for more Page *Phantoms*. "The Murder Syndicate" (December 1938) might be watered-down Page. But there are also Emile C. Tepperman vibes about it. "The Web of Murder" (February 1939) struck me as Page-esque too, but I'm pretty confident that this is Tepperman's work.

"The Radio Murders" (April 1939) is very interesting. Again, I suspected Tepperman, but can't exclude Chadwick or someone else. But it's definitely not Don Cameron, whose diary listed him as writing an untitled *Phantom* in 1939. The diary entry was made in the spring—too late in the year to have been the April issue. The only unidentified *Phantom* over the next year that might fit is "The Phantom Comes Through" (January 1940).

"The Phantom and the Uniformed Killers" (May 1940) smacks of Whit Ellsworth, yet also suggests George Fielding Eliot and even once again Tepperman.

A lot of strange people took a whack at a *Phantom* over the years. A few didn't work out. *Doctor Death* creator Harold Ward submitted a few chapters to one tentatively called "Framed for Murder" about *Clarion* reporter Steve Huston being framed for a killing, but for some reason Ward's idea was vetoed. He never tried again.

In 1946, William L. Hopson mentioned in *Writer's Digest* that he had written lead novels for *Black Book Detective* as well as having "flopped miserably on a *Phantom* yarn." If his Black Book stories are Black Bat novels, that would put that work around 1940-41. I have not identified any Hopson *Phantom*, if in fact it was published as a *Phantom*—or published at all. There are a number of odd, seemingly one-shot *Phantoms* published, especially during the 1940-41 period when they opened the series wide to new writers.

Don Tracy was mentioned as one of Margulies' top writers in 1939, but he didn't seem to get going writing Dan Fowlers until a year or so later, so it's natural to think of him as another of the mysterious Robert Wallaces. The only clue to Tracy I have discovered at this time is a reference to a character in "The Phantom and the Vampire Murders" (July 1940) named Clyde Fiske who was killed in Chapter 1. Tracy's full name was Donald Fiske Tracy. It's an admittedly slim clue, but there it is. If Tracy did that one, he might also have written "The Phantom and the Green Glare Murders" (November 1940). They read much alike.

Standard editor Sam Mines recalled that Sam Merwin, Jr. did a *Phantom* or more. Tom thought he detected the Merwin style in 1949's "Murder Set to Music" (Summer 1949). Beyond that, I have no clue. But Merwin started showing up in Thrilling mags circa 1941, so he could have been lurking around for a while. This inevitably leads me to the mystery of the Phantom ghost Tom Johnson dubbed Author O.

Author O starts showing up in 1942, during the Great Purge. *The Phantom Detective* goes bi-monthly with the war, and the previous regulars, who included Laurence Donovan and perhaps a lingering George McDonald, are abruptly gone.

Author O takes over the series beginning with "Murder Makes the Bets" (January 1943), and writes every novel until the return of Norman Daniels, who writes alternately with C.S. Montayne, beginning in 1943.

When Tom Johnson first read this block of stories, he thought it read like Charles Greenberg's work, and solicited my opinion. I had only one of those stories to refer to but thought it highly improbable. Greenberg himself had given me a list of his *Phantoms* and the last one, "The Phantom and the Melody Murders" appeared in September 1940, whereupon he recalled dumping *The Phantom* for the better-paying *Batman* comics. Tom accepted my opinion even while noting the strange similarities to Greenberg's previous work.

I myself tackled this mystery later. Various writers were considered and rejected—Robert Sydney Bowen, Ray Cummings, Joe Archibald, etc. None fit. It was very frustrating.

In the interim, Greenberg had died, but I came into contact with a colleague and friend of his, Alvin Schwartz. Schwartz, himself a scripter of *Batman* comics throughout the 1940s and 1950s, had expressed surprise when I casually mentioned Greenberg's claim to have written *Batman*.

Schwartz insisted either Greenberg or I was in error. The only *Batman* script Greenberg had ever written was through Schwartz's intercession—and there was only one, he insisted.

This was strange. Greenberg was very clear that he had left the lucrative world of pulps for the more lucrative comics field. One *Batman* story a career change does not make.

This puzzled me greatly. Memories do fade, recall does collapse and mental machinery can rust. Moreover, Schwartz remembered that around the time he started writing *Batman* himself in 1940-41, Greenberg was churning out *Phantoms* at a furious rate, one after another. Yet by 1940, Greenberg had all but quit *The Phantom*. Over time, I questioned Schwartz closely over his recollections. He remained steadfast in his recall.

There really wasn't much room for undiscovered Charles Greenberg *Phantoms* in the 1940-41 period. This stretch was dominated by Laurence Donovan and a sprinkling of guys who come and go. But 1942-43 is a different matter. Those six Author O novels had to be somebody who was pretty well-seasoned because it was rare for one lone ghost to carry the series.

So I began combing my Greenberg *Phantoms,* comparing them with the Author O stories I could lay hands on. At first, the clues were circumstantial.

Author O introduces the Mr. Gray alias that the Phantom comes to rely on. Greenberg had previously toyed with the mythical Hugh Gray. The villain of "Stones of Satan" (March 1943), the Satan, strongly resembled the bat-cloaked Bat from Greenberg's "The Yacht Club Murders" (January 1939). As Tom has pointed out, several Author O stories recycle Greenberg *Phantom* plots.

Certain boilerplate descriptions recur and recur. When Richard Curtis Van Loan adopts a new disguise, he goes through the same routine, including the inserting of nose-transforming pellets into his aristocratic nostrils. So did Author O.

Other stylistic and thematic correspondences continued to mount up. Individually, they were meaningless, but as they added up they were almost mathematical in their certainty.

Consider this line from Greenberg's "The Yellow Shadows of Death" (July 1938):

> The little Chinese, a crimson devil's stitch across his chest, was hurled a dozen feet by the terrific impact of that spray of lead.

Now this from Author O's "The Phantom's Murder Money" (August 1940):

> He had practically been decapitated by bullets, and there was also a crimson devil's stitch of machine-gun lead across his chest.

The circumstances seem to fit the known facts. Author O disappears after a six-book spurt of *Phantoms,* only to return to the series in the latter months of 1945—exactly what you'd expect of a man who was about to be drafted and would later be mustered out of the Army at war's end. Greenberg appeared to continue writing *Phantoms* until 1950, whereupon he no doubt began his true *Batman* work in earnest.

Now that we seem to have put the pieces of the puzzle together, Charles Greenberg now stands revealed as one of the major *Phantom* authors of the entire series!

Lest we forget: in addition to those novels Greenberg himself identified, and the Author O stories, there are his revisions of the works of others. These will probably never be completely identified. But Bob Sampson once told me he suspected Greenberg's revisatory hand in "The Beast King Murders" (July 1937). No doubt there are others.

We've come a long way indeed since the authorship ice was first cracked way back in 1971. Without question, unknown *Phantom* ghosts yet lurk in the crumbling pages of *The Phantom Detective.* The research will go on. Speaking for myself, I'm very pleased to have been a part of it all.

CHAPTER VIII

JACK SCHIFF: EDITOR AT STANDARD

P ULPCON 13 WAS held in Cherry Hill, New Jersey from August 16 to August 19, 1984. The guest of honor was Jack Schiff, who was an editor at Standard Magazines, Inc., better known as the Thrilling Group. Jack Schiff worked there during the 1930s. The Editor-in-Chief was Leo Margulies. The following are some of the reminiscences of Jack Schiff during his after dinner talk on Saturday evening and the panel session on Friday evening,

Will Murray: We have never had a representative from The Thrilling Group, that published *Thrilling Mystery, Thrilling Detective, The Phantom Detective, G-Men, The Lone Eagle,* etc. Our Guest of Honor this year is Jack Schiff who started working there in 1934, about two or three years after the company began. He was one of their editors until 1940 when he went off to write on his own and then to work for DC Comics where he edited *Batman* and other chracters.

How did you get a job as editor at Standard?

Jack Schiff: I tried freelancing. But I decided to put away the thought of writing the great American Novel and earn a living. Ned Pines, the President of the company, was a friend of the family. I went to see Ned and he asked me to make some preliminary analyses of some stories. I did. Ned turned them over to Leo Margulies, the editor-in-chief. I met with Leo and he hired me.

Great writers such as Dickens, Balzac, and Mark Twain would have been pulp writers had there been pulp magazines in their day. They were prolific and they wrote for the masses. That is one of the characteristics of the pulps, prolific output by popular writers, molded by the relatively low pay. Even in the pulps, you notice the improvement of the quality of writing when you go to the higher paying magazines, *Argosy* and *Blue Book*. The writers could afford to spend more time polishing their work.

The ingredients of a good pulp story were well plotted, imaginative stories with action, suspense, and some humor, to hold the interest of the reader to the end. Characterization was not a prime factor, although not missing. Of course, there were "hacks" who got into a formula rut and required quite a bit of editorial rewriting. For the most part, the professional pulp writer was conscious of the basic facts pointed out in my article for *Writer's Digest*, "A Trained Seal Explains His Tricks," in the October 1939 issue. In that article, I differentiated between writing that produced the bare skeleton of a story, and writing that dressed it up and fleshed it out with more vivid language and subtle touches.

Unfortunately, the mystery, adventure, and science fiction writers began to deviate from the basic ingredients of a good pulp story in their efforts to win acclaim in the literary world. Some of this was valid, combining good pulp technique with literary technique to flesh out the skeleton. But in the process many writers go in for descriptive characterizations (not action characterizations stemming from the story), for half baked philosophical or psychological observations that bore you stiff. I have gotten to the point where I have learned to skim through irrelevant, minute descriptions of locale, clothing, food, or liquor to get to the storyline for which I read the book.

I am afraid that the comics field (into which I went for twenty five years after the pulps) has succumbed to the same kind of evolution. Mort Weisinger and I carried our pulp training into the comics field. We developed the same kind of gimmicky, fast-paced storylines with startling twists and turns and sensational villains for the heroes to combat. Our editorial director was Whit Ellsworth, who had written the Black Bat for us back at Standard. In an effort to publish comic stories with so-called characterization and human interest (perfectly valid requirements if the basics are kept), comics have lost touch with the broad readership and are catering to a narrow in-group of the fanzine world. Innovation and change are always legitimate aspects of any writing field, but when you disregard the basics, you lose your mass readership.

One of the most important aspects of the pulps was the excellent training ground it provided for the writers. A number of them went on to the slicks, the movies, books, and television. Just to name a few, that I knew very well; Alfred Bester, Hank Kuttner, Charles Marquis Warren, Major George Fielding Eliot, Steve Fisher, Frank Gruber, Jean Francis Webb, W. Ryerson Johnson, and Oscar Schisgall. All of them acknowledged their debt to the pulps; the discipline of regular writing; of solid, entertaining stories that underlay the frills and embellishments that came afterwards. A number of times, when a writer would submit an exceptionally fine story, we would suggest he try to sell it to a slick magazine. Almost always they sold, for which the writers were grateful. Many wrote for us even after thay hit the jackpot.

Usually, there were some writers, such as William Saroyan, who were determined to "make the pulps." I recall a sport story sent in by Saroyan's agent; Saroyan was a well established writer at the time. A note from the agent stated that Saroyan was anxious to get a sport story published in a pulp magazine. To my dismay, the story did not come up to our standards, I turned it down. But Leo Margulies, our editorial director, accepted it. He knew that the name of William Saroyan on a cover would not mean much to the pulp readers, but it would mean a lot to our publisher, Ned Pines. With pride, Ned could show his friends that his lowly pulp magazine featured the noted author, William Saroyan.

Incidently, I do not know if it is well known that the initials for one of Standard's much used house names, C. K. M. Scanlon, stood for Cylvia Kieinman Margulies, Leo's lovely wife. In later years, she was his partner in his publishing ventures. They started the *Mike Shayne Mystery Magazine, The Man From U.N.C.L.E. Magazine,* the *Zane Grey Western Magazine,* and a number of others.

Will Murray: Can you tell us something about Leo Margulies?

Jack Schiff: Leo Margulies was our editorial director, a giant in the field, an innovator and always on the lookout for new advances. He was instrumental in bringing Leslie Charteris, of *The Saint* fame, over to this country.

He was a marvelous human being. Many writers owe him tremendous debts. Pulp writers lived through hard times and depended upon that check. Leo was always there to help them out with an advance, if necessary. The writers swore by him even after they left the field. He was the boss of the editors, but the working relationship was one of cooperation.

There were some great men on that staff. Among them was Alex Samalman, who is not well known today. Generally, he was considered a production chief, which involved many aspects of producing a good pulp magazine, including display, illustrations, layout, etc. But in addition to all that, Alex had one of the shrewdest editorial instincts that I have ever encountered. If any question came up about a story, Alex, in the midst of all his many duties, would take time to read the story and come up with a shrewd analysis. I am indebted to him particularly, because he encouraged me to do some writing. I learned a lot of writing tricks from him. I would like to pay a tribute to Alex Samalman.

Will Murray: Why did they call Leo Margulies the "little giant of the pulps"?

Jack Schiff: Because he was small in stature, but was large in heart. The appellation, "little," referred only to his size. Incidently, his wife, Cylvia, was taller than he.

Will Murray: Which magazines did you edit?

Jack Schiff: At one time or another, I worked on all of them except for the love magazines. Charlotte Rogers handled those. She started as Charlotte Lane, secretary to the Editorial Director. She was the wife of Wayne Rogers, a pulp writer, who was chief copy editor at Standard when I joined.

For unsolicited stories we had a slush pile. These would be read by Donald Bayne Hobart, who was a western writer. He was an amazingly fast reader and managed to weed out the completely unacceptable stories. After that they passed through the hands of two or three editors for reading and comment. Then Leo made the final decision on whether we should purchase them. We encouraged new writers. We depended upon several agents to send in stories from established writers.

The lead story for magazines with continuing characters was handled differently. These were magazines like *The Phantom Detective*, *The Lone Eagle* and *G-Men*. Rarely did we get unsolicited stories for these characters. These stories came from established authors, with whom we worked closely. First they sent in an outline. We would send back suggestions. Then the author would send in a manuscript. These went through several readings. There was some editing or rewriting afterwards. Usually there was quite a bit of rewriting on stories from relatively unknown authors.

After a few years we specialized. Mort Weisinger took over the science fiction magazines. We had hired him as a result of a short story contest. He was very young at the time. He had been involved with science fiction fans. I took over the detective magazines *Thrilling Detective, Popular Detective, Thrilling Mystery,* in addition to *Popular Western, Thrilling Western, Thrilling Sports, Popular Sports*. Even so, the stories always got some additional readings with comments. If there were any reservations, Leo made the final decision.

Will Murray: I hear a persistant story that Margulies liked to buy up other editor's rejects at a cut-rate and have them rewritten in house—as a cost saving thing; as a way of helping writers; as a way to help train editors. One pulp writer once said to me that to a certain extent, the Margulies group could become a dump market because they would take your rejects and they would buy them at a lower fee.

Jack Schiff: We did some of that, but I must make a definite revision of what you said. It was not at cut-rate. That was something on which Leo insisted. He would pay a writer who had a story that we saw was worthwhile but did not think that the writer could revise it. Sometimes we tried to get the writer to revise it, but the revision was unsuccessful. If it still seemed to be a good yarn, he would buy it. We had several excellent rewrite people: Charlie Strong, Bernie Breslauer and one other person, I can't remember his name (I did some of it). The writer learned from this rewriting. A number of them approved of what Leo was doing and became some of our regular writers.

Will Murray: There was a man named Charles Greenberg who was rewriting and then went on to freelancing.

Jack Schiff: Charlie Greenberg was not on the staff. We did sometimes give him something to rewrite, because Charlie was an excellent writer. He had a good editorial sense too.

Unknown: How much interaction was there between the editorial department and the art department? Did you give much input into the covers that you would like or the interior art, or was the art department fairly autonomous?

Jack Schiff: We had some, but for the most part Alex Samalman and Leo controlled the covers and illustrations on the inside. We would offer suggestions and sometimes the writers had some notes on possible illustrations. Very often it depended on what artists were available. Certain ones we knew could do a bang-up job on certain types of things. We could not always get Virgil Finlay.

Will Murray: Thrilling's big gun as far as super heroes is concerned was *The Phantom Detective*. That was the second hero pulp created. It followed *The Shadow* by about a year and beat out *Doc Savage* by three months. It started in 1933. You came on board in 1934. Was Jack D'Arcy doing *The Phantom* at that time?

Jack Schiff: Yes, Jack was a giant in the field (he was a giant of a man as well). His spelling was atrocious as was his syllabication. But we forgave him for these things because his stories were really excellent. He had a good plotting sense and a vivid imagination.

Marcus Goldsmith was a co-publisher with Ned Pines of a few of the magazines: *The Phantom Detective* and *Popular Detective*.[2] Goldsmith wanted to read the stories before they were published. Jack knew Marcus very well and would play tricks on him. He turned in a locked room mystery. Goldsmith thought it a marvelous story. "But, Jack, you never explain the locked room mystery. How did the murderer get in?" Jack said, "Mr. Goldsmith, you are correct. How would you suggest?" Goldsmith offered, "Why don't you leave the rear window latch off?" Jack did this deliberately because Goldsmith was always asking for changes. Jack wanted Marcus to seize on this point to the exclusion of all others. We editors would not accept the suggestion. We had to dope out a clever solution to the locked room.

At another time, Jack and I were involved in a hazardous adventure. Mort Weisinger and I had been plotting a *Phantom Detective* novel with Jack. Jack had submitted an outline. (Mort and I plotted most of the detective and G-men stories.) At noon we adjourned for lunch. We continued the discussion in the restaurant. At one point I said, "Jack, you can not use cyanide to kill the grandmother. You used that a couple of months ago. Let us think of another way to knock off the old lady." We became absorbed in a pleasanter method of murder. Suddenly we noticed two grim policemen standing by our booth. Jack tried to stand up. Even though Jack was a big man, the cop pushed him down. Jack asked, "What is wrong, officer?" "That is what we want to know. These ladies are complaining that you fellows are planning a murder." We looked and saw, outside of the booth, three little old ladies, with their arms akimbo, glaring at us. We burst into laughter. The officer became uspet. "What is so funny? This is a serious matter. We are going to haul you down to the precinct."

First Jack, and then I, and then Mort tried to explain the situation. As we were talking, we realized it sounded peculiar. The officers did not buy the explanation. Finally I said, "We are only a few blocks from the office. Why don't we run up there and you can verify it. Or better yet, I will give you the phone

---

2. *The magazines co-published by Goldsmith and Pines might explain those books published by Beacon Magazines.*

number. You can call and check our names and descriptions." The younger officer did not like the idea, but the older one thought it reasonable. He went to the phone booth and called. On his way back, I saw his face was relaxed. He said to his partner, "They are okay, Bill. It is a mistake. This guy is actually the writer of *The Phantom Detective*. And the others are editors." Then he turned to Jack and said, "Are you really the guy that writes *The Phantom Detective?* My kid loves that magazine. Oh boy, will he be tickled when I tell him I met the guy who writes the stories." Jack smiled and took out a sheet of paper and a pen and said, "I wil do better than that. Give me your son's name and I will give him my autograph." Afterwards, this incident provided us with many moments of hilarity.

Will Murray: Aren't there some stories about Jack D'Arcy when he needed money?

Jack Schiff: Yes. Mort Weisinger was the kind of guy that would give you the shirt off his back if he thought you needed help. Jack had a way with words. He was always trying to borrow money from the editors. We resisted his pleas, but Jack could always get money from Mort. It began to add up. Finally Mort said to Jack, "You owe me sixty dollars." Jack apologized and said he was strapped for cash at the moment. He suggested an additional loan of $40 to make it an even hundred. Mort fell for the line. Jack could have been a terrific salesman.

Will Murray: I heard a story about Jack D'Arcy and Leo Margulies. Jack was aware that Leo did not read *The Phantom Detective* stories. He would flip through the corners of the manuscript to make sure that all the page numbers were there and pay for the story.

When Jack needed money for the rent, he would type a *Phantom* story with the first five pages and the last three and leave the others blank. He would bring it in and give it to Leo. Leo would check the page numbers, glance at the beginning and ending to ensure it seemed to be a good story, and issue a check. When the manuscript went through channels, the missing pages were discovered.

Jack Schiff: That story is apocryphal. Leo did not get angry at Jack's tricks. He was used to them. Jack always came through in a pinch when we needed him.

We had some fantastic writers in our stable. D'Arcy was one of them when he was not in his cups. Another was George Bruce who wrote sports, mystery, detective, anything. I could call him up on a Monday night and say, "George, I absolutely need a 10,000 worder. We have to replace something that is interfering with another story. I need it by tomorrow." He would say, "Okay." The next afternoon, he was in with a 10,000 word story and a damn good one at that.

Will Murray: They say Jack D'Arcy was a very funny guy. For a while he wrote very serious pulp, but later on he wrote for *Black Mask* and other magazines and he put humor in his stories. Humor became his forté.

Jack Schiff: He used to tell hilarious stories, some off color. He would have everyone in stitches. He was a real charmer.

When he was writing *The Phantom* he was deadly serious about that character. He never allowed himself to fall into a formula rut, although it was easy to do so.

Will Murray: Did he create the character? I know the character was created before you came to the company. I am sure you heard stories. Marcus Goldsmith considered *The Phantom* as his pet. Did he have something to do with creating the character? Or Leo Margulies?

Jack Schiff: Jack defintely did. That is why he was on it so long. Leo defintely had a hand in it. He was looking for that kind of character. I remember speaking to him about it. He believed in two aspects of the pulps. One was creating these characters in different fields. For example, Craig Kennedy is the scientific sleuther. The second was, he wanted unusual villains for the hero to combat.

Will Murray: Charlie Greenberg did *Phantoms*. He had a *Phantom* story with a villain called the Bat. He went on to do some *Batman* stories, which I thought was a funny coincidence. Charlie used unusual villains. One of his *Phantom* stories was called "Melody Murders." The villain was the Keyboard Killer. Using songs he would let the police and the Phantom know what he would do next, where he would strike, and challenge the good guys to beat him to the punch. He was the kind of villain that was a lot like the early *Batman* villains such as the Riddler or the Joker. I always wondered how much of *Phantom* Charlie Greenberg had brought into *Batman*.

Jack Schiff: Charlie Greenberg came to DC a few times and did some comic stories for us. Probably he did bring some of the fantastic villains idea with him. However long before, Mort and I had brought the idea with us. We thought that type of character would go well in the comic media, and it did.

Tony Tollin: Was there a *Phantom Detective* radio show?

Jack Schiff: I do not remember that.

Will Murray: I have heard that there was such a show in the thirties. It was not successful and short lived. No one seems to know anything about it.

The Lone Eagle. That must have started about the time you came into the outfit. What do you remember about *The Lone Eagle* and the men who wrote the character?

Jack Schiff: I did not deal a lot with that magazine. The names escape me. I think Robert Sydney Bowen was among the authors. There was one other guy who had some experience in fighting who wrote a number of them.

Will Murray: Was that Ferd Reichnitzer? It is said that he was the original author of *The Lone Eagle* and maybe the creator or co-creator.

Jack Schiff: Reichnitzer, that is the name. He had probably the most authentic war stories. In addition, he had a good style of writing. It fit the type of story he was writing.

This is another trick, to change your style. For example, a man of many styles was Joe Archibald, a good friend of mine. He could write the most humorous stories and he could write the toughest, most hard-boiled detective stories. We had several people who managed to adapt their style to the kind of story.

Will Murray: One of the later heroes was Dan Fowler, the F.B.I. agent in *G-Men*. One writer, who I know left the pulps and eventually came back, was a man named Edward Churchill. Do you remember him?

Jack Schiff: Oh yes. Eddie Churchill was a real character. He went to Hollywood in the late thirties. He was a good friend of Leo's. I remember almost getting thrown out of a restaurant when Ed Churchill came into town from Hollywood. We went out to a restaurant and he did not have a tie. They would not allow us into the restaurant. He said, "What do you mean? I go into the best restaurants in Hollywood dressed this way." He put up such a fuss that the Maitre D' told us to be seated. I do not think he did any work for us after he went to Hollywood.

Will Murray: After you left he came back. He was one of the early writers on the Dan Fowler stories. He and George Fielding Eliot, for the first year or so, pretty much alternated on the stories.

Jack Schiff: George did most of them.

Will Murray: Dan Fowler started in 1936. Churchill left for Hollywood about 1938. He had done about eight *G-Men* at that point. He did well in Hollywood, but he ended up not liking it. He came back about 1943 or 1944. At that point, he did more *G-Men* plus other stuff. He did an article for *Writer's Digest* on "A Writer Turns Forty" or something like that. I do not know where he ended up nor what he did.

Jack Schiff: I think Robert Leslie Bellem did something like that. He left the pulps for a while and then came back.

Will Murray: He was in TV. He did *Superman, Dick Tracy, The Lone Ranger.*

Tell us a little about Major George Fielding Eliot. He was the first writer to do Dan Fowler.

Jack Schiff: He was an Army man. I guess most of you are familiar with his writing during World War II. He was an analyst on the battles that were taking place. George had a very ordered mind, maybe that was part of his military training. His *G-Men* were meticulous; meticulously plotted, meticulously written. At first glance he seemed brusque and reserved, but when you got to know him and he let his hair down, he turned out to be a darn nice human being. Although he won honors after he left the field, when we would meet him later he never put on airs.

Albert Tonik: Who was the bridge expert among your authors? The first Dan Fowler story I read started out with Dan playing a bridge game. The author did a good job of describing how to bid a grand slam using pre-emptive bids.

Jack Schiff: I am not a bridge expert, but I played a lot. George Fielding Eliot played a lot.

Will Murray: One of the writers who worked for the Thrilling Group in the thirties and the forties was Johnston McCulley, the creator of Zorro, one of the most famous pulp characters. He did a lot of series characters for the Thrilling group like the Green Ghost for *Thrilling Detective* in the early thirties, the Crimson Clown later (a whole host of masked heroic characters). I would guess McCulley looked at *The Scarlet Pimpernel* and decided, we could do this in the pulps.

Jack Schiff: I can not recollect too much about Johnston McCulley except his sense of humor. He had a great sense of humor and he injected it into his stories. After a while he went to Hollywood. I do not remember when.

Will Murray: He was in Hollywood with the *Zorro* TV show, in the late fifties. He probably was in Hollywood before then. He was doing pulps as late as just after World War II.

Jack Schiff: People drifted back to the pulps. Take someone like Frank Gruber, whom Mort Weisinger and I knew very well. After he had a number of successes he used to come into town and have lunch with us. Frank was a very conscientious researcher. Every one of his mystery books had a theme. He did thorough research on it as a background. I came up with two themes for which he paid me something like $50 apiece. I came up with clocks which went into one of his mystery stories, and then with keys which became his famous French Key story.

Wooda Carr: Do you remember Emile C. Tepperman? We do not know what happened to him.

Jack Schiff: I remember Emile very well, very fondly. Emile was a very sweet guy and a hell of a good writer.

Will Murray: Was he a full time writer? He went into radio, we understand, in the forties. What ever happened to him?

Jack Schiff: Yes he was a full time writer. I do not know what happened to him. I did not keep up with a number of the writers. A few of them I had as lifelong friends. Many of them I lost contact with because I was absorbed at DC.

Will Murray: Was Tepperman a good writer by the standards of the day?

Jack Schiff: Tepperman was an excellent writer and certainly could have written for *Argosy* or *Blue Book* or any of the other magazines.

I remember a story by Oscar Schisgall. I did not read the story because it was in *Love*, but the love department thought the story was so good that they "rejected it." They told him to send it over to a slick magazine. I think he sold it to *Saturday Evening Post*. He is the guy who later became editor of *Esquire*. He often commented on the fairness with which we dealt with writers.

Will Murray: A lot of the Thrilling writers had to be very versatile. I notice that they did not always specialize in one genre or another. They crossed from Air War to Detective to even the Horror Mystery type of thing.

Jack Schiff: That is true for the most part. Although in the westerns there was more specialization. A. Leslie, Sly MacDowell and a few others stuck strictly to the western.

Some of the latter overlapped into *Thrilling Mystery* where we had supernatural type of stories more along the lines of Ambrose Bierce than some of the things you have today. Ed Bodin was not only an agent but very interested in the eerie field, and he wrote about true supernatural events.

Will Murray: Did you work much on *Thrilling Mystery*, which was their horror type of magazine?

Jack Schiff: So-called, horror. It really was not in the sense of horror today. That is why I tried to qualify it. We tried to follow the Ambrose Bierce tradition whose stories had a supernatural or a mysterioso quality. In a sense it was closer to *Weird Tales* than some of the out-and-out horror magazines.

Will Murray: Like *Horror Stories* and *Terror Tales,* which were Popular Publications' main entries. They were really into horror.

Jack Schiff: We did not want anything like that. Leo, absolutely, put his foot down on that.

Will Murray: Why did he make that judgement call? Obviously that formula worked for Popular.

Jack Schiff: I have been fortunate in the publishers and editors for whom I have worked. Both Leo and Ned Pines had a publishing conscience. That is not true of all publishers. I had the same thing with Jack Liebowitz and Whit Ellsworth at DC. The stories had to be in good taste. Since the overwhelming majority of our readers were teenagers or youngsters, we felt we had an obligation not to give them the kind of horror stuff that was being perpetrated by some of the magazines. Some of the publishers were overwhelmed by the desire to earn a quick buck by using the ultra sensational. We did not like it because it hurt the field, especially the sex and horror stuff.

Will Murray: When you worked in the field, there were a number of other publishers. Some publishers had gone under, like Clayton in 1933. There was Street & Smith, an old line dime novel publisher, doing pulps. Munsey was the first pulp house and a very famous house. Popular had started around 1932, so it was young. The Margulies group started around 1931, so it was young. The rest were a lot of fly-by-nights, such as Goodman's group which was Manvis and later became Marvel Comics. From the perspective of the Thrilling offices how did you see your competition?

Jack Schiff: We had good relations with Street & Smith and Popular. We felt we were on an equal par with them. We did not feel the same about the Goodman group and some of the others, especially when they started paying a half cent per word and publishing reprints. Not only was it bad for the writers but we felt it cheapened the whole field. The same thing happened later in comics. It seems to follow a pattern.

Will Murray: Which of your competition was the most respected among the people in the Thrilling office?

Jack Schiff: I guess it would be Street & Smith. We knew some of the editors pretty well. Johnny Campbell had written science fiction for us before he became editor at Street & Smith. John Nanovic had a reputation that was excellent. With Popular, there was some friction at times, but for the most part, I think we respected each other. I do not know whether you are including *Argosy* in this discussion. We considered *Argosy* and *Blue Book* to be on a higher level, because they paid more, which meant the quality of their stories was better. This better quality was not true all the time, but they did it more consistently than we did. I think that Dave Vern and Alfie Bester wrote stories that we directed to *Argosy*. There was not the cutthroat competition that often appears in some other fields. When we got together at a convention, there was an amicable feeling, not a hostile type of reaction.

Will Murray: Was it necessary to read a lot of the competition to see what they were doing, to keep abreast of them, to avoid duplicating something that they had done?

Jack Schiff: We had their magazines and we read them. Sometimes we sneered at them. Sometimes we said there is a damn good idea and maybe we had better think along those lines. They did the same with us. In fact, I remember we would exchange calls and say that was a hell of a good novel or novelette you had in this issue. So there was that kind of mutual respect.

Will Murray: Occasionally it did happen that a writer would plagiarize a story from one magazine and try to foist it on another publisher. I am aware of a couple of instances where a Thrilling story ended up in a Street & Smith magazine and vice versa. Do you recall any instances like that? Did you have to watch submissions very carefully?

Jack Schiff: There were a few instances of this. The editors at Street & Smith and Popular and Standard did not start any accusations or anything like that. We understood it could happen. There were a few cases where the writer was actually blackballed, because there was a deliberate effort to put something across. We determined this after some investigation. I do not want to mention any names.

What did happen was inevitable. We all had what I call a stable of writers, who wrote mostly for us but did so some writing elsewhere. This was true especially with some of the authors who were handled by agents. The agents would submit stuff to one outfit or another. Sometimes you did have a story that was kind of similar to another that had appeared by the same author. I do not know whether he had done it deliberately or whether it was just the matter of writing a similar story, perhaps six months later, for another magazine. We used to spot that.

Will Murray: Was one of the reasons that publishers used reprints the notion that the pulp audience changed every five years?

Jack Schiff: I do not think so. I think it was purely a question of profit. Since the magazines were not selling as well as before, at least the overhead was lower. I do not recall our using reprints. I do not know whether they did it after I left. (Note: Standard began using reprints in 1951, just after cutting the word rate.)

Will Murray: The rates had already dropped a lot with the Depression. Even the Clayton magazines, which were not in the class of *Argosy* or *Adventure* or *Blue Book,* were paying 4 or 5 cents a word. But all of them went to a penny a word, two cents tops. So by the thirties all the rates were cut.

Jack Schiff: The result of getting into the half cent a word rate was that it drove writers into other fields. They could not make a living on that. Some of the writers we had, did have jobs and wrote on the side, but most of them were professional writers who depended on writing for a living. While they were doing pulps they were also trying their hand at something like a novel or a movie scenario or something like that. At half a cent a word, they said, "The hell with this field."

Will Murray: Those that could not move on had to become faster producers and became sloppier writers to make the same amount of money. That had to be detrimental.

Jack Schiff: I think the quality suffered.

Will Murray: The Thrilling group is interesting because it came about, as I understand it, as a result of Street & Smith dropping American News as a distributor. American News went to Ned Pines saying we want to distribute pulps. Put out a line of pulps. At that time Ned Pines was doing *College Stories.*

So the whole group was created because of the gap that Street & Smith had left at American News. It was essentially the distributor saying we want pulps as opposed to the publisher saying he wants to publish pulps.

Jack Schiff: I would say it was more a case of mutual desires. We wanted to get in the market and the distributor wanted pulps.

Will Murray: The interesting thing though was the success. This occured at the very depth of the Depression, 1931-32. Pines came in with this whole fresh line of pulps, with a whole different look, a different type of cover art and the Thrilling title: *Thrilling Western, Thrilling Mystery, Thrilling Love, Thrilling Adventure, Thrilling Detective, Thrilling Ranch Stories.* He made it work. All of his early magazines were successful. He did not start having any duds until the late thirties. He was successful when old line publishers like Munsey were folding. How did he do that?

Jack Schiff: I do not know. I know at one point, when we heard about some of the market slipping, instead of cutting back, we increased. We put out the Popular line: *Popular Western, Popular Love, Popular Detective.* This was about 1934. I was not privy to the sales figures. Leo would get the results from Ned and sometimes, depending on whether he wanted to cheer us up or make us work harder, he would tell us how things were going. For the most part, we were not privy to sales and frankly, we did not care. Our objective was to turn out a good magazine. The selling aspect was up to the publisher and the distributor.

Will Murray: What was the best selling of the Thrilling genres: western, love, detective? Which magazines carried the line?

Jack Schiff: The magazines, which featured characters like the Phantom, the Lone Eagle, the Black Bat, Dan Fowler, generally had the highest, most consistent sales. After that *Thrilling Wonder* in the science fiction field did very well. The westerns did better than some of the others for a while. Then they fell down and the detectives came up. There did not seem to be any real consistency. As editors we did not favor one group over another.

Will Murray: You never knew what the sales figures were?

Jack Schiff: Not really. Once Leo got very angry with Ned because he had tried to keep the true figures from him. When I got into comics, I made it my business to know.

Will Murray: Why would a publisher be so concerned about not letting his own staff know how well his magazines were doing? I know that Street & Smith did the same thing. John Nanovic told us that the only reason he could figure out the sales figures was because he was a Catholic and all the boys in the press room were Catholic. Street & Smith printed their own magazines. The press people would tell Nanovic how many they were printing. He used that to gauge his approximate sales. Why not let your own people know how well you were doing? Encourage them when they are doing a good job and showing them why they should work harder when the sales are slipping.

Jack Schiff: I do not know the answer to that. It seemed to be a publisher's privilege to keep the profits of the company to himself. I guess it is the same in any business. We assumed from the fact that we were putting out more magazines, that we were doing well. When you begin to cut back or to cut rates, then you know you are in trouble. We held the line. I must give Leo a lot of credit for that. Just as I gave Whit Ellsworth, in the comics, credit for that. They were concerned about the writer and it paid off. I do not know the answer to the psychology of the publisher as far as not telling. I know in comics, we managed to get those things and we proved it a good idea. When we knew sales were behind, we made definite efforts to do something about the situation. When we were doing well, we knew we were in a good type of yarn. We proceeded in that direction.

Will Murray: Some of your pulp writers did go over to the comics with you. You brought Mort Weisinger into Standard. Later Mort brought you into DC Comics.

Jack Schiff: During the war Joe Archibald and Arthur Zagat went to the War Information Office. While I was at DC, Joe wrote me asking if I had somebody who could write comics for the War Effort. He knew I had done some work with the State Department under Nelson Rockefeller on the history of the United States, printed in Portugese and Spanish. This was a ten page comic magazine. I recommended, to Joe, that he contact W. Ryerson Johnson. But Johnny could not do it because of his freelance schedules.

Do you know how kids used to read comics? We found out in interviewing teenagers and children. They used to flip through the magazine and look at the pictures first. They never read the text. That was the clue, to us, to have the artwork clear enough so that the kid could follow it. Only afterwards do they settle down and read it.

The preceding carries the essence of the remarks made by Jack Schiff. It is interesting to note that John Nanovic at Pulpcon 11 states what he called the "Street & Smith method of producing a novel." He had the author write an outline and come in and discuss it. Then the author was sure of having the story accepted. It seems the Standard method for character novels was very similar. All in all, Jack Schiff has provided an interesting look into the workings at the offices of Standard and Street & Smith.

CHAPTER IX

THE CRIMSON
CALL TO CRIME

High above the city's skyline a red light winked. Strangely like the leering, crimson eye of some giant devil. It seemed to hint of malignant things, of bloody horror in the night.

On and off, it pulsed, glowing, darkening, stabbing the lofty gloom. It was in the *Clarion* Building, at the top of the tower—the light used by publisher Frank Havens to signal election returns. Tonight it was being employed for another purpose.

The people in the streets below who saw it merely thought it was advertising something, or acting as a beacon for airplanes or ships at sea. They didn't guess that it was a signal for one man alone in all of New York's teeming millions.

—"The Counterfeit Killers" (September 1938)

FROM THE TIME it was first introduced in "Dealers in Death" (July 1936) to the end of the series, the red signal light atop the *Clarion* tower signaled mystery and menace for Richard Curtis Van Loan in the pages of *The Phantom Detective Magazine.*

Originally the red light was simply a selective use of existing multicolored tower lights. When the *Clarion's* top crime reporter, Ace Duveen, is gunned down in the City Room, Frank Havens orders his office cleared and grabs his desk phone:

"Get me Feeney," he rasped. "The power house." He stared at the mouth-piece grimly. "Feeney? This is Frank Havens. Now listen close, Feeney, and get this right. Those lights on the tower of the building—the ones we use to signal election returns—I want them turned on, Feeney. Use the red ones only, the ones that blink. And keep them burning day and night until I give further orders!"

On the tall tower of the *Clarion* Building, those red lights danced and blinked and shuddered. Red as blood. Evil eyes winking in the early morning black—

The stay-awakes in the Bronx could see them. To the Jersey shore their jumbled signal carried. Freighters on the harbor and palatial liners at dock along the river spied their lambent glow.

Over the next several years, Van Loan will be squiring many an admiring debutante only to spot the blood-red beacon, forcing him to make lame excuses in order to slip off to become the Phantom. In this instance, he's escorting one comely specimen from Harlem's Jungle Club when Van spies the red blinkers. He hastily makes excuses:

> The woman looked at him with narrowed eyes. She was Nita Wayne—*the* Nita Wayne of Hollywood. Men sought after her, begged for ten minutes of her presence, yet this man—

Once that's done:

> ...his glance returned to the signal beacon. Red lights on the *Clarion* tower— Havens' S. O. S.—and here the Phantom had been dancing the hours away while an urgent hell was brewing.

With its second appearance in "Specter of Death" (August 1936), the blinkers had apparently been replaced by a solitary red beacon. But the soon-to-be-stock situation is much the same:

> [Richard Curtis Van Loan] was standing this moment by the rail, gazing with moody speculation at a spot in the Manhattan heavens where flamed a gleaming red planet.
>
> But the crimson light wasn't starlike in the way it would flash on for a moment, and then wink out again, at mathematically regular intervals. It had been doing that for perhaps two full minutes, a patient, nervous summons, blood-red tocsin of danger in a tinted, unreal heaven.
>
> It said, more plainly than words, "Come, Phantom. Come. There is danger. You are needed." It could be seen all over metropolitan New York, was visible even, so tall was the tower from which it flashed, as far as Connecticut and New Jersey. Never before had the Phantom failed to answer its summons. And he wouldn't now!

Van goes to meet Havens at a prearranged spot—in this case a parked sedan in front of a darkened house south of Columbus Circle. But the usual procedure calls for Van to disguise himself into unrecognizability and show up at Havens' *Clarion* office. However, there are situations when a conference with Havens is inadvisable—not to mention that it will slow down the action.

Such is the case with "The Sign of the Scar" (September 1936). The light is definitely said to be a solitary beacon and is now backed up by a shortwave radio signal telling Van where to report:

> Like an enigmatic, giant star poised above the city, the powerful beacon light atop the *Clarion* Building had begun to blink off and on, off and on. Van Loan's eyes sharpened. His finger tightened on the control stick as he began lettering the secret code signals of that towering light.
>
> But instantly the constant radio beam buzz in his ear phones cut out, replaced by the stronger coded dots and dashes from the powerful *Clarion* press station.

The tall, long-legged pilot's lips tightened across his teeth as he decoded the two identical messages.

Phantom. Fire at One Sutton Place. Scar suspected. Hurry. Waiting at Queensborough Bridge dock. Havens. Phantom. Fire at One Sutton Place.

But the signal beacon atop the towering spire of Frank Havens' newspaper building in the heart of Manhattan kept on blinking its secret code. It would continue to flash that repeated message until Havens—the only man alive who knows the Phantom's identity—contacted Richard Curtis Van Loan.

It was a double system of quick, effective communication devised by Van Loan that enabled Havens to reach him, even on a purely pleasure flight such as this, whenever the murderous tentacles of crime broke past the perpetual barriers of the police.

The Phantom's probing eyes were never long astray from that continuously illuminated beacon. He kept the radio sets on each of his several cars, speedboats and planes vigilantly tuned in on the *Clarion's* shortwave.

Later in the story, a variation is lit:

Letting his motor idle, [Van] looked up at the towers of Manhattan, jeweled turrets, thrusting up spikes of light into the night.

One of them was a red spike, blinking and darting in staccato rhythm. The signal for the Phantom. The signal of dire emergency, a signal that had never been given before!

In this case, it was the kidnapping of Frank Havens' daughter, Muriel. Throughout the series, when the red light flares for a second time after first summoning the Phantom, it will be because danger has ensnarled poor Muriel.

In the very next novel, "Empire of Doom" (October 1936), the light is again modified. Van is attending a reception at Frank Havens' Fifth Avenue residence when the signal flares to life:

Out across Central Park, rising high above the skyscrapers of the Roaring Forties to the south, blinking red lights on Frank Havens' towering *Clarion* Press Building gleamed now, flashing warningly, vividly against the purplish background of foreboding storm clouds.

The Phantom's signal!

Neither exclamation nor tremor betrayed the vitalizing shock that whipped Dick Van Loan's nerves into tensed alertness. His signal—from Frank Havens—

Around him the gay party went on, heedless and merrily ignorant of the dire call. Even Muriel Havens, the nationally powerful publisher's daughter, had no inkling of the grim Phantom drama being signaled in by those rapidly winking lights atop her father's *Clarion* tower.

Dick Van Loan's cryptic smile gave no hint of the driving turmoil seething within him as he deciphered that flashing code message:

Calling the Phantom—Come to my office—Hurry—This is a murder call—

Havens—Calling the Phantom—

The dots and dashes kept on winking ominously, would continue to blink that secret message until the Phantom himself contacted Frank Havens. Van Loan damned himself mentally. He's been idling here, dancing, unalert to that urgent message.

In this story, the *Clarion* Building is renamed the *Clarion Press* Building. It's called that again in "The Torch of Doom" (February 1937). The name will not stick.

Even with this new simplified system, the signal light will in the future sometimes merely wink mutely, bringing Van rushing to Havens' side for a briefing. And for years to come, some writers will continue to insist on using the old discarded multiple blinkers.

It soon becomes clear that the radio backup system has been abolished. This seems to have taken place by the time of "The Beast King Murders" (July 1937):

> Not more than a minute had elapsed since that phone call when a brilliant red beacon leaped into life on the tower of the *Clarion* building in mid-town Manhattan!
>
> High over the heads of the scurrying, late night throngs on Broadway, that red glow flashed, sending its long-traveling rays far and wide, so that they were visible from one end of Manhattan to the other.
>
> Long flashes and short flashes. They required no sensitive radio sets to be picked up: they were for all eyes to see. Yet in all New York only one pair of eyes would be able to interpret the signal which would have awed the unknowing multitudes:
>
> Phantom: come to Grand Central! Phantom: come to Grand Central!
>
> Urgent, imperative, that message was flashed again and again.

But there was more to the *Clarion* signal than just a suggestive scarlet pulsing against the Manhattan skyline. One of the writers—or perhaps it was an overseeing editor—had some fun over the years with variations on what soon becomes a cliché scene.

In "The Torch of Doom" (February 1937), Van Loan is at a Grand Central

Palace automobile showroom, looking to trade in his Deusenberg for a newer model, when someone is murdered in the building. Van is sniffing around the crime scene when:

> And suddenly a sharp tension gripped him. For, out across the roofs of Manhattan, red lights were blinking atop the *Clarion Press* Building—a coded call in crimson!
>
> Watching narrowly, he decoded that winking red Phantom message, and a sardonic smile played for a moment across his thin lips. Frank Havens, owner of the *Clarion*, was calling him, directing him to the Grand Central Palace killings!
>
> There was irony in that. For the first time since Van Loan had inaugurated this secret signal of crime, he was already at the murder scene. And with a clue in his possession that even the police had not muddled.

Van has to duck out to avoid compromising his true persona and return to the crime scene as a fictitious *Clarion* reporter.

Trouble rears its ugly head at daybreak, a time when the red light would scarcely be noticed, in "Hammers of Doom" (September 1937). It turns out Havens had prepared for that eventuality. Van is riding along Central Park's bridle path when the unusual call comes:

> The bridle path ascended to a little crest which gave the riders an impressive vista of the midtown sky-line beyond the park walls. Van Loan's bored eyes lifted to the tall skyscrapers, their upper parts bright in the sun which had not yet completely lighted the streets. The chrome spire of the Chrysler Building shimmered and glinted and—
>
> Suddenly Van's gaze sharpened, his hands instinctively pulled up the reins of his mount. Into his eyes came a look so keen and wide-awake that, had his laughing companions seen it, they would have been astonished.
>
> For that shimmer of the Chrysler had been rivaled now by another glinting shimmer. A shimmer which at intervals, reflecting the sun's rays, sent them flashing in all directions—and with strange, blinking rhythm!
>
> A heliograph! A mechanical mirror device which, in sunlight, could send its flashed messages for hundreds of miles. High atop the *Clarion* Building, it was blinking now as it revolved.
>
> Van's horse was already lagging behind the others again as, unmindful of the mount, he watched those flashes. He had to wait until the heliograph started to send in his direction again.
>
> Then he caught the flashes, and read them as easily as if they were boldly written words.
>
> PHANTOM—GO TO RECTOR AND BROADWAY—PHANTOM— GO TO RECTOR AND BROADWAY—
>
> Urgently came that summons, as the heliograph sought out the greatest of all sleuths wherever he might be in the city.

Van feigns a fall from his mount, makes the usual lame excuses and heads for his Park Avenue digs, from which he calls Havens on the private wire that links home and publisher. This line is used when Havens needs Van, and the latter is known to be home. It's also for Van's use on those rare occasions he stumbles across a crime first.

In "Tycoon of Crime" (February 1938), for example, Van discovers a corpse on the doorstep of his Park Avenue duplex penthouse and for a change rushes upstairs to alert Havens:

> This was a private line, one which connected him, as soon as he lifted the receiver, directly with the executive office of the *New York Clarion,* automatically causing the phone at that end to ring.

Havens keeps his telephone in a desk drawer. There's another line that connects the Bendix lab in the Bronx with the *Clarion.* These connections have the advantage of being untraceable and untappable, but of course they're not as dramatic as the signal light and its variations, so the writers don't invoke this device very much.

At the start of "Minions of Murder" (November 1938), a fog envelops Gotham and Frank Havens is temporarily stripped of his only method of reaching Dick Van Loan:

> The elderly but vigorous publisher moved in his pacing to a French casement window with an outer balcony.
>
> He pulled it open, strode out into the chill grey mist which floated weirdly in space, screening off the great city far below. Ignoring the penetrating chill of the air, Havens turned his eyes upwards, following the building wall into the enveloping clouds. Faintly, ever so faintly, where the spire thrust up there, he could detect a tiny glimmer of red, blinking spasmodically on and off, on and off.
>
> He gave a weary, inchoate sigh, went back inside to his desk, to an inter-office telephone.
>
> "Give me the tower again," he spoke heavily.
>
> And the response came:
>
> "Brady? That light up there! Can't you make it stronger?"
>
> He gripped the phone fiercely. "That red light must be seen, fog or no fog!"
>
> "Sorry, Mr. Havens, but ten lights like that couldn't pierce this mist! Have to wait until it lifts."
>
> Haven shook his head, said, "Well, keep it going! Keep repeating the flashes I gave you!"
>
> [...]
>
> The publisher continued to pace, helpless, agitated. That red blinking beacon on top of the *Clarion* Building had hitherto been a signal which had never failed to bring the man he sought. But now the fog had defeated the code-

blinking light—futilely, it winked unseen in the surrounding clouds. And the telephone calls to every place Havens could think of had proved equally fruitless.

"If only I knew where he was!" the publisher gritted now, shaking his head, raising his hands in a helpless gesture. But the determination had not left his eyes. "I must get word to him, somehow, while the trail is still fresh!"

Emerging from a party across town, Van hears the caterwaul of river sirens. The deeper siren of the transatlantic superliner Queen Anne lifts above the others, spelling out in special code one word over and over: P-H-A-N-T-O-M.

And off he goes.

In the next issue, "The Corpse Parade" (December 1938), this limitation is being attended to when crime once more rears its ugly head:

...Frank Havens strode to the French windows of his office and pushed out onto a balcony. Just overhead, the spire of the *Clarion's* tower jutted into the dark sky. It was there Havens' glance focused, on a huge, dark beacon-globe.

And he cursed as he saw, on a scaffold up there, two mechanics busily working at that beacon.

The beacon was being newly installed, substituted for an old one because the former had not been powerful enough, with its special beam, to penetrate fogs. Now it was dark.

Havens looked from the beacon down to the lights of the city and streaming traffic far below. Somewhere out there must be the man he sought; somewhere out there must he be watching, ever alert for the *Clarion's* red light. And now that light, that signal, was not working.

Spurred by haste, Frank Havens strode back into his office. For a moment he paced. Then slowly, a dawning gleam came into his eyes. He hastened back to his desk, made a call direct to Police Headquarters.

"Connect me with the Commissioner," he demanded, giving his name.

Tooling down upper Fifth Avenue in his flashy Deusenberg, Dick Van Loan is brought up short. All traffic has been brought to a bewildered halt. Once Van, stuck at an intersection, demands of a traffic cop the meaning of all those blazing red lights, and is told the commissioner ordered a full minute of two-way red, he apprehends their true significance. Stymied again, the resourceful Havens had requested all stop signs in the city turned red for one minute. (Good thing Van wasn't in the shower!)

Sometimes the Phantom is out of town and far from the *Clarion* Building's "far-traveling" rays. It was so in "The Phantom's Gamble With Death" (February 1940). Vacationing on the Connecticut shore, Richard Curtis Van Loan is oblivious to the signal light's incessant coded blinking, calling, "Phantom— you're needed... Phantom—you're needed... Phantom—you're needed...

Fortunately, Havens has a new backup. At 15 minute intervals, his commercial radio station broadcasts the identical message verbally. The announcer's urgent appeal finally reaches Van Loan's ears and the Phantom swings into action again.

On other occasions, Van is out of radio range. In "The Phantom and the Uniformed Killers" (May 1940) he's on a Miami golf course when a coded telegram from Havens causes him to break off his game and hop into his private plane.

In "The Phantom and the Crime Legion" (October 1940), Havens is confronted with his biggest challenge yet when a series of influentials are murdered by a new criminal force:

> Even now Havens was considering ways and means of summoning the Phantom. The publisher strode out through the French doors to a terrace just under the high spire of the *Clarion's* tower. Below, the city churned with toy like life. Atop the tower was a great beacon which at Havens' command could flash a powerful red light, in coded signal. Often had that red light summoned the Phantom from some corner of Manhattan or its environs. But it could not summon him now. For, as Havens well knew, the Phantom was beyond the range even of that powerful light.

Moreover, he could not be reached by telephone, telegraph, or even radio!

It turns out that after Van's last harrowing case, Havens suggested he get away from it all for a while. Thus, Van is holed up in an Adirondack hunting lodge with a group of swells who, in trying to escape business worries and the growing war in Europe, don't even have a radio at hand! Then:

> The drone of the airmail plane which regularly passed overhead at this hour drifted from the darkening sky. Van, seeing the wing-tip light of the craft, thought again how shut-in this place was from all news, even from mail. Twice he had considered going down to the nearest village and contacting Havens— or at least hearing the current news. But he remembered Havens' words:

> "You stay there, get crime out of your mind, so you'll be fresh for your next case. If anything comes up, I'll find some way to contact the Phantom."

> As Van moved across the porch to the screen door, he noted that the roar of the mail plane's motors seemed unusually loud. The ship was flying low. That was odd, because visibility was good, and the plane usually flew much higher to make certain of clearing the mountain-tops. It was sweeping overhead now, a great winged shape in the dusk, its red and green wing-tip lights.

> Van's lithe body stiffened suddenly, eyes widening. The red wing-tip light on that plane was flashing! It was winking on and off, in short dots and dashes—a code that was not Morse, but which Van knew well!

> The big mail plane wheeled in its course, flying low and noisily overhead, so noisily that Van's host suddenly peered out of the opening screen door.

> "Say, is something the matter with the mail plane tonight?" he asked.

> "Guess he's just correcting his route," Van drawled indifferently.

> But he realized now that even had he been in the house, that plane would have attracted his notice. Its red light continued to wink. It circled once more

before it zoomed sharply into the darkening sky.

But Van had read its flashed message in the code known only to Frank Havens and himself:

"Phantom! Come at once!"

That had been the terse signal, repeated over and over.

How Havens had contrived to have the mail plane flash that secret code, Van did not know. But he did know that some major crime must have broken—that no time must be lost!

When Van lands his private monoplane at LaGuardia Airport, Havens is there to meet him, while the author explains:

> From his office at the *Clarion*, Frank Havens had pulled the strings that had sent his message to the Phantom—via airmail! This he had done through the Federal authorities, and even the few high officials contacted did not know that the purpose of the device was to summon the Phantom. The aviators were told to flash the wing-light in a certain given rhythm, but were unaware of its meaning.

By this time, Havens has installed a button in his office to activate the light. It's mentioned in "The Phantom and the Green Glare Murders" (November 1940). While driving through Times Square, Van has an unusual vehicular accident. The body of a U. S. senator falls from a clear sky and lands smack on the hood of his car. While Van is investigating the bizarre, inexplicable death, "his eye caught a winking blot of red, pulsing on and off from one of the highest towers on the Manhattan skyline."

Havens' powerful news-gathering organization had alerted him to the tragedy, never dreaming that this is one of those rare times when the Phantom is already on the case.

As the 1940s came on, the *Clarion* light was used less and less. Too pulpy for those grim war times, one suspects. Or perhaps it's because in those years the bulk of the *Phantoms* were written by the two writers who went to great lengths to avoid using the red light—Laurence Donovan and Charles Greenberg. When it calls Van into the case recorded in "Arsenals of Death" (April 1942), the light has not been seen in over a year. There was no explanation.

Starting in "Murder of a Plaster Saint" (February 1944), the signal light—not seen now for two years—has been replaced by a radio sending set located in the *Clarion* tower. Van has a receiver in his car and apartment. It seems the signal light has at last been mothballed, perhaps as a wartime "blackout" precaution. After a few issues' sporadic use, the radio set is phased out and the red beacon is back in "Murder of a Marionette" (December 1944). It's used on and off after this. According to "Death to a Diplomat" (October 1945), criminals now know the red light is meant to summon the dreaded Phantom. In "The Case of the Poison Formula" (December 1945), both contact methods are in evidence, but radio is on the way out as a medium. The Phantom is summoned in "Death Rides the Winner" (August 1946) by both signal light and transmission over TV broadcast stations!

In "Murder Set to Music" (Summer 1949), it's said the *Clarion* beacon is used only in dire emergencies, and its infrequent use over the previous four years attests to the truth of this. In "The Deadly Diamonds" (Summer 1950), it flares one final time and bows out, though the Phantom soldiers on in his relentless war against crime for another three years.

One of the most intriguing questions in the series was where was the *Clarion* tower located? There are many clues salted here and there in the double columns of cold type. Virtually every story places it in midtown Manhattan. "The Broadway Murders" says it's off Broadway. That hardly narrows it. "The Radio Murders" describes it thusly:

> South of Times Square, towering in the soft mist of night like a bodiless head, was the lighted tower of the *Clarion* Building. It was one of the city's exploited night sights with its spire aglow from the indirect lighting of the battery of hooded lamps around the cornices.
>
> But this picture was not what claimed Dick Van Loan's attention. In the very top of the tower a huge red light was winking on and off, like the baleful glare of a blinking Cyclops. To others among the teeming millions who might notice this queer beacon it was just an ornamental light, for a directional beam for some aircraft hook-up. But to Richard Van Loan it meant something entirely different. It was a direct message that Frank Havens was urgently trying to get in touch with the Phantom.

This makes it sound like a well-known Manhattan landmark of the period. But the *Clarion* tower is not a doublet of the Times Building in Times Square, because that famous landmark is mentioned earlier in the same scene.

Illustrations aren't much help. The earliest cut shows a rather baroque building that might have been a mid-sized 1930s office building. A later oft-reprinted drawing depicts the Phantom with a red signal light behind him. It resembles the top of the Empire State Building sans the mooring mast.

Both "The Forty Thieves" and "The Phantom's Gamble With Death" (February 1940) describe the *Clarion* Building as one of the "taller" or "tallest" towers in Manhattan. In mid-Depression, that would seem to narrow it down to either the Empire State Building or the Chrysler Building, the two tallest skyscrapers of that era.

Could it have been one of those two? "Murder Makes a Movie" (February 1942) makes passing reference to the 63rd floor of the *Clarion* Tower, as this particular Robert Wallace styled it. Only two New York City towers had a 63rd floor in those days. We can be sure it's not the Chrysler Building because that spire is mentioned in the same breath as the *Clarion* Building in "Hammers of Doom" (September 1937). Additionally, "The Silent Death" (December 1936) mentions a clock tower, which neither building boasted.

There are other clues. The *Clarion* beacon is visible from the laboratory of the mythical Dr. Paul Bendix, up in the Bronx. Van can spy it from his Park Avenue penthouse apartment, according to several stories. But that only tells us it was a very prominent building.

When he spots the crimson call-light in "Empire of Terror" (October 1936), Van makes excuses to Muriel and heads off to the *Clarion* Building:

> South of Central Park, the *Clarion* tower lights were still flashing their urgent secret code for the Phantom.
>
> And the Phantom was answering that call! Answering it now in the fast run of Dick Van Loan's dark blue coupe down Fifth Avenue and across town to Eighth.

The author doesn't stipulate where Van finally arrives, only to note that he parked a block from the building. Moments later, he is on the corner of Eighth Avenue. Ducking into a subway kiosk, he crosses Eighth Avenue underground to avoid a drenching downpour and arrives at the *Clarion's* entrance.

> The editorial offices of the *Clarion* were on the eleventh floor and Frank Havens had a bullet-proof glass cubicle there, raised above the floor level in a far corner.
>
> But the publisher's real office was a triplex suite on the eighty-fifth and top floors of the towering press building, reached only by a private express elevator entered through a sliding glass cubicle overlooking the editorial rooms.

Therein lies a major clue: the eighty-fifth and top floors. Later, Van emerges into the rain of Eighth Avenue, cementing the location.

It starts to sound like the Empire State Building, which is both south of Central Park and Times Square. But it's not on Eighth Avenue, but Fifth. Nor is it among the Roaring Forties, being situated between 33rd and 34th Streets. Technically, the "Empire of Doom" author doesn't explicitly state the tower is in the 40s, only that it rises above them. That could only mean it's very, very tall.

Or maybe not. For it seems the Phantom's casebooks, which Robert Wallace ransacked for twenty solid years, do not agree on the height of the *Clarion* Building. "Minions of Murder" (November 1937) said this:

> The towering New York *Clarion* Building jutted forty stories into the low-hanging fog of clouds, a fog which completely enveloped its spire, obscuring it from visibility on all sides.

I think we have to dismiss the "Empire of Terror" identification, especially as it seems to be a Dan Fowler novel recast as a Phantom. The *Clarion* Building may or may not stand on Eighth Avenue.

Perhaps a clue might be found in the true identity of the *Clarion* itself. During the Depression, New York was a hotbed of newspapers, with the Times at the top of the heap and the yellow tabloids at the very bottom. The second-largest daily of that era was the suggestively-titled *New York Herald-Tribune. Herald—Clarion.* Sounds like we're in the same ballpark. Especially when you learn that the *Herald* had been once owned by Frank A. Munsey, publisher of the original pulp magazine *The Argosy.* He sold it in 1924 to the

Reid family, who merged it with their *New York Tribune* to form the *New York Herald-Tribune*. (Must be a branch of the same newspaper family that owned the *Daily Sentinel* and spawned the Green Hornet.)

So where were the *Herald-Tribune's* offices located?

Well, directly south of Times Square on Broadway one finds another square: Herald Square! It's in the Thirties, not the Forties, at the intersection of Broadway and Sixth Avenue, now called the Avenue of the Americas. Research uncovers what must by now be obvious: Herald Square takes its name from the original newspaper, the *Herald*.

Further research uncovers the fact that the *Herald* vacated its two-story Italianate headquarters near Herald Square around the time of the merger. After being absorbed into the *Tribune,* the combined newspaper eventually occupied the *Tribune* building on West 40th Street. But this building was but seven stories tall. The *Herald-Tribune* soon outgrew it, and a 20-story addition was incorporated into it, having a West 41st Street frontage. The location fits the *Clarion* setup, but the edifice is woefully stunted for our purposes.

A check of microfilm file copies of the *Herald-Tribune* for 1933-35—the early years of *The Phantom Detective Magazine*—show not one but two addresses of record for that illustrious newspaper—154 Nassau Street in lower Manhattan and 230 West 41st Street.

The second address places the paper's headquarters firmly in the area alluded to in several stories—smack in the Roaring Forties, between Seventh and Eighth Streets, a scant three blocks from the *Times* building. Evidently the *Herald-Tribune* Building formed with the *New York Times* part of what was then called Newspaper Square in the heart of midtown.

However, the Nassau address brings us to what used to be called Newspaper Row. This is the address of the original *Tribune*—at the time of its construction, the largest tower in all of Manhattan. Unfortunately it was built in 1875, and was only five floors tall. Evidently they held onto that landmark even after its usefulness had ended. However, a cluster of baroque-looking skyscrapers still standing today in the immediate vicinity look promising. One bears a striking resemblance to the earliest cuts of the signal-generating *Clarion* Building found in 1936-37 issues of *The Phantom Detective* with its neo-Gothic Cathedral-like spire. It's not hard to identify: at 60 stories, it was the tallest building in the world when it was erected in 1913. The record stood until the Chrysler Building went up in 1930. But this particular structure was built by dime-store magnate F. W. Woolworth and had nothing to do with newspapering. And it's either 20 stories too tall or 20 stories too short, depending on how high the *Clarion* actually was.

Alas, it seems there is in real life no exact counterpart to the famous *Clarion* tower. Perhaps like all great fictional concepts, it's not meant to be found on a map, or discovered in real life. As for its true-life doublet, the colorful *New York Herald-Tribune* was folded in 1966.

But if my researches are true, to this day—almost seventy years after that scarlet summons of death first illuminated the Manhattan skyline, the crimson beacon still shines—from the top of the Woolworth Building.

CHAPTER X

FEAR HAS FOUR FINGERS

ASK A GROUP of pulp fans to name the greatest pulp hero and you get a variety of pleasantly conflicting opinions, fueled and fired by nostalgia and personal tastes. But ask them who they consider the greatest disguise master of the pulps and you have to brace yourself for acrimonious debate, backed up by anecdote and analysis. Nostalgic choice is one thing, specific character skills quite another.

It's funny how among characters as dissimilar as Doc Savage and the Phantom Detective, the Green Lama and the Lone Eagle, they all had one big thing in common. At the drop of a wig, they'd jump into disguise. Even some of the long-running Western characters couldn't resist adopting spare identities or resorting to disguise as an infiltration tactic.

I guess it all goes back to the dime novel days of Nick Carter. Nick was the original quick-change artist. In those days, it was a snap process. You just donned false hair and greasepaint. The authors had it easy, too. All they had to write was, "Nick became a grizzled old man," and presto the reader's imagination happily filled in the wrinkles and grizzles. It went down easier because the authors practically never described old Nick. I guess it was the same holding back of specific details that, years later, led the scribblers behind *Secret Agent "X"* and *G-8* to skip lightly over the physiognomy of their heroes. By that time, popular fiction readers demanded more concrete details, and so they were treated to endlessly repetitive scenes of chracters hunched in front of lightbulb-festooned mirrors, applying wrinkling putty to their strong smooth necks, with nostril-dilators, ear-benders, eye-discolorers, false teeth and all manner of complicated stuff hanging like Christmas tree ornaments off their countenances.

Some pulp heroes were such great disguise artists, they didn't need mirrors and direct lighting. They simply whipped out their handy disguise kit, slapped their faces with clay, and became Blackie Durtt—or some other hardcase—in a dimly lit back alley.

This sometimes led to problems.

No one would quibble with the thought that Richard Curtis Van Loan, as the Phantom, is maybe one of the four or five greatest pulp disguise masters. He was called the Man of a Thousand Faces. True, so were Secret Agent "X" and actor Lon Chaney, but the Phantom outlasted Secret Agent "X" handily. In fact, the *Phantom Detective* magazine was truly the second hero pulp, slipping stealthily onto the newsstands in November 1932, well before any one else jumped on the "let's imitate *The Shadow*" bandwagon. And the Phantom was the only hero pulp to run twenty years, sprawling across three decades, the thirties to the early fifties.

The Phantom's approach to disguise was to slide from false face to alternate identity, disguising himself as anything on legs to pursue his manhunts. He had a few fake identities of his own, Dr. Paul Bendix, gangster Gunner McGlone and the seldom-seen Lester Cornwell, but mostly he liked to infiltrate groups of suspects and victims as one of their own number, be that a scarfaced torpedo or kindly Uncle Ralph.

Many of the Phantom's disguise shifts occurred on the fly. A lot of times— too many compared to the Shadow or Secret Agent "X"—the Phantom was exposed for what he was. The Phantom—never Richard Curtis Van Loan. At least he was competent to that extent, which is more than I can say for the Spider. Even lowly pickpockets knew he was Richard Wentworth!

I guess if you're a pulp hero moving from disguise to disguise and seldom fighting crime in your true identity or cloaked up in some night-blending regalia, there's not much drama or action unless your false face slips a time or two. And for plot purposes, the Phantom was frequently cornered in dark rooms, flashlights and firearms pointing his way as it slowly sinks in that the greasepaint could have been a smidgen thicker this time out.

A typical Phantom dilemma occurred in "The Dancing Doll Murders" from June 1937. It went like this:

> Though his face betrayed no emotion, Richard Curtis Van Loan's heart was hammering. This smiling man in front of him whom they called "Doc" was bringing him close to the brink of destruction.
>
> Then another voice that cut like a knife through the now quiet room brought him closer still. It was the voice of one of the hopheads who had come back from Channel Point.
>
> The man's lips were slack, he was staring not at Van's face, but at his hands.
>
> "Look!" he screamed suddenly. "That guy ain't Dopey! He can't be! Dopey's got a sliced-off finger!"
>
> There hadn't been time for Dick Van Loan to make a close study of his subject. He had played his cards as they came to him—played them bravely, recklessly—and had lost.

If my life depended on it, were I a pulp crimebuster, you can bet I would be damned sure to count the fingers of every unconscious felon I elected to impersonate from that point on. Not so, Dick Van Loan. Compare the above scene with this from the May 1941 issue, "The Trail to Death":

Van, playing his role, was relaxing with the other men. Fletchley the Englishman spoke to him in an accent that upheld his nickname.

"I say, Charlie, do you have a light?"

"Surely." Van took out Charlie Kane's lighter, flicked it, extended it with his left hand while he accepted a cigarette from Fletchley with his right.

And Fletchley stepped back with a cry:

"By Jove—you're not Charlie Kane! You can't be Charlie Kane!"

Every man in the room whirled. And the Phantom's heart seemed suddenly turned to ice. He knew he had played his role to perfection. He was smiling, outwardly calm.

"Have you gone crazy, Fletchley?" he demanded. "Listen to him, fellows. He says I'm not Charlie Kane!"

The tension relaxed as eyes studied Van's flawlessly disguised face.

"You must be balmy, Fletchley!" Henry Latisse turned from the table. "Of course he's Kane. Unless Kane has a twin."

Fletchley himself looked bewildered now.

"But I tell you he can't be Kane! You all know Kane lost the whole middle finger of his left hand only three days ago, when that door jammed on him during a holdup!"

As every man froze, the Phantom knew that for once the long arm of coincidence had reached out to betray him—with mocking irony. In his haste to assume the role of Charlie Kane before the police captain returned to remove the body, the Phantom had been unable to make a minute examination of the remains. Otherwise he could have made this present exposure impossible.

Excuses, excuses. About five years seperated these two incidents. Readers no doubt never noticed. There were too many mind-numbingly similar traps for the Phantom to escape. And escape he did, from both of these tight spots. First time around, he grabbed a chair and used it to slap out a hanging naked lightbulb. The second time, he shot out a cluster of bare bulbs. Thank God for bare bulbs! In the darkness, Van Loan made typical hectic escapes.

I guess Van Loan finally learned to count fingers because as far as I know, he never messed up this badly after that. I can't vouch for the Spider. Somewhere in the dimness of my memory, it seems to be that the Spider once impersonated a four-fingered felon and ended up dodging lead, too.

Maybe I'm thinking of the peculiar incident in "Secret City of Crime" (February 1943). The Spider infiltrates an underground criminal enterprise, and disguises himself as a minor underling he has killed. Joining the criminals, Richard Wentworth is at first accepted as one of them. Then suddenly, a hood looks at him strangely.

"You!" he suddenly yells. "You're not Jenks! You gotta be... the Spider!"

I would have guessed the Phantom myself. But no matter. Suddenly the hoods open fire and we cut to the next chapter, detailing the travails of Spider aides Ronald Jackson and Nita Van Sloan. When we finally return to Richard Wentworth, he's jumping all over the place in a manic effort to dodge a zillion whining slugs. His exertions are so intense, the reader never does learn how the bad guys recognized that our hero was not the real Jenks.

Can't blame author Norvell Page here. This was one of the last Spider novels and was revised by editor Robert Turner. Probably Turner let the telltale reference to a missing finger, or whatever, slip off the page. We'll never know....

But I'm blaming the character when I probably should be blaming the author. I don't know for certain who wrote "The Dancing Doll Murders" or "The Trail to Death." It seems to be the same writer. I venture to guess it's George A. McDonald, one of the more prolific "Robert Wallaces." But one can't be sure of that. Pulp writers of the hero pulp school cross-pollenated one another busily. An *Operator #5* plot resurfaced in *Doc Savage,* a Phantom trick in a Jim Anthony novel. And everybody stole from The Shadow.

Who was the greatest disguise master in the pulps? I would immediately disqualify the Phantom based on this article. G-8, Secret Agent "X" and most of the others all seem equally adept in my mind. Doc Savage had some of the most unusual disguises, but he was limited by his great size and herculean physique.

In my estimation, the Shadow had to be the greatest. Not only because of the quality of his disguises—no pulp hero ever had such a memorable group of alternate psuedo-identities—but because the Shadow had to overcome a major handicap. His huge nose. It's a tribute to the Shadow and his creator, Walter B. Gibson, that readers could accept without blinking hawk-nosed Kent Allard as a vast array of dissimilar characters. That's talent!

CHAPTER XI

BLUE GHOST
BUSTER

T HE IMPORTANCE OF the *Phantom Detective* novel, "Dealers in
Death" (July 1936) was that it transformed the series by introducing several new characters; *Clarion* crime reporter Steve Huston, who would remain
with the series to its end in 1953; Nita Wayne, who would briefly supplant
Muriel Havens as Richard Curtis Van Loan's girlfriend; and Phantom aliases
Gunner McGlone and Dr. Paul Bendix, an elderly chemist whose Bronx laboratory would be the Phantom's chief hideout. Most importantly, this novel
introduced the red signal light atop the *Clarion* building that would summon
the Phantom whenever crime reared its Hydra head over the next fifteen or
sixteen years.

I had been banging my head against the wall on this novel for about two
years and was growing frustrated, when I decided around Halloween 1996 to
write an article on the subject.

Normally when I set out to unmask the author of a pseudonymous novel
I have my suspect already identified, and it's only a matter of presenting the
mystery citing the evidence and unmasking the culprit.

So frustrated was I by my inability to come up with a final answer that I
decided, on the theory that I sometimes think better on paper, of starting the
article, laying out the multiple suspects, and following the chain of evidence
to wherever it took me. I vowed to myself: I will have it all figured out or die
tying. I was pretty sick of reading and rereading *Phantoms* without getting any-
where.

There ensued the most bizarre quest I have ever undertaken. One that
would bring me in contact with the world of the paranormal in my quest to
bust this stubborn ghost.

You'll recall I chiefly considered Norvell W. Page, Paul Ernst, and Ray
Cummings, among others, ultimately deciding that Cummings was the most
likely writer responsible for "Dealers in Death" and "Death Rides the Blizzard"
(November 1936).

As it happened strange things began transpiring during the drafting and
redrafting, and even after turning in the article, they kept on happening.

I can't explain anything of the hows and whys of what I am about to relate. I can only vouch for its truthfulness and authenticity.

Here goes:

Chiefly, I was attempting to identify "Dealers in Death" and "Death Rides the Blizzard"; the former reading somewhat like Paul Ernst and the latter showing signs of Ray Cummings' cunning hand. Yet they were clearly the work of the same writer, and unlike any other *Phantoms* I'd ever read.

Certain novels that followed displayed echoes of this writer, but were not perfect matches. This might have been explained by the fact that Standard Magazines used rewrite men on the *Phantom* series, creating the illusion of multiple styles in the work of a single ghost. Among these novels were "The Dancing Doll Murders" (June 1937), "Cavalcade of Death" (August 1937) and "The Counterfeit Killers" (September 1938).

The first strange thing that happened was truly strange. I happened to be re-reading "Doll" in the company of a girlfriend who was demonstrably psychic. Just take my word for it! She was!

As I was reading the novel, she expressed curiosity in my choice of reading matter. So I told her my reasons for reading it.

Then it hit me! "You're supposed to be psychic. You tell me who wrote it."

She takes the book, holds it for about three seconds and says: "Paul wrote this."

I looked at her in amazement. I had two suspects. Paul Ernst and Ray Cummings; I hadn't told her that. I had hardly told her anything except the name on the book, Robert Wallace, was fictitious.

"Paul Ernst?" I blurt.

"I just get Paul," she says.

I read further and came across the unusual word, "tocsin," which I had recently discovered in a Paul Ernst short story. It was also present in "Dealers in Death" and other Phantoms in this sub-set, all the way down to "The Counterfeit Killers."

"Maybe you're right," I muttered.

I decided to attack the problem in a new way. Forget Ray Cummings. Concentrate on Paul Ernst.

I spent several days skimming old Ernst stories and novels. It was a lot of work, but it was worth it because it enabled me to come to a clear and final conclusion.

My conclusion: Ernst didn't write any of the *Phantoms* in question!

I recalled the subject with my supposedly psychic paramour, saying, "You were wrong."

My girlfriend takes a stack of Phantoms and tries again. She was not doing well. "I never heard of *Phantom* authors with names like Lenny and Jacob," I tell her. But when she takes hold of the last one in the stack (I think it was "Milestones of Murder," April 1938) she asked a very important question:

"Was there another Paul?"

I reflected. I thought there was. Paul Chadwick. But a *Phantom* editor named Jack Schiff once assured me he only did short stories for the Thrilling Group.

That seemed to be the dead end of that rather unorthodox line of investigation. Live and learn! Right?

Not long after, I happened to be glancing over "Cavalcade of Death." I note with surprise that although the tone of the story is very different, stylistically it bore a strong resemblance to "The Dancing Doll Murders."

This blew me away. Before that editor had made his comment, I had thought I detected Chadwick's style in "Cavalcade." But his assertion persuaded me to abandon the investigation. I had since begun to lean towards Emile C. Tepperman, because the story had strong *Secret Agent "X"* characteristics. Both Chadwick and Tepperman were *Secret Agent "X"* writers.

I also noted with interest that the two stories were published only two months apart in 1937.

Could it be...?

With a mounting sense of expectation, I pulled out every Chadwick story I owned.

Bingo! The styles matched. There was no doubt. There were tons of indicators. Chadwick liked to use phrases like "sub-calibre machine gun," "mummery," "crime hunter," and others that were salted through his *Secret Agent "X"* novels.

The skeptical among you may require further proof. Try this:

In "Dancing Doll Murders," the following passage had haunted me for years. I knew I had read something similar elsewhere but could never place it:

The helmeted head turned toward him. The single round glass eye in front goggled at him like those of some giant crustacean.

Now compare this underwater scene from Paul Chadwick's December 1932 Wade Hammond story, "The Corpses' Carnival":

He switched on his helmet light and found himself staring at the glass lens of another diving helmet with a man's eyes behind it, eyes distorted like those of some giant crustacean.

And this from Chadwick's *Secret Agent "X"* novel, "The Death-Torch Terror" (April 1934):

But Agent "X" caught sight of a light glittering on goggles. For an instant he looked into an expressionless, masklike face—a face that was crustacean, monstrous, distorted and made inhuman by some sort of weird helmet.

I rest my case.

So I relearn a lesson I need to relearn from time to time. Stylistic matches are unmistakable. A lot of pulp writers write a little like one another. But if you know what to look for two works by the same author will match to perfection.

Armed with this knowledge, I scanned my admittedly incomplete stack of *Phantoms* and soon I had determined that Chadwick was the author of "The Dancing Doll Murders," "Cavalcade of Death," and "The Counterfeit Killers."

As a side benefit, I solved the nagging riddle of who wrote the very Lester Dent-esque *Secret Agent "X"* novel, "Kingdom of Blue Corpses" (January 1935). It was Paul Chadwick. The Dent flavor was probably gotten from Chadwick's wife, Dorothy Lester, who was Dent's secretary and typist during the first two years of *Doc Savage*.

Unfortunately, despite the presence of the word tocsin, Chadwick proved not to be the author of "Dealers in Death" or "Death Rides the Blizzard." Too bad. I was rooting for him.

It was amazing. The author I was seeking was the last person I would have suspected. I had been blocked by bad information and a psychic had unblocked me.

You may wonder why that editor was wrong. I did too, at first. Then I realized. Schiff was not the editor of *The Phantom Detective*. Thrilling pulps were edited by roving assistant editors under Leo Margulies' stewardship. Schiff flitted from *The Phantom Detective* to *Thrilling Love* to *The Lone Eagle* and back again. Chadwick's *Phantoms* probably came through while he was toiling on *Thrilling Ranch Stories,* or something.

Since I was pursuing the author of "Dealers in Death," I decided to leave this whole spooky Chadwick discovery out of my well reasoned article. Who would believe me?

The next strange thing that happened was the discovery of an old letter from the late Bob Sampson I had saved. I came across it during a file reorganization.

Dated June 6, 1985, it was in reply to a question I'd posed. I'd heard a rumor of a pulp character called the Blue Ghost and wondered if Bob (a human pulp encyclopedia if one ever existed) was familiar with him. I needed the info for my interminable reworking of *The Hero Pulp Index*.

Bob replied that there were two Blue Ghosts, one in *Clues* and the other in *Detective Fiction Weekly*. The *Detective Fiction Weekly* Blue Ghost ran in two 1940 serials, "The Blue Ghost" (February 3 through March 2) and "Blue Ghost Beware" (November 16 through December 21).

I quote from Bob's letter:

Both these serials are written by Myles Hudson, secretary to broadcasting magnate Adam Wilde and using the casebooks of the Blue Ghost. Wilde's name and that of the Ghost, Charles Dexter Bradford, are pseudonyms.

Background: An automobile accident left Bradford an orphan when he was barely 14. His appointed guardian, Adam Wide, handled the boy's money so well that it became a fortune, yielding about $40,000 a year.

When he was in his late twenties, criminals kidnapped a young girl, a child, and murdered her before the ransom was paid. The mother went insane, the father shot himself. Because of this case, Bradford swore to fight crime. He trained intensively in arts and science. Learned the secrets of disguise from Troissard in Paris. Had voice lessons from Thoens, a Dutchman, and Ludeen of London. Following a physical breakdown from overwork, Bradford went to Switzerland, where he learned bodily and muscular control, including detail control of facial muscles which considerably aided his disguise abilities.

Returning to the States, he began operations, killing big shot gangster, Big Augie, as he was sailing from the U. S. In Big Augie's fingers the police found a white calling card with "a gleaming blue splotch like a blob of brilliant ink" in a lower corner. Thus the Blue Ghost, the Death Blot (both those names are cited about once a serial part and always in tandem; elsewhere he is merely called the Blue Ghost). In spite of several of these justice killings, he is in good standing with the authorities, although they do not share as openly with him as with the Phantom. When he meets with them he takes care to disguise his ears, voice, and wears a dark blue suit, and blue tinted glasses. He is however a human chameleon, who can disguise himself to closely resemble almost any man.

He is given to vanishing for long spells, like Cleek. When the need for him is great, the early editions of the *New York Express* print the weather report in the upper left of the page instead of the upper right. At the same time, at night, the searchlights on top of the Federated Broadcasting Building sweep the Fed Broadcasting sign more rapidly than usual. The sign was a huge representation of the globe, with the lightning streaked letters FBC endlessly girding it. Normally the mock lightning was a yellow flame. "Tonight it was brilliant blue." ("The Blue Ghost" p. 12) The lights are only used to signal intense need, immediate danger.

The Ghost's headquarters is in a three story brownstone in the Fifties, east of Park Avenue. The brass plate at the entrance says Chemical Associates, below is the name Milo Hackett. The brownstone is about as secure as a bank vault, full of steel and triple locks, with burglar proof windows, and inside, a corridor filled with mirrors and a television device which scans all visitors. A mirror slides back automatically back to reveal a closet or elevator. There are no staircases to the upper floors. The main floor front is a huge, luxurious townhouse, capable of entertaining 60 people, complete with a huge literary and technical library. The laboratories with all their specialized equipment are on the second floor. The basement is classed as one of the three floors. Milo Hackett, a Ghost disguise, is old, short, humpbacked, with yellow skin, a broad nose and bulging lips. Hair and eyebrows are grey. All this comes off under the application of solvents to reveal Bradford's face.

The Ghost carries a gun but doesn't often use it and then not very effectively. He seems rather easily captured but slides out of trouble with equal ease. He is second generation Phantom of course.

Now when I first read this back in 1985, I was not as familiar with *The Phantom Detective* as I am today. So I completely missed the fact that the FBC signal is a more elaborate version of the red signal light emitted by the *Clarion* building. Or that elderly chemist Milo Hackett is a virtual clone of Dr. Paul Bendix. In fact they shared a similar secret laboratory. And there's the fact that the Blue Ghost was trained by experts who sounded suspiciously like those who trained Richard Curtis Van Loan in "Dealers in Death," like hypnosis expert Emmanuel Helmont and disguise master Professor Muhl of Vienna.

Now I'm pretty intuitive myself. I've had some uncanny experiences along that line. When I read this description, my first thought was, why would a *Detective Fiction Weekly* author rip off the Phantom so blatantly?

My second thought, intuition if you will, ran as follows: he wouldn't dare. Unless he were the author of "Dealers in Death" and was recycling his own concepts.

The problem was, Myles Hudson was listed in all pulp indexes as the author of those two Blue Ghost serials, but nothing else. This suggested a pseudonym, rather than a house name.

I made a mental note to seek out any and all Blue Ghost chapters at the next Pulpcon. There was nothing I could do with my vague theory until then. Bob Sampson was no longer with us, and his *Detective Fiction Weekly* set scattered to the winds.

Days passed. I worked on my article. The Thanksgiving and Christmas holidays filled up my time. I planned to sit my psychic raconteur down with copies of "Dealers in Death" and "Death Rides the Blizzard," but unfortunately our relationship turned spookier and spookier. By New Year she was out of my life and that was that.

In January, I happened to spot a classified ad in the *Comic Buyers Guide* for a pulp and paperback show down in the Tampa, Florida area. Normally I would never travel that far for a one day con of doubtful reputation, but it happened that 1) I needed a vacation, 2) I had two friends in that area in need of visiting and 3) One had made me a standing offer to stay with him any time.

That last person was Chuck Juzek, a long time friend and correspondent of mine.

I made the calls and set up a week long vacation in sunny Florida. I should add that I had an additional impetus to do this. A certain psychic someone had predicted that I would go to a tropical clime in February. Alone.

Florida was as tropical as I cared to get. I decided to go with the psychic flow, as it were.

I never imagined that I would start to find the answers to my questions in a Spanish style house on the Gulf of Mexico, but I've had stranger experiences in my life.

I don't know if you could call any of what follows psychic. It certainly is uncanny.

A weird thing happened as I was preparing to depart. That night I packed. I realized I would need a bigger suitcase than usual and pulled out from storage one I rarely use. To my surprise, it was stuffed with old papers and correspondence. I had squirreled them away years before, and promptly forgot all about them. I tend to do that.

While glancing through the accumulation, I came across a printout of Norman A. Daniels' *Phantom* stories compiled by Al Tonik from Daniels' own card files.

I looked it over because a question had come up in regards to Daniels' authorship of the March 1936 *Phantom*, "The Circus Murders." Tom Johnson had told me it didn't read like Daniels' work. Since the villain, the Crimson Clown, bore the same name as the old Johnston McCulley crime fighter, this suggested a possibility of McCulley's involvement with *The Phantom Detective.*

Sure enough, "The Circus Murders" was on the list. But I soon forgot it, and McCulley.

For I saw to my astonishment that "Dealers in Death" was also listed as Norman Daniels' work.

More importantly, it, along with "Specter of Death" (August 1936), were logged as having been revised by an unknown author!

Here are the facts:

"Specter of Death" was submitted as "The Chameleon" on January 1, 1936 and accepted on February 3. Daniels was paid half his normal fee, $200, and he noted that the tale was revised by another author.

"Dealers in Death" was submitted on March 15, but was not paid for until May 25, indicating real problems with the story. Again Daniels was paid half his customary $400 fee and another author was brought in to salvage the story.

A partial answer to my quest had been in my possession all along. I might never have stumbled across it except I needed that damned suitcase for Florida.

Mind reeling, I packed. I also scribbled a hasty postcard to Tom, telling him of the discovery and asking him to hold my article for revisions.

On the flight to Florida I revised the article by hand. I still lacked a complete answer. "Dealers" bore no Daniels earmarks. It had to have been completely revised. I suspected this unknown rewriter was the guy who created the red signal light, *Clarion* reporter Steve Huston, Van's occasional girlfriend, Nita Wayne, Phantom aliases Gunner McGlone and Dr. Bendix, and other trappings. I didn't see Daniels coming up with all this stuff. His only previous Phantom innovation was the creation of the short-lived alias, Lester Cornwell.

Maybe, I thought, it was Ray Cummings who then went on to pen "Death Rides the Blizzard," which I still felt strongly was Cummings' work.

But there were numberless possibilities. Editor in Chief Leo Margulies once boasted that he never published a story that hadn't needed editorial revisions. He had tons of rewrite men on his staff, ranging from staff writers to associate editors. Two editors, Mort Weisinger and Jack Schiff, claimed *Phantoms* were revised in house left and right. One of the chief guys doing this was Bernard Breslauer. So he was a possibility.

At the same time, *Phantom* writer Charles Greenberg once told me that he would be called upon to punch up inferior *Phantoms*. It might well have been him, since he started writing *Phantoms* circa 1936. Except for one thing: Greenberg's *Phantom* novels never, or almost never, included the *Clarion* signal light, Nita Wayne or Dr. Bendix and Gunner McGlone. So I think we can safely excuse him from the lineup of suspects.

During my stay at Chuck's, I naturally prowled through his extensive pulp collection. At one point, I saw he had a short stack of *Detective Fiction Weekly*, some of them dated 1940, the year of the two Blue Ghost serials.

Maybe, I thought, pulling the bagged copies off their shelf, I'll get lucky and there'll be a Blue Ghost chapter in this stack. Since *Detective Fiction Weekly* was a weekly, the odds were long.

To my utter delight, I spied the name Myles Hudson on one cover. And to my profound astonishment, I saw that Chuck owned chapters from both serials! In fact, he was missing only one installment of "Blue Ghost Beware"!

Eagerly, I unbagged these elusive prizes and settled down to scan the text.

It wasn't long before I started seeing stylistics that matched "Dealers" and "Blizzards."

For example, the Blue Ghost was forever "oozing" in and out of places. In "Dealers" the Phantom was so described. Where in "Dealers," the Phantom was called "the machine of justice," Myles Hudson referred to the Blue Ghost as "the machine of wrath."

I read on. There were scenes in common!

Take this passage from "The Blue Ghost" where Charles Dexter Bradford is discussing the fine art of disguise with his patron, radio magnate Adam Wilde:

> "How do you do it?" (Wilde) asked. "What's the secret, Dex?"
>
> Bradford smiled into the rear view mirror. "What do you mean?"
>
> "I—well, that impersonation of Manuel. You had no makeup, a mere touch of stain on your skin, and yet if I hadn't known he was back at the hotel I could have sworn..."
>
> The other shrugged. "Ask any actor how they let a certain facial muscle sag and tighten the other one. Go to your own mirror and see how your features alter if you droop a corner of your mouth or lift the slant of your brow. I studied those details and practiced them, that's all." He shrugged. "But I chiefly depend on the blindness of my fellow men which makes them see what they expect to see."

Now compare it to this excerpt from "Dealers in Death" where reporter, Steve Huston, has a similar conversation with a disguised Richard Curtis Van Loan:

> "It's my business to see things, Phantom. I've noticed, for instance, each of the three times I've seen you how cleverly you manage to keep your face in the shadows. You arrange your chair, as you did just now, so that you're never under the light. Is that part of the reason why they call you "the Man of a Thousand Masks?"

"That's the chief reason," Van said. "Awareness of light is part of second nature now to me. Disguise is mainly illusion. Ask the average man to describe his brother, his best friend, and see how little he really knows their features. Changing your voice is really more of an art. It's there that my studies in ventriloquism and language help me."

Sounds like the same writer to me.

Myles Hudson was addicted to paragraphs beginning with the stilted phrase, "There was a..." Such as:

"There was a sense of time the Blue Ghost had developed which told him perhaps ten minutes had elapsed when he heard the first sound from somewhere above."

"There was a dream the Phantom had that he dived his plane from the highest roof of the sky into a vast and endless hurricane of darkness,"

is a line from "Dealers in Death."

Most tellingly for me, the Blue Ghost serials were riddled with the same compound words that littered "Dealers in Death." Words like "cat-quick," "panic-sense," "brain-buzzing," etc. Compare those to "Dealers'" "snake-quick," "doom-shout," and "maniac-minded." These were absolute proof positive signs to me. Pulp writers of the '30s didn't use them. They belonged to an earlier era of popular writing.

There were other parallels. The action in "The Blue Ghost" and "Dealers in Death," both move to Florida after the New York action is over with. A lot of scenes had a similar "feel."

Clearly, I concluded, Myles Hudson was the man who revised both these *Phantoms*.

But who was Myles Hudson? A glance through an index of *Detective Fiction Weekly* gave me a whole raft of suspects, not the least of which was Ken Crossen, author of the Green Lama stories. Footnotes in the Blue Ghost serials referred to past cases as "monographs," a concept Crossen employed in his heavily footnoted Green Lama stories published that same year.

I studied these stories at length, photocopied key pages and felt I was getting closer to the elusive answer.

The Florida pulp and paperback show wasn't much to speak of. I renewed some acquaintances and made some new friends. I did pick up an *Argosy* with a George Fielding Eliot story and skimmed Chuck's copy of "Snatch," the first Dan Fowler novel, also by Eliot, another of my *Phantom* suspects. I had been considering Eliot, a bridge fan, as the author of "Dealers" because it opens with a robbery at a bridge game.

Since Eliot had written for *Detective Fiction Weekly*, I naturally attempted to match Eliot's style to Hudson's. There were similarities, to be sure. But I needed a bigger pool of Eliot's work to make a perfect match.

Returning home, I again revised my article. I had a lot more information, but a definitive answer still eluded me. After some thought, I decided to revise my article lightly, leaving the piece basically as it was. The new discoveries would destroy the flow of the writing. Besides, there were enough new lines of speculation to call for a sequel. Getting into the Daniels find and the Blue Ghost alone would complicate the article too much.

I mailed the rewrite to Tom and told him to expect a sequel. Someday. I still hadn't laid this ghost. Only the Daniels half of him.

The mystery of Myles Hudson puzzled me for several weeks. I really wanted to attribute his work to George Fielding Eliot, but I didn't have a perfect stylistic match. And I had learned the hard way not to put too much stock in general similarities.

Then I remembered something. Back when I had first heard of the Blue Ghost, many years before, I had contacted Bob Weinberg about looking through the old Munsey payment checks in his possession to see who Hudson might be. Bob had demurred. There were a ton of those checks. Too much to go through for such a minor character. Dead end.

I recalled that the true owner of the Munsey/Popular files was Argosy Communications owner Joel Frieman. Figuring he might yet have some of these records, I called him, explained my quest and wondered where they were.

Joel replied the files had been in storage, but there had been a fire.

My heart sank.

So, Joel quickly added, he moved them to the New York Public Library for their safety and the benefit of pulp scholars.

Eagerly, I took the information from Joel, and called the library Monday morning. It took a few days to get to the right person who transferred me to the proper office.

Yes, I was told those files were accessible. They were alphabetized by author and pseudonym, making the task of tracing the mythical Myles Hudson comparatively simple. It was only a matter of calling up the correct box of files.

The catch was they wouldn't do it for me. I had to come down to Manhattan and do it myself. Groan.

"How about if I sent a representative?" I inquired.

That would be fine, I was told. I immediately called my good friend and fellow Lovecraft scholar, S.T. Joshi, who was very intrigued to learn the Munsey files existed. As it happened, he had been in the process of trying to track down the *Argosy* appearances of California poet George Sterling, and was at a dead end since it involved examining literally hundreds of tough to locate issues. Here was a one stop place to find his answers. And mine.

"You can kill two birds with one stone," I assured him.

Eagerly I supplied S.T. with the names Myles Hudson as well as a long list of suspects, ranging from Paul Ernst to Richard Sale, in case Myles Hudson did not have a file, and waited several anxious, agonizing days.

As it happened, S.T.'s call came when I couldn't answer the phone. But he left a message.

I'll never forget my shock and amazement when I played back the message in which S. T. blurted out: "Myles Hudson is—Jack Byrne!"

Joshi's voice sounded puzzled. Byrne was not on my long suspect list. How could he be? I knew the name as John F. Byrne, Lester Dent's Fiction House editor who later went to work for Munsey, editing *Argosy*, in which capacity he snared Dent's services once more. I never dreamed he was also a writer.

A later conversation with S. T. brought to light the payment and other data on the series. "The Blue Ghost" for example, was submitted as "The House of 1,000 Horrors" on November 16, 1939. "Blue Ghost Beware" was sold on May 24, 1940. In both cases Byrne was paid six hundred dollars.

What was Jack Byrne doing writing a shameless Phantom knockoff for *Detective Fiction Weekly?* Good question. I don't know if he was still Munsey managing editor then. I doubt it. Managing editors don't have the time or inclination to write serials for their own magazines, and the last market listing I find showing Byrne still managing Munsey was in 1939. Whether he was still attached to Munsey in some lesser capacity or not, the pen name was mandatory anyway.

Of course this was the year when Munsey was launching its string of new pulp super heroes, the Green Lama in *Double Detective*, the Scarlet Wizard in *Red Star Mystery*, Mataala in *Red Star Adventures*, etc. The Blue Ghost, it seems, was a hitherto unsuspected participant of that minor wave.

I wonder if he had been conceived for *Double Detective* or *Red Star Mystery* and dumped in *Detective Fiction Weekly* when someone realized he was too close to the Phantom to survive in his own magazine without being sued out of existence? So he was quietly slipped into *Detective Fiction Weekly*, the last place anyone would expect a clone of the Phantom.

Was Byrne let go in 1939 and did he fall back on his writing skills for the short term? Did he perhaps attempt to write a couple of *Phantom Detective* novels, only to have them rejected? This latter seems unlikely. Complete *Phantoms* are not rejected; they are rewritten.

And why did the Blue Ghost series end after only two serials? Was he considered to be a failure like the Scarlet Wizard? Or did Margulies sue Munsey?

These are questions I fear may never be resolved.

As for Byrne, here's what I was able to dig up on him:

He started working in the pulp field in 1925, after being asked to resign from West Virginia Wesleyan College over the rather unorthodox manner in which he edited the school paper. After stints at coal mining, newspaper work and semi-pro baseball, Byrne entered the pulp world in 1925. By 1930, he was editorial director of 14 Fiction House titles. When Fiction House collapsed in 1932 he was at *Liberty*. When it was revived in the fall of 1933, Byrne was reinstated as editor in chief.

There he remained until mid 1936. It was at that point, according to an unpublished letter from Munsey contributor Howard Wandrei, Byrne engineered a kind of takeover at Munsey by allying himself with a certain faction, which resulted in wholesale executive and editorial firings.

As Wandrei explained it in an April 3, 1936 letter, Byrne, "in search of a better job," insinuated himself into an ongoing power struggle over the direction of the company:

"A new system is being set up at Munseys to correspond to that which appears to have made so much money for Standard Magazines. Byrne will hold a position over all the magazine like that of Margulies at Standard, at a good salary. His underlings will get a salary of not better than $25 per week. The standard of the Munsey magazines is to be cut down to the lowest pulp level in an effort to get mass circulation among the moronic reading public. All salaries are to be cut. Authors' rates to be likewise pared down to the howling quick. Apparently a 1 cent minimum from now on, 1 and a half cent maximum. The possible casualties of this wonderful idiocy need no mention, either as far as the soundness of the company is concerned, or among Munsey's "name" writers who won't take an unkind cut like that from anyone. Other magazines are increasing their rates.

"This scheme cannot work. If this is really the squirrely jamboree that Byrne and the efficiency expert cooked up between them, I hope it boomerangs with impeccable elan or something."

Wandrei's prediction proved correct. Munsey fell on hard times and was bought out by rival Popular Publications in 1942. Byrne's Munsey stint seemed to have ended circa 1939. I understand he later went back to Fiction House. What ultimately became of him I do not know.

There remained but one problem. Placing Byrne at Standard. I had never heard of him working there. In fact, looking him up in various indexes show him to be the author of no mystery stories under his honest name and a solitary tale in Fiction House's *Soldier Stories,* "Brass Hat," May 1929. He did write as John B. Starr, however.

It's probable Byrne worked at Standard circa 1933, when Fiction House was on hiatus. But that is three years before his *Phantom* revisions. Since according to Wandrei, Byrne had been agitating for the Munsey slot for some six months. He might have been moonlighting at Standard during the transition.

Around the time I was planning to call Jack Schiff with whom I had not been in touch in quite a while, I received an e-mail from a guy researching Martin Goodman's pulp publishing career. I gave this researcher several leads, including Jack Schiff's phone number. Since you are calling him, I requested, ask him for me if he recalls Jack Byrne.

The answer came back a day or so later. Schiff did indeed remember Byrne. He was a staff writer at Standard. But he couldn't recall if he had worked on the *Phantoms* or not. But I really didn't need that final confirmation. I had nailed down the last item in my chain of evidence.

Sometime after leaving Fiction House, Byrne went to work at Standard. He not only revised "Dealers," but the novel submitted before it, "Specter of Death." How do I know this? Well, other than the use of the word "tocsin," and a light smattering of other stylistic similarities, the story was published immediately after "Dealers," yet included the signal light which Daniels could not have included since his version was written before "Dealers!" However, "Specter" was not as heavily revised as the others.

This also explains why Daniels, who had been carrying the *Phantom* series through much of 1939 and 1936, abruptly left the series. He had written two novels in a row that needed rescuing. In fact, "The Circus Murders," also by Daniels, shows signs of serious revisions. But I don't think Byrne did that revise.

It also explains why the Byrne style disappears abruptly from the *Phantom* series with "Death Rides the Blizzard." Byrne joined Munsey in mid 1936. The October dated "Blizzard" was probably his last *Phantom* rewrite before he jumped ship.

As for my identification of Ray Cummings as the author of "Dealers in Death" and "Death Rides the Blizzard," despite strong clues pointing to the former, clearly I was wrong. We know Daniels didn't pen "Blizzard." I suspect Byrne wrote no *Phantoms* from scratch; ergo "Blizzard" was originally the work of another failed *Phantom* ghost. Who? I still cling to Ray Cummings as a high probability. The sole Cummings *Phantom* I know about, "The Phantom's Murder Trail," is pretty weak. Maybe "Blizzard" was his first *Phantom* and it really needed work.

There may be other Jack Byrne *Phantom* revisions in the period before "Blizzard." I do not have access to every *Phantom* in that period.

Walter Gibson used to talk about a phenomenon he called "psycho magnetic force" or "psycho proximity." He had some spooky experiences along that line like the time he hit a dead end writing a true crime article about an old British murder, only to stumble across the murder victim's elderly son that very day at a Long Island party, as he related to me in *Duende #2*.

"It seems to me that when you're really after something and you want to learn about it," Gibson told me, "something begins drawing you like an attraction."

I don't know if there is such a thing. I do know that if Walter were alive today, he would greatly appreciate and understand my strange search for the author of "Dealers in Death." Maybe he could explain it to us all too!

So! My long quest was over. I had started out to lay a *Phantom* ghost and ended up laying two. And rediscovering a third (the Blue Ghost) as well! What did it all mean? Search me. I still have a hard time believing any of it happened. But it did.

Explaining it is another matter.

What still makes me shiver with disbelief is that I spent two frustrating years trying to identify a string of *Phantoms* that were the work of two writers, Paul Chadwick and John F. Byrne, neither of whom I would have suspected in a million years because I had mistakenly taken Chadwick off my list of suspects and I never would have thought of Byrne as a pulp writer, never mind a *Phantom* ghost writer.

If it were not for all this weirdness, I would still be at it with no end in sight.

But the punch line to my spooky search is something that came in the closing hours of my Florida stay when I casually asked Chuck Juzek how he came to have acquired both Blue Ghost serials; a character hardly anyone but Bob Sampson and I ever heard of.

"Don't you remember?" he replied. "You mentioned him in a letter to me about ten years ago. He sounded so intriguing that I started buying them up."

I had laid the groundwork for solving the mystery years before I set out to solve it!

Walter would have loved that!

CHAPTER XII

FRAMED FOR MURDER

A S NOTED ELSEWHERE in *The Phantom Detective Companion*, Standard editors put out an open call for new *Phantom Detective* contributors circa 1935. One of those authors was Harold Ward, author of Dell's *Doctor Death* pulp. A long-time pulp scribe, Ward wrote a three-chapter, 23 page treatment for a *Phantom* entitled "Framed for Murder." It's curious to compare Ward's effort to Charles Strong's (which follows "Framed for Murder") in order to gain an insight to Standard's editorial methods. While Ward wrote the first three chapters to a longer piece, Strong's "Money Mad Murders" was a synopsis of the complete story. Perhaps this can be explained by Strong being an in-house rewriter at Standard.

Sadly, there is no known synopsis for Ward's story, so it's impossible to know where the plot would have gone. But the "corpse-like face" that makes an appearance at the end of Chapter III almost sounds like a return appearance of Doctor Death!

Chapter I

Jobbed.

STEVE HUSTON, STAR reporter on the *Clarion*, steered his battered fliver to the curb and climbed wearily out. Officer Patrick Casey, leaning against a lamp post, turned his head at the unwonted excitement. Then, spitting his quid of fine-cut into the gutter, he lumbered forward, his big hand outstretched.

"By all that's good and holy, if it isn't me old pal!" he exclaimed, pumping the reporter's arm happily. "Sure, and it's a sight for sore eyes to see yez. And what brings you over here at this time of the night?"

"You," Huston smiled. "Frankly, Pat, I know damned well that they framed you in that Hartshorn case. You happened to be an honest policeman, so they tore your stripes off and sent you over here to wear your heart out. I want the low-down."

Casey leaned against the lamp post again, his honest Irish face twisted in thought.

"Stand a bit closer till I cadge a drag from a cigarette," he commanded. "I can think better when I've a bit of smoke in me lungs. I 'spose you're up t' your old tricks, workin' up a yarn f'r your paper? And stand close, Steve, me boy. The sergeant has a bad habit of sneakin' up on a man and I don't want any demerits against me name... again."

"That's the point," Huston growled, waiting while the older man lighted his fag. "Next time they'll get you—if

you stay honest. You're only a small cog in a big machine, but they've got to get rid of you, just as they're trying to ditch Farragut and the other honest coppers on the force. There's going to be hell popping in this town unless we can stop it. And that's what the *Clarion's* out to do. You know something about that Hartshorn case—something that you haven't told. And you know that I'll never give you away."

Casey cast a quick glance up and down the dimly lighted street.

"Frankly, Steve, I'm afraid to talk," he said after a minutes' hesitation. "Me boy—he's all the wife and I've got since Eileen died. Next year he's due for college. I've got to keep me job. True, it was a comedown to lose me chevrons, and it's not so pleasant pounding a beat out here on the Gold Coast—but it might be worse. I've stood it a week now, and I'm getting used to it. The people here-abouts aren't so bad, even if they are rich. They—"

He stopped suddenly, his eyes almost bulging from their sockets.

"F'r th' love of God—look!" he exclaimed.

Huston whirled on his heel. They were standing almost in front of a darkened house. Beside it, separated only by a wrought-iron fence, was another so like it that it might have been cast in the same mold.

A light had suddenly appeared in one of the side windows of the second house. From where they stood, they could see into it at an angle.

Framed in the open window—brought out in bold relief by the brilliancy of the lamp—a dying man was slumped in a huge arm chair. The blood was gushing from a gaping wound in his throat; it trickled down over his white shirt-front in an ever widening stream.

Casey plunged forward, the reporter at his heels. Then, side by side, they raced through the narrow gate and up the broad stone steps.

As they reached the porch, the front door opened and a woman rushed out. They caught a glimpse of her face; it was strained and filled with panic. She gasped at sight of them, then seized Casey by the arm.

"Quick!" she exclaimed hysterically. "There's been a—a murder!"

Casey pushed her aside and ran through the broad hall, past the darkened parlor, into what appeared to be the living room. He stopped suddenly, almost stumbling over the body of a woman. Clad in evening attire, the blood was trickling from a stab wound in her chest just above the heart. Beside her lay an overturned decanter; its alcoholic contents mingled with the crimson that ran down over her white corsage.

Casey said: "My God!" His trained eye told him at a glance that she was past help. He stepped gingerly around her and stood for a moment in front of the man in the chair. Like the woman, he was dead. His head had been almost severed from his body. Every minute detail was brought out by the single lamp in the center of the room. Of the indirect variety, its brilliant, yet suffused glow, was shadowless—white instead of yellow; it added to the horror of the diabolical ensemble.

The dead man was almost a giant in stature and, like the woman, clad in evening grab. His big body had slid part way down in the chair and was twisted a bit so that his right hand and arm hung limply, the fingers almost touching the carpet. His jaw had dropped and his eyes were open and staring straight ahead.

The blood was still spurting a tiny stream from the severed jugular, forming an ever-widening pool on the green carpet close to his feet. A half-smoked cigarette, which had apparently fallen from his fingers when he was struck down, smoldered just outside the edge of the crimson stain. The burning wool gave forth a peculiar, nauseating smell. Casey mechanically picked it up and laid it on the ash tray.

"I'll 'phone headquarters," he said, half to himself. "Who are they, lady?"

He turned to speak to the woman.

She was gone.

A car door slammed.

"By God, she killed 'em and now she's getting away!" Casey roared to Steve. "After her, boy! Catch th' number of the license if you can."

He stopped suddenly, a dazed expression creeping into his honest face, his fingers clawing for his gun. There was a peculiar popping noise like a cork being drawn from a bottle. He pitched forward on his face, pulled himself to his knees, still fighting to get his gun out. A second slug struck him. This time he slumped, gave a gurgling moan and was quiet.

Steve Huston, turning, took a step toward the door. A hot iron seemed to sear the side of his head. A million stars crossed his line of vision.

Then oblivion.

HUSTON DRIFTED BACK to consciousness slowly. There was a trickle of liquor down his throat. He swallowed painfully, gagged, opened his eyes. He was lying on the davenport, a white-coated ambulance surgeon bending over him. The room was filled with blue-coated policemen and detectives. Representatives of rival papers mingled with them; they gazed at him sadly, gathering in little groups and conversing in low whispers. He wondered if he had been hit in a vital spot? That was probably the reason for their sorrowful looks, he decided.

A million little devils were beating a mad tattoo inside his skull. The doctor put an arm under his shoulders and raised him to a sitting position.

"Drink this, boy," he commanded.

Steve gulped the bitter medicine down. He felt better instantly.

"How bad am I hit, doc?" he asked, bracing himself for the fatal news.

The young physician shook his head—sadly, it seemed.

"You'll be all right in a few minutes," he answered gruffly. "Unfortunately—for you—Casey's slug just creased you, making a scalp wound and laying you out temporarily."

Steve swung his legs off the couch. The movement made him dizzy and, for a moment, the room swam around him in ever-widening circles. The hellish hammering continued inside his skull, making thinking almost impossible.

"Just what was the meaning of that remark?" he finally managed to ejaculate. He tried to stand erect, but the effort was too great and he dropped back to the davenport again.

The surgeon was shouldered aside as Inspector Frawley took the center of the stage with the eagerness of an unleashed bloodhound on a hot scent.

"Is he able to talk?" he demanded.

The doctor nodded.

"Sure," he grunted. "Only better not rough him for an hour or two."

Frawley's wicked little eyes glistened like those of a snake.

"Huston, you lousy scandlemonger, what the hell did you do it for?" he snapped.

Steve scowled. Thinking was hard with his head aching as it was. He looked up at the bulky inspector, a blank stare on his thin face.

"Are you trying to be funny?" he responded thickly. "If you are, you've got a bum sense of humor. In plain words, I don't get you—and don't be so careless with your vocal organs."

Frawley's thick arm made a semi-circle—pointed to the dead man in the chair, the woman on the floor, to Officer Casey, his stubby fingers still clasped around the handle of his gun.

"What did you kill 'em for?" he demanded.

Steve Huston's eyes widened. A look of astonishment crept into his face.

"My God!" he exclaimed. "Do you think that I—that I'm responsible for this?"

"Ain't you?" Frawley snapped.

Steve shook his head.

"I came over here to see Casey," he responded. "We were standing outside on the walk talking when a light suddenly appeared in this room and we saw that dead man in the chair. Casey charged in and I followed. A woman met us on the porch, directed us inside, then made her getaway just as we discovered the second body—that of the woman on the floor. Casey yelled to me to catch her—get the number of the car she was making her escape in. Just then I heard a shot. I turned. Casey was down, clawing for his rod. Something hit my head and that's all I know until I recovered consciousness just now."

Frawley shook his head.

"You'll have to think up a better one than that," he growled. "In the first place, your yarn about seeing the dead man in the window is horseradish. I'll tell you why. Because the shade is down. I'll tell you what happened. You came in here to meet Walter Buck—"

"Walter Buck?" Steve said excitedly. "I don't get you."

Frawley jerked his thick thumb in the direction of the dead man.

"Don't lie, you rat!" he thundered. "You know damned well that Buck's one of the men—higher-up in that city hall deal your lousy sheet's been trying to uncover. You came here to meet him—to get your take for double-crossing the *Clarion*. You fought over something—I'll not pretend to say what—and you killed him. The woman screamed and you got her. Casey, pounding the beat outside, heard the commotion and came in. You put the heat on him and he went down. But he went down fighting, as a good cop always does. His slug creased your skull and put you out—long enough for somebody who heard the shooting to put in a telephone call and for us to get here. Now what's your answer to that, wise guy?"

Steve Huston brushed his hand wearily across his eyes.

"It don't click, Frawley," he said finally. "In the first place, I didn't have a gun. In the second place, if you had brains enough to look, you'd find that Casey went down without firing a shot—"

Frawley shrugged his shoulders.

"Oh, yeah?" he chortled. "Your head must still be thick from Casey's bullet, wise guy. You say you didn't have a rod. Where did the one come from, then, that we found in your hand?"

Steve's jaw dropped.

"Gun—in my hand?" he ejaculated.

Frawley nodded.

"Exactly," he answered. "With two empty chambers corresponding to the two bullets in poor Casey. And, it happens, we took a squint at Casey's rod, then put it back in his hand so the photographer could get a picture. There's one empty chamber. That's the bullet that creased your dome.

"And that's not all," he went on. Whirling on his heel, he stepped to the table in the center of the room and picked up a thick sheaf of greenbacks, all of large denomination. "We found this money in your pocket," he snapped. "Until you can prove to the contrary, we are assuming that it was the bribe Walter Buck gave you just before you killed him."

He laid the roll back on the table and picked up a knife.

"Here's the last and final bit of evidence," he snapped.

"Its still bloody, you see—stained with the gore of your two victims. You didn't have time to wipe it off before Casey came charging in, so you jammed it into your pocket as you reached for your gun. It's got your fingerprints on it, and the pocket into which you dropped it is smeared with blood."

Chapter II

A Sudden Summons.

THE EXTENSION TELEPHONE in the sleeping quarters of Richard Curtis Van Loan's Fifth Avenue penthouse tinkled like a silvery, low-pitched Chinese gong. Van Loan, slumbering soundly, awoke with every faculty alert. With a single motion of his arm he pressed the button of the reading lamp beside the bed, then jerked the receiver to his ear.

"Van Loan speaking!" he snapped into the mouthpiece.

"I beg your pardon," a guttural voice responded. "Id iss the wrong number. I was trying to get Schmidt's bakery."

There was a click as the receiver at the other end was put back into place.

Van Loan swung his legs off the bed. He crossed the room with long, muscular strides. Every movement was coordinated—efficient. His pajama jacket was tossed over a chair. By the time he reached his bathroom door, his pajama belt was unbuttoned; he stepped out of the trousers, left them where they lay and plunged under a tepid shower. His valet would know, when he put the room to rights in the morning, that his master had received a sudden summons. At the end of twenty-four hours, unless word was received to the contrary, the information was to be given to the man who answered a certain telephone number. Aside from that, the valet was to pay no attention to his eccentric young master's frequent and sudden absences from home.

THE SUDDEN CHANGE from warm to icy-cold water caused a pleasant tingle to chase through Van Loan's body. The shower lasted but a moment. Then he rubbed himself down with a coarse towel.

His hand went out automatically for his shaving kit. Then, as he mechanically ran his fingers across the twelve-hour growth of stubble on his chin, he whirled on his bare heel to the full length mirror. For just a second he paused, surveying his bared fitness once more. He flexed his muscles; they rippled beneath the velvety skin like coiled springs. He smiled grimly at the mass of scars upon his chest—remembrances of adventures similar to that upon which he was about to embark. He was proud of those scars, was Richard Curtis Van Loan. Each was a mark of valor, each a souvenir of some great wrong that he had righted.

For Richard Curtis Van Loan, dilettante, sportsman, follower of the fine arts and wealthy young man about town, was that internationally known personality who called himself the Phantom—grim Nemesis of Crime, more feared by the underworld than the combined might of every law-enforcing agency in the world. Honor among his own kind awaited the hoodlum who could lay him low. Nor would there be any great danger in so doing. For not even the police knew the identity of the strange being who often came to their assistance solving their puzzles with a swiftly spoken word or two, risking his life in the cause of justice, never appearing twice in the same disguise and always disappearing when a case was completed. His exploits were legendary throughout the length and width of the nation.

And in the anonymity of the Phantom lay his chief weapon. Only one man was aware of his true identity. That man was Frank Havens, publisher of the *Clarion* and a great string of other papers scattered throughout the east and middle west. Van Loan's most intimate friend, Havens' policy was, and always had been, one of fearless enmity toward crime and corruption. He it was who had guided the orphaned Van Loan through childhood and youth. He it was who, when polo, tennis, yachting, mountain-climbing and other manly sports failed to satisfy the younger man's craving for activity, had suggested a crusade against crime.

The telephone call had been a code message. To Richard Curtis Van Loan it meant that Frank Havens had called. Decoded, it said: "It is vitally urgent that I see you immediately. Come to my office at once."

And when Frank Havens called, Richard Curtis Van Loan was always ready to obey the summons.

VAN STEPPED FROM the shower into his bed room. He gave a peculiar twist to one of the ornamental knobs on the head of the bed. Noiselessly a section of the adjoining wall swung outward, revealing a large closet equipped as a makeup room. On a shelf before the mirror were materials for every sort of disguise. It took but a second to darken the stubble on his chin. A second more to slip a set of false teeth over his own white ones. They changed the appearance of his entire face. A dark line beneath his eyes and the transformation was complete.

A dozen suits hung in the closet. He slipped into one of conspicuous design, vastly different from the carefully tailored outfits worn by the elegantly attired Richard Curtis Van Loan. A soft hat, brim pulled down over his eyes, added to the metamorphosis. He gave a final glance into the mirror, nodded his approval, stepped back into the bedroom and twisted the knob again. The door swung back into place.

He glanced at his wrist watch. Less than ten minutes had elapsed since he received Havens' call. He walked down three flights of stairs before taking the all-night elevator. Leaving the building by a side entrance, he caught a prowling taxi and in five minutes was at the garage where he kept his cars. The attendant looked at him curiously.

"Car number three," he said in a low voice, allowing the man a sight of the tiny, diamond-encrusted, platinum badge which had been presented to him by the police in order that he might identify himself to them.

The attendant gave a start of surprise, saluted and hurried away. A moment later he drove an ancient car down the ramp—a car that had the outward appearance of thousands of others to be seen daily on the streets. But there the similarity ended, for it was of steel, bullet-proof construction and its hood masked an engine that could do ninety without an effort.

Van slipped the attendant a bill, slid his legs beneath the wheel and, pressing his toe on the gas pedal, piloted the car through the door and onto the almost deserted street.

FRANK HAVENS, GREY-HAIRED, heavy-set—a veritable dynamo of energy—looked up with a start at the man who entered his office unannounced.

"What the—" he exclaimed.

Van Loan interrupted him with a gesture.

"Okay, Frank," he snapped. "What's up?"

Havens breathed a sigh of relief.

"I'll never get used to you, you young devil," he said, extending his hand. "I didn't expect you for another thirty minutes. Nice of you to come."

He waved his visitor to a chair across the desk from his own.

"They've jobbed Steve Huston," he went on.

Van Loan's eyes narrowed.

"Meaning—what?" he demanded.

The lines of worry etched themselves deeper into the publisher's face.

"Less than an hour ago Steve Huston was found unconscious in Henry Doddlestone's mansion on the Gold Coast," he said. "His head was creased with a bullet. Mrs. Doddlestone was dead. So, too, was Walter Buck—Buck, the plunger, you know—a rat, if there ever was one. Both had been stabbed. Beside them lay a policeman, a man named Casey, who had been recently demoted from sergeant. Casey's gun was in his hand with one chamber empty. He had two bullets in his body.

"Here's the terrible part of the affair, Phantom: the gun from which the bullets had been fired was in Steve's hand. The bloody knife with which Mrs. Doddlestone and Buck had been killed was in his pocket. So, too, was a roll of greenbacks—two thousand dollars in all. In plain words, they got Steve into that house and framed him."

"What's his story?"

"I haven't been able to find out. Kidd, who was covering police tonight in Steve's absence, 'phoned me and gave me the bare details. Frawley, the inspector on the job, is holding Steve incommunicado. I've got my lawyer working on the case, but it's doubtful if we will be able to get an order from a judge before morning. Meanwhile—"

He stopped in the middle of the sentence, his fingers strumming nervously on the top of the desk. For a moment Van Loan sat in stunned silence.

"You think—what?" he said finally. "We both know that Steve's innocent. We know him too well to think otherwise. But who would job him? What leads you to such a conclusion?"

Havens got up and paced the floor nervously.

"They are hitting at me over Steve's shoulders," he said. "They know that I'd go to hell for that kid—that he's been with me for years. I'd go to hell for any of my men, for that matter. But Steve's closer to me than any of them. He's almost a son to me.

"You know, my friend, that I've been after that crooked political ring that's been grafting on the new annex to the municipal building. The mayor is with me to the finish. He knows that they've got their dirty claws into the heart of things, but he's been unable to get his fingers on them. It's the same outfit that put over that bridge contract last year—the bridge that went down, killing half a dozen innocent people. Arrests followed, as you remember, but nothing could be proven.

"They preferred charges against Inspector Farragut—-as honest a police-man as ever wore a uniform. Jobbed him—got him transferred to an outlying district. They're getting their slimy tentacles into every branch of city government. Steve's been working on the case. I've given him a free hand and only yesterday he told me that he'd be ready to start publication of the exposé within a few days."

He went back to his chair and, dropping into it, pulled open the drawer of his desk.

"This tells the story," he said, laying a sheet of paper before his visitor. It came only a few minutes ago. The elevator attendant heard what he thought was a call for help out in front of the building. He left his post for a moment to investigate. When he returned that letter, addressed to me, was sticking between the edge of the elevator and the lever."

Van spread the message out on the desk and read:

It's up to you, Havens. We can furnish a man who will come forward and take the rap in place of Huston—a man who will confess that he killed the others and framed Steve. Later, when the excitement has died down we will spring him out of jail and he will disappear.

All that is needed is for you to publish a personal in the 'Help Wanted' column of the *Clarion* tomorrow morning or any morning during the coming week. After that it will be too late. Have it read as follows: 'Wanted: Competent jackhammer operator. Write H care of this paper.'

The publication of that personal will mean that you have given your word of honor to drop your investigation of the annex contract and to turn over the evidence collected by Huston in the manner to be dictated by us.

Failure to do this means that Huston's trial will be rushed. Witnesses will be produced to swear that they actually saw him murder Mrs. Doddlestone and

Walter Buck. They will swear that they summoned Officer Casey, entered the house with him, saw him battle with Huston and, when he went down fighting, ran to the nearest telephone and called Headquarters.

In plain words, Steve Huston will be electrocuted for the triple murder unless you agree to our terms.

The message was unsigned.

FOR A MOMENT there was silence. Then Van Loan pushed his chair back from the desk. "You want me to take the case?" he said.

Havens nodded. "Naturally."

"I refuse. It's too dangerous. I'm tired of risking my life for a lot of bums like Steve Huston."

Havens' jaw dropped in astonishment. His face flushed angrily. He was about to make reply, when he glanced down at the note Van had hastily scribbled and pushed across the desk to him.

There's a dictograph disc hidden under the picture of Charles A. Dana just behind you. Don't let your voice betray the discovery, but play up to me.

Havens nodded. Rising, he turned. Now that Van had called it to his attention, he saw the tiny wire, as thin as a thread and colored to match the wall, leading from behind the picture to the base board and, running along its top, disappearing beneath the door.

His enemies, feeling certain that he would summon the Phantom, had thus arranged in advance to overhear their conversation.

For a moment or two Havens begged his visitor to take the case. Van's voice grew louder as he argued. Finally, with an oath, he whirled on his heel and went out, slamming the door behind him.

He believed that he had accomplished his objective. Whoever was listening at the other end would be certain to think that the Phantom had refused the assignment.

But on the other hand they knew, now, that the man with whom Havens had been talking was the Phantom. They would be waiting for him. The opportunity was too good to be missed.

The elevator whisked him to the street. Stopping for a second just outside the door, he cast a quick glance up and down the deserted street. Then, running across the sidewalk, he jerked open the door of his car.

Something—that weird, inexplicable sixth sense that had saved him so many times in the past—warned him in the nick of time. He threw himself backward. There was a dull roar. The car leaped into the air like a bucking bronco; it came down a battered, tangled mass of steel and iron.

From up the street came the shrilling of a policeman's whistle, the patter of feet as the officer charged down the sidewalk. Another whistle answered in the distance. Doors opened. Men, coatless, hatless, rushed out of the *Clarion* office as the building shook from the violence of the detonation.

The Phantom had been saved by a miracle. He stopped only for a second—long enough to note the thin wire that ran from the wreckage to a darkened building across the street. His keen brain told him what had happened. A charge of some high explosive had been placed under the hood and detonated by means of an electric spark.

His enemies were at the other end of the wire. He tore himself from the hands of the men who would have held him for questioning. Thinking that he was responsible for the outrage, the oncoming officer shouted for him to halt. Bending almost double, he raced onward. The policeman drew his gun—fired. The bullet crashed against a brick close to the Phantom's head. The door of the darkened building opened suddenly. He leaped inside.

There was a click as the key was turned in the lock. He twisted himself to one side as a blackjack descended. The sudden movement saved him from a knockout. The weapon landed on his shoulder. For a moment his arm was paralyzed. Then he went down under the weight of several men.

A pencil flashlight beam blinded him. The blackjack descended again. This time it hit its mark.

Chapter III

The House Next Door.

WHEN VAN RECOVERED consciousness, he was lying face downward on the floor of a swiftly moving car. His hands were tightly bound behind his back, while a rope was twisted about his ankles. His head ached dully from the terrific beating he had received.

He managed to twist his body and caught a glimpse of two men in the front seat, while the back of the car was empty save for himself. He caught snatches of conversation above the low hum of the motor.

"The boss'll probably raise the devil because we didn't bump the Phantom off," one of them was saying. "But he seems to have as many lives as a cat."

The other chuckled.

"I'll say he has," he responded. "It was clever the way the boss had that dictograph planted in Havens' office so that we'd get wise to him. But how the devil did he escape that charge of soup we planted in his car? It cracked the windows in the surrounding buildings, but he got off without a scratch, and his foot was on the running board when I pressed the switch. But the boss'll be pleased to see him, dead or alive. He'll hold him as a hostage. That'll be one more leverage he'll have on Havens."

He raised a bottle to his lips and allowed the liquor to gurgle down his gullet.

"Empty," he growled.

"Good thing it is," the other remarked. "You know how sore it makes the boss when he finds his men drinking on duty."

The other swore again. He turned to hurl the empty bottle through the open window when the driver stopped him with a sharp command.

"That's one thing I'll not stand for," he snapped. "I've been driving ever since prohibition days—when I used to haul alky—and I never got caught, thanks to decent roads and good tires. I might want to come back over this road in a hell of a hurry and damned if I'm going to allow anybody to put the pavement on the fritz with a lot of broken glassware."

The man beside him grunted an unintelligible reply. Turning, he hurled the bottle viciously at the bound man on the floor in the rear. A sudden lurch of the car caused him to miss his aim; the bottle struck a jack that was lying with a pile of other tools beside the captive. It smashed into a dozen pieces.

"I'd never make a baseball player," he growled. "Do you think we ought to tie something around that guy's mouth?"

"Naw. He'll be out for another hour at least. And by that time we'll have him at Headquarters."

They drove in silence for a moment. The man beside the driver lit a cigarette.

"Why do you suppose he raced across the street—straight into our hands?" he demanded.

The other chuckled again.

"Dazed by the explosion," he said. "The cop played our game unknowingly by shooting at him. That added to his panic."

Again there was silence as the big car lurched and swayed through the night. A trickle of rain commenced to patter against the windows. Van's brain was racing—keeping up with the motion of the machine even though his head was still splitting—in an effort to figure a way out of his predicament. Realization came with terrible clarity—that he was in desperate straits—that only a miracle could save him.

The miracle happened.

As he twisted his body to relieve his cramped position, the car, turning a corner too rapidly, skidded. It threw him backward against the rear seat. A stabbing sensation shot through one of his bound hands like the jab of a needle.

He realized what had happened. His hand had come in contact with a piece of the broken whisky bottle the man in the front seat had hurled at him.

The pain was excruciating. Yet he was unable to move, for the other had turned around, probably attracted by the noise, and was gazing down at him. They were passing beneath a lamp. Van kept his eyes closed and his jaws set. And all the time the jagged bit of glass was digging deeper into his flesh.

Finally, after what seemed ages, the man in the front seat turned his head again, and Van was able to shift his weight.

An idea came to him, born of his suffering. Moving slowly, he managed to maneuver his bound wrists in such a manner that the rope came in contact with the jagged edge of the glass. Then, painstakingly, he rubbed the hemp across the sharp edge of the bottle. Time after time it slipped away; he finally got it wedged against the jack and his task was easier.

Excitement started his heart pounding like a trip-hammer when he felt the strands finally give way.

The men in the front seat were still engaged in conversation. Twisting his body slightly, he managed to reach into his pocket. His knife was still there. Apparently in their hurry to get away from the building across from the *Clarion* office they had merely deprived him of his gun, waiting for a more auspicious time to make a search of his pockets.

Opening the knife, he cut the thongs that bound his ankles.

His fingers came in contact with the heavy iron jack. He seized it and pulled himself to his feet. The man beside the driver, sensing the alien presence at his shoulder, turned—made a grab for his gun. Van brought the heavy jack down upon his head with all his strength. The fellow slumped forward to the floor.

The driver was fighting hard to keep control of the car and, at the same time, get his fingers on his gun. Van reached over his shoulder and gave the wheel a sudden twist to the right. At the same time he swung the jack. The other dodged. The extemporized weapon landed against his arm.

The car, uncontrolled, lunged toward the curb. A lamp post loomed in its pathway. The big machine struck it with the force of a battering ram as Van, timing his movement to a split second, jerked open the door on the left side and jumped out.

There was a splintering, slithering impact. The crash of broken glass. The car, sliding on the wet pavement, seemed to wrap itself around the post, then toppled over to the right.

The man at the wheel, pinned beneath the wreckage, screamed in agony. A tiny tongue of flame leaped from beneath the hood. Van saw the red and white of a fire alarm box a little distance down the block. To reach it was but a matter of seconds. Smashing the glass, he twisted the key, opened the door and jerked down the hook.

He stopped... listened. From the distance came the wail of a siren as the first piece of apparatus left the station. He waited a moment longer. The howling of the siren grew louder. Far down the street he saw the red light of the wig-wag on the oncoming truck as it rounded the corner.

Satisfied that he had given his enemies better than an even break, he turned.

A second later the Phantom had disappeared in the darkness.

The police were still in possession of the Doddlestone mansion when the Phantom, dismissing his taxi in the middle of the next block, slid through the darkness of the adjoining alley and cautiously approached the brilliantly lighted house from the rear.

He halted beneath the window where the murdered man had been found, attracted by the sound of voices from within. The curtain had been moved aside and the shade raised because of the heat.

As yet he had made no plans for his campaign. But intuition told him that the solution of the problem was to be found where the trouble had commenced—at the Doddlestone home. Now that he was there, he was waiting for the break he was certain would come—the break that would lead him unerringly straight to the heart of the mystery.

Two men were engaged in low-voiced conversation in the window just above his head.

"But are you certain that it's safe?" one of them was questioning. "With the house filled with cops, who knows what's liable to happen. Frawley's dumb—dumber than hell. That much I'll admit. But he's honest in spite of his thick-headishness. Once you let him get an intimation that everything isn't as plain as it appears on the surface, and—"

"Stop worrying," the other man interrupted. "Remember Poe's *Purloined Letter?* He proved that the safest place to hide a thing is in the open. That's why I rented that other place. I—"

An exclamation of alarm from the other halted him in the middle of the sentence.

"That face! Did you see it—glaring at us from the window of the house next door?"

The Phantom, hidden in the darkness, whirled.

A man was staring out of the unlighted window of the house next door. The darkness contorted his face until it took on the appearance of a wild animal. A mass of unkempt hair fell about his shoulders; his beard was long and tangled and seemed to stand out in every direction. His eyes were maniacal—deeply sunken and shining like those of some nocturnal beast. There was a strange, questing look in them—the look of a haunted creature.

Another face appeared in the background—a face that was white and pasty, like that of a corpse walking in the darkness. For an instant the two pairs of eyes glared across the intervening space.

Then both faces disappeared in the darkness.

CHAPTER XIII

MONEY MAD
MURDERS

WRITTEN BY STANDARD editor Charles S. Strong circa 1936, the following synopsis for "Money Mad Murders" never got the green light. But as Mark Trost noted in *Blood 'n' Thunder* #17 (Spring 2007), the story did not go to waste, as elements were subsequently used in "The Henchmen of Death" (March 1937) and Norman Daniels' own "Money Mad Murders" (November 1939).

CHARACTER SHEET:

Sidney Talbot, President of the Talbot National Bank

Arthur Barron, his son-in-law

Marion Barron, his grand-daughter

Conrad Webster, Chairman of the Board of the Chase Trust Company

Virgil Twyfort, President of the Pacific Coast Bank and Trust Company

Mrs. Edna Twyfort

Gaston Le Clerc, Director of the Amalgamated Bank of Paris

Alexander Torney, owner of Villa Torney

Malvin Burgess, F.B.I.

Frank Kelly, F.B.I.

Chief Burke, F.B.I.

AS A CLOSING fete to the annual convention of the International Bankers Association, Sidney Talbot, President of the Talbot National Bank is the host to a party of bankers and their wives at the Villa Torney on the outskirts of New York City. The party is a masquerade ball. Assisting Talbot with the entertaining is his son-in-law, Arthur Barron, head cashier at the Talbot Bank, and Barron's daughter, Marion. Among the outstanding guests are Mr. and Mrs. Conrad Webster. Webster is a well known race-horse owner, and the proud possessor of the champion three year old, Shah of Persia. In public life he is the Chairman of the Board of the Chase Trust Company. Mr. and Mrs. Virgil Twyfort are other important guests. Twyfort is the President of the Pacific

Coast Bank and Trust Company, and has come to the convention on his yacht, which is moored in the yacht basin at Manhasset, Long Islandf, a short distance from the Villa. Mons. and Mme. Gaston La Clerc are also present. Le Clerc is the Director of the Amalgamated Bank of Paris.

Various costumes are worn by the guests, but the most impressive are those of Mons. Le Clerc, who had come as Louis XVI, and Arthur Barron who appears as a Union Army General. While the clebration is going on, a reproduction of a guillotine is wheeled into the room by a number of people made up as members of the Paris mob. They set upon Le Clerc, and he is hurried off to the guillotine. He pleads for his life in a melodramatic manner, and is permitted to return to his table amid the laughter of the crowd. A few moments later another group of men come into the room robed as members of the Ku Klux Klan. They take Arthur Barron as their prisoner and announce that he has been a traitor to the South. A rope is thrown over a curtain pole at one end of the room, the lights are rather low, and Marion rushes over to her father. She is taking her cue from Mme. Le Clerc and the guillotine scene. The rope is fastened about Barron's neck, he is placed upon a char, and then pushed off, and left dangling. The killers gather up Marion Barron and make their escape in several cars that have been standing at a side entrance with motors running. The guests are horrified for a moment, but then hasten to cut Barron down. They are too late, his neck is broken.

The kidnappers make their way across the island, and finally come to a point where several large moving vans are parked alongside the road. The kidnappers' cars are run into these vans, so that if the license numbers have been caught, it will be impossible to check them. One of the trucks has the legend of a horse trucking company on its side, and several of the Klansmen, now minus their hoods, pile into this and drive to the Belmont Park Racetrack where the Shah of Persia is preparing for a big race on the following Saturday. The gangsters shoot down the stable boy and a couple of handlers in cold-blood and make their escape with the horse.

After the horse has been sent on its way, a driver meets the outlaws with another car not previously employed in either of the jobs, and the party drives to the Manhasset Yacht Basin, where, after a struggle with Twyfort, his wife is taken prisoner. One of the gansters is anxious to blow up the yacht to "simplify" matters, but the leader reminds him that the "have their orders."

Sidney Talbot, President of the Talbot Nat'l Bank
Arthur Barron, his son-in-law
Marion Barron, his grand-daughter.
Conrad Webster, — Chairman of the Bd of the Chase Trust Company
Virgil Twyfort — President of the Pacific Coast Bank and Trust Company.
Mrs. Edna Twyfort.
Gaston Le Clerc — Director of the Amalgamated Bank of Paris.
Alexander Torney — Owner of Villa Torney
Malvin Burgess.— } F.B.I.
Frank Kelly }

Steve Huston, the reporter for the New York *Clarion,* has been attending the masquerade in his professional capacity, and reports the murder of Barron and the kidnapping to his boss, Frank Havens. He is sent to check on the murders at the race-track and the action at the yacht basin, when this information comes in. As he is on his way back to New York he is wondering whether this new string of crimes is going to take him off another case on which he has been working. This case has been with Malvin Burgess, one of the F.B.I. men, who has been assigned to check on the spread of counterfeiting in and about New York City. Steve was a bit disappointed when Havens insisted that he attend the masquerade, but Burgess also put his foot down and indicated that he was going to go on a special assignment and simply would not be able to take him along, much as he might like to.

As Huston approaches the *Clarion* building, he finds that Havens has already turned on the red flashing light to summon the Phantom Detective, and a new lightness grips him. He feels sure that with the Phantom on the job this new menace will be eliminated in a reasonably short time. He gives Havens the meager details he has been able to garner on the new crime wave and then Havens informs him that Chief Burke of the F.B.I. has asked him to come down to the Customs House immediately. Havens doesn't know why, but advises Huston to go immediately. Huston is a bit surprised, too, since the F.B.I. office is on Lexington Avenue in the Mid-town section of the city. He goes there, however, and is ushered into a small room. Several hard-faced individuals are standing about a table. On the table is the mutilated body of Malvin Burgess. Huston examines it with the others, and finds that gobs of flesh have been pulled away from the body here and there, the side of the face is torn to shreds and one of the eyes is missing from the socket. Huston and the other men are unable to determine what might have caused this mutilation. One man remarks grimly that it looks as though Malvin fell into a den of lions. The purpose in summoning Huston is to question his about Malvin's plans, since Huston is presumed to be the last person that saw him alive. Steve explains the situation, and how Malvin kept his secret and it probably died with him. Chief Burke assigns Frank Kelly to go over Malvin's reports and papers at his hotel, and to go on with the case.

Richard Curtis Van Loan, the Phantom, had been working in his laboratory during the afternoon preceding the crimes, and had spent the evening at a fraternity stagg. As he is leaving the party at about four o'clock in the morning, he sees the early editions with the announcement of the crimes, and also notes the flashing lights. He digests as much of the story as the papers have, phones Havens to expect him early the following morning, and also gives him instructions to have Huston ready to help him. He knows that the bankers will be familiar with his identity, so goes to his laboratory and undergoes one of his changes. He decides to impersonate a bespectacled and not too smart appearing journalism student looking for a job as a cub reporter.

On the way down the next morning, the Phantom reads a later edition of his favorite paper which gives him the news of Malvin's death, and the fact that Steve Huston was one of the last people to see him alive. He arrives at the office of the *Clarion* just as a United Parcel Service truck is leaving. He goes upstairs and meets Steve. The latter tells him that Havens is in the office with Sidney Talbot, Conrad Webster, Virgil Twyfort, and Gaston Le Clerc. Steve then takes Van around the place as though explaining the workings of a newspaper, and then steers him into Havens' office. There Havens seems to be upset by his appearance—to calm the other occupants of the room, and then agrees with Steve that the present situation may help Van to learn something about the newspaper business. While they are together an office boy comes in with a paper carton containing a small radio set. Havens is a bit surprised to receive this, but a note in the package, and apparently intended for all present says:

"Take this radio set to the lounge of the American Bankers Club, and keep it turned on as it is now, and you will receive a message that will be of interest to you."

Havens looks at the card, and finds that it is similar to the gift cards placed in packages in most of the large department stores. Van feels sure that a check back will not give any immediate results, since the set was probably purchased by cash, and its immediate delivery ordered. He is interested in the dial setting, however, and expects to determine the wave-length that the murderers will use in broadcasting what he believes will be a ransom demand. He secures this from an examination of the set with Huston as he is wrapping it up. He excuses himself, and immediately gets in touch with the Federal Communications Commission, in order to determine whether any commercial station is entitled to broadcast on the wave band. It is a low wave length confined to amateurs. He tells the employee at the Commission that an attempt to broadcast a bootleg message over that channel is to be made within a short time, and asks to have the broadcast checked.

Van is a bit surprised at the location of the ransom announcement in the Bankers Club, because it seems like an impossibility to order bankers to leave their own club room. The killers made no mention of limiting the audience so Van cannot be sure that they do not want the other bankers to hear it, too. He arrives there a short time later, and the set is placed on a table in the center of the room, and is plugged into the electric circuit. Nothing happens for some time, then there is a crackle as of a new station coming on the air, and a voice begins speaking:

"This broadcast has been especially prepared for Sidney Talbot, Conrad Webster, Virgil Twyfort, and Gaston Le Clerc, and for any other members of the International Bankers Association who may be inclined to listen to a warning that is for their own good. Sidney Talbot, you want to prevent your grand-daughter from suffering the death that came to her father. Conrad Webster, you want to get the Shah of Persia back in time to run him on Saturday in the Sweepstakes; Virgil Twyfort, you want to see your wife again; and you, Gaston Le Clerc, realize that we might have chopped off your head at the Villa Torney just we broke Arthur Barron's neck. We can extend out atrocities to other of those now listening, and will, unless our demands are complied with. The Coiner has thousands of dollars of counterfeit money which he is anxious to get into circulation in the United States, and in foreign exchange offices abroad as quickly as possible. The Coiner represents an international ring that is not satisfied with selling a hundred dollars worth of money here and there to small time crooks on street corners. He is anxious to get distribution over as wide a scale as possible. Therefore, Mr. Talbot, you will go to the vaults of the Talbot National Bank and secure $250,000 in cash, which you will prepare to deliver to a place that will be appointed for you. Mr. Webster will be prepared to deliver a similar amount later on. Since Mr. Twyfort will have to get back to the coast before he can fulfill his part of the bargain, we will give him a bit longer to make his trip. You, Mr. Le Clerc, can make a draft on the credit of your bank with their New York correspondents.

"As each one of these payments is made, you will be supplied with its equivalent in perfect counterfeits which can be replaced in your vaults and distributed by your tellers, thus avoiding the possibility of a shortage when the examiners check on you. Should any of you hearing this broadcast decide to interfere, it will mean the destruction of the hostages we now hold. Mr. Talbot will take this special receiving set with him, to receive further instructions for the delivery of the money. When his grand-daughter has been returned to him, he will then be asked to turn it over to Mr. Webster. This rotation will be continued until we have distributed all of the currency we now have in our possession. You are listening, my friends, to the Coiner. You will hear from me again."

The broadcast concluded. Van's eyes went about the room to all those present. They were all stunned by the enormity of the situation. The set-up was almost fool-proof. Suddenly Talbot turned to Havens and said: "That accounts for Arthur's death." He then explained how Arthur, as head-cashier for the bank had been approached by a man that asked for a package of five dollar bills in exchange for a package of fifties. The amount was ten thousand dollars. "This fellow," explained Talbot, "was probably connected with the ring, and was afraid that Arthur would recognize him." Van whispered a few words to Huston and the other nodded, then the Phantom went to the phone and called the Federal Communications Commission to check on the location of the transmitter. A voice at the other end of the line asked him to come to the office immediately.

Van hurries to the office and laboratory, and gets into the control room, and is about to talk with a man on duty when the other's face lights up in horror, and Van turns to see several masked men in the doorway, and to catch the flash of Tommy guns. He is slightly wounded in the shoulder, and rolls up on the floor. He whips out his own gun and begins firing at the invaders. He is certain that he has nipped one or two of them, but the others withdraw with the wounded, leaving Van and the radio man for dead. Before he dies, the man advises him that the broadcasting equipment was probably in an automobile or a truck, since the checking apparatus found it to be located in several different streets during the broadcast.

Van does his best for the fellow, but is not able to save his life. Other men from other parts of the building come in for an explanation of the situation, and Van explains things to them. They take charge of the body. He realizes that his present identity is no longer of any use to him, so returns to his laboratory to adopt another role. The counterfeit scheme that he has just heard discussed strikes him as being something that might have interested Malvin Burgess, and he wonders whether there is any connection between the Burgess and Barron killings. He knows of Huston's connection with the situation, and after he has rigged himself out as a French gentleman, he gets in touch with the newspaper reporter and asks to have him meet him at a given point. Huston meets him, and they go to see Chief Burke. Van is introduced as the Phantom, and Burke is glad to have him working with them. They discuss the plan for distributing the counterfeit money, and Burke is astounded. He explains that the government is chiefly interested in the plates and engravers, and with these it will be a simple matter to have all of the counterfeit money stopped at the banks, even if it does go out. Burke seems to know how to handle the matter, but Van wants to know how they are going to tell the good money from the bad. The F.B.I. man says that it will be possible to lock up all the money in the banks at present, and issue new money from the Mints and Bureau of Printing and Engraving. Van is doubtful whether the government would be willing to do this, and Burke reminds him that should any of the banks be weakened because of the withdrawal of the huge amounts of money, the Federal Deposit Insurance Corp. would be liable for the loss to the amount of $5,000 for each depositor, and that any considerable number of defalcations of this kind would considerably embarrass the government in view of the present financial situation. This makes it a government matter in several ways.

At the point Frank Kelly arrives on the scene to report that he has checked Malvin's records, and that he apparently had an appointment with someone on the previous night at Torney's Villa. He is going out there to see if he can pick up the thread from there, and that they might have disposed of Burgess before or after making the raid on the masquerade. Kelly is not convinced. He tells something of the things that Malvin has discovered, and among them is the fact that Torney is not only the owner of the Villa Torney, but also has a chain of restaurants throughout the country, and in Paris and at the European watering places. Van cannot see how this effects the situation except to indicate that Alexander Torney is a responsible individual, and might naturally come into contact with all kinds of people. Van then offers to change places with Frank Kelly, but Kelly will hear nothing of it. He is even somewhat disappointed when Burke agrees to let Van and Steve tail him, to see that nothing happens to him.

Steve is called to the phone by Havens, and asked to come back to the office. He takes his departure reluctantly, but informs Van that he will follow along and meet him at the Villa Torney. Kelly is on his way, and Van decides to maintain his French disguise (which he adopted partly because he intended to make a call on Torney himself). He follows Kelly to the place on Long Island, and notes that the G-man is going to reconnoiter about the place before going in. He goes on to the Villa, finds Torney, and identifies himself as an agent of the French Surete. He has all the necessary credentials and Torney meets him with mixed feelings. They get into conversation, and Van describes the man he is seeking as Gaston Le Clerc. Torney is imediately interested, and recalls Gaston's presence in the place on the previous evening dressed as Louis XVI.

Van is then escorted into a private office and is almost immediately set upon by a couple of burly individuals. A tap on the head removes him from any interest in proceedings for the moment, and when he comes to, he finds that besides Torney in the room, there are several other people, among them Gaston Le Clerc. That worthy begins baiting Van, and asks him whether he expects to send him to Devil's Island. Van does not know whether his stab in the dark has struck fire, or whether Gaston is merely making game of him, secure in the fact that he is not a representative of the Surete. Suddenly a thought comes to him in the light of Burke's remark that the government has been looking for the counterfeiter's plant. If Le Clerc is actually mixed up with the counterfeiters, the plant may be on the island of St. Pierre or Miquelon, off the coast of Canada, and the money smuggled in, or it may be one of the French Island in the West Indies. This would account for the failure of the G-Men to locate the plant, and to trace any well-known engravers to a connection with the counterfeit money. He realizes, at the same time, that he is going to have to proceed rather cautiously, so that the lives of Mrs. Twyfort and Miss Brown will not be forfeit!

Kelly is then brought in, and it is obvious that he, too, is a prisoner. He accuses Van of having tricked him, and Van is afraid that he is going to give away his identity. He is saved from embarrassment by one of Kelly's guards who knocks him over the head with a pistol butt. The outburst from Kelly, who is known to be a G-Man has a rather salutary effect, however, since Van is asked for some sort of an explanation. He then tells Torney and Le Clerc that he came to warn them about Kelly's presence, but was not quite sure just who he should contact. He draws upon his knowledge of France and of the French colonies to draw a convincing picture, and feels that he has half-convinced his hearers. They apologize for the rough treatment they have given him, and tell him that as a test of his friendship, and a warning concerning what may happen to him, they are going to permit him to see Kelly put to death.

When they get out of the inner room, Van discovers that it is late at night, and that the Villa is closed. He sees mysterious figures moving about outside apparently on guard, and the party, with Kelly in their midst is heading for a bulky building on the shores of Long Island Sound. Van is wondering whether together they can make a break and get away from their captors, or just what should be done. He has seen Malvin's body, and realizes that if this is the same sort of killing it is going to be a horrible spectacle. As they approach the building they hear a strange rumbling sound, and while Van is looking about in an effort to determine just what is responsible for this, the others appear to be entirely familiar with it. Gaston smiles quizzically, and nods to Van. At the building itself, the only light is from a flashlight being carried by one of the party. The rumbling noise increases, and when the door is opened is extremely loud. Van is aware of huge bodies in an enclosure some distance below the floor, and apparently with access to the lapping waters of the sound. He soon finds that the occupants of the building are large sea turtles. Torney explains that his restaurants are famous for their turtle soup, and mentions that their diet may have something to do with the taste of the soup. Before Van can reply, Kelly is lifted up bodily and thrown to the turtles. This, then, is the explanation of the mutilation of his body, and Kelly is apparently headed for the same fate.

The gang does not appear to feel that it is necessary for anyone to watch the festivities, and the gloom in the pit, marked only by the thrashing animals makes any observation difficult. It seems that the turtles merely go into their shells if any light is shined upon them. At the door, there is a scuffle, and then the sound of pistol shots. Van immediately disarms one of his companions, and a general free-for-all results. In the flash of fire, Van recognizes this new element in the mystery as Steve Huston, and immediately fights his way to his side. They manage to get into an automobile and make their escape. Steve tells Van that Havens has discovered that Virgil Twyfort has a shortage in his accounts at the bank, and that the present draft, if it is discovered will practically ruin him. Van then reminds him that if Virgil is mixed up in the counterfeiting, that the $750,000 he is to collect from the other bankers, will probably take care of things, and permit him to continue his life as a responsible and representative citizen. Van tells Steve something of his discoveries at Villa Torney, but asks him to say nothing about it, unless he fails to show up within a given time. He then has Steve drive him to a dock several miles from Torney's, and leaves him to make his way back to town alone. He secures a speed boat and starts back up to the turtle store-house. He douses his lights, and gets in under the building, which is raised up on piles. When he feels sure that the walls of the building will shield him, he turns on all the lights he has, to bewilder the turtles. He does not know whether Kelly is still alive, but is anxious to save him, if he can. A cry from the turtle pen cheers him, and he uses a pair of pliers found in the boat's tool kit, to cut through a portion of the chicken wire that serves as a barrier to prevent the turtles from getting back into their native element. Kelly has been nipped in several places, and is tired and wan, but more than thankful for his rescue. They rewind the chicken wire as well as they can, to mystify the gang, and then start to make good their escape.

While talking about the turtle death, Van decides that Malvin was probably unconscious when thrown into the turtles, and therefore had no opportunity to fight for his life as Kelly did. Kelly's attitude toward Van has changed considerably, and he is now willing to listen to him, since the ramifications of the case are far beyond his usual experience. They get back to their pier and secure a car. Van drives Kelly to the railroad station, and then goes up to the Manhasset Yachet Club to talk to Twyfort. The latter is not on his boat, but the captain informs him that he will be in New York for several days, in fact that he has ordered the boat brought down the Sound and through the Harlem River to the New York Yacht Club anchorage.

Van realizes that with his discovery of the apparent connection between Torney, Le Clerc and the gangsters, that he must break the case without delay if he is going to prevent the deaths of the hostages. Thus far he has been unable to check on their possible whereabouts. Since Le Clerc was with the other bankers at the Bankers Club, obviously he could not have been broadcasting from the car or truck. The business of Twyfort's shortage might have had nothing whatever to do with the counterfeiting, and might merely have been a coincidence. Van knows enough about "honest bankers" to know that most of them would probably be caught short if they happened to be investigated on a moment's notice.

He decides to get back to Talbot's house to determine whether he has received any information in regard to the delivery of the $250,000 and the receipt of the counterfeit money. When he gets there he finds Talbot in his studio, ear bent to the radio set, and some time later the announcement comes through:

"Hello, Talbot, this is the Coiner. You will take the money you have secured from the bank, packed in a new leather suit-case, and leave your house alone. You will get into your limousine, drive to the George Washington Bridge, cross the bridge, and turn north on route #2. Along the way you will be passed by an automobile with the license number N.J.E-2112. Sound your horn when this car pulls alongside of you, then turn off at the next cross road, and you will be overtaken again, and the transfer will be made." There was a pause, then as an after-thought, the words came, "If you warn the police, or fail to come alone, you will sacrifice your grand-daughter's life. You will be watched from the moment you leave your house, and your car will be searched when the chauffeur leaves it at the gate."

Talbot looks at Van, not knowing what to do. Van had hoped to get the banker to permit him to accompany him on the drive, but the thoroughness of the precautions taken by the counterfeiters made this impossible. Van then suggests that he be permitted to take the place of Talbot. Talbot is afraid that the substitution will be noticed, but when Van completes his make-up, the banker is so amazed, that he has no objection to the change. They pack the money and Van leaves with it. He tries to spot the gangsters that are presumably watching him, but is unable to discover anything. He follows the directions given and is met on route #3 by the Jersey car. He turns off, and a car pulls up alongside of him. He hands over his grip, another grip is given to him, and then the curtained rear door of the other car opens and Marion Barron is passed over to him. She embraces him, but Van tells her that they had better get away before the gang thinks of any other things. He turns the car and starts back to the main highway. On the highway he picks up speed until he is going at about eighty miles an hour. Satisfied that he not being followed, he pulls the car to the side of the road, jumps out with the girl and the money and starts to run for the cover of the trees alongside the road. Marion thinks he is crazy, but they are hardly back in the woods when there is a terrific explosion, and the car is blown to smithereens. Marion is white from the shock, but Van insists that they stay under cover. A number of motorists on the parkway stop to examine the ruins, attracted by the blast. Several motorcycle officers pull up, and then a car comes up that bears the E-2112 license.

Ordering Marion to remain behind him, Van comes out from under cover and closes in upon the occupants of the car, who have come to check on the effectiveness of their plan. He covers the four men and orders them to submit, but they refuse to do so, preferring to shoot it out. The policemen on the scene join in the melee, and the men are either killed or captured. Van explains the situation to the police, then two wounded men are taken to the police station for questioning, and the bag of money is also brought along. Marion is sent home under a police escort. Van phones Havens to tell him to keep an eye on Talbot so that no one tries to commit any reprisals. Van then decides to try a daring plan, and gets permission from the police officers to try it. He goes to the cell and has one of the men brought out for questioning. Then Van makes himself up as this individual, dons his clothes, and is returned to the cell. The other fellow wants to know what they questioned him about, and Van tells him. He warns the other fellow to keep mum. A check on the license number has been made, and the supposed owner has been notified, and promises to come and bail out his friends. He shows up, and Van and the other man go with him. They drive to a road-house and Van and the other man are taken into an inner room where a meeting is in progress. There are a number of men from all over the country, listening to a masked individual, who is explaining to them just how they can operate the counterfeit ring in their own states. He asks Van and his henchmen to explain how smoothly the whole thing worked out. But the henchman chimes in with the bad news. Van is meanwhile trying to spot the voice of the leader, but is unable to do so. He has discovered some sort of a different quality in the tone that is addressing him and his companion, and the voice that was previously addressing the group. He suddenly decides that the original voice, and the voice in the two radio broadcasts he has heard were not real, but were electrical transcriptions, intended to disguise the real characteristics of the speaker.

A telephone call from Long Island also reports the disappearance of Kelly when the men went to get his body to drop it on the steps of the Customs House. The leader is in something of a panic, but keeps his head, and tells the boys they will remove the money in trucks to other cities. Van follows the others out to a large garage in the rear of the roadhouse and discovers a number of trucks. (These are the same trucks that were used to pick up the autos on Long Island.) Glancing into one of the trucks, he notices that they are loaded with turtle shells. Apparently Torney's statement that his restaurants were famous for their turtle soup were justified. He climbs into the driver's seat of one of the trucks, and the masked leader comes to him and his partner and says: "Take this to New Haven." Van drives off with the truck, and they are making fairly good time toward the George Washington Bridge. When they approach the toll gate Van hands the other man the money, and as he turns to pay the toll, he snaps him over the head with the butt of a gun. He then orders the bridge police to set out a radio alarm for the other trucks over several states, and to take no chances. He gets rid of this assistant, and continues on over the bridge. He heads for the New York Yacht Club dock, and is not at all surprised to see the Twyfort yacht anchored at the pier. He parks the truck, and starts down the gangway. He has left the truck far enough away from the dock so that its presence will not excite suspicion. As he is coming down the dock, another vehicle pulls up at the end of the pier, and two people step out of it. One is a man and the other is a woman.

Van manages to get aboard the boat without being detected, and finds that Virgil has apparently received his radio set from Talbot and has been waiting for instructions. A new suit-case the same as that which Talbot had stands close to his chair. As the other party arrives at the gang plank, Van sees that they are Conrad Webster and Mrs. Twyfort. Webster is masked, and a couple of his pug-uglies are followed down the dock. Mrs. Twyfort is ushered onto the boat, and into the presence of her husband. They are ordered to cast off immediately and to head downstream in the yacht. The boat gets under way. Conrad takes care of the good money, and places the phony money in the cabin with the reunited couple. Van is curious about this, and is wondering just what Huston, Kelly and Havens are doing.

The yacht get down off Sandy Hook, and a motorboat pulls alongside to take off Conrad and his men. As Conrad is preparing to leave, Van comes out of hiding and covers him with his gun. He expects trouble from the men in the boat, particularly when he recognizes the leader as Gaston Le Clerc. But he hands a gun to Twyfort and tells him to keep the others covered so that they cannot come aboard. After rounding up the outlaws on the boat, Van is able to give more consideration to those in the boat. He sees that besides Le Clerc the occupants are Kelly, Huston, Burke and Havens. They vouch for Le Clerc, and come aboard the yacht. Conrad is exposed as the leader of the gang. (He has been trying to make Twyfort believe that he is a hero, and has rescued his wife.) Van explains the theft of the horse as a cover-up, so that Conrad could work a big betting coup with his part of the money from the bankers on the following Saturday. He mentions that the men at the stable were killed because they would have recognized some of Webster's employees in the gang. Conrad is defiant and says that when he gets ashore and sees his attorney things will be different. Van accuses Conrad of mining the ship, and telling him that he has exactly five minutes to "kill the mine" and permits him to go below. The others get into the launch for safety. There is the sound of a pistol shot and Van is prompted to go below and investigate it.

Le Clerc pulls him over the side of the boat and they start to back away. Van then decides that Conrad did not have time to stop the bomb, and committed suicide as the easiest way out. Le Clerc is then identified as an officer of the Surete, which accounts for the reason he knew Van was an impostor. He had gotten in with the counterfeiters on the French island of Martinique, and they were willing to play ball with him, because they thought he was a big shot in France. He had located the plant and destroyed it, but wanted to secure the money that had been pirated, and came to New York for this reason. Huston and the others are curious as to how the money has been brought into the United States. Le Clerc looks at Van. Van nods and then says it was brought into the country in the shells of the giant sea turtles. The shield plates can be opened in one of several ways, such as by applying boiling water, and various oils and chemical solutions. Since the turtles were permitted to live after their counterfeit cargo was stored in their shells, they aroused no suspicion with the customs or other authorities upon arrival, and Torney's chain of restaurants provided a legitimate means of keeping them without any further concealment. The trucks that were to be driven away from the Jersey hide-out contained the balance of the counterfeit money to be distributed. While they are explaining matters, the planted bomb goes off and Conrad goes down with the Twyfort yacht. The others return to New York, a new menace conquered.

CHAPTER XIV

THE PHANTOM
OF THE COMICS

T HE PHANTOM DETECTIVE enjoyed a long life in the pages of
his own magazine, as did several other of Standard's successful pulp characters. Yet, not many fans recall the comic book versions of them, which ran in
several of Standard's comics of the day.

Characters such as Captain Future, the Rio Kid, the Lone Eagle, Jim Hatfield and the Black Bat (as the Mask) appeared in near obscurity in the back
pages of titles such as *America's Best Comics*, *Thrilling Comics*, *Exciting Comics*
and *The Fighting Yank*. Some characters, such as the Black Bat and Captain
Future, were drastically changed, while others, such as the Phantom Detective,
remained fairly true to their pulp roots.

The Phantom Detective ran in *Thrilling Comics* #54-62 and 65-70, with a
one-off appearance in *America's Best Comics* #26, which was published after a
period when *Thrilling Comics* was on hiatus (no doubt this Phantom was an
inventory story). Most of the stories were unsigned, but *The Grand Comic-
Book Database* credits Lin Streeter, Edmond Good, and Everett Hibbard as
the primary artists on these stories. According to Jerry Bails' *The Who's Who of
American Comic Books*, Streeter was a journeyman artist who worked at most
of the major publishers during the 1940s, Goode worked on a varierty of titles
and comic strips in the 40s and 50s, and Hibbard was best known for his DC
Comics work, most notably on the Flash.

Included here are nearly all the appearances of the Phantom Detective
from the pages of *Thrilling Comics* and *America's Best Comics*.

Thrilling Comics #54 (June 1946)

YES, PHANTOM, I'M SURE HE WAS ALONE, BECAUSE HE ALWAYS RODE BY HIMSELF!

OKAY, I'LL TAKE YOUR WORD FOR IT!

AT THE OFFICES OF THE MURDERED GIFFORD MANWARING ... THE NEXT DAY...

HOW DO YOU DO, MR. TERRY! MIND IF I ASK YOU A FEW QUESTIONS ABOUT YOUR UNCLE?

THE PHANTOM DETECTIVE! NOT AT ALL! I'D BE HAPPY TO DO ANYTHING TO HELP FIND HIS MURDERER!

I UNDERSTAND MR. MANWARING RODE QUITE A BIT IN THE PARK! IS THERE ANYONE ELSE IN THE OFFICE WHO ALSO RODE THERE ... NOT NECESSARILY WITH HIM?

YES, I RIDE MYSELF SOMETIMES ... AND MR. HARDY, MY UNCLE'S PARTNER, RIDES TWO OR THREE TIMES A WEEK! I'LL INTRODUCE YOU TO HIM, IF YOU LIKE!

RICHARD HARDY, MANWARING'S PARTNER ...

GIFFORD AND I HAD BEEN PARTNERS FOR FIFTEEN YEARS ... I ... I WAS TERRIBLY UPSET TO HEAR OF HIS DEATH!

OF COURSE, MR. HARDY, I CAN WELL UNDERSTAND! THIS PICTURE IS OF YOU, I SEE, RIDING IN THE SAME PARK WHERE MR. MANWARING WAS KILLED!

YES, THAT PICTURE WAS TAKEN RECENTLY! I WISH I HAD BEEN WITH GIFFORD LAST NIGHT ... I MIGHT HAVE SAVED HIM! BUT HE ALWAYS PREFERRED TO RIDE ALONE ... HE SAID HE COULD THINK BETTER!

I SEE ... THANK YOU VERY MUCH FOR YOUR HELP, GENTLEMEN! I HOPE TO SEE YOU BOTH AGAIN SOON! GOOD DAY!

I'D BETTER STOP BY POLICE HEADQUARTERS TO PICK UP A FEW FINGERPRINT SAMPLES, AND ALSO TO GET SOME MORE DATA ON HARDY AND TERRY!

TERRY DISAPPEARS!

OF ALL THE STUPID BLUNDERS...LETTING HIM GET AWAY! HE'S THE MURDERER, ALL RIGHT; AND NO DOUBT THAT "CARPENTER" OF YESTERDAY, TOO!

NOTHING ELSE TO DO BUT SEE WHAT THE AIRLINES HAVE TO SAY ABOUT TERRY'S ACTIVITIES FOR THE LAST DAY OR SO! IT *MIGHT* PROVIDE A LEAD!

MR. TERRY HAS BEEN IN CANADA FOR THE LAST TWO DAYS, SIR! IT'S HIS VACATION...I BELIEVE YOU'LL FIND HIM AT THE ST. PIERRE LODGE, NEAR QUEBEC!

UH-HUH!... THANK YOU VERY MUCH!

Then...A LONG DISTANCE TELEPHONE CALL TO QUEBEC!

HELLO, THE ST. PIERRE LODGE? THIS IS RICHARD CURTIS VAN LOAN! I'D LIKE TO RESERVE A ROOM FOR MYSELF, PERHAPS FOR THE WHOLE WEEKEND! I'LL ARRIVE TONIGHT ABOUT NINE O'CLOCK!

BACK TO VAN LOAN FOR THIS ONE! IT'S GOING TO BE A CINCH...BECAUSE MR. TERRY WOULDN'T *DARE* NOT BE THERE!

A RAPID PLANE TRIP TAKES VAN LOAN TO THE ST. PIERRE LODGE!

HAVE YOU HAD DINNER, SIR? THE DINING ROOM IS STILL OPEN!

THANKS, I'VE EATEN! I THINK I'LL JUST GO UP TO MY ROOM!

Thrilling Comics #55 (August 1946)

AS THE INTRUDERS FLEE...

THEY GOT AWAY, ALL RIGHT! MAYBE I CAN GET SOMETHING OUT OF THE BUTLER! COME ON---SNAP OUT OF IT!

WHEN THE BUTLER REGAINS CONSCIOUSNESS, THE PHANTOM IDENTIFIES HIMSELF...

YOU'RE ALL RIGHT NOW! THIS BADGE SHOULD TELL YOU WHO I AM! TELL ME WHAT HAPPENED, AS YOU REMEMBER IT!

THE PHANTOM DETECTIVE! YES, SIR···

YES, SIR! THOSE MEN··· THEY CAME TO THE DOOR, AND WHEN I OPENED IT THEY PUSHED IT OPEN AND DEMANDED A SWORD WITH A FOREIGN NAME! I SAID THEY'D HAVE TO WAIT FOR THE MASTER AND THEN··· THAT'S ALL I REMEMBER!

SORRY TO TELL YOU SO ABRUPTLY, JENSON---BUT YOUR EMPLOYER IS DEAD! MURDERED, I'M INCLINED TO BELIEVE! WHERE DOES MR. NELSON KEEP HIS WAR TROPHIES?

MURDERED! POOR MR. NELSON!···THEY'RE UP THERE, SIR···IN THE ATTIC! I'LL SHOW YOU!

I'VE NEVER SEEN IT OPEN, SIR! MR. NELSON TOLD ME I WAS TO LEAVE IT ALONE! HE DID SAY THAT HE HAD HIS WAR THINGS IN THERE! BUT IT'S LOCKED!

IT WON'T BE FOR LONG!

NOTHING HERE THAT WOULD--- *WAIT···A SECRET COMPARTMENT!*

HERE IT IS! THE SWORD OF ADJABAB! WHATEVER IT IS---SOMEBODY WANTS IT BAD ENOUGH TO MURDER FOR IT! *WHAT A PRIZE!* THERE'S AN INSCRIPTION ON THE HANDLE!

Death to alien hands that touch the sword of Adjabab!

SO THAT'S WHY THEY KILLED NELSON! I'M TAKING THIS, JENSON! IT'S GOING TO HELP ME CATCH UP WITH THOSE KILLERS!

Thrilling Comics #56 (October 1946)

THE FOLLOWING DAY ... IN THE GUISE OF A WORKMAN ...

THE MUNGO RIVER BEND--- WHERE THE KILLER HIT THE SILK! I'LL BET HE'S GOT SOME PALS IN THIS AREA! ---MAYBE THEY KNOW SOMETHING AT THAT GAS STATION!

NO SWIMMING

YES-- I SHOULD SAY I DO REMEMBER THAT FELLOW WHO JUMPED! HE HURT HIS FOOT WHEN HE LANDED! I GOT OUT OF BED AT TWO IN THE MORNING TO HELP HIM!

HURT HIS FOOT, EH? WHERE DID HE GO?

I CALLED JAKE AND HIS TAXI TO GET HIM TO A DOCTOR! RECKON JAKE MIGHT KNOW SOMETHING! I'LL PHONE HIM!

TEN MINUTES LATER...

YEP-- I PICKED HIM UP ALL RIGHT! BUT HE WOULDN'T GO TO THE DOCTOR'S! INSISTED I TAKE HIM TO THE OLD HAYS HOUSE... DOWN THERE A PIECE!

DID YOU DRIVE HIM RIGHT UP TO THE HOUSE?

NOPE--HE GOT OUT! MUST HAVE LIMPED ABOUT A QUARTER OF A MILE! DIDN'T WANT ME TO GO NEAR THE PLACE! --- *WHAT? THE PHANTOM!*

RIGHT! TAKE ME TO THAT HAYS HOUSE, MY FRIEND--- AND DROP ME OFF IN THE EXACT SAME SPOT!

Thrilling Comics #57 (December 1946)

THE PHANTOM OF THE COMICS 327

Thrilling Comics #59 (April 1947)

Thrilling Comics #60 (June 1947)

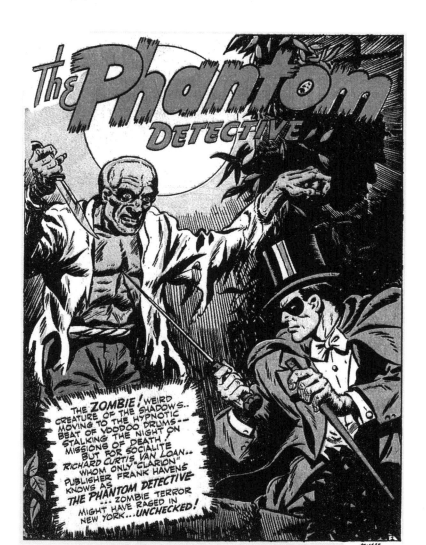

Thrilling Comics #62 (October 1947)

Thrilling Comics #65 (April 1948)

America's Best Comics #26 (May 1948)

Thrilling Comics #66 (June 1948)

Thrilling Comics #68 (October 1948)

When the police and coroner arrive...

NOT A SIGN OF VIOLENCE ON HIM, MR. HAVENS! I'D SAY IT WAS A HEART ATTACK!

N-- NO! I TELL YOU I HEARD HIM SCREAM, AS IF IN PAIN!

HMMM -- HE ASKED FOR THE PHANTOM! THAT WAS HIS LAST REQUEST!

TOO BAD ABOUT JOHNSON-- I UNDERSTAND HE WAS ABOUT TO CRACK A BIG WHEEL! THERE WAS TALK HE WAS AFTER SOMEBODY PRETTY POWERFUL AND WAS ABOUT TO INDICT!

Only Frank Havens publisher of the "Daily Clarion" knows the Phantom's true identity as Richard Curtis Van Loan, society playboy!

THIS IS HAVENS! SEND OUT A CALL FOR THE PHANTOM!

Radio stations begin to blanket the area, urgently seeking the nemesis of the Underworld!

STAND BY, PLEASE! WE INTERRUPT THIS PROGRAM FOR A SPECIAL ANNOUNCEMENT! CALLING THE PHANTOM DETECTIVE! CALLING THE PHANTOM!

Somewhere in the city, Richard Van Loan relaxes with a society playmate...

GOOD HEAVENS! DICK, WE SEEM TO HIT EVERY RED LIGHT!

CALLING THE PHANTOM DETECTIVE

EXCUSE ME, GLORIA! I JUST REMEMBERED I HAVE TO ATTEND TO SOMETHING!

B-BUT DICK --- WHERE ARE YOU GOING! THE -- THE --PARTY---!

Shortly afterward, at the home of Red Larson...

THIS IS HIS PLACE, ALL RIGHT! I'LL RING HIM AND SEE IF HE'S IN!

YEAH -- THIS IS RED LARSON ... WHO? -- *THE PHANTOM!* ... WELL -- ALL RIGHT -- COME ON UP..!

Then..

EEEEAHHHH!

HELLO -- *HELLO!* -- THEY *GOT* HIM! -- I'D BETTER GET UP THERE --!

Dashing up a flight of stairs...

THE DOOR'S LOCKED!

TOO LATE!

CRASH!

As the *PHANTOM* attempts to take the phone out of Red's hand...

OWWWW! -- THAT'S BURNING HOT!

THE PHANTOM OF THE COMICS 399

Printed in Great Britain
by Amazon